W9-CBB-522
Decatur, Michigan 49045

A CARDINAL OFFENSE

FATHER DOWLING MYSTERIES
by Ralph McInerny:

Her Death of Cold
The Seventh Station
Bishop as Pawn
Lying Three
Second Vespers
Thicker Than Water
A Loss of Patients
The Grass Widow
Getting A Way With Murder
Rest in Pieces
The Basket Case
Abracadaver
Four on the Floor
Judas Priest
Desert Sinner
Seed of Doubt

A CARDINAL OFFENSE

Ralph McInerny

St. Martin's Press
New York

 For information, address St. Martin's Press, 175 Fifth Avenue, New York, N.Y. 10010.

LIBRARY OF CONGRESS CATALOGING IN PUBLICATION DATA
McInerny, Ralph M.
A cardinal offense/Ralph McInerny.
p. cm.
ISBN 0-312-11283-1 (hardcover)
1. Dowling, Father (Fictitious character)—Fiction. 2. University of Notre Dame—Football—Fiction. 3. Catholic Church—Illinois—Clergy—Fiction. 4. South Bend (Ind.)—Fiction. I. Title.
PS3563.A3116C36 1994
813'.54—dc20 94-3481
CIP

First Edition: November 1994

10 9 8 7 6 5 4 3 2 1

For Fathers Ted Hesburgh and Ned Joyce

A CARDINAL OFFENSE

Prologue

The rising sun crept across Rome, dividing light from darkness, touching the Castel Sant'Angelo and moving up the wide, still empty Via della Conciliazione toward the Vatican, St. Peter's Square and the great basilica.

The city like the sun had moved through many cycles and by the reckoning of man was accounted eternal. Etruscans, then Romans, first pagan then Christian, had dwelt here, one empire giving way to another. The Middle Ages had ceded to the Renaissance, to both worldly and saintly popes, to warriors and patrons of the arts, to rulers in both the sacred and secular realms. As late as the nineteenth century, Pius IX, *il papa bello,* had been drawn through the streets of his city in a magnificent open carriage. Goethe, Stendhal, Hawthorne, Henry James recorded their glimpses of popes. After the Risorgimento, the pope became a prisoner in the Vatican—and was liberated to the world.

His city, a postage-stamp principality whose chief secular product was postage stamps, remained the center of a Catholic world which had undergone radical change since the closing of the Second Vatican Council in 1965. The call to renewal had received an equivocal response. In the Western countries, priests and nuns abandoned their consecrated lives and returned to the world, while elsewhere vocations flourished.

The number of practicing faithful fell dramatically in the old Catholic countries, but conversions in the hundreds of thousands were made in Africa and the East. Catholic marriages, once a synonym of stability, now fractured as frequently as any others.

Petitions for annulments increased. In the United States of America some forty thousand annulments a year were being granted.

At exactly eight o'clock on this summer morning a tall figure wearing a black coat over a black cassock, a beret pulled down on his prematurely white hair, came out of a building on the Via della Conciliazione and started in the direction of St. Peter's Basilica. He cast a long shadow. He cradled a briefcase in his arm, pressing it against his chest. The morning traffic was not yet heavy when he crossed into the square, nodded reverently toward the basilica, then entered the Bernini colonnade to the left. Shafts of sunlight alternated with the shadow of columns in chiaroscuro as he passed through the passageway. When he emerged, he crossed to the unassuming building that housed the Sacred Congregation for the Doctrine of the Faith, of which he was the cardinal prefect. He was the much loved and much hated Josef Hildebrand.

His secretary, Monsignor Tracy, greeted him with an Irish smile several generations removed from its country of origin. On the cardinal's desk was his schedule for the day. The first appointment would begin in five minutes.

"Bishop Ambrose Ravel, one of the Chicago auxiliaries."

Hildebrand looked up, waiting.

"He is secretary of the American Bishops' Committee on Marriage and the Family."

If Tracy elicited thoughts of the Irish monks who had wandered over Europe during the Dark Ages, Ravel brought with him the great mystery of America, still one of the bastions of Catholic orthodoxy, though not what it had been before the council.

"Annulments," the cardinal said.

"Annulments."

Bishop Ravel was shown in and after the amenities Cardinal Hildebrand went straight to the point.

"The Holy Father is alarmed by the ease with which annulments are granted in your country, Bishop Ravel."

"We are all concerned, Your Eminence."

"Yes. And what is being done about it?"

"Your Eminence, there will be a special meeting of our committee with representatives of the Canon Law Society in the fall. We would very much like you to come and address the participants."

Monsignor Tracy was called in; the cardinal's future commitments were checked against the dates of the meeting; there was no conflict. Hildebrand sat in silence for a moment. Every decision was preceded by at least a silent prayer. His eyes lifted to the Chicago auxiliary.

"Where is the meeting to be held?"

"Notre Dame, Your Eminence. The University of Notre Dame."

"Ah." Another silence. "I shall be delighted to come."

Father Dowling was in no mood when Marie Murkin told him there was a visitor waiting for him in the parlor. In the mail was the official notice of the death and coming funeral of old Father Tuohy, but that wasn't it. From the envelope he'd saved until last, the pastor of St. Hilary's parish in Fox River, Illinois, had just taken two pieces of colored pasteboard and was regarding them with the awe medieval pilgrims had reserved for worthier objects. In his trembling hand were undeniably two tickets for the Notre Dame–Southern California game, the surprising gift of Ambrose Ravel, one of the auxiliary bishops of the Archdiocese of Chicago. Roger Dowling's first instinct was to pick up his phone and relay the astounding good news to Phil Keegan, but here was Marie Murkin calling him back to the humdrum duties of his rectory. It was one of those moments when moral character is gained or lost. With an effort, he returned the tickets to the envelope and slipped it into the inside pocket of his jacket.

"The front parlor?"

Marie lowered her head and looked at him over her glasses. There was only one parlor. A stupid remark, granted, but preferable to letting out a yell or intoning the Notre Dame fight song. He left his study and started up the hallway, managing not to skip.

Before Father Dowling could greet him the man awaiting him in the parlor stood and, arms at his side and head tilted forward, glared at the priest.

"I'm getting an annulment!"

Father Dowling nodded as if this were a perfectly reasonable opening remark, sat, got out his pipe and began to fill it carefully with tobacco. The man followed this with impatience.

"My name is Father Dowling," the priest said before striking a match. "I'm the pastor here."

"I *know* who you are."

"That's where you have an advantage over me."

The man stared, as if he had not understood.

"What's your name?"

"Geary. Michael Geary."

The visitor slumped into a chair and tension suddenly left him. His expression was the saddest Father Dowling had seen in weeks. It seemed to say something about the universe that while Michael Geary was near tears, he himself was finding it difficult not to grin because of the bonanza of those Notre Dame tickets. By hunching his shoulder he could feel the reassuring resistance of the envelope in his pocket.

"Are you a member of the parish?" The status of parishioner was becoming flexible. People the pastor had never seen before showed up to arrange weddings and funerals, assuring Roger Dowling that they belonged to St. Hilary's. ("For years, Father. Since I was a kid.")

But Geary shook his head. "I'm from Chicago."

"What brings you to Fox River?"

"Father Noonan advised me to talk with you."

Noonan! The name brought first a face—lean with heavy-lidded eyes, a wide mouth dimpled at the corners, a bald head that looked like a penitent's knee—and then memories of the days Roger Dowling had spent as a member of the archdiocesan marriage tribunal. He had been appointed to it on his return from Washington with his J.C.D., *Juris Canonici Doctor*, a certified expert in Church law. Jerome Noonan had been his colleague on the tribunal, a Torquemada of the marriage bond, seemingly taking deep satisfaction in assuring the poor devils who came to them that there wasn't a chance in the world that their marriage would be declared null and void. Even if there were a chance, the resolution of the case lay years in the future, the final disposition up to Rome. Roger Dowling had entertained no illusions about the invalidity of the marriages of those who came before them, but the very fact that the husbands or wives were there, seeking to have their marriages annulled and their lives to that point redefined, brought home the tragedy that can lurk in the most ordinary lives. The tribunal came to seem a metaphor for life in general. Who has never felt the desire to undo what he has done and make it as if it had never been? How poignant the hope with which a new start was spoken of, as if life would be transformed once one was free of a spouse.

The day came when nuns and priests began to speak of their vocations in similar terms, but for them a canonical remedy was more easily available. After the council, laicizations and dispensations from vows became common and nuns and priests seemed to flow from convents and rectories into the world. Soon annulments too were more easily had, with final jurisdiction given to diocesan courts, no longer a need to send each case to Rome. Before that happened, undone by the agony of the job, having for too long sought solace in drink, Roger Dowling was off the court, rehabilitated in Wisconsin, and assigned to St. Hilary's in Fox River, at the western extreme of the archdiocese. The pits, as he might once have thought, but he had come to cherish his post as one where he was far more likely to save his own soul and, God willing, help others save theirs. He felt a bit ashamed now of his reaction minutes before when Marie had interrupted his first delighted reaction to Bishop Ravel's gift of Notre Dame tickets. At that moment he had resented being forever at the beck and call of anyone who showed up at the rectory door.

"I'm not on the tribunal anymore, Mr. Geary."

"I know that."

"Father Noonan told you?"

Geary nodded. His eye followed the upward drift of the smoke from Father Dowling's pipe. "Is it okay if I smoke?"

"Of course."

"I only smoke cigarettes." Did he regard cigarettes as merely a venial sin? How strange the evaluation of human deeds was becoming with the waning of the Judeo-Christian ethic.

"What did Father Noonan tell you?"

"He said this was the place to start. I'm not a parishioner but we were married here. In that church." He looked toward the window but quickly looked away. "She lived here."

"Your wife?"

"My contention is that we were never married!"

"Your putative wife, then. What was her maiden name?"

"Ha. Maiden name."

Roger Dowling waited, feeling his insides tighten. He had forgotten the dreadful stories spouses told on each other when they came before the tribunal. But Geary changed tack.

"It doesn't matter. Her name was Furey. It still is." Again the joyless laugh. "As in 'hell hath no fury'?"

Father Dowling emitted a smoke ring and followed its progress through the sun-filled parlor. It was important not to be enlisted on the side of one of the litigants.

Geary leaned forward. "Father, I am the injured party, okay?" He sat back when he was sure this point was established. "It's an Irish name. With an e."

If there were Fureys in the parish still, Roger Dowling did not know them.

"Where did you meet?"

"At a CYO dance." Geary shook his head. "I assumed she was what she seemed, a Catholic girl, Irish. The kind of girl anybody's mother would approve of. And she could dance."

A little smile reluctantly formed on Geary's face, where faded freckles suggested that the now gray hair had once been red.

"How old were you then?"

Geary had been twenty-three, Maureen Furey twenty-one. "I don't say I didn't know what I was doing. No, that's not right. I went into it with wide-open eyes, but the facts were hidden from me."

Had Geary been coached? Life looked at through the lens of the law, whether civil or canon, is distorted into clear chains of causality, simple motives, sharp contrasts between guilt and innocence. The aggrieved party had to portray himself or herself as innocent and put-upon, the spouse as the opposite.

"Father Noonan must have told you that a bride's not being a virgin is no impediment to a valid marriage. Nor need she tell the groom if she is not."

"Virgin!" This time Geary could not give even a semblance of a laugh. "It wasn't her body, Father, it was her soul."

"Her soul!"

"Can you validly contract a Catholic marriage if you don't believe a word of it?"

"Is your wife non-Catholic?"

Geary closed his eyes. He might have been praying for patience. "The woman I went through a marriage ceremony with claimed to be a Catholic at the time, but it has since become evident that she is no more a Catholic than she's a . . ." He inhaled. "I was going to say witch, but that ruins my point."

"She lost her faith?"

"She had none to lose. She hasn't been to Mass for fifteen years."

There was no escaping the dreary interview. Roger Dowling had no right to turn away someone who sought him out in his role of pastor. Over the course of the next hour he got one version of the married life of Maureen Furey and Michael Geary.

Michael Geary was the youngest of five sons. There had been no daughters, and Roger Dowling imagined that life for Mrs. Geary must have been like living in a fraternity house. Patrick Geary, the father, had been an electrician, active in his union, a Knight of Columbus.

"He was big in the Serra Society too. Fostering vocations to the priesthood? He would have given anything if one of us had become a priest. I myself thought of going to Quigley . . ."

Quigley was the preparatory seminary of the archdiocese. Roger Dowling had attended Quigley; it was where he had met Phil Keegan, now the Fox River captain of detectives, widowed, lonely, a frequent visitor at the rectory. An inability to learn Latin had kept Phil Keegan from the priesthood. His life was now spent in terms of crime and punishment rather than sin and forgiveness, but for all that he and Roger Dowling enjoyed each other's company.

"Maybe if it hadn't been for celibacy I would have," Geary said.

It was not often that husbands or wives spoke of marriage as the bed of roses disgruntled celibates imagined it to be. That Michael Geary, here to shed his wife because living with her was allegedly hell, should remember himself balking at celibacy was mildly surprising. In such circumstances, even inveterate spouses expressed a hankering for the monastic life or even for that of a desert hermit. Of course Geary was speaking of a time before he knew Maureen Furey.

Maureen's family was a social notch above Michael Geary's, her father a graduate of DePaul Law who was employed in the city attorney's office. One of two children, Maureen was the only daughter, pampered and spoiled as such things were measured by Geary standards.

"My mother never liked her. Mothers know."

"Know what?"

"She was the product of a mixed marriage."

Having too much to say, Michael Geary found it difficult to say anything. But the message was clear. Maureen had not intended to enter into the marriage contract with Michael, not as the Church understood it.

"We agreed to have kids, right?"

"Do you have any?"

"If test-tube babies were possible then, she would have had them that way."

She had gone through the ceremony, but not with the intention of being faithful to him alone. In retrospect, it seemed to Michael Geary that she had been a flirt at her own wedding, eagerly responding to requests to kiss the bride. One of his ushers had dug Geary in the ribs and said he'd just had a sample of what was waiting for the groom. Within weeks Geary wondered if the remark hadn't meant more than he took it to mean at the time.

"Marrying me was a lark. Better than finishing school. She never intended to have children."

"But you do have children?"

"Two. She said they were mistakes. 'I never could count.' " He adopted a falsetto tone as he quoted her.

A depression that had grown blessedly unfamiliar settled over Father Dowling as he listened to this tale. When he had been on the marriage tribunal this had been daily fare, one spouse going on and on about the defects of the other. So many of the complaints were petty and even taken cumulatively did not seem reason to jettison the marriage vows. But of course the marriage tribunal was not a divorce court, and litanies however long of the peccadilloes of the spouse did nothing to establish that a true marriage did not exist. Those who appealed to the marriage court were required to show that the marriage contract, despite appearances, had never truly been entered into. A shotgun wedding is no wedding, of course, but the tribunal never heard such clear cases. The duress under which the marriage ceremony had been gone through was more often claimed to be psychological, and in Roger Dowling's day, that basis had never been allowed. Claims to nonconsummation, if they could be proved, would make the judgment as easy as a shotgun ceremony. Once a woman with three children had claimed nonconsummation. To the embarrassment of the tribunal, it turned out that she meant she had never experienced an orgasm. Sensitivity courses at the Y had alerted her to what she was missing. It had fallen to Noonan to explain to the woman that the erotic delights she had been hearing of were not a condition of the marriage contract. In recent years Roger Dowling had heard that Noonan, the onetime naysayer, had completely reversed his stand and was now a champion of the easy annulment.

"These are serious charges, Mr. Geary. And almost impossible to prove. It would have to be shown that at the time of the wedding she had no intention of having children."

"She didn't."

"Did she indicate this to anyone?"

"Sure. To me."

"To anyone else?"

He seemed to run through a mental list. "She must have."

"Witnesses would have to swear to that fact."

"She never intended to be faithful either."

"That might be even more difficult to prove."

Geary lit a third cigarette. He blew out the match and shook his head. "There's no need to prove it. She'll admit it."

"Have you told Monsignor Noonan that?"

A quizzical smile formed on Geary's thin lips. "Is he a monsignor?"

Once those who received this title of honor had relished it. Noonan himself had lobbied shamelessly with the previous archbishop and taken great pride in the sartorial side of being a domestic prelate—red piping and a shoulder cape on his cassock, a red pompom on his biretta—but came to think that monsignors were a drug on the market and now as often as not referred to himself simply as Father Noonan. In any case, in street clothes, there was no distinguishing mark between monsignor and simple priest.

Michael Geary said he had indeed told Father Noonan of his wife's admission that at the time they married she was determined not to have children and to take her pleasure where she found it.

"She just wanted to get out from under her parents' thumb."

"I'm not at all clear why he asked you to come to me." Father Dowling turned in his chair and felt again the envelope in his pocket, the envelope with two tickets to the Notre Dame–Southern California game to be played in South Bend. He had not hurried Michael Geary through this interview; he had listened with patience and interest; he had tried however unsuccessfully to feel sympathy with the man.

"I need a letter indicating the name of the priest who presided at our wedding," Geary said.

This could have been accomplished with a phone call. Father Dowling forbore telling Geary this. He got out the ledger for the relevant year, checked the entry, and wrote on parish stationery that Father Gerald O'Neil had said the nuptial Mass and witnessed the exchange of vows between Maureen Furey and Michael Geary. Having shown the letter to Geary, he took it, folded it and put it into an envelope. Taking the envelope in one hand, Geary pulled another from his pocket and showed it to Father Dowling. It was addressed to Rev. Melvin Gorce, in care of a Michigan diocese. Father Dowling looked at Geary.

"What's this?"

"I'll mail it to them."

"You're filing in Michigan?"

"Yes."

"Didn't you say your residence is in Chicago?"

"We have a summer place up there. Father Noonan put me onto Father Gorce."

A summer cottage seemed a flimsy basis on which to claim residence, but the Michigan diocese had become notorious for the ease with which it granted annulments. The fact that Melvin Gorce was involved made it less mystifying that Noonan had sent Geary to Roger Dowling.

"I'll appreciate any help you can give me, Father Dowling."

"The proof that you were married at St. Hilary's may be the extent of it."

"Has she been here? Maureen?"

Not to answer the question would be to feed Geary's suspicions, although he had no right to expect an answer.

"No."

This brightened Geary considerably. As he showed his visitor out, Roger Dowling's hand went involuntarily to his chest and patted the pocketed tickets. In minutes he could be on the phone to Phil Keegan.

Back in his study, his visitor gone, he sat behind his desk to revel briefly in the unexpected bonanza. And then, inevitably, it occurred to him to wonder why Bishop Ravel had decided to send these tickets to the pastor of St. Hilary's in Fox River. Ambrose Ravel had also been on the marriage tribunal, and his career had developed in the fashion Roger Dowling's might have if he had not been undone by the sadness of dealing with couples striving to get free of one another. Roger Dowling's path had diverged from Ravel's, to put it mildly. Possibly the auxiliary bishop thought with sadness of what he would pardonably consider the ruined career of Roger Dowling. Bishop Ravel would probably think Father Dowling was only making the best of a bad thing if he told him how content he was in Fox River, doing the work of a priest, saying Mass and dispensing the sacraments to people he had come to know. Such thoughts delivered no explanation of why these tickets had arrived in today's mail. It would be churlish to call Ravel and ask why he had sent them. Perhaps it was simply an example of the largess an auxiliary bishop could now from time to time dispense.

But uneasiness grew in Roger Dowling until he found himself reluctant to call Phil Keegan with the news. Once Keegan had been told of the tickets and understood that the two of them would be sitting on the forty-five-yard line on the Notre Dame side of the field, the die would be cast. There would be no way in the world he could withdraw the invitation. But why would he want to? It was ridiculous to look a gift horse in the mouth. The image of the Trojan horse formed in his mind, perhaps prompted by the fact that Southern Cal's team was known as the Trojans and its mascot was a horse. He was almost relieved to hear the doorbell ring, but before he could stir Marie burst from her kitchen and went clattering down the hall to the door.

He waited for her clattering return. She came to a stop in the doorway of the study, her hands on the frame, leaning into the room. She whispered what she said and he did not hear her. She frowned and tried again. He shook his head.

"Maureen Geary," she said aloud. Then she added, "In the *front* parlor."

Ash-blond hair, clear gray eyes, a brow that seemed to harbor only noble thoughts—Maureen Geary was not at all what her husband's heated description would have prepared him for. He shook her gloved hand, asked her to be seated, went around behind the desk, glancing toward the street as he did so.

"I waited until he left, Father."

Father Dowling sat down, relieved. Things would go more quickly because she knew her husband had been here first.

"And what can I do for you?"

"You must know why I'm here."

"Tell me."

"Michael is filing for an annulment."

"In Michigan."

"We spend our summers there. It's the only place."

"To spend the summer?"

She smiled suddenly and her eyes crinkled nicely. "No. I meant for him to get an annulment. Or so I've heard. I will fight it, Father. It is a farce to claim that we were never married. Where does he suppose our children came from? I've offered him a divorce, but he won't hear of it. Only if the Church says we're not married will he be happy."

"Why?"

She made a little face. "What's the usual reason? He wants to marry someone else."

"Is that what you want?"

Her smile was gone. She sat back. "Do I imagine I smell tobacco smoke?"

Father Dowling did not relish the thought of being lectured about smoking in his own home, but he knew the bumptious zeal of the new Puritans.

"Yes."

"May I?" She took cigarettes from her purse. Well, the Gearys had that in common anyway. He waited for her to light the cigarette she took from the pack.

"You're willing to divorce your husband?"

"I don't *want* to, no. But I can't stop him from leaving me. Anyone can get a divorce. Can anyone get an annulment?"

"Well, they're certainly more frequent now; the procedures have changed."

She shuddered. "Oh, I've heard all that from Michael. The new Church. Well, I don't believe in the new Church, if that's what it is."

"You're both practicing?"

"Practicing? Michael's an expert."

This was said to be the age of the layman in the church and doubtless it was a good thing, but Father Dowling had learned that there are laymen and laymen. The bad kind really wanted to take over the pastor's duties, swarmed over the sacristy, longed to do everything but say Mass and suggested that even that was only a matter of time. It was the view of the pastor of St. Hilary's that in the age of the layman what was wanted was not imitation priests but laypeople taking the faith into their various walks of life and making it felt there. He gathered that Michael Geary was the first sort.

"A spoiled priest?"

She sat back. "I never heard the phrase."

"A man who might have been a priest but didn't and can never quite forget it."

"Oh, that's Michael to a T."

"You suggested there's another woman."

"There's always been another woman."

"Which is why you would file for a divorce?"

"Or at least consent to one. It would only be to acknowledge what has been true for years." A small smile this time. "What has been true for years is that Michael has been untrue for years."

"Unfaithful?"

"Faithless. To me and to a series of playmates."

"That may be grounds for divorce but not for annulment."

"It's Michael who wants the annulment, Father, not me."

"He would have to bring charges against you."

"Oh, he'll say I'm not a real Catholic."

"What does that mean?"

She sighed. "Do you really want to hear all this?"

"No."

Surprise gave way to a sad laugh. "I don't suppose it is much fun having people break in on you like this and babble about one another."

"It's not a matter of wanting to hear it. But tell me."

"Well, the craziest complaint is what I think about annulments. He accuses me of accusing the Church of annulling valid marriages. Well, it's true I've said that if he can get our marriage annulled the Church will be wrong. But, Michael insists, for a real Catholic the Church can do no wrong. Therefore, I am not a real Catholic."

"Let's hope the Church deserves your confidence."

"Father Gorce thinks Michael has a very good chance."

"Your husband should have filed for an annulment in Chicago. Your lawyer should make that the first point of business."

"My lawyer?"

"A defender of the bond. You are not alone before a marriage tribunal. The burden of proof is on your husband."

"Why did he come to you?"

"Weren't you married here?"

"I suppose he hoped it wasn't recorded." She looked at him. "Was it?"

"If you'd like proof, I could give you a copy of your marriage certificate."

"Proof! Why should I need proof? But that is why I came. I looked all through the house, I checked our safe-deposit box and didn't find it. I even suspected Michael of destroying it."

Michael Geary had invoked the name of Noonan; he had begun their conversation with the statement that he wanted an annulment; he had made grave accusations against his wife; he had shown Father Dowling the envelope addressed to Melvin Gorce. Despite all this, the pastor of St. Hilary's found Maureen Geary a more credible informant than her husband, though the basis for this was certainly superficial. She looked honest; she did not seem the faithless wanton Geary had portrayed; her charges against him were more plausible than his against her. Husbands are more likely to be untrue than wives.

"You talked to Father Gorce?"

"Yes."

"I am sure he explained to you how unlikely it is that the Church will annul a marriage. Divorce is the dissolution of an existing contract. The Church does not recognize divorce where a marriage has been validly entered into. An annulment is possible only if a marriage never really existed. It can be granted only if, despite appearances, the consent of one or both parties was not really given."

"Father Gorce didn't talk that way at all. But then Michael got to him first too."

"But you think there really is a marriage between you and Michael?"

"Father, if the Church says we aren't married, then the Church won't be what I always thought she was. Michael and I are married. Sometimes I tell myself, why not just go along with it, tell them what they want to hear, let Michael have his way." She smiled vaguely. "Maybe I'd marry again myself."

"What you say to the tribunal would be under oath."

She looked away and drew thoughtfully on her cigarette. Smoke slid from her lips like some portion of her soul. She looked at him.

"I wonder if Michael realizes that. It would be like lying in confession, wouldn't it?"

"Not every problem has a solution, Maureen. Not even large problems. But if life together has become impossible, a separation . . ."

She held up the hand from which she had not removed the glove. She smiled wistfully.

"I came here just to get a copy of our marriage certificate. You're lucky I waited for Michael to leave or you would have had two crazy people here at once."

"I would like to talk to you together."

"You're kidding."

He wasn't. Speaking with her, he was able to believe that whatever had gone wrong with the Gearys, and obviously something very serious had, it was not irreparable. Would people divorce in such great numbers if it were more difficult to do so, if they could be reminded of what they had undertaken and be persuaded to take up the burden anew? Of course, it seemed preposterous to suggest that there weren't enough marriage counselors in the country. But then marriage counselors were not exactly what he had in mind.

"How old are you?"

"Fifty-two." She hadn't hesitated. "Fifty-two next month."

Once that would have been thought an almost patriarchal—or matriarchal—age. Did Maureen or Michael or both see themselves as still on the threshold of life, or at least able to begin again as if for the first time? People get out of marriages because they wrongly think they can revert to what they were before. But we are what we do. And what we do sometimes gets us into impossible circumstances, although less often than is thought. Difficult, perhaps, but not impossible.

She listened while he said these things, and there was no rejection or defiance in her manner. But when he paused, she made a little face.

"Father, it's not just a matter of what I think."

"I know."

"What did Michael say?"

"You wouldn't want me to repeat our conversation to him."

"Oh, I know what he would have said. When he drank too much, he would tell people I had a little problem. The first time he was unfaithful, or at least the first time I learned of it, he began to spread little stories about me."

Roger Dowling could wring Gorce's neck for encouraging Michael Geary to apply for an annulment. He did not want to believe that they were as easily gotten in the Michigan diocese as rumor had it. The marriage bond is a sacred thing, and it was unthinkable that any diocesan tribunal would treat it cavalierly. At the moment, his inclination was to believe Maureen and consider Michael a pathological liar. Imagine what the man had sat here and said about his wife.

On the other hand, it was unwise to think that when a marriage sours it is the fault of one party alone. Finally, each of the Gearys blamed the other. The question was whether they were interested in repairing the damage and living the promises they had made to one another long ago in St. Hilary's parish.

"I'll give you what I gave him, proof that you were married here."

"Okay." She sighed. "I suppose I should have proof."

He asked about her children then Kate, the daughter, was married and living in South Bend, where her husband was a student at Notre Dame.

"What will she make of this, Father? That's what really bothers me.

I try to imagine what I would have thought of my parents if they had done anything remotely like this."

"The annulment?"

"Marriage is hard, Father, sometimes it seems impossible, but if we can just walk away from it, well, that's what we're likely to do whenever things get rough. I don't want my kids to be like that."

"Perhaps I could arrange—"

But she was shaking her head, eyes closed, before he finished. "No. No, Father, please. It's too late." She looked at him. "Whatever damage we can do to Kate and Brian is done."

"Where is Brian?"

"He is living in Minnesota, in a place overlooking the Mississippi."

"Is he in school?"

Her eyes were on him when she said, "No. He left school to enter the monastery. He was going to become a monk."

"Ah."

"Now he wants to be a hermit. He'd have to explain it to you."

After he had shown her out, it occurred to Father Dowling that it was a mark against Michael Geary that he intended to pursue an annulment in Michigan. Procedures in Chicago were not what they were, but it was not the ecclesiastical Reno Gorce was running. The depression all this caused Father Dowling was partially assuaged when he took from his pocket the Notre Dame tickets as if making certain that they were real.

He put through a call to Bishop Ravel and was told he was out of town.

"Any message, Father?"

"Cheer, cheer for old Notre Dame."

"I beg your pardon?"

"He'll understand."

Marie Murkin sat at her kitchen table, moving a spoon about in her cooling cup of tea, preoccupied with the odd goings-on in St. Hilary's rectory. Her problem was not that she didn't know what was going on but that she knew just enough to make her deeply uneasy. First had been the letter from downtown, from the Most Reverend Ambrose Ravel, one of the platoon of auxiliary bishops who helped the cardinal run the largest diocese in the world. Marie had been housekeeper since before Roger Dowling was assigned to the parish. She had willingly bade good-bye to two of his predecessors, but the thought of Father Dowling's being reassigned and leaving the rectory had the aspect of a nightmare. Any letter from downtown was thus cause for some anxiety, and matters were not helped by the pastor's practice of teasing her about them. Her only defense was to feign total indifference to their contents.

This morning that had been particularly difficult because of the name typed above the printed legend: "Most Reverend Ambrose Ravel, D.D." Phil Keegan had once given her to understand that Ravel had gotten the advancement meant for Roger Dowling if he had remained on the marriage tribunal. If Marie Murkin *had* permitted herself to entertain the nightmare of Father Dowling's transfer, rather than drive it from consciousness like an impure thought, she would imagine his being summoned back to the marriage court and put once more on the path to honor and promotion. It might have been "Most Rev. Roger Dowling, D.D.," typed in the upper left-hand-corner of envelopes. It was all too easy imagining the bureaucrats downtown asking themselves what they were doing wasting a man with a doctorate in canon law as pastor of St. Hilary's in Fox River.

This fear had been fed by the fact that the overwrought Michael Geary had told Father Dowling he had been sent to Fox River by Noonan. Monsignor Jerome Noonan, that is. In the hallway, where she was dusting and couldn't help overhearing the beginning at least of Geary's conference with the pastor, the name caused her to gasp. Fearful she might have been heard, she slipped away to her kitchen.

If Father Dowling left St. Hilary's, so would she. She had no fear of the future. Marie Murkin could always support herself. Not that she would take another rectory job. She just couldn't imagine giving her all to another parish. She had put away a bit, and Father Dowling had set up a retirement fund for her, worked out by Amos Cadbury, the distinguished Fox River lawyer. She would just go off to a warmer climate and sit in the sun. For part of the year, anyway. She could not leave the Chicago area for good.

She hated these thoughts, but she had been driven to them by the names Ravel and Noonan. She sought distraction in an item printed in a special left-hand column on page three of *The Fox River Tribune* under the title "Jeopardized Virgins." The item began, "In the past week three reports have been made of disappearing lawn statues of the Virgin Mary. No connection between the thefts of the inexpensive images has been discovered but, according to police, neither has a connection been ruled out." Marie shook her head, as much at the events reported as the sassy way in which the *Tribune* exploited it for a laugh.

After Geary had gone, Father Dowling returned to his study and just sat at his desk. Marie was determined not to be the first to give in, to go in there and beg him to tell her what Bishop Ravel had wanted. She had of course noticed the way he slipped the envelope into his pocket, lest her eye happen to fall upon it and learn its contents. Waiting was torture, minute following minute until she thought she would scream. She had to know her fate! When the doorbell rang she ran for it as if Father Dowling would try to beat her to the door.

And there on the doorstep was a woman announcing that she was Mrs. Michael Geary! What in heaven's name was going on? Marie had to practically shout the woman's name before Father Dowling understood. But then his reaction was appropriate to the surprise of the caller. And that was why Marie sat at her kitchen table, stirring her tea over and over again, just worried sick.

She got up and turned on the radio, WBBM, her favorite station, nonstop news or, as Father Dowling complained, nonstop commercials, but Marie liked the banter between male and female announcer, listened avidly to the weather reports and took what the pastor called culpable pleasure in following the accounts of traffic jams throughout the Chicago area during rush hour. Reported from a vantage point in the Sears Tower, the conditions on the Eisenhower and Stevenson expressways brought cheer to the heart of St. Hilary's housekeeper, sipping tea at her kitchen table.

The phone in the kitchen gave off the little sound that indicated someone somewhere in the house was on the line. Since Father Dowling was the only other person in the house, it was a pretty safe bet that he was calling someone. But how could she be absolutely sure? Thoughts of an intruder, entering by an upstairs window and making a furtive phone call, justified picking up the kitchen phone. No need to make a production of it, of course, which is why she eased the instrument off the hook, covered the mouthpiece and listened.

When she heard the pastor's joyful voice asking to speak to Bishop Ravel, Marie actually cried out. Thank God she had covered the mouthpiece. She put the phone gently back on the hook, slumped into her chair and sipped her lukewarm tea, a look of devastation on her face.

Phil Keegan showed up for the noon Mass and Roger Dowling asked him to come to lunch. It was then that he told Keegan about the Notre Dame tickets.

"How would you like to watch Notre Dame play Southern Cal, Phil?"

"That's not until next month. Is it on the tube?"

"I meant in person."

"Oh sure."

"I've got two tickets."

Phil Keegan said warily, "We going to be chauffeured down in a stretch limousine?"

"I don't think Bishop Ravel has one."

Marie appeared in the kitchen doorway.

"Ravel?" Keegan asked. "What's he got to do with it?"

"The tickets are a gift from him."

"What for?" Marie cried, rushing into the dining room.

"The Notre Dame–Southern Cal game."

"That isn't what I meant."

But Father Dowling was looking at Phil Keegan, whose expression had become beatific. His unseeing eyes were fixed on the wall, but it was clear that in his mind he was already jammed into the stadium watching what sportswriters were calling the game of the decade.

"Why would Bishop Ravel give you tickets to a game like that?"

Marie's reaction renewed his own wonder about the reason for this unexpected bonanza. But before he could call his benefactor again Bishop Ambrose Ravel telephoned him.

"Roger! Ambrose Ravel."

"Hello, Bishop. I've been trying to reach you."

"You got the tickets?"

"Yes! And thank you. What a surprise."

"After I mailed them, I thought I should have sent them Federal Express. That game is really being talked up."

"Well, after all, Notre Dame."

"Do you get down there often, Roger?"

"Not at all since coming to St. Hilary's."

A pause. "Are you liking it there?"

"Very much." Emphatic, but not overly so; it would not do to suggest how contented he was.

"You don't miss the tribunal?"

"Does a paroled prisoner miss his chains?"

Merry laughter. "That would be more appropriately said of the petitioners."

"Not in my time. Most of them left with their chains intact."

"Roger, there are forty thousand annulments in this country every year."

"Good Lord."

"Exactly. Out of fifty thousand worldwide. The Holy Father has several times pointed out that North America has by far most of the Church annulments granted. As we did awhile back of laicizations. He sees a connection."

Roger Dowling had of course avidly followed the pope's trips to the United States. On the first visit, he had seen the pontiff in downtown Chicago, and it had brought back those glimpses one got during the Angelus in St. Peter's Square.

"I had an ulterior motive in sending you those tickets, Roger."

His heart sank. "Oh?"

"Yes. Roger, the Bishops' Committee on Marriage and the Family will be holding a special meeting at Notre Dame with some members of the Canon Law Society for several days just before that game. Cardinal Hildebrand is coming from the Vatican. Of course, that's very hush-hush. The topic is annulment procedures in this country. I am representing the bishops' committee. I want you there at my side, as my *peritus*."

"You're as expert in canon law as I am, Bishop. More so."

"Your experience on the tribunal was in stricter times. Now you have pastoral experience as well. That's a rare combination."

In moments of gratitude for the life he led at St. Hilary's—a life of obscurity that had enabled him to recapture his vocation and grow, or so at least he hoped, closer to God—Roger Dowling had reminded himself that he was at the disposal of his superiors. If the cardinal—or the appropriate committee on clerical appointments—sent him elsewhere, he would of course have to go. And the elsewhere he most dreaded was back to the marriage tribunal.

He told Ambrose Ravel he hoped he was doing some good in this parish. "I know it's been good for me."

"You're certainly eligible for a better assignment, Roger. Have you ever applied?"

"I am exactly where I want to be."

"You are a fortunate man. But I want to disturb the even tenor of your ways just this once. Will you accompany me to the Notre Dame meeting?"

That this was a request he could refuse was clear from the tone of Ravel's voice. Roger Dowling took a minute and when he answered had the ominous feeling that he was agreeing to far more than was being asked.

"Sure. I'll be at Notre Dame to see the game anyway. I'll kill two birds."

Ravel laughed. "That was the idea, Roger."

Old Father Tuohy, who had spent almost as much time in a retirement home as he had as pastor of St. Paul's, had endeared himself to everyone he ever met, even his fellow priests, and his funeral had the dimensions of an archdiocesan event. Of course the cardinal usually celebrated the Mass on such occasions, particularly now that he had been in Chicago long enough to have had at least some acquaintance with the deceased. But he had been unable to attend and Bishop Ambrose Ravel was the celebrant.

The Cathedral was packed. The sanctuary was full of prelates and half the church with priests. The laity had to take what they could get, except of course Tuohy's twin sister, who hobbled down the aisle to the front pew, looking from side to side as if she might start blessing the lot of them.

In the sacristy, Bishop Ravel came up to Roger Dowling and put out his hand. Did he expect Father Dowling to kiss the episcopal ring? But Ravel had the look of a man who had made a deal. The handshake was to confirm it.

"Notre Dame is favored by ten points."

"I'll settle for one."

" 'The game of the decade.' I quote *Sports Illustrated*."

"There seems to be a game of the decade every week."

"Ho ho," Ravel said and drifted away. From across the crowded sacristy, Jerome Noonan had been watching, and he now lifted his brows significantly.

When they formed the procession Noonan fell in behind Roger Dowling, so they ended up side by side in the same pew.

"Roger," Noonan whispered, squeezing his arm. His general air was that of a coconspirator. How little he had changed, a benefit perhaps of going bald early.

"Monsignor Noonan," Roger Dowling replied.

Noonan looked more than half a bishop in his monsignorial regalia.

"And you know which half," Tuohy had chuckled the last time Roger Dowling had visited him. That had been before the Gearys' visit to the rectory reminded Father Dowling what he had talked with the older priest about. Tuohy had frowned when the marriage tribunal had come up.

"Anyway, Noonan should be a restraining force."

"I don't know, Roger. I hear they're calling him Wolsey the way he argues for nullity."

Tuohy had taught at Quigley before becoming a pastor, so his priestly life was divided into thirds: teacher, pastor, emeritus.

"Our court is still strict compared to others," Roger Dowling remarked.

"At least when a priest leaves we don't say he never was ordained."

But Tuohy was not one to dwell on the troubles of the present and the delights of the *vita ante acta*. His equable temper was an achievement, not a natural gift, and it arose from an unshakable confidence that all would come right with the Church in the end.

"And with ourselves too, Father, let us hope."

Tuohy's end had come at eighty-three, and here they all were, fellow priests and laymen, in a festive mood, certain that if anyone had been ready to give an account of himself, it was Tuohy.

Ambrose Ravel preached, his performance given generally high marks by the clerical audience, most of whom thought they could have done at least as well.

"Do you have a car, Roger?" Noonan asked after the Mass.

"Don't you?"

"I walked."

"Well, you can't walk to the cemetery."

"Is that an invitation?"

And up the street they went to where Roger Dowling had parked.

"The Gearys have been to see me," Father Dowling said, once they had gotten into the trail of cars headed for the cemetery. Police were everywhere, busily making sure that the funeral procession was given right-of-way.

"Tuohy would have loved this," Noonan said as patrol cars maneuvered, lights flashing, with now and then the guttural growl of a siren.

"Did you suggest to Geary that he apply for an annulment in Michigan?"

"Remember Gorce?"

"Is that why you sent Geary there?"

Noonan turned sideways. In street clothes he might have been a senior partner in a law firm, a banker, someone whose success did not depend upon dealing directly with the public.

"You got out at the right time, Roger."

"It wasn't exactly my decision."

"Subconsciously it was."

"Well, I don't know about subconscious, but I wasn't always as clearheaded as I might have been, then."

"All that in the past?"

There was a tinge of condescension in Noonan's voice and anger leapt in Roger Dowling, but he suppressed it. Noonan had known him in his time of weakness. But that weakness had, in God's providence, turned out to be his salvation. What if he had stayed on the marriage court? He found himself less censorious of Noonan.

"Thank God."

"Geary wants out, Roger. It's that simple."

"Is there anything wrong with their marriage?"

"Canonically? I doubt it."

"So why encourage him?"

"Maybe he wants to marry an organist." Noonan's eyebrows continued to lift as Roger Dowling looked at him. "That may be why he decided not to file in Chicago."

Noonan either thought Father Dowling understood this enigmatic remark or expected him to ask about it. Father Dowling decided not to. Noonan had always been a conduit of unreliable gossip.

"Would he have gotten a declaration of nullity in Chicago?"

"Maybe Gorce will see it differently."

"How about the wife?"

"She's divorcing him anyway."

"What they need is a good talking-to."

"That's why I sent him to you."

The funeral cortege was slow but required Roger Dowling's attention because every once in a while it seemed they would speed it up. But he had time to think that he had not performed well with either of the Gearys.

"I don't think I was much help."

"Oh yes you were."

"How so?"

"Geary came back to me. He'd sent the papers to Gorce but now he wants me to assure him that he's doing the right thing. In the eyes of the Church."

"Tell him to reconcile with his wife."

"Is that what you told him?"

"I wish I had. What are the children like?"

Noonan shrugged. "Never met them. It hadn't come to that point. Ambrose seemed to single you out in the sacristy, Roger."

"He said hello."

"You see much of him?"

"I don't see many monsignors, let alone bishops."

Noonan misunderstood the remark. "We'll have to get together more often, not just funerals."

"Come have dinner at the rectory."

Noonan let that pass. "Ambrose is the best of the bunch. I mean of the auxiliaries. He's going places."

There was a shade of envy in Noonan's voice, regret for what might have been, but Roger found himself grateful that he had escaped ecclesiastical advancement—auxiliary bishop in Chicago, then a small diocese of one's own, after which a large city, an archbishopric, maybe cardinal . . . Is that what awaited Ravel? It seemed oddly plausible. And Roger Dowling realized he wouldn't trade St. Hilary's in Fox River for any of it.

"Well, he's going to the Notre Dame–Southern Cal game."

"The best deal I found was five hundred dollars for a pair."

"I didn't know you were a fan."

"I'll be there for a Canon Law meeting that week."

Roger Dowling busied himself with the car, though they were moving along smoothly now, the procession convoyed by police officers on motorcycles.

The crowd of mourners surrounded the grave and the bishop's voice came and went on the slight breeze. Autumn seemed a good season in which to die, going out with the summer, waiting for winter. A silly thought. Tuohy was beyond seasons now.

"I'll catch a ride back with Flannery, Roger."

"It was good to see you."

"Remember about dinner."

"There's always a place set."

"Keep me posted on the Gearys."

It puzzled Father Dowling that Noonan acted as if the Geary marriage had now become the concern of the pastor of St. Hilary's. Maybe he was right.

Kate Geary had stopped going to Mass sometime during her sophomore year at St. Mary's. No religious crisis had been involved, no solemn decision of the kind involved when she quit smoking. She just stopped going. One Sunday she slept in and nobody noticed; the sky didn't fall; she felt pretty much as she had before. Insofar as she thought of it at all, it was to notice that not many others went to Mass either. Or if they did it was to midnight jammie Masses in the dorm, some special occasion, the ceremony vaguely reminiscent of Girl Scouts and Camp Minnetonka. A theology course convinced her that she hadn't just stopped the practice of her religion. She no longer believed any of it either. As far as she could see, neither did the professor, who explained that the Resurrection didn't mean that Christ had actually risen from the dead, and that the miracles narrated in the Gospels were doubtless later inventions to gain a hearing for Jesus as a wonderworker. Nor had Jesus thought that he was divine; he hadn't meant to found a church or any of that. All that came later, the invention of the first generation of Christians. Or maybe the second. None of this matched what Kate had once believed, and she had no interest in this laundered version of Christianity. She had lost her faith, and it bothered her a little that the loss didn't mean more to her than it did.

So she talked with Ginny, who was forty and a nun and seemed to think she was still a coed. She wore her graying hair long, dressed with expensive casualness, saw her role in the dorm as providing an ear for students in times of crisis.

"Don't be so sure," Ginny said when Kate told her she had lost her faith. "I've often thought the same thing."

And she was off. A feature of bringing your troubles to Ginny was that they were soon eclipsed by the nun's own. Ginny obviously paid a great deal of attention to the events of her own life, all of which she took to be fraught with significance. Kate listened as the nun sketched the dark night of the soul she had passed through many many times. To take just one example, there was a time when she had walked down the cinder path toward the river, stopped and looked up and imagined the sky, space, emptiness, just going on and on and on forever, just infinitely out there, not needing anything or anyone to explain it. So where was the need for God? Ginny made funny little faces to punctuate her story and ended with a helpless smile.

"Maybe there isn't any need," Kate said.

"That's what I thought! And *then* I thought, maybe I was just produced and I'll grow old and eventually die and my body will return to the common pool of stuff, and that's all there is to life."

Kate nodded. It sufficed.

"So then why am I a nun? Why am I living my life in this way?"

"Would it really matter?"

"What do you mean?" Ginny was shocked.

"What difference would it make if instead you'd married and had a zillion kids and—"

But Ginny was distracted by a knock on her door and Kate gladly ceded her place to the next poor soul in need of counsel.

"Everything all right?" Ginny asked a week later, a funny little worried frown on her face.

"Supercalifragilisticexpialidocious."

"Cool."

It was not until the second time she went out with Mark that he told her he was a seminarian at Moreau, the seminary on the shore of one of the lakes on the Notre Dame campus.

"You're going to be a priest?"

"I'm thinking of it."

"Do they know you date?"

"I'm supposed to. It's part of the training."

Kate thought it must be a line, but it wasn't, and then she got mad.

"What am I, some sort of lab animal to help you test your capacity to be celibate?"

"I thought we had fun together."

They did. She liked him. If he had a vocation she would become a medical missionary to Zaire. Any date is a way of considering a boy in a more permanent role, however remote the speculation. But if he was speculating about living the life of a priest, well, that didn't seem fair. On the other hand, it undeniably added zest to what he always called their relationship. She was cast in the role of the feminine principle, the powerful deterrent to the pointless ascetic aspirations of males. It made her feel sexy. The first time he stayed over in her room she felt she had seduced him.

Losing her faith made sex seem more important, not less. She definitely did not want to be a toy, an instrument to gratify a man. As her own life took on the nature of a project if not a problem, she found herself looking forward to having kids. The way you raised your kids told you all about yourself, that was her new theory, one she would not have told Ginny.

Nor did she tell Mark the truth about her parents. The wonder was that the nonstop quarrel that was her parents' marriage hadn't driven Kate into the convent. The phrase "married bliss" always sounded ironic to Kate, but then that is how her father used it, ironically.

"Fifteen years of married bliss," he had said mordantly the first time she heard him use the phrase, in the dead of night, awakened by their quarrel. Her father sounded as if he were throwing in the towel, conceding the argument to her mother, or at least signaling that he did not want to go on with it. Not much later Kate realized that the recurrent reason for the quarrel was her mother's objections to the way her father acted with other women. At first she had imagined the flaw was something like bad grammar or a lack of social graces, which made some sense. If either of her parents was at ease in the company of others it was her mother. And then she learned what it was. She thought her father was fighting with Mrs. Wallace when she came upon them grappling in the front hall, but the way they jumped at the sight of her and fell all over themselves greeting her told her otherwise.

"We were just playing a game," her father said later, and that was that.

Her brother, Brian, developed a capacity to ignore the constant bickering of their parents. It was possible he really didn't notice, or care, he became such a weirdo so soon, building a chemistry lab in the basement and stinking up the house with mad concoctions. But he had developed a rocket that actually flew, zinging straight up and out of sight and then drifting back to earth on a beautiful striped parachute. Brian always won at science fairs; he got a Merit scholarship, and when he went off to Berkeley he in effect resigned from the family. Then out of the blue he left graduate school to enter a monastery in Iowa. Kate hadn't realized there still were monasteries anywhere, let alone in Iowa. It had been at least two years since Kate had seen her brother when her mother told Kate she was going to divorce her father because he threatened to apply for an annulment.

"What's the point, Mom?"

"The point?"

Maybe her mother didn't see herself at fifty-two as over the hill in the sex department. It seemed a strange age to be wanting to trade in a husband for someone new.

"Kate, I don't want to divorce him."

Not even after the embarrassment she must have felt when the parish organist publicly accused Michael Geary of sexual harassment? Her father's very visible and much honored service had apparently sufficed to snuff the accusation.

"Don't do anything, Mom. Let him do it."

"Do you know what an annulment means? It would mean your father and I were never married, and what would that make you and Brian?"

"Your children?"

"I stayed with him as long as I have for the sake of you and Brian."

"Oh, come on."

"I mean it. I didn't want you to be the product of a broken home."

Was the broken home a product of them? "Why an annulment?"

"The Church doesn't recognize divorce."

"Will Dad try to get an annulment even if you get a divorce?"

"What do you think?"

It had the air of a rhetorical question. If her father had never been married at all, in the eyes of the Church, then he would really be free. And if anyone lived his life in the eyes of the Church, it was her father. He had been unhappy about what had happened to St. Mary's, so far as being a Catholic college went. Kate defended it, trying not to think of her theology professor and Ginny and other things she doubted her father even suspected. The secularization of the school was just fine with Kate. It made her own slipping away from the faith of her father easier to do.

"Kate, don't you even care?" her mother asked.

"What will you do?"

Kate thought of Mrs. Wallace. Apparently there had been a regiment of Mrs. Wallaces. It was strange to think that her father was still like a teenager in the sex department. Marriage domesticated sex, put it in a wider context, made you grow up. At least it was supposed to. Kate thought this had nothing to do with religion; it was a promise a couple made to one another, obligations they took on to their kids. Not that it was just duty. Kate loved being married and she was darned if she and Mark were going to turn out like her parents.

It pained Kate to think of her father the way she and her girlfriends had thought of Mr. Oliver when they baby-sat the Oliver kids. When he drove the baby-sitter home, he asked funny questions. Kate and a friend had exchanged giggling confidences.

"Did he touch you?"

"He put his hand on my knee, as if by accident. He was driving. He wanted to know about my boyfriends and what we did."

Kate hadn't said anything about this to her parents. Like the story of her drifting away from the faith, it seemed to be hers alone. When she married Mark they had a big wedding in Sacred Heart church on campus; her father spent a ton of money and wept at the rehearsal dinner, wept during the ceremony and went around damp-eyed at the reception afterward.

"Make it work, kids," he said to them more than once, his advice floating to them on the scent of champagne.

By then she had let Mark in on a few of the family secrets. Having left the seminary, he was doing graduate work at Notre Dame, in theology, of all things. ("It's what I know. It was my undergraduate major.") Hers had been economics, but she didn't imagine that committed her to a lifelong attachment to the subject. Her interest had barely lasted through her senior year. Now she was married; they were living in graduate student housing; she was pregnant and her mother had told her she was divorcing her father and there might be an annulment besides. It didn't seem the best time to tell her mother of the grandchild forming now in her womb.

She got another version of events from her father.

"It's only technical," he said, when she asked about his applying for an annulment.

He sounded like Gatsby dismissing Daisy's husband. "It's only personal." She would not discuss religion with her father.

"Don't do it, Dad."

"Kate, it's nothing I can do anyway. If the Church says—"

"The Church! Forget the Church. We're talking about Mom."

He paused and she could see a dozen bad arguments flit behind his eyes.

"The process has already begun."

"If you're not her husband, you're not my father either."

"Kate."

"I mean it."

There had to be some way of stopping him. The way her mother spoke of Father Dowling made Kate want to talk to the priest. She had to talk to someone, and Ginny wasn't available anymore. She had finally gone over the wall and was sharing an apartment in Phoenix with Maxine, who had been in the art department. Kate told Mark she was going to Chicago to shop, which she intended to do, but her chief destination was Fox River. And here she was, stashed in the parlor of St. Hilary's rectory by a housekeeper who had greeted her as if she were a ghost, waiting for Father Dowling.

She had her father's flat face and clear blue eyes, but there were other strains in Kate as well, doubtless those coming from her mother's side. Father Dowling found her a mature young woman, at ease, though watching him closely as if she wasn't at all sure what he might say or do.

"It's been a while since I saw a priest in a Roman collar. Except for Father Hesburgh, of course, but he's not on campus much since he retired."

"So you're at Notre Dame?"

"My husband is doing graduate work." She hesitated. "In theology."

"Good God."

"Amen."

He was grateful for her cheerful reaction. It was a mistake, commenting on a whole department like that, particularly when one only heard of the bad apples, but if Kate was bothered, she concealed it well.

"I'm here about my parents."

"They've both been here to see me."

"That's why I've come. Is there any way to stop my father from getting an annulment?"

"I don't know."

"They've been married thirty years, they have two children."

He could have told her stories, but the story of her parents was bad enough for her. Her father had let her know he was asking for a declaration of nullity.

"In Michigan."

Obviously her father hadn't told her that. She thought Father Dowling was kidding her until the silence grew.

"I understand you have a summer place in Michigan."

"My parents do."

"The marriage court in the diocese up there has a considerably less crowded calendar than the Chicago tribunal."

"She's willing to divorce him, against her will. Shouldn't that be enough for him?"

"Perhaps he plans to marry again."

Her mouth opened and closed. She looked at the sparsely filled bookshelves behind him. The books there were more decorative than functional. Who had a chance to read in the parlor? His library was in the study. Her eyes came back to him.

"I'm no longer a Catholic, Father. I lost my faith. Even so, this shocks me."

She spoke as if she owed him the information. It proved to be a welcome diversion from her parents' troubles. Listening to her account of the fitful practice of religion coupled with the heterodox accounts of Christianity, both under apparently official auspices, Father Dowling found it easy to understand why Kate would do what she had done, wash her hands of the whole business. But what she had discarded was not Catholicism. Had she talked about these things with her husband the theologian?

"Oh, it's just research for him. Papers to be written, classes to be taken, and, in a year or two, on the job market."

He did not ask her if her husband too had abandoned the faith. How many of those teaching theology still believed? *When the Son of Man comes again will he find faith upon the earth?*

"I'd like to talk with you about it."

She made a face. "I'm so tired of talk about religion."

He laughed. "That's one of the definitions of sloth. Do you know Dante?"

"I know who he is."

"Have you ever read him?"

She hesitated, then shook her head. "Not really."

"You should. I recommend the Dorothy Sayers translation of the *Divine Comedy*." There was a set on the shelves behind him. He put the three paperbacks on the desk and pushed them toward Kate. "You can take those."

She leafed through the top volume. "You're right about him marrying again. I mean, if he ever did, he would want it to be kosher with the Church. I pity the poor woman."

"Is there a woman?"

"I guess there's always been a woman, Father. That's my mother's claim anyway. It's why they fought."

"Do you know if it's true?"

She thought about that. "Would they quarrel about something that wasn't true?" She shook her head. "He's like a little kid."

Her sympathies were apparently with her mother. He thought of the distraught man with whom he had spoken in this parlor. A daughter would never see a parent the way a stranger does, and by and large the assessment would be unrealistically positive or negative. Whatever grievances Maureen Geary had, they were compensated somewhat by her daughter's devotion. Father Dowling had thought Michael Geary a somewhat farcical character; what must it be like to think of your father as a clown?

"Your father seems to take his religion more seriously than your mother does."

"He's a professional Catholic, one hundred percent, hurrah for the pope. Always busy around the parish."

Is that what she thought it was, a tribal loyalty, keeping rules, going by the book? Michael Geary had made himself into a guardhouse lawyer on the annulment canons. Not that Father Dowling had anything against keeping rules. He suspected that Kate had come to him in the hope that he would call her parents to order.

"I shouldn't think the Church would want to do him any favors."

"Why not?"

She ran her finger along the edge of the table. "Because of what the organist at his parish accused him of."

"What parish is that?"

"Blessed Sacrament."

And Father Dowling now understood Noonan's enigmatic remark at Tuohy's funeral. Of course. He had not made the connection when he talked with Geary and it was odd his wife hadn't mentioned it. At first it had seemed a charge against Panzica, the pastor, but he was just being blamed for whatever happened on parish property. As suddenly as it had first appeared, it disappeared, but not before it was clear that a pillar of the parish was being accused. Michael Geary.

Kate stared out the parlor windows at St. Hilary's Church.

"That's where they got married, isn't it?"

"Yes."

"If they did." And suddenly she began to sob. It seemed right that someone should weep at the death of a marriage.

After she was gone, Father Dowling said, "She was taking it pretty well until the end when she broke down."

"She's expecting."

"Are you sure?"

Marie just gave him a look.

Alone, he reached for a one-volume Dante—*Tutte le opere*—on his shelf, moving aside a small bronze bust of the great Florentine.

"Keep an eye on that," Phil Keegan had advised recently.

"Do you have designs on it?"

"Ha. You know those little plastic statues with the magnetic base people stick on dashboards? Cy's wife had hers stolen."

"Stolen!"

"Came out of the supermarket and found the wing window of her front door had been forced open. The statue was missing."

"Anything else?"

"Not as far as she could tell."

"Odd."

"It gets odder. She mentioned it to a clerk in the store next time she was there and was told several other people had the same experience."

“She never should have married the sonofabitch in the first place,” Gordon Furey said when his wife told him she’d talked with Maureen and the Geary marital troubles had been topics one, two and three.

“She agrees with you,” Elizabeth Furey replied. “So does Michael.”

“After thirty years!”

“He wants out while he has time left, apparently.”

“Does he think he can start over again with some chick?”

“Maureen thinks his eye is on a matron. Catherine Burger.”

“Come on.”

Gordon Furey’s attitude toward marriage, toward life, was ironic. If people stopped looking for happiness, they’d be happier. What the hell, marriage is most people’s purgatory. His tired joke was to refer to Betty as his current wife, though they had been married longer than the Gearys. He sat now in the soggy costume in which he put in twenty minutes a day in simulated skiing, watching TV as he labored on his suburban treadmill. Sweat ran from his brow—body heat escapes through the skull—and he lifted his sneakered feet slowly, one at a time, staving off the stiffness, while in his chest his heart still pumped hard. He ought to be the fittest broker in town. Betty had started telling him about

Maureen and Michael while he was still on the machine, and his legs became a blur of motion.

"You'll loosen the plaster downstairs."

"I'd like to loosen Michael Geary's teeth."

"At least the kids are grown."

"What started this anyway, the organ-grinder episode?"

Betty made a face. It was her policy not to laugh at his jokes, even the good ones. The sexual harassment charge against Michael Geary by the organist at Blessed Sacrament, the Geary parish, had been a two-day story, followed by silence during which Christopher James, the organist's father, negotiated with the lawyers for the archdiocese. What exactly the charge was had never been made publicly clear.

"When she said 'Stop' he thought she was referring to the Vox Humana button."

"Gordon!"

"Confucius say, lady organist peddles it."

The jokes got worse, but Gordon didn't think it was funny, not really. There were days when he confessed, if only to himself, that he didn't know what the hell was going on anymore. There were days when, like Auden's clerk, he could write on a pink official form, I do not like my work. The poem purportedly was about the fall of Rome. Poets were always the first to sniff out decay. Betty tried to convince him it was just because they were older that the present looked so different, but it *was* different. Once there had been raunchy motels where X-rated movies were piped into the rooms; now every supposedly respectable hotel had pornography available. Just an example.

"Maureen filed for divorce so he would stop talking about an annulment."

"I'm going to have a talk with that sonofabitch."

"That ought to help."

"Can it hurt?"

What Gordon couldn't tell Betty was that once, fifteen years ago, when he himself had been fooling around, Michael got wind of it and cornered him in the locker room of the athletic club.

"Look, Mike, forget it. You don't know what you're talking about." Even now, years later, Gordon remembered the feeling of being justly accused and having no convincing response. And Michael knew it. He was in the catbird seat and loved it.

"She's my sister."

"I'm aware of that."

"Whom you married, Gordon. You stood in front of the priest and before God and—"

Gordon had grabbed Michael's arm and pulled him into the steamy anteroom of the showers.

"For Christ's sake, Mike, take it easy." He had clients here. Who would trust him if his wife could not?

"Exactly. For Christ's sake."

"You missed your vocation."

"I'm more interested in you being true to yours."

Gordon was cornered but at least Michael was speaking in lower tones, telling him marriage was a vocation, like the priesthood, a once-and-for-all deal. "Souls are involved here."

"And bodies." Little Karen was plump and uninhibited. Gordon made a damned fool of himself with her and he loved it.

Michael shook his head, more in sorrow than whatever. "I've spoken to the girl, Gordon."

"You what!"

"She took it a lot better than you. You know she's a Catholic?"

Gordon couldn't believe it. But it was true. The final conversation he had with Karen was brief and on the phone. She said she didn't like people calling her a sinner and a scarlet woman. "Especially when it's true."

He refused to win her back with theology, even if he could. Time passed and he got over it and so far as he knew Michael had never said a word to Betty. And now the sanctimonious ass wanted the Church to pretend he had never married Maureen and was really free as the breeze. Now it was Gordon's turn, and by God he intended to throw the book at his brother-in-law.

"Who'd you say the woman was?" he asked Betty.

"Catherine Burger."

"Burger Drugs?"

"The first wife thereof."

"Burger's still alive."

"And married a third time."

So what was the point of threatening an annulment?

"She was the first Mrs. Burger."

"Panzica?" Marie's voice rose on the second syllable and her nose wrinkled.

"Father Panzica, pastor of Blessed Sacrament. I've asked him for dinner."

"What kind of a name is that?"

"Blessed Sacrament?"

She turned her head and looked at him out of a corner of her eye. "Panzica." The accent on *zeek* was less exaggerated this time, and Marie's nose scarcely twitched.

"A family name."

Marie inhaled, and half a minute went by before she exhaled. Someday her face would turn blue. She started for the kitchen, asking over her shoulder, "What time is he coming?"

"About six, if he can find the place. I am quoting our guest."

"Hmmph."

"I suppose he's heard of your cooking."

She straightened and turned and looked sharply at him, as if she wasn't sure how the remark was meant. But Roger Dowling had pushed back from the table and bowed his head in thanksgiving. It was a questionable use of prayer, to end a teasing exchange with Marie, but then he was a little sheepish about his motives for inviting Larry Panzica.

Blessed Sacrament was the parish of the Geary family and had been since they bought their first house. Kate and Brian had attended the parish school; Michael had been a parish stalwart—usher, finance committee, extraordinary minister, golfing host of a succession of assistants (the pastor himself did not golf)—a pillar of the parish but apparently, like so many pillars, eventually a pillar of salt.

"He didn't look back, but he looked around," Panzica said as they sat in the study before dinner. He had taken a tentative sip and now held his glass before him for inspection. He looked at Father Dowling.

"Jameson's."

"God save Ireland."

"Panzica is an Irish name?"

"On my mother's side." He winked, then added, "And there's a mole on my father's side."

Panzica roared with laughter. He was a large swarthy man who walked on the balls of his feet and when seated looked as if he were ready to spring into action at the sound of a bell.

As soon as he had stepped inside the house, he had stopped, closed his eyes and inhaled the aromas emanating from the kitchen.

"*Sit nomen Domini benedictum,*" he whispered reverently.

"*Ex hoc nunc et usque in saecula.*"

Father Dowling wished Marie had been there to overhear this eruditely pious endorsement of her efforts, but she was avenging herself on him by working in silent servitude, something going on every burner of her stove while she moved around with the distracted expression of one about to be turned over to the lions.

In the doorway of the kitchen, he managed to get Marie's attention. She turned and lifted the back of her wrist to her forehead and looked meekly at the two priests.

"This is Father Panzica, Marie."

Larry took her hand and pressed it to his lips. "There are gods even here," he cried. "Heraclitus. Marie, I can hardly wait." He threw back his head and with closed eyes inhaled deeply, a beatific smile spreading across his meaty face.

Marie melted under this effusion and soon the two priests were shooed off to Father Dowling's study, where Panzica lauded the liquor he had been served. Was it too obvious that Roger Dowling had asked Larry Panzica here in order to quiz him? He put off the purpose of the invitation until later, when the table was cleared and they were sitting over coffee, with Marie offstage but doubtless tuned in.

"Tell me about the Gearys."

Panzica looked closedly at his host. "What have you heard?"

"He came to see me. So did the wife and daughter."

"How about Brian? Have you met him?" Panzica dipped his head and rolled an eye toward his host as he asked this.

"What's he like?"

"Remember Sorrell at Mundelein?"

The name did not ring a bell. Panzica was several years Roger Dowling's junior and their seminary careers had overlapped, but Roger remembered no Stephen Sorrell.

"Saint Stephen. The face of an altar boy, clothes out of St. Vincent de Paul's, a whiz in moral, nuttier than a fruitcake. He must have slept sometime but this was never established. All-night vigils in the chapel, bouts of fasting, scrupulous as a nun."

Panzica summoned these memories with relish, and Roger Dowling waited to learn their relevance. Brian Geary was another Sorrell, that was the point.

"Sorrell publicly asked the rector if he could justify the amount of money spent on our meals. That was the beginning of the end. He tried to organize the kitchen help and grounds crew. One visiting Sunday he picketed the faculty residence, carrying a sign listing the unjust practices of Mundelein."

"What happened to him?"

But Panzica was not to be hurried. "We called him the cereal killer. He ate nothing but Wheaties. Anyway, there was a story about him in *The Wall Street Journal* a couple years ago. Something about margin calls he couldn't meet. On paper he was a millionaire, until his margins were called."

It wasn't until they were once again ensconced in the study that the relevance of all this became clear. Roger Dowling left the door open, in deference to Marie, who had doubtless now settled down at the dining room table, within range.

Brian Geary had been a strange boy since grade school. He refused to serve Mass, saying he was unworthy.

"This was prior to puberty too. I told him no one is worthy. He offered to scrub the sacristy." Panzica shook his head. "The father was a more standard kind of zealot. Being a big man in the parish was a kind of disguise."

"Disguise for what?"

Panzica hesitated, mulling it over, and Roger Dowling repeated that the parents had come to see him, and Kate as well.

"She's down at Notre Dame," Panzica said.

"Yes."

"Why did they all come here?"

"He said Noonan had sent him. About the annulment."

Panzica sat back. "Annulment!"

"They were married here."

"The bastard talked about an annulment?"

Roger Dowling was surprised that Michael Geary's pastor had not known this. "He talked to Noonan but he's applied in Michigan."

It was all too obvious that Michael Geary's pastor had not been made privy to his plans to have his marriage declared null and void. Panzica shook his head slowly, a cigar at a jaunty angle between his teeth.

"Why am I surprised? He's just the type. If you can't or won't do what you promised to do, ask for a change of rules. If that guy can get an annulment . . ." Panzica shook his head. How many pastors had been as confused as the faithful by marriage tribunal decisions in recent years? Not that it had been a local problem, but as in the case of Geary it was all too easy to enter a plea in another jurisdiction, one like the Michigan diocese that was notorious for swift and uncomplicated declarations of nullity.

"What's the wife like?" Roger Dowling asked.

"A saint. So's the daughter. Roger, it's the men in the family I can't stand, and they're always around. At least Brian was until he went away to school."

"And the monastery?"

Panzica's great almond eyes rolled upward. "I'll do time in purgatory for the letters I've written for that boy. Was I supposed to tell some novicemaster Brian Geary was a wacko? Maybe he belonged in a monastery. That's what I told myself. He wasn't meant for the world."

"Geary's seeking an annulment is news to you?"

"But not surprising. They've separated. I knew that, of course. And that she filed for a divorce. I figured that was just a legal move; she knows marriage is forever."

"He says there never was one."

Panzica muttered profanely. "I suppose he could claim he meant to go on playing the field."

"Oh, he says the defective assent would have been on her part."

"What a jerk. Despite all the professional Catholic stance, the guy played around. He's got a thing for musicians."

"Oh?"

"The sonofagun seduced my music teacher, for crying out loud. Now she's playing piano in a dive on the North Side. When I confronted him with that, he dropped to his knees and demanded I hear his confession. He knew I couldn't refuse him." Panzica looked at Roger Dowling. "A real sweetheart. I tell you this because I knew of it, and so did others, before he tried to silence me with the seal."

"How long ago was this?"

"Three, four years."

"Did his wife know of it?"

"In my experience, Roger, husbands have very few secrets from their wives."

"You may be right."

"Then he seduced my organist and choir director. In the church!"

"Good Lord."

"I thought that's what you had in mind when you brought up the Gearys. It was in the paper until it got hushed up."

"Geary could do that?"

"Ha. No, it was the cardinal."

Panzica's expression was pained and sorrowful. The woman brought suit against the parish and the archdiocese, not against Geary. Or he was a lesser figure in the charge.

"Roger, when the story broke it sounded as if I had been up to something."

"What happened?"

"The archdiocese settled. The woman was a convert, against the wishes of her father. I'm sure it was his idea to sue, and to leave Geary more or less out of it. You can imagine what they must think of me downtown, costing them that kind of money."

"Did Geary have to come up with any money?"

"You'd have to ask him."

"The wife put up with a lot."

"And the kids. Well, the girl, Kate. I don't know her that well. Her husband is studying theology at Notre Dame."

The Notre Dame connection was obviously commendation enough for Panzica. What would he say if he knew of the two Notre Dame–Southern Cal tickets in the drawer of Roger Dowling's desk?

Panzica wanted to hear all about Geary's plans to get an annulment, but there wasn't much to tell. He knew that the wife had moved out; he thought it overdue, and she had talked to him about that.

"How did she explain it?"

Panzica made a face. "I suppose I should have asked. After all, she had put up with him all these years."

When Roger Dowling got them off the subject of the Gearys and asked Panzica what he thought the outcome of the Notre Dame–Southern Cal game would be, the pastor of Blessed Sacrament proved to be extremely knowledgeable. Roger Dowling could get absorbed in a game while it was going on, but thought little of sports at other times. He had always marveled at people who rattled off statistics and could give a play-by-play account of games played a decade before. At nine-thirty, Panzica rose.

"I've got to say goodbye to Marie," he said.

"Marie!"

But she was already in the doorway.

"Marie," Panzica said, "you're mine. I won you fair and square at cribbage. You will report to the Blessed Sacrament kitchen Monday morning."

"I know I lost," Father Dowling said. "But I thought that means I have to keep her here."

Marie Murkin had long experience with clerical humor and took all this with good grace. But there was nothing but sincerity in Panzica's praise for her cooking, and Marie was aglow when the door was closed and Panzica's big black car was backing out of the driveway.

"What a lovely man."

"It's too bad about his taste buds. He was in his twenties before he realized that other people tasted as well as smelled the food when they ate. Apparently he can't tell the difference between grits and tapioca."

Marie just glared, not dignifying this with a reply. But from the kitchen, before she opened the door to the stairway leading to her apartment, she called, "You're just jealous."

The house was outside La Crescent, Minnesota, high on a bluff overlooking the river. Originally it had been a two-bedroom ranch, built on a slab, but a series of owners had added wings and rooms without paying much attention to the heating plant. Already in fall, Brian could tell how cold the house must be in winter. Maybe even well-insulated walls and a better furnace wouldn't have kept it warm, with the wind sweeping up from the river, gathering force as it came and rattling windows and making the aluminum siding buckle and complain. Brian loved the place.

He had left the monastery, but he didn't want to go home, he didn't want to face his parents again after yet another defeat of his hope that he had a vocation to the religious life. Even his father had lost enthusiasm for the effort.

"Maybe God's trying to tell you something," he suggested when Brian decided the Franciscans weren't for him. But then had come the Dominicans—a week had sufficed to convince him to leave—and most recently the Trappists in New Mount Mellary outside Dubuque.

As he sat by the picture window—a single pane that seemed to ripple under the force of the gale—watching the landscape grow bleaker while the trees were stripped of leaves and the colorless uncut grass flattened, it was bitter to remember that he had come to think the religious orders he had tried did not demand enough of him. He wanted a contemplative cloistered order. Of course he had thought of the Trappists, but he had not known of the Iowa monastery, founded more than a century ago by a group of monks come over from Mellary in Ireland. The first time he saw the forbidding buildings, the austerity of the guesthouse and then the chapel, he had been sure that this was where he would spend the rest of his life.

The chapel was narrow and high and bare. The stalls seemed pushed back against the walls. A dozen monks at best were singing in the office when he arrived, their hands lost in their sleeves, the great cowls pulled over their heads, huge psalters propped up before them. At the great doxology they dipped forward, swimmers about to enter the pool, and Brian bowed too. His body responded as if in some previous life he had been a choir monk accustomed to making a right angle of his upper and lower body.

His eye trailed toward the far altar, a simple sacrificial slab in the otherwise empty sanctuary. The world he longed to leave seemed far behind him here, this monastery the very anteroom of eternity.

Gabriel, the guestmaster, spoke to him, spoke quite a lot, but Brian had thought it was only a concession to his function. But when he moved out of the guesthouse and into the monastery and was assigned a bed in the great bare dormitory, a monk who was not Gabriel chattered away, explaining everything. Again, that seemed called for by the occasion. But that evening in the common room he learned that silence was no longer the mark of the Trappist monks.

"It's what you say, not whether you talk."

An old monk giggled. "We had sign language before and our hands never shut up. If you're going to talk with your hands, you might as well talk with your mouth."

Brian was oddly disappointed and for the first time he found himself regarding this austere demanding life as somehow gone soft. His image of the Trappist was a gaunt man who slept in his coffin, had a shaved head and large eyes that seemed to see beyond time. A man who never used his voice except in praise of God.

He noted with disapproval that there was always coffee on in the common room and a Dubuque paper. The library was unheated, and Brian inspected the stacks, his breathing visible in the morning just after Mass when the others were sipping coffee in the common room and checking the sports page. Brian ran his hand over the spines of the volumes of Migne's Patrology and imagined himself reading through that great collection, volume after volume. He pulled one out at random,

Augustine on the Psalms. His Latin was insufficient for the task, but what difference did that make? He had the rest of his life to devote to it.

The abbot's name was Ramirez, and he was from Guadalajara.

"Spain?"

"Mexico. My father was a wetback." His smile revealed a golden tooth. Brian hoped that had been put in before the abbot became a monk. "Do you smoke?"

"I used to."

"You quit?"

"Yes, Father Abbot." He felt that he was acknowledging a high rank in a disreputable army, like a Mexican general.

"Cold turkey?"

"Yes."

The abbot opened his desk and pushed a package of cigarettes toward Brian. "It might be better to taper off."

"I stopped smoking two years ago."

"Why?"

Brian told him about the Franciscans. He told him about the Dominicans too. He had resolved to be totally candid.

"They made you stop smoking?"

"I wanted to."

The abbot had taken a cigarette from the pack. He rolled it in his fingers, then put it in his mouth. He produced a lighter and thumbed it into flame. The acrid smell of burning tobacco seemed almost sacrilegious. The abbot watched him through a cloud of smoke. There was little in the office to distract Brian. A bookshelf between two windows that looked out on a courtyard, opposite a great crucifix before which stood a prie-dieu. Brian imagined the abbot kneeling there for hours, lost in contemplative prayer. The cigarette was meant to mislead him, to mock the pride that can go with ascetic effort.

"May I?" he said, nodding toward the pack of cigarettes.

"How long did you say it had been?"

"Two years."

He did not push the cigarettes toward Brian. "Tell me about your graduate studies."

Did astronauts have trouble later believing that they had really been in space? Did those who had walked on the moon come to doubt they had actually stood on that lifeless surface? Brian had difficulty believing his memories of Berkeley.

"I studied physics. Theoretical physics. Astronomy."

"Would I understand any of it?"

"If you can follow a story."

The abbot thought he was kidding, but he was serious. The theoretical physicist imagines accounts of data, trying to include as much as possible in the plot. Reduced to mathematics, such stories took on rigor, and it was easy to forget that they had been spun out of thin air. Thin air. The phrase seemed akin to those which prompted one to devise a story. Light showing up where it did on the spectrum suggested distance from the observer, and soon a vast system of galaxies emerged, rushing away even as one tried to account for them.

"Is it true that a falling star fell centuries ago and we only see it now?"

Brian had not come to the monastery to talk about the life he was fleeing. The abbot had lit the cigarette, but he didn't smoke it. One puff and then he let it burn, and finally he put it out.

"Have you met the novicemaster?"

It was an excuse to end the interview. That night, sleepless in his narrow bed, the dormitory filled with the noises and smells of sleeping men, he told himself that the abbot was a saint who had smoked only to ease a newcomer into the demanding routine of the house. Where had the cigarettes come from?

There were days, weeks, the first month really, when Brian had been almost completely content, sure that at last he had found the niche God had made for him from all eternity. It would have been perfect if he could have overlooked the annoyance of living with the others. Borromeo beside him in chapel had breath so bad it was impossible to ignore. The organist played awfully, and the Gregorian chant adapted to the psalms in English required a knack no one in the community seemed to possess. It was painful to sit through the reading, in chapel, in the refectory; words were mispronounced, the cadence suggested incomprehension of what was being read. Brian's day became an effort to keep away from the other monks. But there was no escape from the snoring and farting in the dormitory. On a solitary walk he came upon the hermitage.

He hadn't known what it was, a simple stone building, with a slate roof like the main building, all alone in the woods.

"Gabriel built it," he was told. "He'd been reading Merton."

Like Merton at Gethsemani, Gabriel had wanted to spend weeks in solitude in the woods, away from the community, exchanging the cenobitic life for the hermetic.

"Could I see it?"

"Ask Gabriel."

Gabriel seemed oddly defensive when Brian asked to see the hermitage.

"It's just a stone hut."

"How often do you go there?"

"It's been a while."

Gabriel gave him the key, and Brian went with great excitement through the woods. The door opened with some difficulty; it was not hung properly; and inside was a chill musty smell, but sunlight fell across the main room, which was dominated by a fireplace. There were a bedroom and chapel and a small kitchen. From the window Brian saw the privy twenty yards away. He stood in the sunlight and opened his arms as if to embrace the room, the hermitage, the solitude.

"Who told you about it?" the abbot asked when Brian asked permission to spend some days at the hermitage.

"I came upon it on a walk."

"How did you get inside?"

"Gabriel gave me the key."

"Do you still have it?"

"Yes."

The abbot extended his hand. Brian hesitated before handing it over.

"This is a monastic community. We live and pray together."

"But Gabriel . . ."

The abbot smiled. "Talk with Gabriel about it."

"I just wanted to get away from the others," Gabriel said. "I thought I wanted to be alone with God but what I really wanted was to be apart from the community."

Brian told himself that the abbot had talked Gabriel out of the idea of the hermitage, shaming him with the suggestion that he was shunning the others and thus deficient in charity. The thought grew upon Brian that he was meant for a life of solitude. The problem was how to live like a hermit in the world.

The house on the bluff overlooking the Mississippi River was the answer to that. He had never felt so alone in his life. Or so cold. He resolved not to start the furnace until the temperature dropped to freezing. After a few nights, he put an electric blanket on his bed and that made sleep possible.

The trouble with solitude was that there was so much time to think. Had he imagined that nonstop prayer was possible? Human nature is incapable of that. Odd aches and pains made themselves felt; he found himself thinking and thinking about the cold. Efforts to get out of himself brought thoughts of his family, of his father's incredible desire to have his marriage annulled and his mother's compromise offer of a divorce. Had his parents been unhappy? Of course they had, but they had been happy too. He had never thought before that their being husband and wife depended on their being happy. Kate's long letter made it clear how hurt she was by what their father was doing.

Sitting by his window, looking at the Father of Waters, he thought that what his father needed was a retreat, time in a monastery, a few days down there at New Mount Mellary among men who knew that this life is soon ended in death. *Memento mori.* Remember that you must die.

Amanda James was nineteen years old when she returned from school at Thanksgiving break and told her father she was going to become a Catholic. They were dining at the club. Holidays always brought back his sense of loss, Marge's swift and painful death from leukemia, and Christopher James cherished these times with his daughter. He had excluded any thought of remarrying because he didn't want Amanda to think he had so easily gotten over his loss. Her announcement came without prelude, and immediately he associated it with the loss of her mother.

"I suppose most people think of it at some time in their lives."

"Have you?" The spark in her eye seemed to suggest that they might go in together. He sensed that it was important to handle this with great care.

"Yes, I have." This wasn't quite true. He had examined the preposterous claims of the Roman church, not because he felt any attraction to it, but because it seemed the sort of analysis a man ought to have at his disposal. He had never dreamed that he might use those refutations on his daughter. And he didn't, certainly not on that occasion. The arguments were barbed and incisive and he knew they would have anything but the desired effect.

She spoke with great seriousness of the attraction the Catholic Church had for her. Unsurprisingly, it was the liturgy and the music that drew her: Gregorian chant, Palestrina. She actually hummed a little there at the table while he nodded tolerantly. She might have been chanting mantras, telling him she was going to put on a yellow robe and pester people in airports. He didn't know what to say that would not sound cruel and make things worse.

"You mustn't do anything rash."

"Oh, I'll have to wait until Easter. Holy Saturday."

Would those intervening months change her mind? Her mind. It was the first time he realized that his daughter was an autonomous person, having thoughts and desires that were out of his reach. Her mother had been plain, but Amanda was pretty in a wispy way. Her hair was light in color and not abundant and her coloring suggested pastels rather than primary colors, pale blue eyes, brows that lacked strong definition, a nose that just escaped being pug, narrow lips. She had never done anything without consulting him before. Her choice of school, her major subject, had been as much his decision as hers. Not that he had felt he was imposing on her. He had never before felt any mystery in her, any depth he did not know.

"They told me to speak to you about it, but I would have done that anyway."

She meant the chaplain of the Newman Club. That there were religious centers on campus was inevitable, he supposed, but he had never imagined they would pose a danger to Amanda.

"I would be disappointed if Renaissance art did not have an effect on you."

"I told the priest we're Protestants. Is that right?"

"Well, non-Catholics."

"Was I ever baptized?"

"No."

Her lips parted in wonder. "Then I'm a pagan."

Good God. But he remained calm, at the table, and during the week she was home. In her room he found a rosary. He picked it up with his fountain pen and held it at arm's length, staring at it. Did she mumble prayers over those beads?

What was the point of a university education in the twentieth century if young people were not made immune to medieval superstition? On Sunday morning he was wakened by the sound of her car starting. From his window he watched her back out the driveway.

"I've been to Mass," she said when she returned. He was in the kitchen, in his robe, eggs and bacon ready, both Chicago papers waiting to be read.

"Better get going on your breakfast. I've been keeping it warm."

"I'm always surprised how crowded Catholic churches are."

Threaten people with hell if they don't come and you could fill any church.

He associated her susceptibility with the loss of her mother, but there was more. Marge's parents had been Catholics, not very fervent ones, and she had thought of herself as one until he talked sense into her. She let it go without difficulty. Nor was there any objection from her parents when they had just a civil ceremony. The issue had never come up again—until leukemia struck.

Protecting her from priests seemed the least he could do for her, and he had been successful, he was sure of it. Once he had come into her room to find a bearded fellow standing at the end of her bed. He was too scruffy and unkempt to be on the staff. James thought he was a visitor who had wandered into the wrong room, or some kind of kook who liked to stare at people in pain. And then he saw the wooden cross hanging around the man's neck on a leather thong. He just stared at the hand the man extended to him.

"Leave her alone."

"I'm the Catholic chaplain. Your wife mentioned to the nurse that she's Catholic."

"Get out of here."

For a moment he thought he would have to pitch the fellow into the hallway. It sickened him to think of priests and ministers preying on the ill, catching people when they were afraid.

Had he sneaked back when James wasn't on guard? James had told them at the nurses' station that his wife did not want to be bothered by any chaplains. The reaction had been impassive. It was as important to keep all this from Amanda as it had been to prevent that bearded chaplain from snaring Marge in her final moments.

"I see you're saying your beads."

"The rosary? Mama gave me that."

"When?"

"Just before she went back to the hospital the last time."

"I never saw her use them."

"She wouldn't have wanted to disturb you."

He laughed. "Why on earth should I be disturbed? Do you know what worry beads are?"

He told her, describing men in Athens running wooden beads through their fingers, swiftly, over and over, a nervous habit.

"That's different," Amanda said.

"I suppose the effect is about the same."

She smiled out of her imagined wisdom, and he wanted to strike her. But it was the sense of having been deceived by Marge that struck him. The suggestion that she had retained some vestige of religious belief after seeming to assent to his dismissal of it was troubling. It altered his sense of what his marriage had been, falsified his memories.

They went to Florida at Christmas, two weeks on Longboat Key. They were hardly settled when she found out where the closest Catholic church was.

"I want to go to Mass Sunday."

"Amanda, sit down."

He spoke to her calmly and with great reasonableness. He surprised himself. Did she really understand what Catholics thought the Mass was? Could any rational person believe that a Galilean who had died two thousand years ago showed up on all these altars at the words of a priest? It was worse than magic. Magic is meant to astonish and entertain. Religion fetters the mind with nonsense, plays on fear and foolish hope. Did Amanda really think that all the people who had died since the beginning of the race would one day leap out of the ground, all the dust and bones coming together again, flesh forming, consciousness returned?

"I believe whatever the Church teaches."

Her pale blue eyes glistened with credulity. Her calmness infuriated him, and the sense that no matter how persuasive what he said might be, she would remain unaffected by it.

He went to a driving range and hit twenty dollars' worth of balls, punishing them, his swing methodic and smooth despite the raging anger within him. Some of the balls went nearly three hundred yards.

"Will you come to my baptism?"

"No."

"That's all right. I understand. But I wanted to ask you."

He did not tell her that he would rather watch her suffer and die than do what she intended to do. This conjured up images of Marge, and he had the irrational certainty that she had capitulated to that chaplain before she died, been blessed and mumbled over and torn definitively from him. And now they were taking Amanda as well.

"I hate the Catholic Church."

"That's better than being lukewarm."

"Have they given you answers for everything?"

"There's only one big question, Dad."

"No. There are a million questions. And most of them have no answers."

The impulse to cut her off, disown her, deny she was his daughter, was strong. But the prospect of being all alone unnerved him. Besides, it would be to give them a double victory.

He decided to pretend it meant little to him. My daughter the Catholic. She graduated and came home and took a job in a parochial school, and her connection actually brought him clients. The priest, Panzica, asked him to draw up contracts for the teachers in his school. When he didn't send a bill, Panzica called him up and asked what he owed.

"That's all right. I did it pro bono."

"Oh no. That's why people don't want to do business with the Church, they think they're expected to contribute their services."

He did send a bill, for less than he might have. Did Panzica think he was a Catholic? Amanda still lived with him, and that softened the blow her defection had been. Once he stood in the vestibule and listened while she played the organ. Ushers kept coming up to him, offering to seat him, but he shook his head, made a face and pointed to his stomach. They left him alone.

Amanda enjoyed teaching in Blessed Sacrament School as much as playing the organ in the church, and he had listened patiently to her anecdotes, happy for the most part. Being a Catholic had something of the aspect of a fairy tale for her. An item in the newspaper brought home to her that not everyone felt the same.

"Daddy, how awful!" With eyes rounded in horror she handed him the paper.

Someone had nailed a pigeon to the street door of a downtown church, apparently while the bird was still alive. He shook his head.

"Why would anyone do such a thing?"

He might have mentioned the offering of birds in the temple of Jerusalem, as well as sheep and oxen. She must have noticed that in the New Testament. Of course he said nothing. He prided himself that she had no idea that her father was numbered among those who thought her religion primitive, an affront to reason. Perhaps the pigeon was a bloody parody of the Mass Amanda daily attended.

Then, one day, out of the blue, Amos Cadbury suggested lunch and made an extraordinary proposal.

"I am quite in sympathy with the organizers, Christopher. On the other hand, should there be litigation with the Church, I could not represent them. My loyalties would be hopelessly divided."

"Sympathy versus loyalty?"

"They are right to call attention to the psychic attrition that has been caused by such judgments. As often as not there are children. Or one spouse is adamantly opposed." Cadbury leaned forward and whispered. "There are forty thousand annulments granted in the United States each year."

All this was news to Christopher James. He had not realized that the Church's jurisdiction actually took the form of tribunals and judges. There was a Code of Canon Law and a long tradition of interpretation and application of it.

"Not that you would be engaged in canon law, Christopher. The group is considering civil redress."

"Amos, I am not a Catholic."

"That is why I've come to you. I think any Catholic lawyer would feel as I do. On the one hand, there have been victims of these declarations of nullity by ecclesiastical courts. On the other, if the correct procedures are followed, if declarations are upheld on appeal, there is no further action possible within the Church."

Christopher James, untrammeled by religion, could give the benefit of his undivided expertise to the group that had formed. There would never be a suspicion that he had, however unconsciously, shortchanged his clients out of reverence for the Church. Thus it was that James had become counsel to Victims of Canon Law, VOCL. The president of VOCL was a young man named Frederick Burger.

"This is Mr. Christopher James," Burger told the some two dozen charter members. There were ex-wives and ex-husbands as well as children of marriages declared never to have existed. The hurt and resentment that had brought them together were palpable. They applauded when he stood, and he looked at them with the sense that they expected much of him. It provided him with his opening.

"I intend to plead your cause with every ounce of energy I have and with every skill I have learned in a quarter of a century of the practice of law. I am not a Catholic. It is not the theology of matrimony or the jurisdiction of ecclesiastical courts that interests me. Like yourselves, I find it surprising that a process that for centuries granted a minuscule number of declarations of nullity now seems to issue them almost casually and without adequate concern for their effect on those concerned. The hardship and heartache this has caused cannot go unaddressed."

How sweet it was to make a principle of his disdain for the Church and to have for clients loyal Catholics who were determined to sue the socks off their Church, for their own benefit, to be sure, but also to stop the flood of annulments. In a litigious age, their cause seemed certain to gain hefty judgments in the courts.

All this was uncharted legal territory. Would the civil courts consider a class-action suit against the Archdiocese of Chicago beyond their jurisdiction, a breach of the constitutional provision for the freedom of religion? When he was permitted to file, inquiries came in from around the nation. Christopher James soon had a team ready to travel and advise local attorneys in suits like the Chicago one.

This turn in his career, the reason Amos Cadbury had come to him, though he never made a point of it, was James's successful handling of Amanda's case. When Michael Geary, a married man, a pillar of the parish, began to show an interest in Amanda, to offer her rides home from choir practice, Christopher James had only suspected the archdiocese's vulnerability. As counsel for VOCL he had been ready and eager to go back to the well again and again.

"Sue the Church?" His mother made a little moue. "What for?"

"Revenge!" But he laughed when he said it, eliciting a laugh from her as well. "And the money."

"I have plenty of money, Freddy."

"Lucky you."

"Now don't start that."

And of course he didn't. Freddy Burger had no intention of distressing his mother. He could not afford to make an enemy of her the way he had of his father. The organizational effort he had put into VOCL should have endeared him to his father, if the paternal parent had given a damn about anything connected with his first marriage. It was his mother who had petitioned for and received an annulment. Freddy sympathized with her desire to have the Church make it official that his father had gone through the marriage ceremony without in any way intending to be faithful to her for a month, let alone a lifetime. But his first reaction to the judgment had remained.

"So what am I, a bastard?"

"Freddy, that doesn't follow."

And she showed him such proof as she had, the statements of canon lawyers and theologians, that the children of annulled marriage were not thereby illegitimate. It was a logical screamer. Legitimacy required a legitimate marriage, but in this case no marriage at all had ever existed. Ergo, he had been born out of wedlock.

"Not in the eyes of the Church."

Ah, the simplicity of his mother's faith. It was because the Church said so that her marriage had never existed. It was because the Church said so that the child of that marriage was nonetheless legitimate. No wonder she also accepted the absurdity of the Church's teaching concerning sexual orientation. As far as Freddy knew, she had never had the least doubt about him, and he had been discreet, painfully discreet. Others rhapsodized about the joys of coming out, of enlisting the support of parents and siblings. But Freddy had witnessed such scenes and sensed in the body language and expressions of the family what their deepest feelings were. It was too much like the heroic acceptance of a retarded child, a defiance by the parents of their own deep sense of shame and inadequacy, no matter the public stance. Freddy had no desire, or need, to put his mother through that.

"If you think your father will appreciate your efforts, you are very much mistaken."

"Can you believe that he and you and I have very little to do with this effort?"

She dipped her head and gave him a lashy look. "No."

He laughed and gave her a noisy kiss on the still taut skin of her cheek. He was proud of her beauty and the way she took care of herself. She golfed in summer, swam throughout the year and twice a week worked out exhaustively at her health club. It was there that she had caught the eye of Michael Geary.

Geary had already caught the eye of Freddy. Well, captured his attention. Geary was a caricature of the gung-ho professional Catholic who made Freddy physically sick. His mother's loyalty at least had the merit of self-interest. Geary could always be counted on for unsolicited endorsements of Church edicts and pronouncements. In the local Catholic press he ranked as a sort of celebrity thanks to his well-publicized generosity to one cause or another. Freddy had developed a fascinated hatred of Geary, the kind of obsession that led him to stay on the lookout for news of the loathsome man. And then, in what could have been an answer to his prayers, if Freddy had still prayed, Michael Geary was accused of sexual harassment by the organist at Blessed Sacrament parish. True, Freddy felt a fleeting solidarity with a newcomer to the ranks of the outcasts. Geary, needless to say, denied everything. That was *de rigueur* in such matters. The photograph of the wronged maiden did not address Freddy's concupiscence, of course, but she was not a femme fatale by any estimation.

Freddy began a folder on the case, clipping out the initial story. The following day there was extensive coverage of Geary's denial, his expressions of sadness coupled with continuing Christian charity toward his accuser. The by now familiar routine.

The folder never thickened. The story was exhausted before four days had passed and sank into a journalistic black hole. Others might be curious as to what had happened, but Freddy was astounded. The diocesan paper carried a résumé of the secular accounts that weekend, and then the story definitively died. Freddy called the papers; he called the television stations; he wrote letters to the editor that were not used, so he called about that.

"Too much Catholic-bashing."

"Hey, I'm a Catholic."

"Lots of bashers are."

Something in the man's tone prompted Freddy to say, nicely, that he sounded like someone who had been bashed himself.

"Well, I've been abashed."

"Ho ho."

His name was Larry. They met for a beer. Freddy had misdescribed himself of course, intending to look around the place to locate Larry. He would only make himself known if . . .

"Freddy?" Slim, thirty, big eyes.

"Larry? Well, you are a surprise."

It gave him a conduit into the kind of local news that interested him. Larry was religion editor, but he did obits and letters as well. They took a booth and had their beer and Larry brought him up to speed on the Geary case.

"A negotiated settlement is being crafted behind closed doors."

"Geary admits guilt?"

"Geary is the least of it. The suit is against the parish and the archdiocese. The woman's lawyer knows what he's doing."

"Who is he?"

"Christopher James."

"James?"

Larry nodded. "Her father."

The rumored settlement bore out what Larry said about James's skill. The problem was that the lawyer's appetite seemed to have been assuaged by the bundle he got for his daughter. How to enlist him for VOCL?

Larry's account and the possibilities it opened up caused Freddy to put an end to the discussions he had been having with a lawyer named Tuttle, a cut-and-slash type, Freddy thought, who might be just what VOCL wanted. He asked the little lawyer if he had any qualms about taking on the Catholic Church. Tuttle put his tweed hat on, then took it off.

"In what way?"

"Legally."

A sly smile. "Son, whatever falls within the purview of the law is my meat and drink."

Maybe, but Tuttle seemed on a vegetarian diet at the moment. Still, a lean and hungry look seemed just the thing. Until it occurred to Freddy that he could get the local best.

"Amos Cadbury wouldn't touch it with a ten-foot pole," his mother cried when he told her he had an appointment with the dean of Fox River lawyers.

"I'm counting on that."

"Then why on earth . . ."

Larry had told him the scuttlebutt to the effect that the patrician lawyer had sometimes said bitter things of his church's altered policy on annulments. Of course he would never state such criticism for publication. This suggested Freddy's tactic.

Amos Cadbury steepled his fingers while Freddy made his case. The old man shut his eyes from time to time, in response to the scandalous statistics Freddy rattled off. Of course Cadbury knew them perfectly well, and he was clearly pained by them.

"We are now ready to hire counsel."

The manicured fingers broke contact; his hands separated. He explained that, sympathetic as he was, it was out of the question for him to represent VOCL.

"Whom would you recommend?"

The noble head of white hair began to move negatively, then stopped. Idea. He thought a moment.

"Let me see what I can do."

Two days later, Freddy had an appointment with Christopher James and VOCL had its counsel.

"Even if it's right it's wrong," Marie told him, shaking her head so vigorously her hair began to dance free of its pins. "And I can tell you most people feel the same way."

"You may be right."

"Of course I'm right."

Marie glared at him, certain he must be up to something, conceding her point so quickly. But the housekeeper was very wrong if she thought Roger Dowling was going to defend the explosion of annulments in recent years.

He might have told her what had brought him to Fox River and St. Hilary's, but he supposed she knew. Housekeepers know everything, particularly about the pastors they serve. Once it had caused him agony to listen to people pleading for what the tribunal would be unable to give them, release from their marriage, the declaration that it had never been and they were free to begin over again and this time do it right. One might have thought he would have welcomed the change of policy that had opened the floodgates. As soon as psychological factors were admitted, it began to seem that no one was capable of making a lifetime commitment.

But the same reasoning had been applied to priests who wanted to leave. Entering Quigley as a teenager, caught up in a process that led inexorably to ordination, was one ever really free to say no? Parents and friends expected the seminarian to go on to ordination. Wasn't there moral suasion there that could intensify to a point where the candidate was acting under duress?

His own vocation, the choice of it, had been a point of reference when Roger Dowling was on the marriage tribunal. A man was ordained at a later age than most men marry, a few years older. At least that had once been the case.

"I can't even remember the day," a man would say. "And I don't mean because of the reception."

Women too claimed their wedding day was a blank. "I look at the photographs and it's like an event in someone else's life."

But it is the nature of the past to sink into obscurity; if it were vividly before us in all detail, the present would be impossible. We bring it back selectively, remembering this and that, forgetting most of it. And the future constantly moves toward us, obscure, unpredictable. We project our plans into it and keep on adjusting to twists and turns we could never foresee. This is not a defect, but the nature of life. Yet the obscurity of the past, the dimness of the future and the chanciness of the present are now regularly evoked as impediments to entering into marriage.

"So what are they going to do about it?" Marie wanted to know.

"Something. The pope is concerned. He is sending a representative to the meeting I shall be attending at Notre Dame."

"Meeting! I thought you were going to a game with Phil Keegan."

"The meeting comes before."

"Well, this is the first I ever heard of it."

"Marie, it's all very confidential. I tell you of it now because of course I can trust you with a secret, but also to assure you that you are not alone in being angry about all these annulments."

"That's what I said."

"I'm only repeating you."

Her eye was on him, waiting for some indication that he was teasing. But he just looked innocently back at her until she turned away. In the doorway of the study she looked back at him.

"Who is the representative?"

He held up his hand. "Marie, I don't want to put your ability to keep a confidence to an unfair test."

"Tell me."

"I'll tell you afterward."

She made an angry noise and disappeared.

Ambrose Ravel had sent on several manila envelopes jammed with papers—minutes of meetings, an offprint of an article on tribunals, clippings, *monita* from Rome, transcripts. They lay unread on his desk. What an enormous price Ravel was exacting for those Notre Dame–Southern Cal tickets. If Phil Keegan had not made the game the point of his life, Roger Dowling might have withdrawn. The prospect of sitting down with Cardinal Hildebrand was an exciting one until he thought of the purpose of the visit.

Noonan called to say the price of tickets was now above five hundred dollars. "Imagine being there and having to leave as the game is about to begin."

"Have you called the university?"

"Roger, they don't want this meeting. They feel they were snookered into it. They live in dread of being identified with Hildebrand."

"Good Lord. The man is prefect of the Congregation of the Faith."

"Formerly the Inquisition, as *The New York Times* always adds. But think of that theology department."

"They're not involved, are they?"

"The university isn't involved. Not technically. The Center for Continuing Education and the Morris Inn are public places. The Jehovah's Witnesses have been meeting down there for years. The university is clean."

"Clean."

"Uninvolved."

"What do you think will come of the meeting?"

"Nothing."

"Something has to be done."

"Sure. Just apply existing law and regulations. There's no need for more regulations. It's the dodging of them that is causing the problem."

"So what's the answer?"

"Get tickets for that game."

The Center for Continuing Education was located on Notre Dame Avenue, just north of the University Club, across the street from the Morris Inn, to which it was connected by tunnel. Despite its name, it was a convention center where lectures were given and academic and other seminars and meetings held. Its auditorium was equipped for simultaneous translation, a capacity put to use during the inaugural meeting involving the *periti* of Vatican II in 1965. The main lobby rose two stories, and during breaks in meetings held in the rooms above, participants could look down on those seated below.

On this Monday morning, with nothing scheduled, Will Lawrence looked into the empty auditorium, passed through the unoccupied lobby, waved at Phyllis fussing behind the reception counter and sailed into his office.

"Hello, hello, hello."

Three women responded in similarly joyful tones—Wanda the Caucasian, Harmony the Black, Pearl the Vietnamese. The CCE was a No Smoking Area, an equal opportunity employer, one of the few units of the university outside the Athletic Department that showed a profit, a model of its kind.

His leather chair received his posterior in an almost obscene embrace. On his desk were, to the left, messages, in the center, correspondence, to the right, his agenda for the day.

"Professor Bieler is due in fifteen minutes," Pearl said.

"The junk mail is on the bottom, first-class on top," Harmony said.

"A Bishop Ravel called," Wanda said. "You might want to return his call before you see Bieler."

"Ravel."

"From Chicago."

"Bishop Ravel from Chicago."

"He's with the canon law group."

The three women groaned in unison, saving Lawrence the trouble. Into their well-ordered life, where meetings were scheduled months, sometimes a year, in advance, had come, a month earlier, the need to arrange a special meeting of the Canon Law Society.

"Impossible" had been Lawrence's first reaction.

"We only need a meeting room."

"The Philosophy Department has a two-and-a-half day meeting on those days, fifty guests have preregistered, the Morris Inn is full."

The impossible became possible when Lawrence was called to the main building by the associate provost. The president and provost and various other myrmidons were already there when he arrived, occupying every chair. For an unsettling moment he feared he was going to be made to stand, but a chair was found in a closet and unfolded for his use.

Sourd of philosophy resumed what he had been saying. The philosophy meeting had been moved to the library auditorium; rooms had been found in local motels. Lawrence resented this usurpation of his function, but was relieved that the reshuffling had already been done.

"Have you scheduled anything else?"

"The Class of seventy-nine is coming in on Wednesday . . ."

"Cancel that."

"Yes sir."

Waddel from security was called on for an inarticulate assurance that his staff would be supplemented by a dozen Pinkerton agents.

"We met with the Vatican advance man," the vice provost told the provost.

"Does the cardinal have a bodyguard?"

"I hope so," the president said, to general laughter.

The cardinal was Josef Hildebrand, and whether he was mentioned by name or title, Lawrence could see he was the bad guy, so why all this fuss over a meeting that featured him? Evidently overtures had been made to hold a special convocation and award him an honorary degree, but the cardinal had declined. He had also declined quarters in Corby Hall, preferring the Morris Inn. "Since I am a guest of the Canon Law Society, not the university." The provost seemed to be imitating a German accent. When the president laughed, everybody laughed.

"They still resent our independence," Bieler explained.

"The country's?"

Bieler took it for a joke, thank God. These were uncharted waters for Lawrence. Bieler was happy to expatiate. The course taken by American Catholic universities, particularly their theologians, had not endeared them to the Vatican. Bieler saw it as a matter of decentralization.

"Subsidiarity," he added. "A time-honored principle of Catholic social doctrine."

"What does it mean?"

"Let the authority closest to the problem handle it."

Later, Lawrence tried to explain it to his staff. Xavier Foy was dumbfounded by the transfer of the philosophy meeting to which he had devoted months. The other two program directors weren't speaking to one another and paid unrelenting attention to what Lawrence had to say.

"I don't get it," Pearl said. "He's coming to Notre Dame but he doesn't want to be the guest of the university and the university doesn't care if he comes, yet they're turning everything inside out for him."

"What about the game?"

"The meeting is due to end on Thursday."

Gill from the Morris Inn had been told to keep six of the rooms commandeered for the Canon Law Society meeting through the weekend, thus uprooting guests whose claim on rooms for football weekends was almost hereditary. It was too late to find other rooms within a hundred miles of South Bend.

"They're offering me rooms in Moreau Seminary," Gill wailed. "These are people who consider staying at the Morris Inn camping out. Have you ever seen a seminary room?"

"No."

"Barebones."

"Bad?"

"They're singles. The beds are as wide as your butt. The best I can say is that the linen is clean. They'll have to go down the hall to the john. Will, these are couples I'm talking about."

"You're going to put women in the seminary?"

"I'm not putting them there, the administration is."

There were threats of changed wills and altered giving to the university. By comparison, Lawrence felt relatively above the fray. All his dirty work had been done for him. Of course philosophers could be counted on to be philosophical. Sourd said he actually preferred meeting in the library. If the departments and other centers had a choice, they might all prefer to avoid the CCE, given the hefty fees. Lawrence resolved to make certain that the present rearrangement would not be considered a precedent.

Bishop Ambrose Ravel arrived in a Lexus at eleven o'clock.

"I want to inspect the scene of the crime."

A joke. Lawrence showed him around, told him of the Vatican advance man and the Pinkertons. Ravel might have been a Pinkerton himself, except for the collar and the gold chain.

"What's Cardinal Hildebrand like, Bishop?"

"He's the pope's right-hand man."

"Will there be a press conference?"

"No no no. This is very hush-hush." Ravel reconsidered. "He doesn't care for publicity. There's no need to make any announcement about this meeting."

"It's closed to the community?"

Ravel nodded. "A private meeting."

"What's the subject?"

Ravel seemed to reject several possible answers before he said, "Some technical points of canon law."

Lawrence decided he wouldn't tell Bishop Ravel of Bieler's threat to picket the CCE while Hildebrand was on campus. He would have preferred that the professor of theology had not told him. But since Ravel was being so damned secretive Lawrence thought he would reserve a little surprise for him.

When she had first learned what her father was up to, Kate had confronted Professor Bieler at a departmental reception in the University Club and before Mark could stop her asked if it was possible for her parents' marriage to be annulled. Bieler's eyes were out of tune with the rest of his face; the eyes twinkled, the rest was frozen.

"Why?"

"They've been married over twenty-five years, they're parents, they're about to be grandparents."

Mark explained to Professor Bieler that Kate's dad had filed for annulment.

"In Chicago? He probably won't get it."

"Michigan."

"Sounds like he's serious."

Bieler hadn't sounded serious enough for Kate, and that had been the start of her obsession with the subject. Soon she was a storehouse of information about the annulment process. One of the unlooked-for results of Vatican II, as she put it, not without sarcasm. Mark preferred the Kate who had put the Church behind her and couldn't care less about what Catholics were now doing or believing.

"Mark, it's the hypocrisy of it. Marriage is forever, unless you want out, and then they'll decide there's nothing to get out of. It just never happened."

"Annulment isn't new."

"Fifty thousand of them a year is new. And forty-plus thousand of those are granted in the United States."

Bieler explained this by the fact that in this country we have a deeper knowledge of the psychology necessary to contract a valid marriage.

"It's due to progress?"

Bieler turned his frozen face on Kate. It was pretty clear to Mark that the professor was trying to figure out how to handle her. Mark had told him Kate had lost her faith. Bieler had nodded.

"Are your parents happy?"

"Happy?"

Bieler spoke of a dark past when couples had been condemned to stay together, no matter the psychic attrition, prisoners of a union entered into with insufficient understanding of what it held in store for them.

"I wonder if there are any happy marriages."

"Kate!"

"Mark, think about it. Remember when I backed into that car at the supermarket and we argued and it was days before we made up."

"But we made up."

"My parents always made up too."

"Always?" Bieler asked. "Children seldom know much about their parents' marriage."

He assumed a knowing look. Omniscience as well as infallibility were now enjoyed by theologians. What a pill. That's what students called him, he was so obsessed with contraception. Bieler had been one of the first to reject *Humanae Vitae* and it angered him when his students failed to understand the battle he had fought. Contraception was going to save marriages. That was the theory. Maybe her parents hadn't practiced contraception. That's why their marriage was on the rocks. But she felt more like crying than laughing.

There are few who would be able to form a mental picture of Northern Illinois University, where Freddy Burger had studied pharmacy, let alone mistake it for the quintessential college campus, but when Freddy came into sight of the golden dome from the Toll Road he could not believe he was seeing something for the first time. As touted, the campus of Notre Dame was beautiful. Freddy lied his way through the gate, getting a visitor's pass, and drove between the golf course and a row of residences that looked like a movie set. When he reached the lake, he pulled off the road, leaving his car in a restricted parking zone. The path along the lake was made for walking.

The place made him feel as he had in Rome, at once at home and in the camp of the enemy. Freddy never ceased to smile, even when alone; it had become his natural expression, the necessary mask to hide the deep resentments he felt when surrounded by things Catholic. Just as he had never wished to make public what he was, so he kept clear of the woeful little bands that deluded themselves into thinking that their protests would alter the teaching of the Church.

Freddy accepted the priestly judgment passed upon him. There was a part of him that agreed with it. What he could not do was allow that he must bend to it. He would defy it, but subtly. Not in words, not by flaunting what was so delicately described as an alternative lifestyle, but by striking back in a way that enlisted the support of the most loyal sons of the Church. When Amos Cadbury had acknowledged the righteousness of his cause, and persuaded Christopher James to represent VOCL, Freddy's success had been assured.

Even if James lost every judgment, the principled case would have been made against the duplicity of marriage tribunals that handed down declarations of nullity on almost any pretext. If it ever occurred to Freddy that it was his ambiguous gender rather than his status as the fruit of an annulled marriage that he protested, he saw that as his own secret. And anyway, what difference did it really make?

He had come to Notre Dame to talk with Michael Geary's daughter. He moved his car to a parking lot behind the bookstore and followed the flow of students to the south dining room, where he had an unwanted lunch in the Oak Room—he wasn't hungry, but he wanted the experience of eating under the murals depicting the history of the place. Then he called the Hanson number in graduate student housing.

"Mrs. Hanson, this is Monsignor Noonan of the Chicago marriage tribunal. You are the daughter of Michael Geary?"

A long pause. "Yes." There was a reassuringly wary tone in her voice.

"Are you aware of your father's petition before the tribunal?"

"Look, there is nothing I will do to help him. Nothing."

Freddy went on. "That was the decision of this tribunal. He has now taken his case elsewhere."

"Yes. To Michigan."

"Mrs. Hanson, one of our investigators will be at Notre Dame later today. It would be very helpful if you would consent to talk to him."

"Helpful to whom?"

"It would help justice to be served."

Freddy sensed he had her, but he did not press. When eventually she agreed, he told her that a Mr. Frederick Burger would call on her.

How easily such things, in a blend of improvisation and planning, were done. There were times when Freddy felt all but invincible, capable of bending anyone to his purposes. He whiled away an hour walking the campus, peeking in classrooms, careful not to give the impression of being too interested in these beautiful young people. A little more than an hour after he had telephoned, he knocked on the Hanson front door.

"Frederick Burger?"

"Don't say I sound like a city in Virginia."

She thought about it, then granted it a small smile. Her obvious pregnancy was a surprise, and Freddy felt unease. But this was no time to lose heart. He went inside, took the seat she offered and gave her his best smile.

"I'm here under false pretenses. I represent VOCL. You haven't heard of it? Well, we're relatively new. Victims of Canon Law. What do you think of your father's request for an annulment?"

She was confused. He watched the flicker of thought across her face. Of course she ought to react to the realization that he had gained entry to her house by pretense. On the other hand, the mention of VOCL in quick conjunction with her father's effort to win an annulment got the response he hoped for.

He told her about his mother and father and loved the sympathy in her eyes. He already was what she was in danger of becoming.

"What are you studying?"

"Oh, it's my husband who's the student. Theology."

"Theology!"

She shrugged and smiled.

"What on earth is it? I mean, what courses does he take?"

"Do you really want to know?"

He laughed. "You're right. My curiosity is exhausted by the subject of annulment."

"There have been rumors of a meeting to be held here on that. Someone coming in from Rome, closed-door, hush-hush. But the topic is annulment. Everyone is all aflutter." And she pressed her elbows to her sides and flapped her arms.

"Tell me more."

"I don't know any more."

"But this could be important. For VOCL."

Freddy felt a sudden vertigo. What if someone lowered the boom and the marriage courts were put under severe restrictions? What if final decisions, not just appeals, had to be made in Rome, the way it had been when annulments were all but impossible to get? The prospect did not please. It was no part of Freddy's campaign to change the procedures he protested.

Mark Hanson came home, a Viking type, both the team and the race.

"I didn't know theologians were so big."

Freddy checked the impulse to engage the man in banter. Even without the wife there, that would have been unwise. Mark seemed nervous when Kate said she had told their visitor about the Cardinal Hildebrand rumors.

Hildebrand! She hadn't mentioned that name before. A thrill went through Freddy. *Der Kommandant* at Notre Dame! The meeting had seemed an opportunity for he knew not what, but if the legendary Cardinal Hildebrand was involved, this was big. Very big.

"It's just a rumor."

"As the landlady said of the man under her bed."

Appreciative groans. By the time he left he had made two friends. Kate had expressed interest in VOCL before her husband came home. Now the three of them seemed bound by the rumored visit of Cardinal Hildebrand.

The Casa del Clero was located just beyond the Piazza Navona, and, as its name indicated, it was occupied by priests—simple priests, monsignors, bishops, archbishops, and an occasional visiting cardinal. Most of the permanent residents worked in one Vatican office or another. Monsignor Sebastian Tracy, as the confidential secretary of Cardinal Josef Hildebrand, enjoyed a kind of participated prestige at table in the Casa del Clero.

"Will you accompany him to the States, Sebastian?" This question was lofted across the table in bored British tones by Tony Booth.

"States?"

"The former colonies."

"I accompany the cardinal whenever he asks me to."

"Then you are going?"

"Where?"

"What is it? Do you think the room is bugged?" Booth checked the salt and pepper, lifted the lid of the sugar bowl, looked beneath the table.

"Tony, I don't know what you're talking about."

Booth rolled his eyes to the ceiling, then sat forward, elbows on table.

"Sebastian's boss, *der Kommandant,* is going to America to defend the marriage bond, close down the annulment mills, and try to get out alive."

"I hadn't heard you'd been taken on to do disinformation for the cardinal."

"Not good enough, Sebastian. Everyone knows."

Well, everyone would know if Tony Booth had his way. Where on earth had he learned of the trip? Tracy was certain there had been no leak from the Congregation. The only possible sources there were himself and the cardinal.

As if in response to these thoughts, Booth drawled, "Ravel stayed at the Casa Stritch."

The oath of secrecy at the Holy Office was binding under pain of sin, as Tony Booth must know. Of course now there was a logical problem involved in keeping secret something others already knew, but Tracy could not enter into the conversation Booth's remarks had generated.

Communication with Bishop Ravel was being carried on by facsimile machine. The following day Tracy sent the Chicago auxiliary a fax telling him that rumors of the scheduled visit had been emanating from the Casa Stritch.

"It is imperative that the cardinal's meeting with your committee not become a media event."

Sebastian, Monsignor Tracy's Christian name, had been suggested to his mother by a character in a popular novel. No image of the martyr, his body perforated by dozens of arrows, had prompted her. He was born in Redwood Falls, Minnesota, went north to St. Thomas College in the Twin Cities, where he realized he had a vocation. His bishop had sent him to the American College for theology, and he had never returned. His entire clerical career had been in Rome. His companions in the Casa del Clero suggested the route he was on. Would he someday as a seasoned archbishop be assigned a diocese in the States? His native land had come to seem a foreign country, a mission territory so far as the Church was concerned. The abortion abattoirs surpassed in horror the practice of exposing female infants in more primitive lands.

The cardinal wrinkled his nose when Tracy told him it was known that he would be making the trip to the United States.

" 'Secret' and 'secrete' have the same root, do they not, Monsignor?"

Tracy was about to remark that he was not responsible, but did not. Instead he showed the cardinal the fax he had sent Ravel.

"Have I made a great mistake, Monsignor?"

"The problem requires action. Direct action."

"Insist on discretion with Bishop Ravel."

"Our meeting will be eclipsed by the football game."

This required explanation. The cardinal seemed unaware of the phenomenon of college sports.

"There is a historic rivalry between Notre Dame and Southern California."

"This game takes place at the university?"

"Right on campus."

"Football crowds," the cardinal said, shaking his head.

But he would be thinking of European soccer. Monsignor Tracy assured him that there was no violence at American college football games.

"Except on the field."

Crinkled blue eyes, wavy hair, thinning and graying but of the unmussable kind Catherine Burger had always liked in a man, all these attracted her, as did his gorgeous smile, which seemed to involve more than the allotted number of teeth, but it was Michael Geary's view of life that made him the first man she had responded to since she was freed of the ineffable Burger.

"Annulment, not divorce," she explained, "so it wasn't really a marriage at all."

She said it because she knew it would be as important to him as it was to her. But she had been planting a seed as well. Things could go only so far between them unless Michael too was free. He made inquiries and was not encouraged. The Chicago tribunal sounded like a different place since her experience with it.

"Is Father Noonan still there?"

"The big bald guy?"

"Ask him about other tribunals."

A slight frown on his face, and Catherine knew she must go slowly. It helped that they were so much alike. He could get out of his marriage only if the Church told him there was nothing to get out of. It had to be absolutely official, no doubt about it, as blessed as any marriage.

"I don't want to shop around."

"Didn't you say you own a place in Michigan?"

He did. Catherine had heard things about the Michigan diocese; Freddy was full of lore on such matters; and she was not surprised when Father Noonan gave Michael an introduction to a Father Gorce, who ran the tribunal.

"I doubt that Michael Geary can get an annulment even there," Freddy told her.

"When I applied, Freddy, I don't think I really believed mine would be granted. I knew the truth of the matter but these things are often difficult to prove."

"The pope in Rome would have given you an annulment."

"He did," Catherine said primly. "In effect."

"How long has Geary been married?"

"The question is whether, not how long."

"Don't get your hopes up."

Freddy could say anything while wearing that sunny smile and punctuating it with a laugh. Catherine had given up trying to understand him. In many ways he seemed indifferent to her annulment, yet there was the role he had played in the founding of VOCL. But there was one negative effect of the annulment Catherine found difficult to express even to herself. Freddy seemed incapable of taking life seriously; he had never gone with a girl long enough to suggest that anything would come of it. Catherine sadly resigned herself to the fact that she had turned her son into a confirmed bachelor. For that matter, apart from Freddy's infectious laugh and suggestion that VOCL was merely making a statement, Catherine felt uneasy about the zeal with which the group sought large judgments against the Church. In this, however, she received assurance from Amos Cadbury.

"It is an expensive lesson but one that must be learned, Catherine. The Holy Father himself has expressed concern." He paused. His ancient skin was still aglow with health; his white hair made her want to run her hand through it. He leaned toward her. "I have reason to think that Cardinal Hildebrand himself is coming to this country to underscore the Vatican's dissatisfaction."

Michael's case was accepted in Michigan. She let him take her in his arms when he brought her the news.

"I wouldn't have had a prayer in Chicago."

"I felt the same way."

"Does the name Amanda James mean anything to you?"

"James?"

"She was the organist at Blessed Sacrament."

Listening to the incredible story, Catherine felt that she must have been aware of it; Michael said the media of course made the most of it.

"I wasn't the target, as it turned out. They went after the parish and the archdiocese. Even so I suspect my name is mud downtown."

"What happened?"

"She was awarded a bundle, more than enough to retire."

"They believed her?"

"It was my word against hers. Gallantry is not dead."

Like most women, Catherine was ambivalent about the rash of charges of sexual harassment. Many of them seemed to involve a hatred of men, the notion that there was a war to the death between the sexes, that all men are fundamentally rotten. On the other hand, she had been married to Lorenzo Burger and knew what the male animal was capable of. Somehow she found herself believing such charges and at the same time suspecting the woman of overstating the facts. In Michael's case, it was easy to think he had been unjustly accused. Catherine was so susceptible to him that she could imagine the old maid organist he described wishfully thinking he was interested in her.

"Who was her lawyer?"

"Her father."

The counsel for Freddy's group was a man named Christopher James. She asked Freddy if he knew whether he had a daughter.

"Amanda?" His smile was radiant. "So he told you."

"Of course."

They seemed to be involved in a contest, but Catherine wasn't sure which of them won. Freddy clearly enjoyed revealing that he had known all about the Amanda James accusation. But she thought she had gained by her response. Why wouldn't Michael Geary tell her of that episode, however trying it must have been?

Praying that Michael might receive his annulment seemed an odd request, and Catherine found herself unable to formulate it when she dropped into old St. Jude's for a noonday visit. She knelt in the oddly unoccupied right side of the church. One or two people looked at her briefly, then turned away. She closed her eyes, trying to pray without praying, when she became aware of the smell. She looked around and caught the eye of a woman wearing a babushka who had looked at her before. The woman made a face and nodded.

Catherine left the pew, stepping into the aisle. When she passed the confessional, the smell was overpowering. It was not in use, there were no lights over the doors. Ten feet past the confessional the smell lessened.

Perhaps she should have done something. The woman in the babushka had stood and looked back at her expectantly. But Catherine left the church.

The following day she read that a dead dog had been found in a confessional in a downtown church.

Gordon Furey felt a little creepy keeping an eye on Catherine Burger, following her around, spying on her, but he wanted to find out what she was like. One thing was clear pretty quick. She was no Karen, who had been a great body and not much else. Catherine was pretty pious, by the looks of things, popping in and out of churches, attending Mass a couple of times a week. Then the young man showed up and Gordon thought he was onto something. The guy was a bit swishy, but some women like that. Maybe she found him a contrast to Mike. It turned out to be her son. Freddy.

But maybe that wasn't a blank after all. What did the son think of his mother carrying on with a married man?

"Carrying on?" The kid's smile got brighter.

"A manner of speaking."

"What's your interest?"

"He's my brother-in-law."

"Oh ho. So why don't you talk to him?"

"What would I say?"

"Well, he's a big Catholic, isn't he? Give him a fire-and-brimstone talk."

"Your mother's Catholic too."

"Oh, she won't make a move unless he gets an annulment. That's what she got. So she's eligible."

Freddy seemed to think the whole thing was a joke. Well, it couldn't hurt him anymore, if it ever had. But Gordon couldn't laugh off what Mike was trying to do to Maureen.

"Your mother know about his wife?"

"Why don't you ask her?"

"Maybe I will."

"Is that why you've been following her?"

"Following her?"

"Isn't it funny we never think someone might be watching us when we're watching someone else?"

"Who was watching you?"

"God?"

It seemed a point of honor now to talk with Catherine Burger. But how and where? He decided to confront her when she was most vulnerable to his appeal, right after Mass.

He was waiting for her when she emerged from church and came down the steps to the sidewalk.

"Michael Geary is married to my sister."

She stepped back and lost her balance and he grabbed her arm, preventing her fall.

"Who are you?"

"Gordon Furey. Can we talk?"

She shook her head. "I think I know what you want to say. And I understand. But I am doing nothing wrong."

"Because you have an annulment?"

"Who told you that?"

"Freddy."

"Freddy!"

"He suggested I talk to you."

She came with him to the junk-food place on the corner and they took Styrofoam cups of coffee to a table by the window. She listened while he told her about all those years ago, when he had misbehaved with Karen and Michael had brought him to his senses.

"What convinced you?"

"He used the indirect method. He talked to the girl."

"Ah. And now you're talking to me. Did you talk with Amanda James too?"

"He told you about her?"

She nodded, looking at him over her Styrofoam cup, as if she were about to tell him what a sincere and honest man Michael Geary was.

"I don't give a damn about Mike. I'm thinking of my sister and their kids."

This moved her. "Life is so cruel, isn't it?"

"There's no way in the world he'll get an annulment."

"Well, if he doesn't, that would settle things between me and him."

"Do you mean it?"

"Of course."

He believed her. He felt disarmed when she added, "So you see it's up to the Church. I'll accept whatever decision they make."

"They'll say no. Meanwhile he is leading my sister and her kids through hell."

"Hasn't your sister filed for a divorce?"

"And made him move out. That was to get him to drop talk of an annulment."

"A divorce wouldn't leave him free to marry."

She loved Michael. She wanted to marry him. Life is cruel, she had said. It's also nuts. What in God's name did she see in a bastard like Michael Geary?

"Michael," he said heartily when he got through to him on the phone. "When can we have lunch?"

It was Tuttle's fate as an angler for legal business to see most of the big ones get away. But he was not a fatalist. Success was possible. Persistence had its rewards. So he put on fresh bait and let out his lines again. His audience was not entirely of this world, for his sainted father, who had financed his prolonged stay in law school and not abandoned him during the years it had taken Tuttle to pass the bar, seemed to speak to him from beyond the grave, to encourage him as he always had, to believe in him.

Even so, it had been a disappointment when Freddy Burger, who had sought Tuttle out, suddenly dropped him like a hot potato. A fallow period gave Tuttle the leisure to follow Freddy's subsequent moves. There was some consolation that he had lost a client to Christopher James, a lawyer whose success brought water to Tuttle's mouth and tears to his eyes. And, given James's recent success in pressing his daughter's suit against the archdiocese, Freddy's fickleness made sense.

"Who is he?" asked Peanuts Pianone, the Fox River cop who was Tuttle's closest friend.

"A client."

"You're tailing a client?"

"Protective surveillance."

Either in Peanuts's patrol car or in his own seasoned Toyota, Tuttle monitored Freddy, marveling at the smiling confidence with which he met the world. It was odd that such a cheerful guy had founded such an angry organization. VOCL. Peanuts kept an eye on Freddy when Tuttle was otherwise occupied.

"What am I looking for?"

"Just keep me posted on what he does."

"He's a snoopy bastard."

"What do you mean?"

"He checks out other people's cars."

"Checks them out?"

"If a door's unlocked, he'll hop in."

"He steals cars?"

"Naw." Peanuts looked at him. "With a Corvette, he should steal cars?"

"So what does he do?"

"Check them out."

Tuttle himself never saw Freddy do any such thing. He did not disbelieve Peanuts. Peanuts never lied. But that didn't mean he always understood what he saw. Not that Tuttle had any explanation of a rich young kid who tried out unlocked cars as if he meant to drive them away, then didn't.

Tuttle's interest was soon absorbed in the fact that Freddy was following some guy around. Not what he might have thought either, given Freddy's manner; this was an older guy. An older guy who was following Freddy's mother!

"Maybe someone's following us too," Peanuts said.

Tuttle could almost believe it. It ended finally when Freddy and the guy—Tuttle now knew he was Gordon Furey—had a talk, Freddy grinning at the guy all the while.

There was something going on and Tuttle couldn't figure out what it was, but the hope grew in him that he could somehow profit from it. Peanuts suggested that if you just started following someone at random, you would always run into something baffling, but Tuttle didn't believe that. Something was afoot, and he was determined to cut himself in on whatever it was.

In his office, sharing a pizza and swilling soda with Peanuts, Tuttle thought it over. Peanuts never talked while he ate, so he was not a distraction at such times. After he had done away with two-thirds of the pizza, Peanuts napped. Tuttle might have been napping too, with his tweed hat pulled over his eyes, his scuffed loafers up on the desk, but he was reviewing the facts.

Freddy Burger had come to him to talk of an organization he was founding of people hurt by annulments. Victims of Canon Law. Their discussions had hardly begun when Freddy paid him off and hired Christopher James as counsel for the organization. Meanwhile, Freddy was a man about town, favoring odd bars and hangouts, taking a rest in unlocked cars from time to time, if Peanuts was right, but then tailing a man named Gordon Furey, who was tailing Freddy's mother, Catherine. Freddy might have been smiling when he confronted Furey, but Tuttle was not deceived. The young man was peeved.

The upshot of this meditation was Tuttle's decision that it was Freddy's mother who was the key to the riddle. She lived in a large house overlooking the river, and there was a parking area on the opposite side of the road that gave an unobstructed view of the house. Well, of its garages. He and Peanuts sometimes watched the house together, sometimes separately. Peanuts was fascinated by the videocam Tuttle brought along, just in case.

"What do you want pictures of, Tuttle?"

"Turn it on whenever anything happens over there."

Thus it was that Tuttle acquired a collection of videotapes recording the comings and goings of automobiles at the Burger house. His guess had been that Gordon Furey would show up to see Freddy's mother. But it was another man who came regularly.

"Who's he?" Peanuts asked.

"Call in his tag number and find out." They were using a patrol car on this occasion.

The owner of the car was Michael Geary.

The 911 was made at 2:23 reporting a dead man in a car parked behind an insurance agency on the West Side.

"Geary," Cy said to Phil Keegan.

"Is that the name of the insurance agency?"

"It's the dead man's name too."

Maybe Phil Keegan would have gone with Cy anyway, but that clinched it.

"Who's Geary?" Cy asked.

Speak well of the dead, Keegan told himself. Geary was a sanctimonious pain in the neck, or at least he had been.

"A dead insurance man."

The agency occupied a converted residence, a beautiful two-story brick house. The gaudy sign in front of it was a kind of desecration. Once this had been prime residential property and these the houses of local movers and shakers. Cy entered a driveway that ran from the street along the side of the house and into the parking lot in back. Police cars, the orange-and-white ambulance, its light pulsing like a watchtower's, were parked at odd angles around the Continental.

The body had been found in the driver's seat of Geary's car, which was parked in its designated spot behind the building that housed Michael Geary Insurance.

Florence Lewis, Geary's secretary, had Shirley Temple hair that didn't seem real, a pretty face and an enormous bosom. Flustered but still very much in charge, she showed Keegan and Cy into her office and pointed to a set of windows framed by flouncy curtains and half obscured by various hanging plants.

"I saw him drive past that window toward the lot in back." She needed air, and she inhaled. "Five minutes later, I went into his office and he wasn't there. I thought he'd gone to the men's room, you know, and came back here."

She had pointed toward Geary's office, where Agnes Lamb was supervising the inspection, and now indicated the room they were in.

"Maybe ten minutes later I tried to transfer a call to him but he didn't pick up his phone. That surprised me. So I went and looked in his office again and he still wasn't there!"

She had asked the two agents at work in the large office area that had once been the dining and living rooms, as well as the typist, but they hadn't seen Mr. Geary come in either. The way she said this indicated a general disapproval of their alertness and dedication.

"I asked Mr. Wadding if he would check the rest room, but he said he'd just been in there."

Really puzzled now, Florence went to the back door and looked out.

"His car was there all right. And he was in it! Well, I was relieved. His son had called long distance, wanting to talk to him, and I told him his father was sitting in his car out back. I gave him his mobile number. I was that relieved. I had begun to doubt I had seen his car go by."

"He was just sitting out there?"

"It sounds funny now, but I guess I figured he had some reason."

"Did he often sit out there in his car?"

"No!" She glared at him. "I did wonder whether Brian got through to him and looked out again. I thought he was using his car phone. He preferred a headset when he drove, he never trusted the microphone he originally had pinned on the sunshade. I figured he might be talking with his son, but I came back here and rang his mobile number anyway. It wasn't busy."

Still she hadn't been worried. She had returned to her desk. During the next half hour she had peeked out at Geary from time to time, more and more puzzled. She just could not imagine what he was doing out there.

"How was I to know anything was wrong?" she wailed. Her eyes darted again toward the parking lot, where Monique Pippen from the medical examiner's office stood beside the open door of the car. Geary had fallen to the ground when Florence had finally gone out there and opened the car door to see what the matter was. After telling them this, she stopped, not closing her mouth, waiting, looking back and forth at the two of them.

"I suppose you're used to dead bodies."

"You thought he was dead?"

"That's what I mean. I didn't know. He fell onto the ground like a sack of cement. Once in a bus I saw a man have a heart attack." She waved the thought away. "Then I saw how the wires were twisted around his neck."

"Had he been ill?" Keegan asked. They would get a report on the body from Monique Pippen.

"He's never been sick a day in his life." Her expression altered. "I'm quoting him."

They checked Geary's calendar to see what his appointments were. There was only one name listed, from two to three, Mrs. Rockhurst, who was now sitting wide-eyed in the waiting area at the front of the office, following it all. What a story this would be for her bridge club. It was her impatience that had finally decided Florence that she should go out and find out what was keeping her boss in his car. According to his calendar, there had been an eleven o'clock appointment, and that was it for the morning.

"Those are his business appointments," Florence said. "The ones in that book."

Cy turned to her. "Is there a record of nonbusiness appointments?"

"He had a little book. He carried it with him."

It was in the inside pocket of his jacket. Cy brought it back after helping Pippen and the paramedics zip Geary into a bag.

"Did they check all his pockets?" Phil Keegan asked.

Cy produced a plastic Ziploc bag. Keegan could see a wallet, a handkerchief, change, a rosary. Geary had had a one-thirty appointment with someone named Noonan.

"And he had an eleven here?"

"He'd scheduled an hour but he didn't need it."

"Who was that with?"

"Father Panzica."

Keegan took the book and looked at the entry. "There's a Panzica who's a priest over at—"

"That's him. Mr. Geary belongs to Blessed Sacrament. He said he hoped to get the parish insurance business."

"What time did he leave?"

"Father Panzica?"

"Geary."

"About a quarter of eleven."

"You see him drive by your windows then?" Cy asked.

"Yes." She looked sharply at Cy, as if his question had expressed skepticism. If it had, she would never know. Cy went through life with one expression and a single tone of voice.

"Who's Noonan?" Cy asked. But Florence was distracted. She was drawn into the larger office by fascinated dread and solemnly watched her employer make his last exit from the agency, enclosed in a rubberized bag, carried by two young men with wild hair who might have been hauling luggage. Cy repeated his question. Florence knew no one named Noonan.

"Any guesses?"

She was suddenly aware that she was being questioned in the middle of the office and that whatever she said was heard by Wadding and Goren, the two agents, and by Pam the typist-receptionist, too. Not only that, Mrs. Rockhurst seemed to think that her appointment entitled her to kibitz on the proceedings. Of course the police would want to talk to everyone there, but Florence was not interested in making a public statement. She took them back into her office and shut the door.

"He was having trouble with his wife. Trouble," she repeated and gave a little laugh. "She has initiated divorce proceedings and he has been talking for months about getting an annulment. From the Church."

"Noonan!" Phil Keegan said. "Monsignor Noonan."

Florence and Cy looked at him, expecting him to say more, but Keegan shut up. He left Cy with Florence and went to speak with Agnes Lamb. Geary's office had been thoroughly photographed and was now being dusted. Keegan told Agnes what Florence had been telling them.

"See that lady sitting up front," Keegan said. Mrs. Rockhurst sat forward on her chair, hands on her knees, looking as if she were about to make her first parachute jump. "Mrs. Rockhurst. She came for an appointment with Geary. Find out what she saw."

For the next twenty minutes, the office was filled with the high nonstop voice of the elderly woman, who seemed to have the gift of total recall. The trouble was, nothing she recalled was at all relevant to the death of Michael Geary.

"She saw him drive in," Agnes said.

"She saw a car drive in," Keegan said.

"At the same time the secretary says she saw Michael Geary drive in. She also says she thought she saw someone in the backseat of the car. She isn't sure, but maybe." Agnes reported this in flat tones. Apparently Mrs. Rockhurst's memory had been stimulated by what she heard had gone on in the parking lot. "She supposes that was whoever strangled him."

The car had been taken away to be inspected under optimum conditions. Agnes called downtown and told them to give special attention to the backseat.

"Maybe she did see someone."

Keegan and Cy had spoken to Wadding and Goren, Geary's two agents. Wadding was in his mid-twenties, full of bullshit about insurance. He seemed to think this was an opportunity to sell Captain Keegan a policy.

"I have a terminal disease," Keegan told him. "What can you tell me about what's gone on here?"

Goren said, "I can't believe this happened." He was pushing forty, thin blond hair, jowly, and there was a film of sweat on his high forehead.

"What's wrong with you?" Wadding asked Keegan.

"You can't believe what happened?" Keegan asked Goren.

The two agents had different versions of what had happened. Wadding was sure it had been Geary's heart. "He smoked. He was over fifty." He shrugged as if he had proved something. Keegan ostentatiously took out a cigar and unwrapped it. Goren was sure Geary had been killed.

"An unhappy customer?"

"You're kidding about being sick, aren't you?" Wadding asked.

Ever since he had made the connection between Noonan and the marriage court, Keegan had been convinced the explanation of what had happened lay elsewhere. By the time they got downtown, the ME had a pretty good idea what had happened.

"It looks as if he was strangled and the wire from his headphones used to do it. They might have been clamped back on his head afterward." Jolson paused, as if he wanted to be asked how he could be sure of that sequence. Neither Phil Keegan nor Cy said anything. "They were on backwards," Jolson said.

"You said looks as if he was strangled."

Jolson nodded. "Dr. Pippen has her doubts." He gave Keegan a little smile. The captain would be aware of the imaginative scenarios Monique Pippen favored.

"What else might it have been?"

"Might have been?" Jolson's eyes rolled as an infinity of possibilities suggested themselves. "What might not have been? We shall take the body apart and determine what it was."

This might have been another comment on Monique Pippen. Keegan didn't like the suggestion that he had been engaged in wild surmise.

"You're the one who mentioned strangling."

"Just quoting, Captain Keegan. Just quoting."

"Who is Noonan?" Cy asked when they were back in the car.

"He works on the archdiocesan marriage tribunal. I know about him from Roger Dowling. I want to talk with him."

"I thought I'd stop by The Crock." Cy was leafing through the appointment book that had been taken from Geary's pocket. "It's where he had lunch." He closed the book. "Or was supposed to."

Keegan would have liked Cy to be there when he talked with Monsignor Noonan. People talked to Cy, telling him more than they intended, as if striving to get some noticeable reaction from his expressionless face. But Keegan fancied the clergy his special province. Keegan himself put through a call to Father Dowling and invited himself to the rectory. It would be a chance to find a good approach to Noonan.

"Just drop me off at St. Hilary's, Cy."

In the dining room only one table was still occupied, but the customers in the bar looked as if they were settled in until the sun went over the yardarm. Depending on which way Cy looked, The Crock smelled like a restaurant or a bar. The little light was still on over the pulpitlike stand holding a book in which reservations were written. Cy was checking it out when someone spoke beside him.

"Can I help you?"

"I'm Lieutenant Horvath."

The woman was as tall as he was, but that might have been the way she wore her hair. Her dress, her manner, her expression, suggested someplace far more exclusive than The Crock.

"Did Michael Geary have lunch here today?"

"Oh God." She stepped back, waiting for him to say more.

"What's wrong?"

"I knew he was angry when he left, just stormed out, but I didn't dream he would go to the police."

"What was he angry about?"

"Could we sit down? I was just having a bite."

Her bite was a toasted cheese sandwich and a diet drink. "I should eat before the customers, that's what they do in Europe. You come early and the chef and waiters, everyone, is eating. When they're done, the customers are admitted."

"You've been to Europe?"

She sighed. "I lived there. Near Sorrento."

"I don't know where that is."

She looked as if she thought he might be kidding. "In Italy. Near Naples."

"Are you Italian?"

"Irish." She touched his arm. "Grace Masterson. I tutored the children of a very distinguished family. In English."

"But you're Irish?"

"I'm as American as you are. What's Horvath?"

"Hungarian."

She narrowed her eyes to study him, then nodded. "Yes."

"What made Michael Geary angry?"

"Did he file a complaint?"

"You answer my questions, then I'll answer yours."

"I don't want this place dragged through the newspapers. I'm sure they'll make it sound like a barroom brawl."

"Who was involved?"

"There were just the two of them. Mr. Geary lunches here often. The other man was his brother-in-law, I gathered. I had never seen him before. But he was stuck with the bill."

"What was his name?"

"I'll check the credit card slip when I've finished." She picked up her sandwich, then put it down. "Would you care for something to eat?"

"A grilled cheese sandwich?"

She dismissed the suggestion with a wave of her multi-braceleted arm. "The special was shepherd's pie." She motioned to a waitress going about on thick-soled white canvas shoes, looking as if she might bound across the room like Michael Jordan. Cy was served; she finished her sandwich and, elbows on the table, talked while he ate.

"Don't ever go into business for yourself. I used to dream of a place like this, when I lived in Italy. I saved and I was left a little by an uncle and I thought, finally, independence, my own boss. If I were shackled to the front door it wouldn't matter. This must be what criminals who get life feel like. There's no torture but there's no end to it either." She looked around. "I don't even know what it seems like to customers anymore. I spent so much time on the decor, but who notices?"

"It's nice."

"The shepherd's pie?"

That was more than nice. By the time Cy had finished and the waitress had swept the table clean, he knew all about Grace Masterson. She had told him everything but her age, but he guessed that was between forty and forty-five. There was no wedding band among the many rings she wore. She was her own woman but she was a woman, no doubt of that. Her whole manner was meant to charm. She went to the register and brought back the credit card slip. The signature was illegible, but the legend from the card was clear. Gordon Furey.

"You never saw him before?"

"Never. I noticed their conversation had grown animated, but that's not unheard of, even at lunch. People in this country do not know how to drink." It was a theme she obviously would have liked to develop, but she checked herself. "They began to get the attention of the other diners."

"What was it about?"

"Oh, it wasn't that you could overhear. It was the intensity with which they spoke. They leaned toward one another, jaw to jaw, like a baseball player and an umpire. Mr. Geary upset a glass of water, I don't think on purpose, and the other jumped to his feet, nearly overturning the table. For a moment I thought they would fight. That's when Mr. Geary left. I don't think he even saw me, he was so angry."

"He's dead."

"What!"

"He was found dead in his car behind his insurance agency about two-thirty."

"My God."

"When did he leave here?"

"It wasn't one o'clock. You saw how early his reservation was."

"He had an appointment at one-thirty."

"Did he keep it?"

"We'll find out."

She looked at the credit card slip, which he had handed back to her. "This man looked as if he could cheerfully have killed Michael Geary."

"And vice versa."

She nodded. "You're right." And then, "Do you think something happened to him too?"

A call to Furey's office yielded the information that Mr. Furey was not available now, did Mr. Horvath wish to make an appointment?

He thanked the receptionist and hung up. Grace Masterson looked at him.

"He's there. Look, we'll have to record what you've told me. It's a nuisance but it has to be done."

"I don't want any publicity. Not of this kind."

"Then don't talk to reporters. Thanks for lunch."

When they stood, she seemed to be thinking they made a nice match. Cy rubbed his chin with his left hand. What the hell was going on? First Monique, now Grace Masterson. He'd have to start showering in cold water in the morning.

The news of Geary's death got a little yelp out of Marie Murkin, but Father Dowling simply listened to Phil Keegan's account. Keegan made it all converge on Geary's one-thirty appointment with Noonan.

"Did he keep it?"

"I haven't checked yet."

"Should I?"

"I was hoping you would."

Roger Dowling consulted his Rolodex, then dialed a number and asked for Monsignor Noonan. Keegan went into the kitchen and listened on Marie's phone. The housekeeper sat at the table, staring mournfully out the window.

"Jerome? Roger Dowling. Remember our talking about the Michael Geary case?"

"Aha. Is this the old fire horse responding to the bell?"

"Did you meet with him this afternoon?"

"He didn't show. Thank God. I had already made it as clear to him as I could that we would not consider his case. I wonder if they turned him down in Michigan."

"He's dead."

"Dead!"

"His body was found in his car this afternoon."

A moment of silence.

"The poor devil. So to speak. May he rest in peace." Noonan sighed. "Well, he wanted out of his marriage."

"Not this way."

"I know, I know. Roger, they all think they'll live as long as Methuselah. The man was in his fifties. I don't suppose it ever occurred to him that he might die. What was it?"

"It looks as if he was murdered."

"Good grief, Roger, why didn't you say so? Murdered." A humming interval. "Yes, I can believe it. There were times when I felt like it myself."

"Careful. The police are very suspicious."

"Ho ho. But how did you know he had an appointment with me?"

"The police told me."

"Are you serious?"

"It was entered on his desk calendar."

"I suppose they'll be pestering me about that."

"Not if you can account for your whereabouts," Roger Dowling said in a mock-serious tone.

Noonan spluttered about that awhile, then wanted to talk about Notre Dame, but Roger Dowling said he'd call him back about that.

"I have the police here now."

"Tell them I'm innocent."

"If they don't put me under oath."

"What did he mean about Notre Dame?" Keegan asked when he went back into the study.

"He's attending the same meeting I am. Before the big game."

"I can hardly wait."

"You won't be prevented from going by the Geary investigation, will you?"

"Who's Geary?"

Marie came in and stood wringing her hands. "Why can't people let well enough alone, Father? Imagine the man frantically trying to pretend that he had never married that lovely woman or had that marvelous daughter. And what does it all matter now?"

"He didn't just die, Marie," Phil Keegan said. "Somebody killed him."

"Well, no wonder, given what he was trying to do. How would you like it if your wife had applied for an annulment?"

Keegan didn't like references made to his late wife, not even by Marie. Roger Dowling hadn't known her either. Those memories were Keegan's alone and he wasn't going to let anyone else in on them. Of course Marie was suggesting that Geary's wife had a motive to kill him.

"She was trying to keep him, Marie, not get rid of him."

"Bah. She was ready to divorce him. It wasn't him she wanted. She wanted him to stop pretending their marriage had never existed."

"Till death do us part."

"It's been changed, Phil. 'As long as we both shall live.' "

"Why do they have to change everything?"

"It's the same thought."

Now that Phil Keegan knew that Geary had not kept his appointment with Noonan, the question arose as to where he had been between lunch and the time Florence saw him drive past her office window at the agency. An hour later Keegan was downtown at his desk when Cy called in and told him of the quarrel between Geary and Gordon Furey at the restaurant.

"Gordon Furey?"

"Mrs. Geary's brother."

"How long after Geary did he leave the restaurant?"

"At most ten minutes."

"Where are you now?"

"At his office."

Gordon Furey was not there, although he had been expected back after lunch. His absence had caused a mild furor, the cancellation of appointments, postponed consultations, messages unanswered. Cy had already circulated Furey's license number on the radio. Gordon Furey was clearly someone they wanted to talk to, but they were going to have to wait until they found him to do that.

Keegan snapped up his phone so quickly he almost anticipated the ring.

"Captain Keegan?"

It was Monique Pippen, but not with news of the autopsy; Jolson hadn't even begun that.

"About the death car?"

Keegan winced. Monique was given to colorful descriptions as well as imaginative explanations. "Geary's vehicle?"

"One of our crew found something odd in it and took it and I know he shouldn't have, not that it's worth anything, I mean it isn't anything expensive, it's—"

"What the hell is it?"

"A statuette. One of those little plastic madonnas you see in cars, you know what I mean."

"Okay. You told me."

"Should I send it down?"

"Send it down."

He returned the phone gently to its cradle. The world was mad, but what of it? A man had been murdered and the assistant medical examiner was worried about a plastic statue someone took from the car in which a body had been found. No, she was right to be conscientious. Give her credit. And forget it.

He sat back and lit a cigar. This murder, like most murders, would be a family affair. Gordon Furey looked like the killer. An autopsy would be performed, Geary's car gone over from bumper to bumper, a careful note made of everything about it, and everything in his office, but in the end it would probably turn out that his brother-in-law killed him after a quarrel over his intention to get an annulment.

Keegan picked up the phone and called Roger Dowling to keep him up on things. Of course he did not tell his old friend that he thought Gordon Furey had done it.

"He's not at his office and he's not at home. But he's somewhere. He should be able to cast light on things."

"There's a search on?"

"It shouldn't take long. Not just because the license number has been broadcast. He's driving a very unusual car. Remember the Avanti?"

"Isn't that made in South Bend?"

"Originally by Studebaker."

Keegan put down the phone and, puffing on his cigar, let thoughts of Avantis and South Bend lead on to the big game between Notre Dame and Southern Cal.

Hearing about the quarrel between Geary and his brother-in-law came as a relief to Father Dowling. Earlier both Phil Keegan and Marie Murkin had assumed that it must have been Mrs. Geary who was responsible for her husband's death. Given the circumstances, as he understood them, Father Dowling had found that implausible. Of course it helped that he didn't know Gordon Furey; awful deeds are always easier to attribute to strangers. Maureen Geary had come to his rectory to talk; he felt he knew her, at least somewhat. She would have had to be overcome with rage to summon the strength to strangle her husband. If indeed he had been strangled. Phil Keegan had cast some doubt on that.

"Wasn't there wire twisted around his neck?"

"Yes."

"Doesn't that suggest strangling?"

"Yes."

"So why do you object to my calling it strangling?"

"It is my professional duty to await the coroner's report."

"And to be contrary," Marie said with disgust.

The quarrel between Gordon Furey and Geary now vindicated Phil Keegan's exaggerated caution. Father Dowling looked up Mrs. Geary's number, picked up the phone and listened.

"Marie?"

There was no answer, but he heard her breathing.

"I am going to call Mrs. Geary if you will put down the phone."

"Father Dowling, are you on? Sorry. Go ahead. I can make my call later."

"Thank you."

He waited ten seconds before she hung up. A moment later she thumped past the study door, her nose in the air. Father Dowling dialed.

No answer. Ten minutes later, he tried again. Ah well. He had thought he might be of some help to her at this difficult time. He put a piece of paper in his typewriter and got to work on his mail.

"Any luck?"

Marie stood in the doorway, wearing her blasé look. The sudden ringing of the phone saved him from making a teasing remark.

"Should I answer it, Father?"

He picked up the phone and said hello.

"Father Dowling?" It was Maureen Geary. "Have you heard?"

"Yes."

"I can't believe it. I just can't believe it." Her voice trembled, but she managed to control it.

"Are you at home?"

"I'm calling you from an oasis on the Indiana Toll Road. I was visiting my daughter when I got the news."

"Your daughter at Notre Dame?"

"Yes."

Undeniably he felt relief, no matter his thought that Geary's quarrel with his brother-in-law had turned suspicion on Gordon Furey.

"Father, I have to talk to someone. I didn't want to stay there with Kate and visit all this on her and her husband. She's expecting." A little tremulous gasp. "When I came there and talked with you it helped me so much."

"Come now."

"Let's see. I'm near Chesterton. How far is that from Fox River, do you know?"

"Look, I'll come to your house. The address looks to be halfway between here and where you are."

"Oh, Father, I can't ask you to do that."

"I'll see you at your house."

When he put down the phone he said to Marie, "That was Mrs. Geary."

"I figured."

"I'm going there."

"I heard."

Priests still make house calls, hospital calls, school calls, jail calls, although this was beyond the call of duty, Maureen Geary not being a member of St. Hilary's parish. But willy-nilly he had become involved in the Geary marital problems, and he could hardly refuse to be of what help he could.

Negotiating the highway toward the northern suburbs, remembering Michael Geary's visit, Roger Dowling reflected that it had never entered his mind that the man had been embarked on a course that would endanger his life. Not from his wife or children, perhaps, but from Maureen's brother. The quarrel in the restaurant had made public what Gordon Furey thought of what Michael was doing. A man who could engage in a quarrel in a public place, one that had threatened violence, could have, in a continuation of that anger, choked the life out of Michael Geary.

That Michael Geary had felt justified in what he was doing was obvious, but then most of us are able to convince ourselves that the course we are following is the right one. Without that, it would be impossible to act. But we can be wrong. Weakness, desire, past misdeeds combine to obscure the transition from the ideal we accept to its demands in the present circumstances. Michael Geary, a Catholic loyalist, doubtless staunch defender of the nuptial bed and the indissolubility of marriage, had come to see his own marriage as the exception, a nullity, nothing that could bind him to the woman with whom he had lived for more than a quarter of a century and with whom he had had two children. He asked the Church to let him walk away from that, into another woman's arms, while shouting the glories of matrimony.

And no doubt Gordon Furey had become convinced that it was imperative that someone stop this idiocy.

The Geary house harmonized with these reflections. A large frame house, two stories and gables on the roof suggesting an attic as well, it was balanced by a one-story wing on each side, one of which, Father Dowling trusted, would be called a sunroom. A car was parked in the drive, and he pulled in beside it.

He turned off the motor and stared at the oddly shaped car. The driver's door flew open and a man hopped out and hurried back to Father Dowling, peering at him. The tall beech trees that flanked the house must be reflected in the windshield. The man stopped abruptly when he got to the car and put his hand on the fender, as if for support. Father Dowling rolled down his window and stuck out his head. The man stepped away from the car.

"I'm Father Roger Dowling."

The man stared at him, then nodded, as if there were a slight delay in the communication. The priest pushed open the door and got out. There was a tooting sound behind him and he turned to see a station wagon draw into the drive. Maureen Geary got out and looked past the priest at the other man.

"Gordon! Of course you would have heard."

Roger Dowling stepped aside while brother and sister embraced, Maureen sobbing, trying to draw her lower lip between her teeth, Gordon Furey, as he must be, looking wide-eyed over her shoulder at the priest.

"It was on the radio," he said.

Freeing herself from her brother's arms, she turned to Father Dowling wearing a tragic expression.

"Thank you for coming, Father. Let's all go inside."

In the house, Maureen busied herself making coffee. The living room was defined by a massive fireplace and looked out on a sweep of lawn that was now mottled with brightly colored leaves. On the other side of the fireplace was a room with several shelves of books and a huge television set.

"Maureen said you talked to the two of them."

Father Dowling turned to Gordon Furey. "What did you hear on the radio?"

"That Michael was dead."

"Someone murdered him."

Furey frowned and shook his head. Was this meant to express disbelief?

"The police are looking for you."

"For me!" He actually leapt backward.

"I understand you had a quarrel with Michael in a restaurant earlier today."

"How did you know that?"

"I also know that you didn't return to your office, nor have you been home."

The slightly patronizing manner that Catholics adopt toward their priests had underlain Gordon Furey's obvious nervousness, but now it was gone and Father Dowling watched the wild anger mount in the man.

"Are you really a priest?"

Roger Dowling touched his collar.

"Anyone can wear one of those."

"What's going on?" Maureen asked, coming into the living room.

"He says the police are looking for me."

"What?!"

"I had lunch with Mike today. We got into an argument, naturally, and he left in a huff."

"And several hours later he was dead," Father Dowling said.

Maureen's expression alternated between disbelief and what looked like the recognition that her brother might have been responsible for Michael Geary's death.

"Gordon," she began, then dropped into a wingbacked chintz chair.

"They are looking for your Avanti," Father Dowling said softly. "Of course they have its tag number. Just now, that is effectively concealed from the street, presuming of course that the Fox River police have enlisted the help of the Winnetka police."

"They think I killed Michael?"

Father Dowling said nothing. Furey walked toward the fireplace, turned and moved rapidly across the room. Soon he was pacing back and forth, looking at his sister and then at the priest. When he stopped, he had obviously made up his mind.

"I've got to get out of here."

"Gordon, don't. Where would you go?"

"Give me your keys."

Father Dowling stood. "You can run but they'll follow. You can hide but they'll find you."

"You're coming with me."

"Gordon!"

"I mean it. Come on. Mo, give me your keys."

"They're on the kitchen table. But you're not going to force Father Dowling to go with you."

"Of course I'll go," Father Dowling said. It seemed imperative to get the man out of the house. Father Dowling walked into the kitchen, picked up the keys from the sideboard and opened the back door.

"Give me those," Gordon Furey growled, hard on his heels.

"Of course."

"Gordon," Maureen wailed. "Stop this."

"Call your daughter," Father Dowling said. "I'm sure she'll want to be with you."

"Call Betty," Furey barked. "Tell her . . ."

"Tell her what?"

"Tell her whatever you want." He took hold of Father Dowling's arm and propelled him down the driveway, around the priest's car, to the station wagon.

Gordon Furey had trouble adjusting the seat, and when he started to back down the driveway, the motor died. Maureen Geary, hugging herself, stood beside Furey's Avanti, a horrified expression on her face. Getting her wild-eyed brother out of the house definitely seemed the right thing to do for her at the moment. Furey got them into the street and gunned the car up the avenue.

"Better slow down."

He did. He got onto an avenue with traffic lights at every intersection, making their progress intermittent, but where were they going? Father Dowling put the question to Furey, who was hunched silently over the wheel, cursing the red lights.

"I didn't kill him."

"Then you have nothing to fear from the police."

"They won't believe me." He glared at the priest. "I *wanted* to kill the bastard. I could have."

"That's not quite as bad as actually doing it."

"He wanted their marriage annulled!"

"I know."

"Do you approve?"

"No."

This relaxed Furey. Until a police cruiser went by, going in the opposite direction.

"They won't be looking for this car."

He began to fumble with the radio. Another police car passed. Father Dowling turned and looked behind. The cruiser was making a U-turn. When Furey came to a stop at yet another red light, Father Dowling pushed the gearshift and turned the key in the ignition. Furey grabbed his hand, twisting it, trying to get the keys.

There was a rap on the window and a huge cop looked down at him.

The passenger door opened; Father Dowling's arm was grabbed and he was pulled roughly from the car. A tall babyfaced cop suddenly stopped trying to look tough.

"Are you a priest?"

"Father Dowling."

The cop called across the roof to his partner, who had Gordon Furey facing the car while he pulled his hands behind him. "This one's a priest."

"Tell them who I am," Gordon Furey demanded. "This is an outrage."

He was still protesting while he was led away to the cruiser. Several other cars now bracketed the station wagon, and the backed-up traffic began to be heard from, horns blowing, angry shouts.

"How did you know about the station wagon?" Father Dowling asked the still puzzled young cop.

"A woman called in."

"I'll take her car back to her. Okay?"

The young cop discussed it with his partners and the other policemen. "We ain't looking for no priest," one said.

The young cop came back. "You're blocking traffic." He said it with a boyish smile.

Father Dowling got behind the wheel, took the key from his pocket and started the engine. Several minutes later he pulled into the Geary driveway.

"Kate's on her way," Maureen said after he told her what happened. "I couldn't call Betty."

"If there's still coffee, I'll have another cup before I go."

They sat at the kitchen table. "I've been thinking," she said. "I'd been talking with the lawyer about divorcing him, and Michael was going to die. Isn't that awful? And now none of it matters, annulment, divorce, nothing."

"Remember the good years," Father Dowling advised.

Her separation from Michael had been a kind of rehearsal for the loneliness she would now know. She talked of her daughter, and of the grandchild Michael would never know.

"Kate insisted on coming."

"Of course she did."

"I haven't been able to reach Brian."

"Your son."

"My son the hermit." A small, wondering smile. "He's not like either of us and he certainly isn't like Kate."

"I'd like to meet him."

"It looks as if you will."

"He had a priest with him when we got him," Runger of Winnetka told Phil Keegan when they transferred the prisoner to the Fox River jail. "A guy named Dowling."

"I know him."

What in hell had Roger Dowling been doing driving through Winnetka with Gordon Furey? It was obvious he would get no answer from Furey, who had come in stone-faced between Runger and another officer and stood glaring at Keegan while he took possession of him.

"Take these goddamn handcuffs off me."

Phil Keegan nodded to Runger, who handed the keys to his deputy.

"That's the first thing he's said."

Furey did not say anything else until the Winnetka cops were gone.

"Captain, this is an outrage. I am an attorney-at-law. If you want to talk to me there is no reason to treat me as a common criminal."

"Why don't you sit down, Mr. Furey, so we can talk. This is Lieutenant Horvath."

Keegan's tone of voice placated Furey. He nodded at Cy, sat and began rubbing his wrists.

"You're Michael Geary's brother-in-law?"

Furey nodded.

"Do you know what's happened to him?"

"I heard something on the radio."

"He's dead."

Gordon Furey looked at Keegan. Furey wore a three-piece suit, the vest of which looked tight. He tugged it down.

"You had lunch with him at The Crock."

"Yes, and we quarreled. If he hadn't left, we might have had a fight in the restaurant."

"What time was it when he left?"

"Why have I been arrested?"

"You argued with Geary, you nearly had a fight, you left the restaurant maybe five minutes after he did, your whereabouts from then on are unknown, Geary is now dead."

"I wouldn't want to prosecute that case."

"How would you defend?"

"That isn't the way it works, Captain. I start off innocent."

"Where did you go when you left the restaurant?"

Furey shook his head. "I want a lawyer present."

Keegan shoved the phone toward him and pushed back from his desk. "We'll leave you alone."

"Thank you."

Keegan followed Cy into the hall and pulled the door shut. "Do we know where he went from the restaurant?"

"We know he didn't go to his office, where he was expected, and he didn't go home."

Cy, checking the paperwork Runger had left, noticed that the car Furey had been driving when he was arrested was not the one they'd had the search on for. A check showed it was registered to Michael Geary.

"But Geary was found dead in his car."

"This one's registered to him too."

Keegan looked at Cy. "His wife's. Where the hell is the Avanti?"

There was no point in asking Furey until his lawyer showed up. Meanwhile Phil Keegan called St. Hilary's.

"I just got in, Phil," Father Dowling said.

"How come you were with Gordon Furey when he was arrested?"

"Have you talked with him?"

"We're waiting for his lawyer to arrive."

"He knew you were looking for him. So he took his sister's car and asked me to go along."

"Asked you?"

"What have you charged him with?"

"Maybe it should be kidnapping. Is his car at the Gearys'?"

That was the last place Roger Dowling had seen it. Keegan had a truck sent to pick it up and left the questioning of Furey to Cy and Agnes Lamb, who had been reviewing the results of the preliminary investigation of the car in which Geary had been found dead.

"What do you make of the plastic statue, Captain?"

"Lots of Catholics have them in their cars, Lamb. Geary was a Catholic."

"In the backseat."

"Say it came loose, lost its magnetism, and he put it back there."

She thought about that. "Yeah. Maybe."

Phil Keegan hoped he didn't have another Monique Pippen on his hands. Fanciful theories developed when irrelevancies began to fascinate.

If Roger Dowling had wanted him to stop by he could have mentioned it when they talked about Furey's car, so Phil Keegan went reluctantly home. He always went reluctantly home. Sometimes he would hear married men talk enviously about the bachelor life. Had he ever felt that way? God forgive him if he had. His girls were married and moved away and all tied up with their families. And he was too busy to visit them often. Or just unwilling to leave his job and its demands. Why would his daughters visit him? There wasn't room enough in his apartment to put them up, and besides, he just wasn't that good with kids. His oldest grandson eyed him in awe, wanting to hear about the bad guys, and his work sounded like a kids' game when he responded, cops and robbers.

He lived in a development situated beside the Fox River, but most of the buildings surrounded an artificial lake with real ducks on it. On with the lights and the television and then a frozen dinner into the microwave. He took it with a beer back to the living room and listened to the "Sportswriters" on TV. By and large he liked them, but they almost never had a good word to say about Notre Dame. They got on to the upcoming game with Southern Cal and agreed four to one that Notre Dame was in for a defeat in its own stadium. Sometimes he thought he watched television only to be aggravated by what he saw.

There was a Dirty Harry movie on cable, and he was watching that when the phone rang. He pressed Mute on the remote control and picked up the phone. It was Cy.

"What did Furey say?"

"Not much. He said he just drove around after leaving the restaurant."

"Just drove around."

"To cool off, after the argument."

"Did Holmer agree to charge him?"

"He got authorization to hold him overnight for more questioning. His lawyer threatens to sue the city out of its shoes."

"Anything on the car?"

"Two things."

The distinctive Avanti had been parked in the garage near Furey's office during the early afternoon, maybe while Geary was getting killed.

"Maybe?"

"Jolson is being cute about establishing a precise time of death."

"Is that what Monique says?"

"The second thing about the car is that they found a plastic madonna in the trunk. Like the one that was found in Geary's car."

Whatever dangers the Church faced from its enemies without paled beside those coming from the aggrieved within. It was a melancholy feature of recent years to see priests of the archdiocese publicly charged with the most dreadful crimes. The clergy were more struck by the moral horror of a priest's leading astray those in his charge, young women, boys, than were the laity. The laity, God bless them, had difficulty believing such things could happen, but their resistance was due to high expectations of priestly conduct. These expectations were justified in the vast majority of cases, but the small fraction guilty of such terrible deeds had brought the priesthood itself under a cloud, at least in the media.

"What's wrong with these guys, Roger?"

Phil Keegan, who might have become a priest himself if he had been able to learn Latin, wore a look of incomprehension.

"All men are sinners."

"Aw, come on, Roger. You sound like Whatshisname. All priests are child abusers?"

Roger Dowling found it impossible to discuss this with even so close a friend as Phil Keegan. At gatherings of clergy, the sense of having been betrayed could be indulged, and theories, wild, wilder, wildest, advanced to explain the unexplainable. Of course all men are sinners, meaning anyone can do anything in certain circumstances, but the life of a priest, his training, his prayers and preaching and daily Mass, made some sins at least unthinkable.

"This is the death knell of celibacy," Green said, and waited out the predictable roar of disagreement. "Whatever can be said for celibacy abstractly, and Paul VI said it as well as anyone, we have to face up to the fact that candidates for the priesthood are drawn from a society that has sex on the brain."

It was easy to agree that things were very different than they had been. Sex had never been a secret, but it was now an obsessive topic of public discussion. Young people were instructed in it as if it were driver training and equipped with the means of engaging in it with alleged impunity. Add to this approving, functional approach the constant assault on the senses from the printed page, the television screen, live entertainment, and it was easy to see Green's point.

The problem with it was that the possibility of a faithful marriage seemed equally under assault.

"It's the seminary," White growled. "Have you been out there lately? It's a goddamn country club. As for the classes . . ."

Moral theology was the favorite culprit. Roger Dowling tended to agree. Ever since 1968 when, after three long years of delay, Paul VI issued *Humanae Vitae*, stating that nothing justified changing the age-old ban on contraception, moral theologians had been in revolt. While waiting for the encyclical, they had anticipated a different verdict. The traditional stand was savaged, its arguments said to be nonsensical. All marital problems would disappear once a couple could separate sexual activity from the possibility of pregnancy. The whole attitude toward sexuality had been wrongheaded, Jansenist, fearful. It was a Christian duty to celebrate the body. Couples should enjoy one another.

That such a theology was developed during the 1960s perhaps diminished the surprise, given the changes in the wider society. But once sex and procreation were separated, prohibitions of pre- and extramarital affairs became difficult to sustain. And, if sex were all, what really was wrong with homosexual couplings? If sex between man and woman could be deliberately rendered infertile, homosexuals seemed already and naturally in the artificially induced condition.

But Paul VI eventually said no, there would be no change, and his encyclical was met with a roar of rejection. Theologians whose professional reputation had become identified with a pro-contraceptive position refused to back down. The Canadian bishops seemed to align themselves with dissident theologians. The American bishops did not do that; they officially accepted the papal verdict; but the increasing defiance of theologians, and the public-opinion polls that claimed to show that most Catholics not only practiced contraception but thought it was okay, presented a delicate pastoral problem. A low episcopal profile became standard. The doctrine was not denied, but it was never preached. Marriage preparation courses distinguished between *official* Church teaching and what Catholics could in conscience do.

For more than a quarter century dissident moral theology had been taught in seminaries, and a whole generation of priests emerged who were wholly indisposed even to inform laypeople about *official* Church teaching on sexual morality.

The results were now all around them. Priests and religious had left their posts, regaining lay status. The practice of contraception did not prevent Catholic couples from matching the dismal marital record of the nation as a whole. Divorces were no longer rare or a scandal. Remarriage became frequent. Annulments became almost as frequent and as easily obtained as civil divorce. Celibacy was attacked on all sides. In the sensuous temper of the time it was taken as an insult that some men actually presumed to live chaste single lives for the glory of God. Celibates themselves became confused.

That was the background against which the current scandals had to be seen, and then they appeared inevitable rather than surprising.

"We're going to be sued back to the Stone Age," Greeley predicted.

Settlements for millions and millions of dollars were being made across the country. The laity bristled at the suggestion that they had a duty to pay excessive court judgments exacted for the misbehavior of the clergy.

"The Catholic Church in America was once favorably compared with Standard Oil for efficiency of operation and management," Green said. "Now it ranks behind *Mad* magazine."

"*Mad* magazine's doing all right, isn't it?"

"I said behind."

Once every parish in the archdiocese of any size had three or four priests in residence. Soon there would be many parishes without any. Inner-city parishes were being shut down, the churches sold off. Bewildered parishioners picketed their closed-up churches. Things were bad and getting worse.

"Roger, what the hell is going on?" Phil Keegan demanded.

"We're going through a rough period."

"Rough period!"

What got to Keegan most, although this might have been due to the Geary murder, was annulment.

"The Chicago record is good, Phil."

"So what? People know where to go. Look at Geary. The Church is supposed to be universal, the same in Peoria and Timbuktu."

It was important not to encourage Phil Keegan when he got in this mood, either on politics or on the Church. Roger Dowling felt like a Pollyanna, insisting things weren't as bad as they seemed.

"Tell it to Mrs. Geary," Phil said.

"Well, death has done the job her husband wanted. And that she too wanted, in a sense. Remember, she had filed for divorce. How's your investigation going?"

"It wasn't her."

"Good Lord, I didn't think so."

"Cy did. At least he wanted to rule it out."

"She was visiting her daughter in South Bend."

"That's what ruled her out."

"And you've arrested Gordon Furey."

Keegan frowned. "Everyone's innocent, Roger. You realize that, don't you?"

"I would have thought everyone is guilty of something or other—everyone past the age of reason, that is."

"Furey has a public argument with Geary that nearly comes to blows. He follows him out of the restaurant. Geary misses a meeting with Monsignor Noonan and Furey can't tell us where he was during the three hours. He shows up at his sister's while you're there, and takes off in her station wagon. Nonetheless he's innocent."

Roger Dowling couldn't help thinking what a defense lawyer would do with such a circumstantial case. "Who is his lawyer?"

"A young associate of Amos Cadbury's. Angela Street."

"I know her."

Keegan frowned, as if this were somehow disloyal. Angela, unmarried, lived in an apartment half a mile from the parish plant. "She very nearly talked the judge out of issuing an indictment," he said. "Of course the prosecutor assigned Hurley to the case."

"Eugene Hurley."

"You remember him?"

"Is Gordon Furey that good a friend of the prosecutor?"

"Hurley avoided a dismissal by mentioning the statue that was found in the trunk of Furey's Avanti."

Marie stepped into the study from the dining room. "I knew those dreadful things would lead to something."

"What dreadful things?"

"There has been an epidemic of sacrilege in this town, Philip Keegan, and you know it. All one has to do is read the newspapers."

Roger Dowling calmed her down. Apparently the dashboard madonna found in Furey's Avanti was like the one found in Geary's car.

"You saying Furey's responsible for those things?"

"Are you saying there's no connection between the two statues?"

Roger Dowling asked Keegan what Cy Horvath made of all this.

Keegan beamed with pride in his protégé. "He is trying to make the best case possible for Furey's innocence."

"Innocence!" Marie put her hands beneath her apron and gave it a toss.

"So Hurley won't get any surprises during trial."

Cy Horvath had been in the detective bureau of the Fox River police ever since the reorganization of the department by Phil Keegan, when he cleaned out the political appointments and assorted deadwood. In one fell swoop, half the force was gone, making room for recruits like Cy. Peanuts Pianone was the only political appointee left, and he was at least good for laughs. Peanuts's uncle had shifted to the reformers before the crucial election and had survived what Bastia called the cleaning of the Augean stables, some sort of classical reference, according to Roger Dowling, but Bastia had won anyway, people were that fed up.

If Peanuts Pianone was good for laughs, Chief Robertson was a pain in the neck, but by and large he left the division alone. By and large. Today he had appeared importantly in Keegan's office.

"That Geary killing is a pretty nasty business, Phil."

"Yes sir."

"How's the investigation going?"

"It's in its preliminary stages."

"Keep me posted."

And Robertson went off for lunch at the Summit Club. Keegan passed this on to Cy deadpan.

"Didn't you tell him about Gordon Furey?"

"He could read that in the newspaper."

"Hasn't he?"

"Cy, you don't understand the tension a chief of police works under. He's got all kind of reports not to read, let alone the newspaper."

"Maybe Furey didn't do it."

"Yeah?"

"He says he didn't. His lawyer will try to show he didn't. How did he do it if he did?"

What they knew about what Furey had done that afternoon, and even what they didn't know, had a big gap in it. It didn't put Furey near where Geary had been killed.

Geary had been killed in his car some minutes after arriving at his insurance agency, passing Florence Lewis's window and parking behind the building. When Florence realized he hadn't come inside, she looked out and saw him seated behind the wheel of his car. He was dead, strangled, apparently by someone in the backseat. Florence had noticed no one other than Geary in the car when it went past her window. The parking lot could be entered from the street in front of the agency by the driveway that passed the office windows. But it could also be entered from the rear, by means of an alley that in turn could be entered either at the south or the north end.

"You think he parked and then someone got in the backseat and strangled him?"

Cy looked expressionlessly at Keegan.

"I mean, isn't that our assumption? Furey was waiting for him in the parking lot."

"How'd he get there?"

The Avanti had been parked at the time in a downtown garage.

"Otherwise the killer had to be in the backseat all along and waited until he parked to do it."

"There's at least one other possibility."

"Yeah?"

"He might have been brought back to the agency already dead and put behind the wheel."

Keegan frowned. He disliked fanciful theories. "The killer was driving when Florence looked out, and she thought it was Geary."

"She knew it was his car."

Cy had taken Agnes Lamb back to the agency and run a little test, driving past the windows several times, with Agnes Lamb seated at Florence's desk.

"And?"

"She identified me every time."

"What's the point?"

"One time it was Peanuts at the wheel."

Agnes had been set up in the sense that it was a police car each time, she was teamed with Cy, Peanuts was not involved. She saw what she had expected to see, so maybe that was how it had been with Geary's secretary as well.

"What's the ME say?"

"It's possible. She checked the reports. He hadn't been dead long but it could have been hours."

"She?"

"Moniqu Pippen."

"Is this her theory?"

Pippen was a beautiful woman Keegan said reminded him of his second daughter who for some reason had decided to join the medical examiner's office. Fear of malpractice, curiosity, who knew? Keegan complained that Dr. Pippen had an inflamed imagination and liked to devise complicated and improbable explanations of how people got dead. Once she had been right and it had spoiled her. If she saw a man shoot another in the middle of an intersection, she would suggest the real gunman was hidden in the crowd at the corner. If Cy had been capable of blushing, he would have blushed. But not because this was Pippen's idea. It wasn't an idea, it was a possibility and he wanted to know if it could have happened.

"Look, Cy, she may be bored with the obvious, but we aren't. If a guy is found strangled in his car, sitting at the wheel, and there is evidence it was done from behind, we're going to assume the killer was in the backseat."

"He wears a size twelve boot."

"Boot?"

"Cowboy boot. Pippen did notice the boot prints on the left side of the car. Whoever was wearing the boots could have got into the backseat."

Or gotten out of the front seat. Forget the boots. What the test with Agnes made possible was that someone other than Geary had driven by Florence's office window in Geary's car with Geary already dead, maybe in the backseat.

"He wasn't strangled," Monique insisted.

"The wire around his neck was a decoration?"

"It was twisted tight enough to strangle him. Only I think he was already dead."

"Of what?"

"I'm running tests, okay?"

That had been the basis of the drive-bys, testing a possibility suggested by what Monique said. Cy imagined Furey behind the wheel, delivering Geary to the parking lot behind his office. The Avanti was downtown in a garage. Geary's car provided a way of getting Furey to the agency, but how did he get back downtown to his Avanti?

"How long do you suppose it would take to walk downtown from here?" he asked Agnes.

"From here?"

"Look, you and Peanuts take your cars and go. I'm going to time the walk."

Peanuts and Agnes looked at him in awe.

"Lieutenant, it's miles. You can't do that. Do part and we'll compute the whole."

"Let him do it," Peanuts said angrily. "I'll do it, Cy. You want me to walk downtown from here? I could do that."

"I'll do it, Peanuts."

He started off and first Peanuts then Agnes drove by. After three blocks he told himself that Agnes had made a very good suggestion. There was no need to actually walk the distance to figure out how long it would take.

He made the walk anyway. To prove a point. To keep busy and drive thoughts of Monique Pippen from his mind.

They agreed that Mark would stay in South Bend and Kate would attend her father's funeral alone. She would be there days before the depressing event and perhaps would stay longer, and Mark was getting ready for an oral examination that would decide his fate so far as going on for the doctorate was concerned.

"I could come up for the funeral itself."

Kate put a hand on his cheek, treating the remark as an expression of goodwill rather than a serious suggestion. Terrible as this news had been, stunned as she still was by the horror of newspaper and television accounts of her father's being found dead in his car in strange circumstances, there was a part of Kate that welcomed a chance to get away from the suffocating atmosphere of graduate student housing and the Theology Department.

Far more distracting to Mark than a family funeral was the constant chatter about the secret meeting to be held the following week on campus. *Der Eisenkardinal,* as Hildebrand was often referred to, had taken on mythic status.

"Beware a defected liberal."

"The Neo-con of theology."

It was assumed that Hildebrand, from an alleged liberal stance immediately after the council, had for career reasons moved rightward, the ultimate reward for this being his current position as number two man in the Vatican.

"Doesn't he say he wants to retire?"

Kate's remark was met by wise smiles.

"There's one more rung to go."

Loss of faith or not, Kate was put off by such cynical talk about religion. Theologians saw themselves as adversaries of a conservative Church establishment; churchmen were seen as ambitious, unprincipled types, clawing their way to the top.

"The top of what?"

"They want power, Kate."

Power? Theologians were powerstruck enough for her, but it was the paltriness of the aim that made it comical. Success for a theologian was ten seconds on the national news bashing the Church. Kate read some articles by Hildebrand and checked one of his books out of the library. She took guilty pleasure in liking what she read. The cardinal preached an old-time religion of the kind Kate had lost.

"Stay here," she told Mark. "You have too much work to do."

He agreed, unsurprisingly, and she wondered if he wanted her out of the way while the Hildebrand matter heated up. She had sensed that her contrariness had made him uneasy.

Well, she found that she wanted to keep him from this grim family event. An image formed in her mind of the three of them, her mother, Brian, herself, huddled around the body of her father. The tableau suggested a final unity before disintegration. Kate would return to Mark, bearing her baby within her, Brian would go off God knew where, and her mother? It was difficult to think of her mother as a widow.

Marian in the next unit had asked her over for coffee. Marian had lost her mother during the summer.

"Thank God you're pregnant, Kate. I don't know what I'd do without him."

"Him" was Matthew, a butterball drooling in his playpen, mesmerized by a plastic bird that hung above him. The death of parents removes one generation from the buffer between the baby and future. Kate was now half an orphan, only her mother between her and the full ravages of time.

Her father's death was graspable only in terms of its effects, on his coming grandchild, on Kate, on her mother. By dying, he had achieved the annulment he wanted. "So long as you both shall live." The contract was fulfilled now, all paid up, her mother as free as her father had wanted to be.

Kate resolutely refused to let her mind dwell on the present condition of her father, if any. He didn't really seem gone at all, no matter the grotesque glimpse of his body flashed on television. Was his soul still going on somewhere? Kate was finding it difficult not to be skeptical about her skepticism. Proofs for the immortality of the soul had been fashioned to accommodate this sense that the dead are not entirely gone.

Mark took her in his arms, but she turned away and went into the kitchen. Why was she picking a fight with him? Because she was now under the disadvantage of having lost her father to violence, under a cloud of infidelity, whereas his parents still flourished in Wisconsin, heavy with virtue and predictability. His parents annoyed her for living the kind of life she was determined to live with Mark. She wanted to be boring and predictable, the two of them glued to each other like Siamese twins, a separate existence unthinkable.

There had been a story in the Fox River paper about her father. A reader could easily think that Michael Geary had been a victim of the random violence that was the daily fare of newspapers. What had she feared would be printed? "Husband Seeking Annulment Meets Violent End?"

What Kate hadn't expected when she went home was to be questioned by a detective from Fox River.

"You been married how long?"

"Three years."

"You lived at home until then?"

The black detective's name was Agnes Lamb, and when she spoke, words seemed to form on the surface of a sustained note, the humming an apology for quizzing Kate like this. On the other hand, the details of Kate's life were approached as if they were simply terribly interesting in themselves.

"Only in the summer. I was away at school."

"Notre Dame?"

She nodded. There seemed to be no need to distinguish between St. Mary's and Notre Dame.

"So three summers ago was the last time you lived in your parents' house?"

"Four."

"But you were married three years ago."

Did Detective Lamb want to hear of the summer spent in Wisconsin, at the camp for city kids, doing something for those less fortunate than herself, as the phrase went, but also able to see Mark because the camp was only an hour from his hometown?

Finally Kate had succumbed to the lure of the questions and tried to reconstruct life in the Geary household, Mom, Dad, Brian and herself. How easy it was to portray it as it might have been, as her parents must have wanted it to be. Her own marriage had taught her that arguments are inevitable in marriage, silences, taking offense, sometimes angry words, but these were minor squalls on an otherwise peaceful surface. Kate had never felt so busy before; even before the baby came there was so much to do. If she didn't do things, who would? That was the realization that altered her life radically. So what if her parents had quarreled? Everybody quarreled.

Except Mark's parents, of course. He frowned and gave it some thought when she asked him if his parents had ever fought. How could she tell him what it was like to lie in bed, wakened by angry voices, and realize that they were at it again, her mother's tearful voice wavering out of control, her father's growing louder and angrier? Of course he was guilty of whatever it was her mother was shouting. Kate never quite heard the words or, if she did, never quite understood them. What she felt was the psychic equivalent of an earthquake, the sense that the very ground on which her life was built was shifting. It made her dizzy.

"Silver anniversary," Detective Lamb murmured when Kate answered the question how long her parents had been married. "What went wrong?"

"Wrong."

"Why did your father move out?"

Kate wanted to say it was a trial, it didn't mean a thing, but that would sound silly.

"What did she tell you?"

The questioning went on for another quarter hour with Kate eluding the effort to see how much she had known of why her parents' marriage had fallen apart after so many years.

"Were you close to your mother?"

"Of course."

"How often did you see her?"

"We talked on the phone several times a week."

"And your father?"

She did not want to talk about her father. She did not want to think about him. She wanted all this to be over, a dreadful event in the past, life returned to its even tenor.

"Your uncle was pretty protective toward your mother, wasn't he?"

"What do you mean?"

"She could call on him in case of trouble, rely on him, you know."

"What are brothers for?"

Did the detective think Uncle Gordie and her mother had conspired to kill her father?

"You have a brother, don't you?"

"Yes."

"Will he be coming home?"

That was what Mark had asked her as she was leaving. "Will Brian be there?"

"Of course."

"Have they found him?"

"Mark, he wasn't lost. He called. He's coming."

Outside, Marian had been strapping Matthew into a car seat, ready to go off somewhere. Beyond, the buildings of the campus loomed, the dome of the main building dominating, atop it the great gold statue of Mary looking ever southward.

"Schuler will say a Mass for your Dad."

"Hmmm."

"He offered."

"That's nice."

She had meant it. She wanted that, suddenly, promises of prayers, priests offering Mass for the repose of her father's soul, the great huddling of the tribe to get her through this terrible tragedy. Schuler was a graduate student like Mark, though a priest as well. A priest like Mark might have been, except that Jimmy Schuler still believed it all. Like her brother, Brian.

The rule against eulogizing the deceased at funerals was seldom strictly honored. Pastors might not make praise of the departed the topic of the homily at the funeral Mass, but there was a second chance at the end of the ceremony, before the casket was wheeled out. It was Panzica's practice to invite the mourners to be seated, after which he would stand for a moment with bowed head and then address the immediate family. Inevitably the suggestion was made that the departed was at that very moment enjoying the vision of God. At the funeral of Michael Geary, Panzica felt no impulse to ignore the canon law on the subject. The only mention of Michael Geary was in the course of the liturgy.

Of course the pastor of Blessed Sacrament sincerely prayed for the soul of his departed parishioner, and he would have been horrified by the thought that Geary's ultimate destination was not the beatific vision. But if ever a man had earned a few cleansing years in purgatory, that man was Michael Geary.

Memories of his sessions with the cardinal and the archdiocesan lawyers over the suit brought against the parish and the cardinal by Amanda James ensured a sleepless night for Father Panzica. It was the only blemish on his priestly record, and it really had nothing to do with him. He had hired Amanda to play the organ and she had been seduced by Michael Geary, a parishioner as well as an inveterate member of various committees. How did that make Blessed Sacrament liable for the real or alleged anguish Amanda suffered as a result of her deflowering?

It was a thirty-eight-year-old woman's claim to have been a virgin when she was seduced that had captured the attention of the media. The original tone of the coverage had been one of skepticism. Since writers found it inconceivable that anyone could abstain from sexual activity, Amanda's accusation against Geary had been treated as the fantasy of a sexually repressed old maid.

Except that Geary had dropped out of the story from the beginning. With uncharacteristic delicacy of taste, the accused was referred to as someone fulfilling certain unspecified functions in the parish. Of course people would imagine this meant the pastor! Panzica was subjected to merciless kidding from his fellow priests, even those who realized it was anything but a joke. Not that the cardinal had any misconception about what had happened. But Amanda's lawyer, her father, saw the parish and archdiocese as a far more attractive target for their suit.

The scandal had faded away during the year and more of negotiations with lawyers. Since the facts were undisputed, the only question was holding the parish and archdiocese responsible for what had happened. A sizable settlement seemed the only way to put the matter to rest. Panzica did not think that the pastor who was linked to the loss of that kind of money, however innocent, would escape consequences. Monsignor Noonan had discussed with him Geary's inquiry into having his marriage annulled.

"Annulled! They've got two kids."

Noonan's expression was one reserved for the naive. "Of course he could never have gotten it done in Chicago."

"I should hope not."

"That's why he entered the plea in Michigan."

The more Panzica thought of the unfortunate Michael Geary, the more difficult he found it to grieve. At the cemetery, when everything was finished and he was shaking Mrs. Geary's hand, it was all he could do not to congratulate her on having got rid of such a man.

"Do you see that woman, Father?"

She nodded at a woman who stood some distance from the gravesite, a dramatic figure in an ankle-length fur coat with a hood that she had pulled over her flowing blond hair.

"Who is she?"

"I suppose she thought of herself as Michael's fiancée. She is why he wanted the annulment."

Thank God Noonan had told him of it. Mrs. Geary probably thought every priest knew all the archdiocesan business. He did not want to think what his reaction to her remark would have been if he had not heard of the annulment.

"Who is she?"

"Mrs. Burger."

"Mrs.!"

The widow shrugged. Behind her a tall bearded man looked at Panzica with round unblinking eyes. It was difficult to recognize the altar boy of yore in this gaunt figure. Standing with his family, Brian seemed all alone, unconnected, remote.

"They gave you leave to come?"

Brian just stared.

"The Trappists."

"I am no longer in the monastery."

"Well, it's a hard life."

"On the contrary."

Geez. Panzica turned to Kate and idiotically asked who would win the game next Saturday. Her brother shifted his feet and his expression suggested he was going to say something dismissive about college athletics.

"Notre Dame, of course."

"I hope you're right."

"Are you coming down for the game?"

"Ha. I heard tickets are going for five hundred dollars."

"Come and you can use Mark's ticket. We'll go together."

Was she serious? "Maybe Brian would like to go."

She laughed. "He's less interested than Mark. Come on down. I mean it." She swung her purse around and took from it a pencil. "Do you have something I can write our number on?"

He would have torn a page from his ritual book. But instead he found Father Tuohy's memorial card in his pocket. He handed it to her.

"Everybody's dying," she remarked before turning it over and writing the number. "Let me know by Wednesday or I'll offer it to someone else."

Panzica had the odd feeling that he was being rewarded for not praising her father from the pulpit. He couldn't believe his good luck.

Mrs. Geary was watching the woman in the fur coat, who was still standing where she had been.

"She's waiting for us to leave," Mrs. Geary whispered to her daughter.

"Well, she must have liked him anyway."

"Who is she?" Brian asked in sepulchral tones.

"No one," Kate said.

"A friend of your father's." There was an edge in Mrs. Geary's voice.

But Panzica felt suddenly capable of surviving the collapse of Western civilization. A man who had seduced the organist and cost the archdiocese tons of money had applied for an annulment in another diocese in order to marry the woman in the fur coat, who also apparently was married.

Gordon Furey came and pressed an envelope into Panzica's hand. "For you, Father." He patted the priest on the arm. Panzica thanked him. He liked Furey. He had tried to talk sense to his brother-in-law Michael Geary, when he was involved with Amanda; he had even talked to the girl. That had taken guts. Too bad he hadn't acted earlier.

But then there wouldn't have been this funeral and Kate Geary Hanson offering him a chance to see the Notre Dame–Southern California game.

"They're not student seats," Kate said. "My father paid for them. They're in the south end zone. Bring binoculars."

"He hasn't said he's coming," her mother said.

"I'll come," Panzica cried. "Of course I'll come. It's just that I find it hard to believe."

He walked the family back to their cars, Brian bringing up the rear.

"I'm sorry about the Trappists."

"Some of them are good men."

"I meant about your leaving."

"It was God's will."

"Have you gone back to California?"

From Brian's look, he might as well have mentioned a previous existence. "I have a hermitage in Minnesota."

Geez. But Panzica let it go. His step was light as he went to his car. The Gearys gave a little toot when they went by. They were followed by the Fureys in their car. Panzica started the motor and looked back at the gravesite. The woman in the fur coat was standing by the still open grave, staring down at the casket holding the mortal remains of Michael Geary.

"I hate cemeteries," Agnes Lamb said.

"People are dying to get into them."

"Don't." Agnes actually shivered.

"It's nearly over."

Cy Horvath was guessing, but Agnes seemed to need reassurance. She was a funny cop. She never flinched from the most unsavory and violent aspects of the job, yet here she was quaking in a cemetery despite the fact that she was behind the wheel of an unmarked police car, snug and warm and out of the weather, just waiting for the priest to get done putting what was left of Michael Geary into the ground.

"I'll come with if you want," she had said at the church, but Cy told her to stay put while he went inside and from the choir loft looked down to see who had shown up. This was the choir loft in which the organist whom Geary had harassed or whatever had played. Maybe they both had played up here. He shook the sacrilegious thought away.

Father Panzica was slow but there were no frills. The sermon was about the readings, no blubbering about what a pillar of the parish Michael Geary had been. The mourners were clustered in the front pews, with just a scattering of others through the church. No media, Cy noted with satisfaction. The blonde in the fur coat, pressed into the corner of a pew, was craning her neck to see. Why didn't she move up?

During communion, Cy went downstairs and out to the car, where Agnes waited for him to say something.

"It won't be long."

"What do they do?"

"Go in and take a look."

She opened her mouth and closed it. Baptists didn't hang around Catholic ceremonies, even in the line of duty.

"I've seen films of President Kennedy's funeral. Is it like that?"

"Well, the congregation's different. And the body."

It was a good thing he didn't telegraph a joke because she sure as hell didn't telegraph her reaction.

"Do you believe in life after death?" she asked.

"Sure. Don't Baptists?"

"Who said I was a Baptist?"

Her employment application for one thing. "You quit?"

"I don't mean heaven and hell and all that. I mean another life."

"Here?"

"Yes."

"My God, I hope not."

"Are you serious?"

"One of the attractions of dying is getting out of Fox River, Illinois."

"You might come back in California."

"I thought you didn't mean hell."

"Sometimes I think I'll switch out there, after I have more experience."

"Of what?"

"As a cop."

"They need cops in California?"

The church doors opened and a silver-haired man in a gray overcoat came out. He skipped down the steps and went out to the curb, where he opened the back door of the hearse. Agnes put her hands on the wheel.

At the cemetery she had gripped the wheel ever since they parked out of sight of the burial party. It was the season for cemeteries, all the leaves turned, grass losing its summer greenness, a chill in the air despite the thin sunlight.

"See the woman in the fur coat?" Cy asked.

"What about her?"

"She was at the church."

"Who is she?"

"I don't know."

"I wonder why she doesn't join the rest of them."

"Maybe she's bashful."

If he hadn't seen her at church he wouldn't have thought anything of the way she stood some distance off watching the final prayers for Michael Geary before he was lowered into the earth.

"Is she why we came out here?" Agnes asked.

"You see anyone else you wouldn't expect to see?"

"Cy, I only recognize the widow."

They were here because the hot idea they had been pursuing had been cooled by Keegan.

"What if Furey isn't our man?" Keegan had said.

"He could have walked from Geary's insurance agency."

"He has varicose veins."

Cy knew what Keegan meant. It wasn't simply that Furey denied harming the man he had threatened in the restaurant; he seemed almost eager to have it proved in court. Furey's smile had been unnerving when Cy had explained to him how he had driven the already dead Geary to his agency and then walked downtown to where his Avanti was parked.

"Why take him back to work if he was dead?" Furey had said.

So he would be found there, far from where Furey had argued with him? But then Furey should have established some kind of alibi. He seemed to think his lack of an alibi established his innocence.

"Not that it has to be established," his lawyer, Angela Street, added.

"Of course he could have killed him," Grace Masterson had said. "I thought he was going to do it right here."

And Keegan had said, "Keep your eyes open, Cy."

"They're leaving," Agnes said now, nodding at the mourners drifting away from the gravesite.

"Wait. No point in attracting attention."

The undertaker's limos took the party away; the other cars moved slowly out the cemetery road. The blonde in the fur coat watched them leave and then walked slowly toward the grave, picking her way among markers, stirring up fallen leaves. At the open grave, she stood with her hands jammed into her coat pockets, her hooded head bowed. From a distance she might have been a monk.

"What's she doing?"

"Praying?"

"Or making sure he's dead."

She stood there maybe five minutes, then turned and kicked her way through the leaves to a van parked twenty-five yards down the road. A van? Cy would have imagined a luxury car. Vans were bought by families with kids.

Without asking, Agnes pulled away when the van began to move. After getting close enough to read the tag number, she dropped back.

"Want to follow her?"

"You got any other appointments?"

Agnes shook her head. "No, I covered them all. Sitting outside a church during a funeral, kibitzing on a burial. That's about it."

Cy liked Agnes, in a professional way. The male menopause or whatever it was that made him want to make a damned fool out of himself with Monique Pippen did not affect him with Agnes. Of course she was black and probably unattracted by Hungarians. And armed.

The blonde obviously never imagined anyone else would be watching her the way she had been watching the mourners. Once out of the cemetery, she goosed the van, going an average of five miles over the speed limit.

"We could pull her over."

"Or shoot out her back tires."

The tag number was worthless. Her destination was the airport, where she dropped the van off at a rental agency's parking area and then wended her way to the short-term lot, where she got into the kind of car Cy had imagined her driving. A Lincoln, black, the boxy one before the streamlined models came out.

"Funny," Agnes said.

"Feminine intuition."

"This was your idea."

"That's what I said. Intuition into the feminine mentality."

"She's leaving a pretty big trail if she's trying to fool someone."

Maybe she thought her own car would be recognized at the cemetery. But anyone who had taken much of a look around would have noticed her standing there.

"Shall I keep on following her?"

"Sure."

He called in the tag number of the Lincoln and had the name before she turned into the driveway at the end of which was a mailbox with the same name on it. Burger.

Jerome Noonan stood before the full-length mirror affixed to the inside of his closet door and surveyed his monsignorial presence. He seldom wore the full regalia to which his title of domestic prelate entitled him—we live in leveling, egalitarian times—save in the privacy of his own rooms. He turned, looked at his reflection over his shoulder, adjusted the door and went to his desk, where he sat and lifted one hand to his chin. Thus had the bishop sat when he discussed the missions with Gregory Peck.

A vocation to the priesthood is a mysterious thing, particularly when it is awakened in prepuberty, as it had been in Jerome Noonan. Oftentimes it was the influence of a nun at school or a priest or the experience of serving at Mass. There were boys who had uncles who were priests, thus bringing the possibility near. Noonan's vocation had come while watching *Keys of the Kingdom* in the Nokomis Theater.

He owned a video of the old black-and-white film but did not need to watch it often. Its scenes and sequences were part of the marrow of his bones. From boyhood, his ambition had vacillated between the lean soutaned figure before the desk and the bishop behind it, his ringed hand fingering his pectoral cross as he spoke to his priest. His life, he supposed, was a dissatisfying mixture of both.

The image that formed before his eyes now was that of Roger Dowling and Ambrose Ravel in conversation at Tuohy's funeral. What was going on? Whatever it was, Noonan felt irrationally responsible. It had seemed an unfair way to get rid of Michael Geary's importunate demands to send him to Roger Dowling.

"St. Hilary's," Geary had answered, when Noonan asked where the marriage he wished to contest had taken place.

"In Fox River?"

"My wife is from there."

And so was Roger Dowling. The name evoked the sweet-sad reaction it had ever since Dowling broke down under the pressure of the marriage tribunal. Apparently he had been seeking solace in the bottle and it had gotten out of hand. So off he went to a place in Wisconsin that specialized in such cases and eventually was assigned to Fox River.

"James Joyce described Ireland as an afterthought of Europe," Ambrose Ravel had sententiously observed. "Fox River is an afterthought of the Archdiocese of Chicago."

Neither Ravel nor Noonan was now overshadowed by Dowling, the upward curve of whose clerical career had seemed inevitable.

"Some are ordained, others are foreordained," Ravel had said.

And some like Ravel are just plain lucky. The chance of advancement had come down to the two of them, or so it seemed, but Noonan had never been able to see Ravel as a rival. For one thing he was younger; he was perfectly content doing what he was asked to do; he lived in the untroubled conviction that his superiors were always right, so that his life was not so much one of disciplined obedience as of doing the only reasonable thing. Everybody liked Ambrose Ravel, in a slightly condescending way. Noonan, who did not expect to be liked, concentrated on being respected and admired.

Ravel had been made bishop and eventually would have his own diocese; Roger Dowling had settled in at St. Hilary's and, reports were, was a new man. He was content. Noonan did not believe this. He went to see for himself and felt like a friend of Job who was greeted not with a catalog of the ills that had befallen him, but with a serenity Noonan found unnerving.

He himself was suspended between success and failure, a mere monsignor who was still stuck on the tribunal.

"You represent continuity," the cardinal had said when Noonan had broached the subject of a change. Those were the days when the cardinal ran the whole show, no nonsense about appointment boards. "God knows what the new regulations mean."

The new regulations invested great power in diocesan tribunals. Once applications ran a tortured course locally and then were sent to the Rota in Rome. It was Ambrose Ravel who had spoken of a musty room stacked to the ceiling with yellowing petitions.

"Like a paper sale."

An inspired image, but one that got them all going on the parish paper sales—drives to collect stacks of old newspapers which were then sold for a pittance to finance some project or another. There was a contest and whichever grade of the parish school won was treated in some way, Noonan couldn't remember how.

"A Cubs game," Ravel said.

The point of the comparison was that petitions for a declaration of nullity went to the Bleak House in the Vatican, where the years rolled over them before they were taken up. There were simply not enough canon lawyers to speed it up. Not that it mattered. Requests were almost inevitably denied. By that time the petitioners might be dead, divorced and remarried, even reconciled. The cardinal had been right to think that things would be different now.

Jerome Noonan remembered vividly the first time they had taken testimony from a psychiatrist on the mental state of the petitioner at the time of the marriage in question. The idea that there was some hidden block to consent that only a professional could discern was a far cry from the traditional instances of involuntary action, violence and fear. Once these new criteria were admitted, they increased and multiplied, until it was possible to wonder if anyone had ever performed a human action in the traditional sense of the phrase.

Ambrose Ravel's opposition and his written rationale to the new cardinal had arguably earned him ordination to bishop. Ravel said nothing that he and Noonan had not discussed again and again. It would have been fairer if Ravel had suggested a joint report. But Noonan's real regret was that he had not beaten Ravel to the punch. In the event, the Chicago court tightened up considerably. If all tribunals had done the same, things would be better. But here and there around the country, often in remote and improbable dioceses, tribunals issued declarations of nullity with the rapidity of a Nevada divorce mill. Noonan felt he should have guessed that Michael Geary would take that route.

When he saw Roger Dowling and Ravel in conversation at Tuohy's funeral, he feared the two men thought he encouraged such latitudinarian shenanigans. His conversation with Dowling had been reassuring. Now Michael Geary was dead.

The matter was over now as definitively as it would have been with an annulment. But now the son was on the case. When he was told that a Mr. Geary wanted to see him, Monsignor Noonan shivered as his mother might have at the thought of a visitation from beyond the grave. But of course it was Brian Geary.

"Ah yes. You're the professor, I understand." Michael Geary had been guardedly proud of this.

"I left a tenure-track position at Berkeley," the staring young man with the beard said. "I entered the Trappists."

Was that the explanation of the beard? Like most diocesan priests, Noonan was alternately attracted and repelled by the image of a more austere life. He told Brian it was too tough a life for him.

"It's not, really."

"People say that about living in Antarctica."

It was the last time Noonan tried a joke. Brian Geary was serious in a single-minded way.

"If I spent my life as a physicist, conducting research, lecturing, I might at the end have advanced knowledge of the physical universe a millimeter or two."

"That's more than most people do."

"We know almost nothing."

Noonan nodded. That was certainly true of his own understanding of the sciences.

"Astronomy is the key. It always has been."

"Ah."

"There we try to look beyond the visible and almost succeed."

Noonan wasn't sure that a smile was the proper expression for this conversation, but he was stuck with it now. It seemed pasted to his face.

Brian had gone to the monastery as to a direct route to what astronomy could not reach. Inner space. The whole thing sounded like a research project, a spiritual lab. With disappointment, he had become a hermit. Noonan thought of Gregory Peck going off to China when Brian told him of the house high above the Mississippi at La Crescent, Minnesota.

"I never heard of it."

"Neither had I. That was the point."

"Of course."

"In my heart I complained about the Trappists, but that was my pride. I was not worthy to live among such holy men."

Noonan nodded. His dealings with the laity had seldom ventured beyond discussions of the difficulties of spouses.

"I am a sinner."

"We all are."

"But not all sins are equal."

Noonan was about to say that it would be another sin of pride to insist that one was worse than everyone else, but the young man's manner did not encourage ill-considered remarks.

"Have you ever thought of Mundelein?"

Brian stared at him, awaiting further explanation.

"The seminary of the archdiocese."

It was obvious that he had disappointed the young man. Brian Geary, jumping from the university to the monastery to a hermitage in Minnesota, seemed a perfect instance of someone who could not make a permanent commitment. There wasn't a chance he would be admitted to Mundelein.

"Did you advise my father to seek an annulment?"

Monsignor Noonan felt they had reached the real point of this visit. "I advised him not to seek one in Chicago."

"Why?"

"I doubted it would be granted."

"So you sent him where it would be."

Anger rose in Noonan, although of course he had had experience of family members who blamed the tribunal when an annulment was granted and just as often when it was not. But he had learned not to expect sympathy and no longer pointed this out to complainers. They were more interested in their own grievance than in his.

"No, I did not tell your father to apply elsewhere."

The bearded young man thought about it. Monsignor Noonan felt that his word was being doubted. He had to get away from this topic.

"I wouldn't advise you to go to the seminary."

"Why?"

"Two things, Brian. Your search for a religious vocation thus far is not encouraging. How long were you with the Trappists, months? That's not much of a trial. The hermitage has lasted a shorter time. Such indecision tells against a vocation. But there is something else."

Brian sat across from him, unblinking, the beard concealing any expression he might have.

"It is natural that the death of a parent, particularly the kind of death your father suffered, should turn your thoughts to eternal things. That is good. But becoming a priest is certainly not the only way to take one's faith seriously. It could permeate your scholarly life . . ."

Brian was shaking his head. "I burned my bridges."

"That was unwise."

"I am not interested in being wise in that way."

Noonan brought the conversation to a close as quickly as he could. He found an old Mundelein brochure and pressed it into Brian's hand. As soon as he was gone, he called Fox River, but Roger Dowling denied sending Brian to Noonan.

"How did he ever hear of me?"

This question had not remained with him and now, seated at his desk, regarding himself in the mirror, Brian Geary was the furthest thing from Noonan's mind.

The church was just a minute away from her kitchen door, but summer or winter Marie Murkin made a point of dressing up at least a bit before hurrying over—in summer a change of shoes and a lace mantilla, in other seasons protection against the elements. This fall day she slipped into her raincoat and eased its hood over her stiffly sprayed hair and stepped onto the porch.

The sky was an upturned bucket, rain falling in waves rather than drops; the sidewalk ran like a creek, and even as she stood there lightning flashed above the dull slate roof of the church, a jagged javelin whose afterimage died before the rumbling of thunder came.

Marie descended the back steps sideways, hand on the ledge, then ducked her head and scampered through the rain. A moment later, inside, more or less unscathed by the rain, she was checking out the bank of vigil lights before the statue of St. Anthony of Padua. Despite her urging, Father Dowling resisted progress, refusing to switch to electric candles that could be timed to go off after fifteen minutes. Marie knelt, closed her eyes and let her thoughts rise with the smell of wax and burned matches.

"Sulfur," Father Dowling had said, when she mentioned this accompaniment of prayer. "Are you sure your prayers are going in the right direction?"

She offered it up, as she always did when she couldn't think of an answer to his kidding. Father Dowling wasn't kidding now. He was over there in his study, filling the room with pipe smoke, a book open before him but not reading it. He didn't agree with Phil Keegan about the murder of Michael Geary, and he had no alternative explanation.

The man was dead by unnatural causes and Gordon Furey had been arrested, yet Phil Keegan acted as if he hadn't the least idea who had done it. The problem, if you listened to him, was that there were too many people who had reason to do it.

"And opportunity."

"There's the immediate family," Keegan began, and Marie, listening from the kitchen, suppressed an impatient cry. Mrs. Geary had been with her daughter in South Bend and her crazy son had been playing hermit in Minnesota. Phil Keegan knew that as well as she did. Or as Father Dowling, who reminded him of it.

"The two women vouch for one another and the son for himself," Keegan said.

"And you haven't ruled out suicide?"

"Suicide!"

"Geary managed to leave an ambiguous scene behind him. But imagine that he came back to his office, parked in the back . . ."

Keegan picked it up, with a sarcastic tone. ". . . wrapped the wire around his neck and strangled himself. Or were you thinking of assisted suicide?"

"Have you pursued that?"

"Roger, what in blazes would be his motive?"

"What motive would his wife or daughter or son have had?"

"You know what kind of guy Geary was."

In the church, Marie got off her knees and sat back in the pew, looking up pleadingly at the saint holding the baby Jesus in his arms. St. Anthony never failed; he always answered her prayers, sometimes in surprising ways, but he never just ignored her. She was here to beg him to solve the Michael Geary murder so that some semblance of normalcy would return to St. Hilary's rectory.

She ran through the list she had come up with, to give the saint a head start. She included the widow and children, just to show she wasn't telling St. Anthony his business, but after that the list just grew and grew. Amanda the molested musician, as Marie cynically thought of her, might be in Florida, but her spiteful father was still in town. Imagine a so-called Catholic holding up the archdiocese the way she did. The payment was made just to get the story out of the papers and the case out of the courts. Marie was of two minds about all these charges being brought against the Church, against priests. She had been a rectory housekeeper long enough to realize that priests are flesh and blood. The less said about the Franciscans who ran the parish for a time the better. But the Amanda James case looked contrived.

If Amanda had been a child it would have been different, but a woman in her late thirties claiming she had been molested by a layman in the choir loft? It was Michael Geary's busy involvement at Blessed Sacrament that enabled him to be described as a member of the parish staff. That had made the archdiocese and the parish liable, according to the charge. Poor Father Panzica. For three days the newspaper story had made it sound as if the pastor were accused of the deed rather than of being Geary's superior. Any man who would put a priest through that was capable of killing the man he thought had abused his daughter.

And now apparently there was Catherine Burger as well, the woman Michael Geary had intended to marry—if he got an annulment, as she apparently already had. Marie did not want to be distracted by the question of annulments. St. Anthony, Father Dowling and God himself knew what she thought of those. Marie's marriage had been worse than most; she had been deserted by her husband, but it had never occurred to her that she could be free of him in the eyes of God or man. And they had had no children. Yet here was Michael Geary, father of two and soon to be grandfather of one, wanting the Church to agree he had never been married at all so that he and Catherine Burger could marry. Would the bride wear white?

Oh, it made Marie so mad, what some people would do to twist the Church to their own designs. It must have made Catherine Burger's former husband or whatever he was equally mad, and there were children there too, and relatives, a whole roster of people with reason to want to harm Michael Geary. Why, it might even have been Father Panzica!

Marie's mouth opened and she glanced up quickly, hoping that St. Anthony hadn't noticed the thought. She just hoped it didn't occur to anyone else, after they realized how silly it was to think Mrs. Geary or her children had done it. Father Panzica had suffered enough.

"Molested," Mrs. Fiori, the housekeeper at Blessed Sacrament, said in an even tone, when she met Marie for coffee at the minimall equidistant between St. Hilary's and Blessed Sacrament.

"How old is she?"

"She will be thirty-eight in December. I checked her employment record at the school."

"So she was a teacher."

"Just music. It was like part-time. She came on Wednesdays and Fridays. A very flighty woman, flighty and flirty."

"Oh?"

This was something Mrs. Fiori had only realized after the event. "I am so innocent, Mrs. Murkin! I had no idea what kind of man Michael Geary was."

"How many kinds are there?"

Mrs. Fiori nodded at the implied wisdom of Marie's question.

"Did Michael Geary still come to Mass?"

"Bold as you please. Imagine. He's cost the diocese millions and there he is . . ."

"Millions?"

"No one knows exactly how much. Not even Father Panzica."

Oh, it was difficult, remembering such things, to keep some semblance of Christian charity. Marie straightened in the pew, eyes closed, her lips moving in prayer. There was a tap on her shoulder.

"Ma'am?"

Marie lurched when she looked up at the bearded staring man who stood beside her. She scrambled to her feet, her heart in her throat. For a frightening moment, she thought she was going to be punished for her skepticism about Amanda James's ordeal in the choir loft.

"Do you have a match?"

"You can't smoke in here." His clothing looked out of St. Vincent de Paul, he looked as if he might have wandered in from anywhere.

"I want to light a vigil light."

"Just take a taper and light it from one already burning."

"I never thought of that."

He seemed more helpless than menacing. Marie got out of the pew and went with him to the vigil light stand and gave him the taper. He hesitated.

"How much are they?"

"Give whatever you wish."

He put the taper in his other hand and jammed his hand in his pocket. He brought out a handful of change.

"Is that enough?"

Marie took a quarter and put it into the slot. The sound of money died away. "Go ahead."

Finally she guided his hand, getting the taper lit, then moving it to an unlit wick. It was eerily like a baptismal ceremony. Or a couple after the wedding lighting a candle before Our Lady's altar.

"Do you want to see the priest?"

The man looked around. Marie could see he was much younger than he had at first appeared, in his twenties? Did he think Father Dowling spent the day in church?

"Come over to the house."

He looked at her as if he hadn't understood.

"To the rectory. I am the housekeeper."

"All right. I want to confess a murder."

The constant fall of the rain made it difficult to stay awake, let alone to give consecutive thought to the events that had followed on Michael Geary's visit some weeks ago. The man was dead, murdered; Gordon Furey had been arrested; but Father Dowling could see why Phil Keegan and his department simply did not know enough yet to make any reasonable guess possible. The sensible thing was to forget about it.

This decision having been made, he put down his pipe just as Marie appeared in the doorway, dripping water, her face a mask of significant silence. And then the tall bearded man appeared behind her. Father Dowling rose slowly.

"Someone to see you, Father."

She stepped aside, providing a full view of the visitor.

"Hello, Brian. Come in and sit down."

"I'm all wet."

"Brian?" Marie squeaked, looking from the pastor to the young man, her head swiveling upward as she did.

"Do you have some fresh coffee, Marie?"

"Brian Geary," Marie said, getting it at last. "Tell Father what you told me."

"I want to confess a murder."

Father Dowling came around the desk and got Brian into a chair. His sweater was soaked through.

"Maybe you better take that off. You'll catch pneumonia."

"I'll get one of your sweaters," Marie said, and scampered off.

"I killed my father."

Father Dowling held up his hand. "Wait until we get you comfortable."

"I don't want to be comfortable. I want to be hanged."

"Well, you're in the wrong state for that."

"I am in a state of mortal sin."

Father Dowling nodded, wishing Marie would hurry up. When he heard her coming, he suggested again that Brian take off his sweater.

"It doesn't matter."

"I'll make the coffee," Marie said, handing Father Dowling the sweater. He closed the door after her and took a chair across from his visitor.

"I was just remembering your father's visit here."

"When was that?"

"A few weeks ago. Your mother came to see me too."

"Why?"

"They were married here."

"In your church?"

"Well, I wasn't here then, of course." He decided not to smile.

"I was just there. In the church. My father pretended the marriage hadn't taken place."

Brian spoke in even, sepulchral tones, with little spaces between the words and a full stop after a sentence.

"Tell me about yourself."

"I killed him."

"I understand you have been in a monastery."

Cool gray eyes regarded Father Dowling. "You think I'm crazy, don't you? No one does wrong anymore, they are victims of what has happened to them. And what has happened to them is nobody else's fault if we turn to that. Everyone's innocent. Or crazy. I have sinned."

"Everyone has sinned."

"It was not for me to decide whether my father should die. What he was doing to my mother could not be undone. And he would not change. Does anyone ever change?"

"Yes."

"I don't. I thought that if I left the world and went into a monastery

I would be different. I thought that if I left the monastery and lived like a hermit I would be different. And then I killed my father."

"How?"

He seemed almost surprised by the question. "I strangled him."

"The police are going to want to know details."

"First I want to confess my sins."

"Why did you come to me?"

"My mother mentioned you. She didn't tell me that she had been married here."

There was a tap on the door and Marie sidled in with a tray. She took it to the desk, but there was no clear space on which to put it. Father Dowling took it and placed it on a footstool.

"Thank you, Marie."

"I'll pour."

"Thank you, Marie."

She closed the door somewhat emphatically. Father Dowling poured a cup of coffee and handed it to Brian, who shook his head, gripping the arms of his chair.

"I'm fasting today."

"Liquids too?"

"I take just water. I fast every other day."

All over the country men and women were on diets; the roadways were clogged with joggers, and health clubs wrung honest sweat from their clients, all this in the interest of shapeliness or a longer life. But fasting would be regarded as grotesque and unnatural, doing penance for the kingdom of heaven's sake. Not that it wasn't excessive to be fasting every other day.

"A carryover from the monastery?"

"I never ate better than I did in the monastery."

"Tell me about it."

Another silence. "You are trying to divert me."

"You have already told me, Brian."

"But not as penitent to priest."

"Do you really want to make this a confessional matter?"

"You don't believe me."

"No."

"Why?"

"I am told you were in Minnesota when your father was killed."

"That was my alibi."

"I needn't tell you that it would be a serious sin to confess something you had not done, something like this."

"Do you think I am just trying to bind you to secrecy? I already told that woman."

Father Dowling took a stole from the bookcase beside his chair, put it around his neck. He turned his chair to one side and waited. The silence grew and then he began.

"Bless me, Father, for I have sinned."

He began as he must always have begun his confessions, accusing himself of sins against charity, of sins of pride, the venial sins and peccadilloes that weigh more heavily on one seeking to become as Christian as he can. There was a long pause during which Father Dowling, eyes pressed shut, prayed that the young man would not abuse the sanctity of the confessional with a fanciful story.

"I killed my father."

"You're sure?"

"How could I be mistaken about a thing like that?"

Father Dowling's duty was clear. "Before I give you absolution, you must tell me that you intend to make recompense for what you have done."

"I will go to the police and confess."

Slowly, reluctantly, certain the young man was confessing a fantasy, Father Dowling lifted his hand and, saying the words of absolution, made the sign of the cross over the bowed head of Brian Geary.

"I want to be punished, Father. I want to go to prison . . ."

"The police have been told that you were in Minnesota at the time."

"When my father was killed?"

"Yes."

Did he never blink? His wide eyes seemed those of an exotic animal, recently captured, staring uncomprehendingly at dangerous and strange surroundings.

"But I wasn't there. I was here in Fox River."

The land may be awash with lawyers, but this was of no concern to Tuttle of Tuttle & Tuttle, a one-man law firm whose title commemorated his late father, not a lawyer, who had never lost faith in his son and had paid his way during the five years it took him to complete the law course and through the grim years before he passed the bar exam. No wonder Tuttle did not consider himself just one lawyer among many. He had served his apprenticeship in a hard school, continued to practice hard-scrabble law, and was ever on the alert for an opportunity.

The Michael Geary murder seemed such an opportunity.

But in what way? This was something Tuttle had been pondering for a week, ever since, with Peanuts Pianone, he had checked the newspaper account of the discovery of the insurance representative's body in a car parked behind his agency, the car he and Peanuts had often seen Geary park at the Burger house along the river road.

Tuttle was reconciled to the fact that Peanuts was his best friend, and vice versa. The Pianones had been powerful in Fox River politics for years. Until reform overwhelmed them, there had always been at least one member of the family on the city council, and they continued to exert a covert and self-interested influence. During the glory days they had placed Peanuts on the police force, managing to have all but the physical examination waived. He had no more status now than he'd had at the beginning of his service, but he knew more than he understood and under appropriate prompting passed it on to Tuttle.

The two men were seated in Tuttle's office. On the desk, half a dozen Styrofoam cartons contained the remnants of the Chinese dinner they had consumed. Peanuts was on his third can of Diet Pepsi, Tuttle on his second. This diuretic liquid would exact discomfort, but no matter. Peanuts was full as a tick and looked ready to doze off.

"What's new on the Geary case?" Tuttle asked.

"Geary?"

"Michael Geary."

"He's dead."

Tuttle nodded. Patience and persistence were needed for a conversation with Peanuts.

"Who's working on it?"

Peanuts chewed methodically. He stopped frowning when he forgot what he was thinking of.

"Agnes Lamb?"

Peanuts unwrapped his feet from the legs of his chair and pushed them out in front of him. His forehead lowered menacingly over his eyes. "That bitch."

"Affirmative action," Tuttle said and shook his head. But if anyone was the beneficiary of special treatment it was Peanuts. As a patrol officer he might have earned his keep, but the deal had been the detective squad and there he had remained all these years. The addition of Agnes Lamb, the black cop, had served to underscore his standing. They had been paired at first, on the assumption that Agnes would prove to be no better than Peanuts, but she had developed into a good cop and was definitely on the rise. Her ascent was the measure of Peanuts's status, and eventually he began to resent it.

"Cy Horvath is stuck with her," Peanuts said with disgust.

"What are they working on?"

"Michael Geary."

"What's new?"

Peanuts didn't know, but he had access to the department records. That, apart from the fellowship of Peanuts and the delights of Chinese food, had been Tuttle's reason for suggesting this midday repast. What Tuttle held within himself, warm as the shrimp fried rice he had just eaten, was the knowledge of Michael Geary's affair with Freddy's mother. It was difficult to think of it as his secret, but so far nothing much was being made of it, and Tuttle cherished the hope that the knowledge he had gained during the surveillance of the Burger house could be turned to advantage.

"I'll take you back," Tuttle offered when Peanuts stirred.

"I got a car."

"Then I'll go with you."

"Where you going?"

"The same place you are."

On the way, Tuttle developed the theme that a review of what was now known of the Geary investigation would reveal that Agnes Lamb was just a fifth wheel.

"Fifth wheel."

"No help to Horvath."

"She's no help to anybody. I won't work with her."

Five minutes later, Tuttle was seated at a departmental computer, calling up what the investigation into Michael Geary's death had revealed thus far. As a student, and in preparing for the bar exam, Tuttle had had trouble retaining the hundreds of items that were supposed to be at a lawyer's fingertips. It had all been too abstract. But when the fingertips were definitely his own and information bore some promise of reward, he had the memory of a computer. His rapid survey of the Geary file transferred it from the monitor screen to his head.

He rapped on his head, having first removed the Irish tweed hat he wore in all seasons. "My hard drive."

Back in his office, he cleared his desk of debris, sat back, put his feet up, pulled his hat over his eyes, and thought, not of facts or precedents or judicial opinions, but of the concrete data at his disposal. Everything he had learned of the police investigation into the death of Michael Geary was indelibly impressed in his memory, and more. Ever since the discovery of Geary's body in a car behind his agency, Tuttle had been thinking of the organist at Blessed Sacrament who had sued the archdiocese because of what Geary had done to her in the line of duty. Tuttle remembered the episode because he had hoped to represent her, but before he'd been able to come up with an angle of approach, the thing had been hushed up. He should have known Christopher James was her father. But the event had not been eradicated from the hard drive in Tuttle's head.

Without really deciding to, he had retained an interest in the doings of Michael Geary. A man who would deflower an organist in a choir loft would strike again. Tuttle's meditations thus became an interesting amalgam of what he had learned of the police investigation and his own continuing observations. Here was the bright side of not being burdened with too many clients.

What were the facts about Michael Geary as only Tuttle knew them; that is, what was the sum total of the police results and his own knowledge?

1. Michael Geary had been found dead in his car, which was parked behind his insurance agency; he had been strangled.

2. The presumption was that the deed had been done where the body was found, but the possibility that it had happened elsewhere and that the body had been brought to the agency had been explored by Lieutenant Cyril Horvath.

3. Geary's wife had filed for divorce. (Tuttle felt a pang of regret that he had not anticipated her action and somehow contrived to represent her.)

4. A memorandum from Captain Phil Keegan indicated that Michael had filed for an annulment not in Chicago but in Michigan, where the Gearys had a summer cottage.

5. The police, without being explicit about it, seemed to have entertained the possibility that Mrs. Geary had killed her husband. That turned out to be impossible because she was out of town at the time, visiting her daughter at Notre Dame.

Tuttle's mind drifted away at the thought of the legendary school whose football team divided the sports fans of the nation into two camps, those who loved the Irish and those who hated them. Tuttle accounted himself a fan, despite his relatively weak attraction to sports. But a feigned mania for Notre Dame was another bond with Peanuts, who was a forcible reminder that "fan" is the diminutive of "fanatic." For Peanuts there were only two possible outcomes of the season. Notre Dame was recognized as number one, or Notre Dame was cheated of recognition as number one. Peanuts often drove ticketless to South Bend in the hope of dealing with a scalper outside the stadium. If he could be believed, he had paid as high as three hundred dollars for a ticket.

"Three hundred dollars!"

Peanuts nodded with pleasure. He had been prepared to go to five hundred. The thought of such abuse of the value of money made Tuttle almost physically ill.

"You could have watched it on television."

"I did. The next day."

It had occurred to Tuttle to doubt Mrs. Geary's alibi. There was no indication that the police had. He might have proposed a trip to South Bend, offering to accompany Peanuts to a game, with an eye to checking out Mrs. Geary's story. But what was the point?

6. Gordon Furey had been put in the slammer, charged with the death of his brother-in-law, Michael Geary.
7. But the latest development, the confession of Brian Geary, had thrown everyone into a tizzy. The first reaction was that he was crazy. Then his boots were found to match prints next to the car in which his father's body had been found.

That should have settled it. Maybe it did for the police. But Tuttle's mind was stuck on something else. Cy Horvath and Agnes Lamb had monitored the Geary funeral, a routine matter when they had their doubts about Gordon Furey and Brian Geary had not yet confessed. And routine had paid off in the person of Mrs. Catherine Burger.

It pleased Tuttle to think that he had anticipated the police by weeks, staking out Catherine Burger's house. He got up, pushed his tweed hat back on his head, and put a video into the VCR. He would run them all, study them, see if there wasn't something there that might clear up matters and make the Gearys and Fureys indebted to him.

After the first video, he decided not to look at all of them now. There were five or six and watching them was no treat. The way Peanuts used the videocam, there was just a jumpy sequence of arriving and departing cars, interspersed with a closeup of a watch, his or Peanuts's, showing the time and day. The trouble was, when you had seen one arriving or departing car, you had seen them all.

Who was the woman in *A Tale of Two Cities* who worked into her knitting the record of hated victims gone to the guillotine? Amanda felt a bit like her. Madame Defarge! Yes. But the vindictive Parisienne had not kept her roll sitting on a Florida beach, a wide-brimmed straw hat and dark glasses protecting her from the sun, with the ceaseless whisper of the surf, the slightest of breezes soothing her oiled body as it bronzed.

Her book lay unopened beside her, her Walkman too. Her mind was in suspension and she was filled with a vast content because of the news Daddy had telephoned to tell her. Michael Geary was dead. Justice had been done at last. Amanda wished only to be—not to think, not to read, not to listen to music; just to be.

The trouble was that you have to put your mind to not thinking. Even asleep, the mind, or at least the imagination, went on. There was no stopping the replaying of the past. But Amanda came closest to nirvana sitting in the sun. In the morning, she sat beside the condominium pool, watching a crew reroofing with palm leaves the open hut where bathers from the beach washed sand from their feet, and older women sat in rows of tipped-back chairs while their husbands ogled Amanda. In the afternoon, she sat on the sand, the great hulking condominiums behind her, the impossibly blue water lapping at the impossibly white sand of the beach.

Michael Geary was dead. Daddy called to tell her.

"He was found strangled in his car behind his insurance agency."

"Good heavens."

"Heaven had nothing to do with it."

"You said strangled?"

"Yes. I tried to reach you all day yesterday and the day before. Where were you?"

"On the mainland, shopping. The next time you're here, we must drive down to Venice."

"I suppose I shouldn't have been so eager to tell you the man is dead."

The sun shattered on the water, spangling the waves, causing her to turn her unshaded eyes away. "Who would do such a thing?"

"The police haven't said." He cleared his throat.

"Are you worried?"

"Worried about what?"

"God knows you had reason."

"Amanda!" He was genuinely shocked. "We have received our compensation."

"Oh, settling was obviously the thing to do."

She had left all that to Daddy. She told him that her life had gone wrong only when she failed to listen to him, but he had turned even the wrong to her advantage. It was strange to be living among the retired and affluent on Marco Island when she had just passed her thirty-ninth birthday.

It was because Michael had betrayed her that she could accept the terrible news of his death, even imagine herself Madame Defarge. She felt vindicated but not vindictive. Daddy had suggested that Michael had led astray another young woman.

"Perhaps a less reasonable one this time."

He had persuaded her that what Michael had done to her cried to heaven for compensation. Of course she had stressed that it had all started in the church, in the loft. Her lips parted with the memory, the sacrilegious memory. She still could not fully believe that she had let him do such a thing to her in such a place. But of course it had been unreal. He was so gallant and persuasive, and had such a tenor voice. Beforehand, he had driven her home several times and brought tears to his own eyes when he sang the ballads his father had sung. John

McCormack, Frank Munn, other Irish tenors whose names were unfamiliar to her. She felt that he was admitting her to the sanctum of his memories.

"Do you sing to your wife?"

After a moment, "I should have known you'd heard."

"Heard what?"

"Ours hasn't been a real marriage, not for years."

Amanda was struck dumb by this. Why had she mentioned his wife? It had been a reminder to herself that he was a nice man with a wife and family who was driving her home from choir practice, never mind the singing in the car.

"I'm sorry," he said. "I thought you knew."

How could she possibly know a thing like that? The tears that had been brought on by "Macushla" continued to flow, and Amanda's heart went out to him.

After that he had avoided her and she was relieved, in a way, but she was also concerned for him, worried that he regretted having said to her what he had. Then his awful brother-in-law had come and accused her of breaking up Michael's marriage. She had to see Michael after that dreadful encounter. She had sought him out and he had driven her home again, this time asking all about her.

"And you live with your father?"

"Do you know him?"

He made a little noise. "Everyone knows him."

Of course they did. All her life she had been the daughter of Christopher James. He had been father and mother to her as well as a successful lawyer, specializing in estates and trusts. Amanda did not know what he would have done if she had ever told him that Michael Geary reminded her of him. Like her father, Michael could be understood best by imagining that he was one of the boys she taught in the parish school. Amanda didn't really care for the girls, even though their voices were more formed. Girls were catty and sly and not to be trusted, not really. These little girls were just like the little girls with whom she had grown up. Amanda had hated the girls' rest room, camp, the dormitory she had slept in during the few months she had lasted in the school Daddy sent her to after her mother's death. By contrast boys were open books, like Daddy, like Michael Geary when she got over the strangeness.

He was shy. And he wanted her. Boys did. They always had. And she always felt sorry for them and did what she could for them. She did what she could for Michael in the choir loft of Blessed Sacrament and afterward they were both horrified by the sinfulness of the act. They had actually gone downstairs and up the aisle and knelt in a front pew and whispered an Act of Contrition together. It was almost as binding as a wedding ceremony. That was why she had just ignored Gordon Furey's threats.

After that, when Michael drove her home, singing, he would always find a place to park so she could do what she could for him. Daddy suspected something, but rather than talk about it he followed them and one night, in the midst of things, he appeared beside the car and with a great roar dragged Michael out of it. It was terrible. With the back of his hand, Daddy had sent Michael reeling. Michael had tried to talk but had been silenced.

"I'll talk to you alone! You'll be hearing from me."

She had driven home with Daddy. In silence. Inside the house, he had taken her in his arms, patting her back, clucking soothingly. His assumption that she was a victim restored her innocence. He had a series of meetings with Michael before filing the suit.

Amanda was mortified. She resigned as organist and as music teacher at Daddy's suggestion, thinking he meant to save her embarrassment. But he told people she had been traumatized by the experience. That Michael had molested her in the choir loft was a description Michael himself seemed to accept.

Of course, as Daddy told her, Michael had somehow gotten the idea that he would share in the settlement. And Amanda had thought how nice it would be if he could come down and enjoy this sun with her, just the two of them. But before the thought went beyond the hazy beachtime thinking of her first weeks here, Daddy called and gave her the news that made her feel like Madame Defarge. It served Michael right, not staying with his wife but finding another woman and then seeking an annulment in order to marry her! Amanda was furious that he hadn't wanted to do that for her.

Until she remembered his Irish tenor and tears formed in her eyes behind the sunglasses.

The man with the fleshy chest covered with gray hair, a curly halo emphasizing the deep tan on his domed head, wearing the male equivalent of a bikini, came down the steps from the pool. He always came down ten minutes after Amanda got settled and paraded around like a peacock. From behind her dark glasses Amanda could watch him to her heart's content. He seemed nice. She had thought he was with one of the women who sat by the pool, but she was sure now he was alone. She imagined that he had lost his wife. She wondered if he could sing.

"You're not bored?" Daddy asked.

"Bored!" She laughed the thought away. Of course he thought of her as marooned on Marco Island. But the airport was forty-five minutes away and she could be anywhere she wanted when she needed a change of scene.

But she was there when Daddy called later to say that Michael hadn't been strangled to death after all.

"It was poison."

"Why did his son claim to have strangled him?"

"Who knows? Well, either way, he's dead."

"Amen."

When he had been arrested and taken downtown, Brian had looked forward to incarceration. A cell—the word itself was a sensuous delight and what it stood for all he wanted. To be alone in solitude and silence, to remove all impediments of imagination and thought and turn his soul into a receiver awaiting signals from inner space.

Jail wasn't at all like that. It was a constant bedlam, metallic noises, groaning and grumbling, the smell of antiseptic, haunted men ignoring one another, hating themselves and everyone else, misfits and failures, the rejects of society. He could not pretend to be one of them. It was by his own choice that he separated himself from the rest of men, and he did so not out of contempt for his fellows, but from a deeper sense of solidarity.

Nor was he alone. He shared a cell with two other men, one reeking of alcohol, the other semiretarded, who carried on an endless conversation with himself. The drunk moaned in his sleep. There was a stool in the cell and he felt that he would rather burst than perform natural functions in so public a manner. But such fastidiousness belonged to the world left outside.

He claimed a corner, adopted the lotus position and shut his eyes to his surroundings. He had been in the monastery because he chose to be; his hermitage too had been his decision, and he could leave either one at will. Here he had lost freedom of movement and put himself into a machinery he did not understand. Still, when the lawyer Tuttle visited he was resigned to spending an indefinite time in jail.

Brian thought he had been told Tuttle came at his mother's behest, but nothing was said of this when they sat across the table from one another. The little lawyer moved his business card about on the table as if it were his hole card. Brian half expected him to turn it over and cry "Full house!" or some other winning combination. Except that it was losing rather than winning that Tuttle's whole manner suggested.

Not guilty by reason of insanity! The prospect of that plea truly alarmed Brian. Sanity seemed a fragile possession in that jail, the loss of it almost welcome. Burdens would lift from the shoulder, remorse and sorrow become inoperative. All one had to do was see oneself as a toy wound up by alien forces, then let go to run amok.

I didn't jump, my feet did. *Lord Jim.* That was the last temptation, to disclaim responsibility. But he was here because he embraced responsibility.

Father Dowling's visit was different from Tuttle's. The priest looked at him sadly, and no wonder.

"I did do it, Father. I didn't lie."

It was the thought that he had lied when making his confession that bothered this priest with the softly penetrating eyes. A sacrilege. Why should he have to prove he had done what he had done?

"There has been a new development. I was asked to tell you. The cause of your father's death was poison."

"But I strangled him."

"You didn't kill him, Brian."

"I murdered my father."

"In your heart, perhaps. But you didn't kill him."

It was like being put into the jail cell and losing his freedom all over again, even though this meant he was free. The deed he had done was not the deed he had done, though he was guilty of it. But he could not be punished. He had to go out into the world again, like Cain, but his mark would not be visible to others.

He felt cheated of the punishment he had earned. He was let go. He looked into the cells as he passed by them, envying their occupants, reluctant to leave. Horvath the detective wanted to talk with him.

"Why did you want to kill him?"

"Do I have to answer?"

"No."

"He wanted an annulment."

Horvath shrugged. "Half the people in the country get divorced, the ones who marry."

"This isn't a divorce."

Father Dowling had thought his confession was sacrilegious. That was what Brian thought of his father's effort to have his marriage declared null and void. The marriage he had entered into before a priest, before God and the Church. To pretend that hadn't happened was to mock God and the sacrament of matrimony, it was to injure the Church as well as his wife and family.

"He wanted to dissolve his marriage. There is only one legitimate way to do that."

"Death?"

"Death."

"Well, someone beat you to it."

Horvath was willing enough to tell Brian what they now knew about his father's death. A poison introduced into the insulin supply.

There was money in the wallet they gave back to Brian. He had forgotten all about it. He walked up the street and when he saw the bus depot, headed for it. Six hours later he was in South Bend. He found Kate's number and called her.

"Where are you?"

"Here."

"In South Bend!"

She came for him and her expression when she walked toward him told him how he must look to her. Her crazy brother.

"Where's your bag?"

"I checked it." He couldn't remember where the things he had brought from Minnesota were. At the house in Fox River, he supposed. But he didn't want to alarm Kate further by telling her that what he wore was what he had with him. "I'm hungry."

They went to a steakhouse on Route 33. It was the first meat he had eaten in two years. He felt like a savage. Bloody juices from the rare meat pooled on his plate.

"Why did you say you did it, Brian?"

"I thought I had."

Her laugh was joyless, half fearful. He must sound crazy to her. But he did not want to go into what had really happened in the car parked behind their father's insurance agency. The memory of looping that wire around his father's neck and then twisting, twisting it tight, made him push his plate away.

"It was because of the annulment, wasn't it?"

"Yes."

Tears formed in her eyes. It was like seeing in her his own feeling of being denied reality. The father who, whatever his faults, had been part of the rock-bottom foundation of their lives had wanted to pretend that nothing had been what it seemed, that there was no marriage or family, that all those years, bound together by blood and memories and the house they lived in, could be swept away like a technicality. It was worse than betrayal. It was to say there was nothing and no one to betray.

"Come on, let's go home."

"No. I'll go get a room. I'll be leaving early in the morning."

"But why did you come?"

"To see you."

The tears ran down her cheeks and his own eyes blurred. This was his sister, this stranger who had a husband and was expecting a child, who lived a life of which he knew nothing, but who was closer to him than anyone else. What memories did she have of their shared life? How he wished now that they had been closer, that they had learned to talk easily to one another, but he had always felt half a stranger to her. She did not understand why he did the things he did. She asked him if he would go back to Berkeley.

"Maybe." Why tell her that he could never go back to that? "What's the place where he applied for the annulment?"

She knew the Michigan town and the name of the priest who had encouraged him. Gorce. Melvin Gorce. The waitress came with the coffeepot, and they waved her away. How many cups had he drunk already? He never drank coffee.

"I'll take you back to the depot so you can get your things."

He stood at the entrance of the depot and waved as she drove off. He got into a cab and asked to be taken to the airport.

"There's no more flights out of here tonight."

"I want to rent a car."

"That you can do. Where you going?"

"Chicago."

"There's a bus you can take. They call it a limo, but it's a bus."

He had had enough of buses. The terminal was all lit up and practically deserted. Forlorn figures were scattered among the seats. Behind the airline counters great posters told of unspeakable bliss to be had somewhere else. The rental-car counters were similarly aglow. He chose one at random and got out his driver's license and a credit card.

"Destination?"

"Can I drop it in Chicago?"

"Sure." The girl's hair looked as if it had been dipped in glue and then worried with a fan. Her face was almost clownish with makeup. She hit the computer oddly because of the long nails she wore. Ten minutes later, she pushed keys across the counter and told him where he would find the car.

The Michigan border was only eleven miles away, and he had the illusion he was almost at his destination. But two hours of driving lay ahead. It was one in the morning when he drove into the parking lot of an all-night diner, locked the doors of the car and curled up in the backseat.

Gorce, Melvin, Rev., was in the book. The address was a house half a block from a large parish plant, church, school, convent, parking lots that served as basketball courts as well. The first Mass was at seven o'clock. The celebrant was an old priest, a monsignor, who moved slowly but said Mass fast. During the Mass a man pushed a wide broom down a side aisle, then propped it against the wall. He looked around the vestibule with a proprietary air. Brian got up and went back to him.

"Is that Father Gorce?"

The man stepped back when he looked at Brian. He seemed to be sniffing for the scent of booze. He thinks I'm a bum, Brian thought, feeling an odd pride. He shook his head.

"He says the seven-thirty."

"Thanks."

"Monsignor hears confessions right after this Mass."

Brian returned to his pew. He did not go forward at communion time. He had been absolved of the murder he had not committed, but there was still a barrier between himself and God. A barrier named Melvin Gorce. He wanted the confrontation he had been denied when he called on Monsignor Noonan.

Half the people who had come to seven o'clock Mass stayed for Gorce's, and there were new arrivals as well. Brian was aware of curious eyes on him, sitting bolt upright, arms folded beneath his beard. He felt he could sleep with his eyes open. Gorce was fat and pink, with a tenor voice. The Gospel reading concerned the unjust steward. Gorce's homily lasted three minutes, was obviously prepared and was delivered in a conversational style.

After the Mass, Brian went around the church to the sacristy side. He stepped forward when the priest came out.

"Father Gorce?"

"Yes?" Uneasiness, as his eyes swept over Brian.

"My name is Geary. Brian Geary. Michael Geary's son."

The name did not register immediately, and Brian felt anger leap within him. It was not possible that he should have forgotten. Then he had it. "Oh, yes." He searched Brian's face. "I said a Mass for him."

So he knew he was dead.

"Why are you here?" Gorce asked.

"I wanted to see you."

"That's right. I remember now. Your family has a cottage near here, don't they?"

"Wasn't that the excuse for applying for the annulment here?"

Gorce pulled back his sleeve and looked at his gold watch. A harried expression came over his face. "Well."

"I won't keep you."

He hadn't expected that. He started to go, then turned. "Look . . ."

But what it was Brian was to look at never emerged. Gorce seemed to be telling himself he owed no explanation to this unkempt wild-eyed young man. Brian noted the make and tag of Gorce's car.

For three days he sat in the front pew during Gorce's Mass. He did not speak to him again. He learned the pattern of his day and from time to time confronted him, at the chancery, at the restaurant where he lunched, came upon him as if by accident, and said nothing. He was getting on Gorce's nerves.

"You're stalking me," Gorce hissed angrily when they had nearly collided as the priest left the church after Mass.

Brian said nothing.

"I've read about your confession."

So Gorce knew that he had claimed to strangle his father, but had been let go.

"Why would you say you had done such a thing?"

"I thought of it as a declaration of nullity."

Gorce's mouth opened, then closed on what he had been going to say. That night, when Gorce turned into the driveway and the garage doors slid up, Brian rose from behind a hedge and was caught in the sweep of the headlights. The car slipped into the garage and then the doors started to close.

Brian was surprised. The side door of the garage was padlocked on the outside. He went to a window and looked in. Gorce was in the car, behind the wheel; the garage light was still on. Brian tapped on the window. Gorce lurched as he turned to the noise and then he clutched his throat, his face distorting as he looked at Brian looking in at him.

It was the last thing Gorce ever saw.

The game of the decade was only a week and a half away and Phil Keegan had come to St. Hilary's in the expectation that he and Roger Dowling would indulge in some serious pregame preparation. But during dinner, he had talked with Marie more than with the pastor, and now that they were in the study, Roger Dowling did not respond at all to Keegan's analysis of the holes in the Southern Cal defense.

"Anything wrong?"

Roger Dowling looked at him. "I'm sorry, Phil. I had a phone call from Bishop Ravel just before you came."

Panic gripped Keegan. Was the bishop asking for the tickets back?

"I knew it," Keegan said angrily.

"Knew what?" Roger Dowling suddenly smiled. "No, no. The tickets are ours, fear not. No, he called to tell me someone had died."

Keegan managed not to cheer. "That's too bad."

"Does the name Melvin Gorce mean anything to you, Phil?"

He thought about it, then shook his head. "Who's he play for?"

Dowling laughed sadly. "He was a priest. In Michigan."

"A classmate of yours?"

"No. Not even a friend. I met him once or twice, I suppose. He's dead."

Phil Keegan sat back. At their age, it was inevitable that from time to time mortality should occupy their thoughts. You might call it a professional obligation on both their parts.

"Gorce was on the marriage tribunal up there and had encouraged Michael Geary to think he could get an annulment."

It might have seemed only a minor irony until Roger Dowling mentioned the way Gorce had died. In his car that was parked in his garage.

"Carbon monoxide?"

"I think it was his heart."

"Want me to check it out?"

Of course he did. That's why he'd brought it up. Now they were free to turn to the big game, and they did. Both teams were approaching the contest with high rankings.

"It could be a battle for number one, depending on what they both do this Saturday."

"I'll be going down next Thursday afternoon."

"Where you staying?"

"I'll be put up at the Morris Inn." Dowling stopped. "Good grief, that's for the meeting of canon lawyers. I hope I can stay on there through Friday night."

He picked up the phone and called Bishop Ravel, but the bishop wasn't in. Father Dowling tried unsuccessfully to get the secretary to speak of the Notre Dame meeting. She wouldn't even admit she knew there was to be such a meeting.

"Why all the secrecy?" Phil Keegan asked.

"Cardinal Hildebrand is coming."

"Yeah?"

"You know who he is?"

"I've heard the name." Keegan was not given to reading what was called the Catholic press, and he always avoided Church news in the secular media.

Roger Dowling's sketch of the cardinal made it clear why there would be a desire for secrecy all around. However much the football team had retained its honorable traditions, the university itself, apparently, had adopted a feisty attitude toward Church authority. If Keegan understood Dowling, the university wouldn't want it known that the high Vatican official would be visiting because it might look as if the university was caving in to pressure from on high. The Vatican, on the other hand, would be reluctant to give the appearance of honoring an institution some of whose theologians had engaged in unrestrained pope-bashing.

"So why's he coming?"

"I assume to read the riot act to canon laywers who had aided and abetted the annulment process."

"It's about time."

Michael Geary would have been a hard guy to lament, given the way he'd been running around, but when Phil Keegan heard he had been trying to get his marriage annulled, he wrote the guy off as a real phony. There had always been laypeople ready and willing to help around the parish, but in recent years a type had become common that Phil Keegan didn't like at all. When he couldn't get to Roger Dowling's Mass he went as early in the day as he could. In his experience, the liturgy began sensibly and became progressively wilder as the day advanced. Evening Masses could be anything. Sometimes you couldn't find a priest on the altar, what with all the lectors and singers and special ministers milling around. Phil Keegan had never received Communion from a layman yet and he didn't plan to start. Michael Geary had been an extraordinary eucharistic minister, meaning he distributed communion on Sunday.

So who killed the sonofabitch? The widow was out, the daughter was out, the son was out, more or less. How could you prove a hermit wasn't in his hermitage? The police force in La Crescent amounted to two guys who raised their salaries by bagging speeders. They thought the bearded stranger had been home during the days mentioned, but they weren't sure.

"Any way to make sure?" Keegan asked.

Silence on the phone. Then, "I can't think of any."

"Thanks."

"Can you?" the Minnesota constable asked.

"Thanks."

The organist Geary had wronged was sitting on the beach in Florida, and her father had a heart that would have given out under the strain required to strangle Geary. Amanda had no brother or lover who might have wanted to avenge her.

"How about the agency?" Cy had asked.

"What do you mean?"

"His business associates."

Keegan okayed it. The two women and the two agents who worked for Geary had been in the building behind which his body was found. The next thing you knew they would be treating Geary's murder as an unmotivated piece of madness by person or persons unknown. Or maybe assisted suicide, with the assistant disappeared.

Monique Pippen had floated into his office on a cloud of perfume, her bosom abundant but proportionate to the rest of her, all woman.

"I can give you a profile of the person who killed Michael Geary."

"I didn't know you drew."

She sat, settled sideways on a chair across from him, keeping her all too visible knees close together.

"The murderer was a small man or a woman, maybe even a child. Shoe size, five; that is one of the things we know for sure."

"Because of the boot found in the backseat?"

"Yes."

"It belongs to Ms. Florence Lewis."

Dr. Pippen touched the back of the chair with her shoulders, then sat forward again. "Is that a joke?"

"Not to her. How would you like to explain one of your boots in the backseat of your boss's car?"

"How did she explain it?"

"She said she'd left it there."

"When?"

"They all went out to lunch together, Geary's treat, Pam was in front, Florence in the back. She slipped out of her boots and into heels before going into the restaurant. She must have taken only one into the office when they returned."

"Do you believe her?"

"What good is one boot?"

"Did the others back her up?"

"Oh, we made her try it on. It fit like a glove. Or a boot. It was like Cinderella."

Dr. Pippen's shoulders slumped, with breathtaking results. "I based everything on that boot."

"Maybe you should stick with the autopsy." Pippen's specialty lent itself to definite answers, facts, pieces of the puzzle, but she wasn't content with that. She wanted to put them all together and spell murder.

"I do know the cause of death."

"Strangling."

"He was diabetic," she said.

"I saw that."

"Saw it?"

"In your boss's report."

"I wrote that. He signs everything."

"The deceased also had a lower partial, varicose veins and was uncircumcised."

She inhaled deeply as if she were inflating water wings. "He was also equipped with an experimental device that automatically released insulin into his system."

"I've heard they were developing those."

"They're ingenious. Part of a whole new medical technology, patches that administer medicine, others that control pain in those suffering from sciatica. His was designed to control his blood sugar automatically."

"So?"

"It was the murder weapon."

They had found electrical wires wrapped around Geary's neck, tightened like a knot.

"I don't get you."

"It was not filled with insulin, not pure insulin; it had been gradually poisoning him for hours before he succumbed."

"Poison? Well, well. That does give us something to go on."

"When I say poison, I don't mean anything exotic. Many things not technically classified as poison would have a deadly effect if introduced directly into the bloodstream. But this was poison. Jolson's guess is a common household rat poison." She smiled.

"Poetic justice."

"He didn't specify a brand name. In any case, that's nonsense. The device had hydrochloric acid mixed with the insulin. Among the household products hydrochloric acid is found in is toilet bowl cleaner."

"Poetic justice."

"Why do you keep saying that?"

"Are you busy?"

"Why?"

"I want to go to the bathroom. At Geary's agency. You can come along."

In the bathroom at the agency, on a triangular shelf in a corner, there was a white plastic bottle on which was a legend promising to make toilet bowls sparkle like the stars of the sky. Keegan searched for a list of ingredients. He read that the product contained poison, could be lethal if swallowed, keep out of reach of children, vapor harmful, contains hydrochloric acid.

"Who could have gotten this into his insulin?"

"Whoever replenished his insulin supply."

"That would most likely be him, wouldn't it?"

"Most likely. Where was he returning from when he drove past the office windows and parked out back?"

"Let's ask."

Florence Lewis reminded him, coldly, that the police had confiscated the appointment book. "And other things."

"Did you get a receipt?"

"I'd rather have the appointment book. But I don't need it to tell you where he was that day." She waited. Coax me. Finally Dr. Pippen did.

"Where?"

"Having a powwow with his wife. That was his word."

"What did he mean by it?" Dr. Pippen asked.

"What anyone means by it."

"A showdown?" Keegan asked.

"Well, a discussion. I remember saying a little prayer that they would be reconciled."

"Did you ever find your other boot?"

"Yes. And I threw them both away." She looked up. "Was that all right?"

Thus it was that, when Roger Dowling asked him how the investigation of Michael Geary's death was going, Phil Keegan did have things to say.

"But Maureen was with her daughter in South Bend."

"So the question is, who did he powwow with that day?"

"But the poison was in the bathroom at the agency."

"There's probably the same poison in every bathroom in this house."

"There is not!" Marie looked in. "Poison in the bathrooms? Never."

But in the bathroom off the back hall there was a bottle of the same cleaner found in the bathroom of the Geary agency.

"So his medicine could have been altered anywhere."

"Well, it needn't have been at the agency."

"Where did he go after lunch?"

"We don't know yet."

Maybe it was his own ambivalent thoughts about Monique Pippen, but Cy thought they had not paid enough attention to the mysterious woman at Michael Geary's funeral. Catherine Burger. To identify her was to learn all kinds of reasons why her attendance at the funeral could not possibly signify any illicit connection with the deceased.

"One of the most principled women I know," Amos Cadbury said, and he might have been canonizing Catherine Burger.

"Amos is a reliable judge of people," Father Dowling said.

"Cyril," Monique said, in her professional voice, "that is just the point. Her relation to Michael Geary, whatever it was, does not jibe with her persona. That's why the secrecy."

Agnes was not eager to recall the day of the funeral, the trip to the cemetery and following the mystery woman to her home.

"They belong to the same crowd, the same club. The Gearys were people she knew, but not friends. That's why she kind of hung back."

In search of a balance to these feminine conjectures, Cy called on Gordon Furey. He was not greeted cordially, of course, but Furey did seem to remember that Cy had given him the benefit of the doubt when the Winnetka police delivered him.

"It's routine to monitor the funeral of someone whose death is under investigation."

"So you saw me there."

"There was a woman at the church, sitting away from the mourners. She went on to the cemetery too, but looked on only from a distance."

"Every parish has them," Gordon Furey said. "Widows, old maids, women with nothing to do. They show up at all the wakes and weddings."

"Her name is Catherine Burger."

Furey had been playing with a letter opener. At the mention of the name, he flipped it into the air and caught it neatly by the handle. He looked at Cy with resignation.

"Michael hoped to marry her."

"She's not married?"

Gordon Furey was suddenly willing to lay before Cy the whole sordid scenario of his brother-in-law's desire to have his marriage annulled. Michael Geary's insistence that the Church assure him that he was free as the breeze was matched by Catherine Burger's, whose marriage had been annulled.

"You think she put the idea in Geary's head?"

"Of the annulment? She wouldn't have to. My sister applied for a divorce, hoping to stop the annulment nonsense, but she knew it wouldn't be enough for Michael, not if he meant to marry again."

"You know Catherine Burger?"

Furey tapped the tip of his nose with his forefinger and made a face. "I talked to her. But first I kept an eye on her for a time. Followed her around. I was damned mad about this, let me tell you, and I wanted to see what it really came down to, a man with a wife and two children. Of course she knew all that, but since she'd been through the same thing, she wasn't likely to think it was all that bad."

"Does she have children?"

"A son. Freddy."

Cy and Agnes acquainted themselves with Freddy, the private and the public Freddy. Agnes would not have been welcome in the kind of bar Freddy favored, and Cy did not go in: he got the picture. The public Freddy was the smiling agitator. Victims of Canon Law suggested what Freddy thought of his parents' annulment.

Freddy was a little alarmed when Cy identified himself, but his smile did not waver.

"What can I do for you, Constable?"

"Did you know Michael Geary?"

"The super-Catholic? How could I not? Did you know he was in the process of seeking an annulment of his marriage? That's a sort of Catholic divorce."

"I'm Catholic."

"Well if you ever want to get rid of your wife, be of good cheer. There are canon lawyers eager to accommodate you."

"Geary hoped to marry your mother."

Laughter bubbled forth from the young man. "Marry the Virgin Queen? Lieutenant, whatever his ambitions, his prospects were dim."

Phil Keegan frowned over the reports of these inquiries. "What the hell does this have to do with anything, Cy?"

"It looks like not much."

"We're looking for a poisoner, right?"

Right. Neither Agnes nor Monique seemed to care that the Catherine Burger inquiry had led nowhere.

Father Dowling took 294, to avoid Loop traffic, warned by the reports on WBBM, but road construction reduced the interstate to a two-lane highway for miles and took away any advantage afforded by the alternate route. It was an experience he would profit from when he drove to South Bend for the game.

That prospect made the present trip seem superfluous. He had been vague in telling Marie Murkin where he was going and how long he would be gone. Of course anything he said to her was likely to be passed on to Phil Keegan, and he had not wanted to tell Keegan he was taking this trip to Michigan. But there had been no response at all on Keegan's part to the mention of Melvin Gorce's death, and Roger Dowling knew that any argument that the Fox River police should interest themselves in the death of a priest a hundred and fifty miles away would sound mad, given the amount of unfinished business they faced. That there might be some connection, well, that was where the madness came in. Marie of course had her own interpretation of his secretiveness.

"If you don't want to tell me, of course you don't have to. I am only the housekeeper."

"I should be home tonight."

"Is that what I should tell the callers?"

"You needn't tell the callers anything."

"So it's some kind of secret."

"What do you usually tell callers?"

"Usually the pastor is in," Marie said primly. "At the disposal of his parishioners."

She knew that would sting. He had dropped efforts to explain to himself how this long drive to Midland, Michigan, related to his responsibilities as pastor of St. Hilary's parish in Fox River.

"I suppose, in an emergency, the chancery will know where you are?"

"The chancery!"

"Isn't that where your bishop friends are? The ones you go to football games with."

Marie pretended to be convinced that Ambrose Ravel wanted to transfer him out of Fox River. She had heard too many people speak of the chances he had lost by the way he left the marriage tribunal and ended up at Fox River. Years had passed; there had been no recurrence; now he could be put back on the fast track to clerical advancement, rising as Ambrose Ravel himself had risen. If there was any possibility at all of that, he would of course refuse. He would go to the Trappists first, like Brian Geary. He told Marie that football games were on weekends.

"I know that," she said in a voice heavy with accusation. "I know you're not off to a football game today, you and your powerful friends."

She was determined to brood and there was nothing he could do about that, so he stopped trying. Huge trucks were to the right and to the left of him on a highway that had now expanded to four lanes. He felt that he was intruding on a route meant only for commerce and the semis that roared along at seventy miles an hour. It was difficult to believe that only a few years ago the speed limit had been fifty-five. Whatever it was, five or ten more miles had to be added to account for the actual flow of traffic. He was beginning to feel that he was being swept away from his duties and the ordinary elements of his life.

"Get a cellular phone," Phil Keegan had suggested when Marie complained of being unable to reach the pastor.

"It would be stolen."

Keegan shook his head. "They've got them so you can carry them in your pocket. They're not tied down to your car."

"So Marie could call me anywhere at any time? What an awful thought."

"I was thinking that you could call her."

"There are telephones everywhere."

He certainly wouldn't want to try talking on the phone while caught up in traffic like this. It was hard enough to think, and that, apart from the need to find out for himself, discreetly, what had happened to Melvin Gorce, was why he was taking this trip. He wanted to think, but there were things he would rather not think of.

The bearded son of Maureen and Michael Geary was in many ways an enigma. By all accounts, a talented scientist, whose education had been provided by fellowships from high school on, whose appointment at Berkeley put him on a track to permanent and lucrative employment in the science that he loved, astronomy, but who within a few years had felt his interest in science drain away as his mind and spirit were drawn beyond the physical world.

But discontent with the academic life had soon become discontent with the monastic life. Brian spoke as if the life of Trappists was not hard enough for him, but that was not the real complaint. He hungered for an experience of something beyond experience, an intimation of which he had had when studying the formation of galaxies. By separating himself from others and retreating into a hermitage he had hoped to erase the distance between himself and God. Behind the impatience was a restless but genuine faith, Father Dowling was sure of it.

And that was why he had found it so difficult to believe Brian's claim that he had killed his father. Until he had solemnly confessed it. To knowingly lie in the confessional was a sacrilege, and Brian knew it. Father Dowling had had no choice but to believe him.

"I strangled him," Brian had said. "I was waiting in the parking lot and got into the backseat. He must have seen who I was, he wasn't alarmed. I put the wire around his neck and throttled him."

"Sure he did," Phil Keegan said. "Only now we know he strangled a dead man. In any case, it was the poison that killed his father, not the wire."

That meant that Brian was morally guilty of murder—that was the act he had intended to perform—but legally innocent, at least of murder.

"We could charge him with mutilating a corpse, something like that," Keegan said. "But what's the point?"

"Have you told him yet?"

"Not yet."

"Can I do it?"

"Be my guest."

Brian ducked when he came through the door into the visiting room, then stood erect. Here he was a monk in a cell again, except that he seemed content as he said he had not been in the monastery. The prison outfit, the beard, the laceless shoes, the staring eyes—Brian seemed to sense that something had changed. He came and sat across the table from Father Dowling.

"You remember when you confessed to me what you had done to your father."

"Yes."

"That you had killed him."

Brian did not answer, just waited.

"What would you say if I told you you did not kill him?"

After half a minute, Brian said, "Areyou saying that?"

"Yes."

"I killed him, Father. I was there."

"You said he did nothing when you got into the backseat."

Again Brian waited.

"Brian, he was already dead."

Had the wall clock behind its mesh of wire been audible all along? The seconds seemed to fill the room while Brian considered what Father Dowling had said.

"It doesn't matter."

Father Dowling nodded. "Not morally, no."

"I made a good confession, Father."

"Yes. And I gave you absolution. But they won't be keeping you here much longer."

Brian looked around, as if he was supremely indifferent to his surroundings. A murderer without a victim, a penitent without a penance, what would he do next?

"Do? I don't want to do anything. I'll go back to Minnesota."

"To your hermitage?"

"I only rent it."

Who knew what theories about man's passage through life Brian had developed in solitude? His monastic vocation seemed to have little to do with the liturgical life monks lead. Father Dowling asked if he said the office in his hermitage, the collection of psalms and readings that make up the prayer of the Church.

"No."

"What prayers, then?"

"None. No words."

"Ah."

Meditation? Perhaps. An inner concentration triggered by images, scenes from the life of Our Lord, and leading on to mysteries only the saints knew. But somehow it was easier to think of Brian on an analogy with the people who had lived along the Mississippi before the settlers came. Blanketed, weatherworn, far-seeing eyes trained on a horizon never to be reached.

The theology of Brian's predicament fascinated Phil Keegan. "You can't kill a dead man, Roger."

"Not according to the law."

"Yeah, physical law. You only die once. Or in this case, you're only killed once."

"But there can be many authors of one death." Had Keegan forgotten the events that had led to the imprisonment of Edna Hospers's husband some years ago?

"Just because he wanted to do it, he did it?"

It seemed unwise to continue along those lines. Roger Dowling remembered the imagined cases discussed long ago in moral theology classes. A husband, thinking his wife a stranger, goes to bed with her. Does he or does he not commit adultery? Conversely, thinking the man is her husband, a woman goes to bed with him. Is this adultery? The discussions had spilled out from the classroom, along the walks, into the recreation room, to the table in the refectory.

"I presume this is a dark room," Green had said facetiously.

"The better for things to develop."

Groans, grudging laughter, but an unwillingness to be diverted. Beyond the game of imaginary scenarios was the mystery of human action, what makes an action the kind of action it is? What the agent thinks he is doing is crucial, but not of course the whole story. Brian Geary was right to think that the fact his father was dead when he looped that wire around his throat did not exonerate him. In his wide staring eyes lay the realization that he had wrought vengeance on his father's corpse.

"Why?"

"He hoped to annul my parents' marriage."

"Your mother had filed for a divorce."

"In order to stop him. It didn't work. So I stopped him."

"Well, somebody did."

But who, and for what reason? The satisfaction of knowing the true cause of death freed Brian Geary but put the police back where they had been at the beginning.

"It looks like the annulment had nothing to do with it."

Perhaps not. But now, some days later, the news of Melvin Gorce's strange death drew Roger Dowling northward to his funeral.

Birdsell, who had served on the diocesan tribunal but like Roger in Chicago had retired from it, had offered to put him up.

"I do my own cooking," he warned.

"I'll take you out."

"Hey, I'm pretty good."

And he was, good and surprisingly elaborate. The casserole looked easy, but the side dishes dispelled that impression. Birdsell had resigned from the tribunal because he didn't like the ease with which annulments were being given.

"One day I noticed how we compared with other dioceses. I noticed the number of cases we were getting that should have gone somewhere else. This was taken to be a sign of our deeper compassion."

"What's the verdict on Gorce?"

"Well, they agree he's dead. There was carbon monoxide in his lungs or blood or wherever it ends up, but the coroner wonders if that's what really killed him. He thinks it was his heart. There was also a high level of alcohol."

"Nothing around his neck?"

"You mean the scarf?"

"What about the scarf?"

"White silk, monogrammed, fringe on the ends. Remember when we all got those for Christmas? He was wearing one."

"Like a noose?"

"Like a scarf."

"What do you think happened?"

"Say he'd been drinking and he comes home, drives into his garage, closes the door and falls asleep. He wakes, turns off the motor, falls asleep again. Death by natural causes."

"Natural?"

"He had a heart attack too."

"He did?"

"He had them all the time, small ones, scary ones. He'd had that balloon surgery twice. The drinking was absolutely forbidden."

Bieler called in the editors of two campus publications to let them in on the real news of the coming weekend.

Wicket, editor in chief of the daily Bieler could not read without wincing, given the typos and syntactical howlers, to say nothing of the level of illiteracy it revealed, seemed to make a point of not listening to him. Howe of the glossy weekly, which looked as if it had been put together by the storied typing monkeys, was eagerly attentive.

"A spy from Rome?"

"Torquemada," Bieler said.

Howe got Wicket's eye, but it was clear they did not get the allusion.

"The Spanish Inquisition?"

No bulbs lit above their heads. The enemies of the Church knew more about her than did this new generation. It was a common lament of the faculty that students knew nothing about their putative faith.

"You have done your job well," Quinlan growled. "You produced the college teachers who produced the high school teachers who produced these students. And you are also responsible for the directors of religious instruction in the parishes. It is trickle-down illiteracy. You should crow with triumph rather than complain."

"Your argument is with Vatican II, not with theologians."

"Vatican II! I would give a lung if they had even heard of Vatican II. They think it is an alternative band on shortwave radio. They have never seen its sixteen documents. They know nothing of the council."

"I meant the spirit of Vatican II."

"Ah. Meaning ignorance of it? I see, I see."

It was always wrong to engage Quinlan in debate, in the faculty senate, in the letters column of the daily, anywhere. The best defense was to let him talk so that his anger could turn the tide against him. Nobody likes to discuss religion, particularly in a Catholic university. Talking with the campus journalists, he found it easy to share Quinlan's disgust, and for a fleeting moment Bieler was willing to take some part of the blame.

Wicket said, "Priests, bishops, cardinals always come to the game."

"Actors, singers, lots of people."

Telling them that the congregation Hildebrand headed had once been called the Inquisition would not work.

"This has to be seen in terms of the long struggle between Catholic universities and Roman oppression."

Wicket made a note, or was it a doodle?

"One of the most hallowed marks of the university is academic freedom. Academic freedom is impossible if there is outside interference. Professors of theology have been engaged in this struggle throughout my lifetime."

It was wrong to allude to one's age. Bieler had seen how colleagues lost touch with students when they mentioned they had kids the age of those in the class, or when they mentioned grandchildren. Bieler's kids lived with their mother, something Marion considered a victory, but the truth was that Bieler was glad to let her have the obligation of raising them.

"They both want to go to Notre Dame," she told him.

"There's no favoritism in admissions."

"Richard, they're smart!"

She was probably raising them as ultramontanes, just to spite him. She was forever faxing him articles from *Crisis* and *First Things*. The thought spurred him on to paint the great battle in colorful terms. Wicket was meeting his eye now, when she wasn't taking notes, and Howe clearly took his cue from her.

With quick broad strokes he put before them the oppressive days before John XXIII. Calling a council had been a way to rally friends of change from around the world and lift the heavy hand of Vatican bureaucrats from the life of the Church.

"Rome was where everything was ultimately decided."

"All roads lead to Rome." Howe said it as if he wasn't sure whether he was remembering it or inventing it. Yipes.

"They did if your marriage went bad and you wanted an annulment."

"My folks got an annulment," Howe said.

Wicket wanted to know what an annulment was. Bieler led into it by describing a situation where spouses were stuck with one another no matter what. "Till death do us part," Howe said. It was a concept Wicket seemed to find attractive, until Bieler spoke of battered wives and abused children. Somehow he didn't think Wicket would be as responsive to the hell that marriage to a shrew could be for a man. Marion had just let herself go and acted as if the point of being married had been achieved with the birth of the kids. Bieler, who had fought the good fight to have sex severed from procreation, hankered for more. Marion once called him a sex maniac. It was the beginning of the end.

"If Hildebrand has his way, battered wives will just have to take it."

"Can't they just leave?"

"And never marry again? Sure. But we've made progress. Why should your whole life be ruined because you stumbled into a disaster? The Church has learned compassion. The Church, but apparently not Rome."

It helped not to think of what someone like Quinlan would say to all this. But these were broad strokes, the heart of the matter. Journalists did not deal in subtleties.

Even so Wicket and Howe seemed unsure what the story was. Bieler tipped back and looked at his ceiling, its sections sprayed with fire-resistant concrete. "Rome Cracks Down?" "Cardinal's Chilling Visit?" Bieler mentally shuffled through the possibilities. Why should he have to do their job for them? When they left, he had the sense of having wasted his time. He picked up the phone and put through a call to the *National Catholic Reporter.*

The *NCR* was to Catholic journalism what Hans Kung was to theology, a gadfly, a pit bull, a wary eye on the centers of power, sassy.

"Hildebrand? Hell no, we hadn't heard."

"Next week. A closed-door meeting in the CCE."

"Right before the big game."

"He's staying for that."

"Which side will he root for?"

Ho ho ho. At least he didn't have to spell out the implications of such a meeting when the subject was annulment. But change is a seamless garment, so to speak, and it was important not to give up on any of the changes that had been so hard-earned since the council. With so many of the oppressive traditional doctrines, it was possible for the faithful to negate them in practice, contraception, birth control, in vitro fertilization, abortion, assisted suicide. Who could stop you if you chose to do any of those? But only a Church court could nullify a marriage and enable you to enter into a new one. Divorce just didn't do it. The divorced could not remarry in the Church, and though there doubtless were cases of it, second marriages performed without fanfare, that was not the same thing as starting over after a declaration of nullity. The United States had led the Church in its enlightened approach to the problem, but now the cold hand of Rome was descending. Most tribunals had tightened their practices, but Rome was still not satisfied. Doubtless Hidlebrand wanted the old practice restored, with all cases decided in Rome.

"Who's involved?"

"Ambrose Ravel seems to be in charge."

"Ravel!" It had been difficult to decide whether Ravel was one of the good guys or not. He had become auxiliary during the Bernardin years, a reassuring sign, but he had lately raised fundamental questions about the bases on which annulments were being granted.

It was too late for any story to appear before the Notre Dame meeting, but they would send a reporter to make sure that the clandestine procedure would be brought to the attention of their readers. When the daily appeared, Bieler didn't even notice the story—he had glanced at the front page—and was surprised by Will Lawrence's call.

"How on earth did they find out?"

"I haven't seen the story." It was pleasant not to have to lie.

"They mentioned Hildebrand! The Main Building is in an uproar. They're accusing me!"

"Did they really expect it to be a secret?"

The story was on page five under an enigmatic headline. "Inquisitive Cardinal to Visit Campus."

Monique had talked with Michael Geary's doctor and run the insulin dispensing device through fingerprinting.

"The woman's prints are not new."

"Mrs. Geary."

"They weren't living together."

"Any other prints?"

"Of course he could wear it during sexual activity."

"Of course?"

"I mean, I don't see why not."

"I always remove mine."

Before disbelief came she stared at him open-mouthed. "You're awful."

He was, too, kidding around like this with an attractive young woman. He was no better than Michael Geary, except that Michael Geary actually goofed around. But no, Cy Horvath did not think of himself as anything at all like the late Michael Geary. Monique prompted strange thoughts and sometimes he said funny things but he hadn't laid a glove on her and by God he never would. That would be a blow at the very foundation of his life, and it would totally disillusion Phil Keegan as well. Phil Keegan was no picnic to work for but he was a good and honest cop and a good man besides. Keegan could make eyes at Monique, he could marry again, no reason at all not to, except he wouldn't. Father Dowling kidded him about Marie Murkin sometimes, but that's all it was, kidding. If Phil Keegan could be faithful to his wife's memory, Cy could be faithful to the wife who was everything he wanted in a wife anyway.

Back to the poisoning of Michael Geary. In order for anyone to do what had to be done, they had to know about the insulin dispenser, that is, of its existence and what it was and did. This could have been long-term knowledge or recently discovered, but adding poison to the insulin did not seem to qualify as a spur-of-the-moment decision. The plan required foreknowledge of the device.

"That ought to narrow the range."

Monique began the list with the doctor, his nurse or nurses, the pharmacist, anyone with access to the pharmacist's records. To these could be added those who worked in the agency.

"He had diabetes, sure," Florence Lewis said; then her mouth opened. "Was that it, insulin shock, a coma?"

"Did he suffer from those?"

"He shouldn't have, but he did. That was the point of the automatic insulin dispenser."

"Ah, you know about that."

Florence regarded that as a strange remark. "Everyone did."

By everyone she meant herself, Pam and the two agents, Wadding and Goren.

"He'd had it all his life, but he never really accepted it. He wanted to think that he could overcome it by willpower. His wife told me this. I always called her when he went into a tailspin."

Monique explained the condition of a diabetic in such a state. "Disoriented, dizzy, incoherent. If you didn't know better, you'd say the person was drunk."

Apparently it had been a regular if infrequent occurrence at the agency. Mrs. Geary would come with food for her husband and in minutes he would be back to normal.

"And they would quarrel about it. This automatic dispenser was supposed to take care of that."

"How long had he had it?"

"Oh, it was relatively new. Experimental."

"Since he and Mrs. Geary began having trouble?"

"Began? If you mean was it since she moved out and filed for divorce, yes."

"So Mrs. Geary wouldn't have known of it."

"Of course she would. It was her idea."

"Had he had any of his spells since getting it?"

"No." Florence shook her head. "It must have run out."

"Like the sands of time," Monique said, and then looked embarrassed when both Cy and Florence turned to look at her. "So to speak."

"Only the container was almost full. Someone had put poison in the insulin, Florence."

Florence, having absorbed this news, sat down as if she had been dropped. "And it was put into him by the thing that was supposed to keep him healthy." She spoke this to the floor, after which she lifted her eyes. "What kind of poison?"

Monique brought the white plastic bottle from the bathroom.

"It came from that?"

"This bowl cleaner contains hydrochloric acid."

"And you can tell if it came from that bottle rather than another."

"Tests will be run," Monique said, having recovered from her rhetorical excess.

But she would tell Cy at the first opportunity that the product was uniform and it was unlikely that the contents of one container could be differentiated from another. "Of course we'll try."

Of course again. She spoke as if she were testifying and it was important to underscore the authority of what she said.

The bottle from the agency bathroom felt full. Cy held it to the light, but it was opaque.

"You got a scale here?"

"Scale?"

"To weigh things."

"Like mail?"

"You got a scale to weigh mail?"

"Unless we threw it away. We don't use it much."

"What do you want it for?" Monique asked.

"I don't think this bottle has ever been used. It contains a quart."

"And you want to weigh it to see if it's a full quart."

"Or find a quart measure, of course."

"Do you have a quart measure, Florence?"

"I'll look."

"I think you're right," Monique said. "This seems full."

There was a full quart in the plastic container. Florence found a container that had held a fluid quart of soft drink. Cy improvised a funnel and transferred the contents. A pungent odor filled the room.

"Be careful of your eyes," Monique warned. "That can damage them."

"Of course."

"Why do you keep saying that?"

"Do I?"

"Of course you do."

"That's why. You're a bad influence on me."

"So I'm told."

He looked at her but she turned away. Cy asked Florence how long this particular product had been used in the agency.

"Apparently not at all."

"I don't mean this bottle. I mean this brand."

"As long as I can remember."

"Who would replace it when necessary?"

"The cleanup lady."

Every weekday evening at six a Mrs. Motzko came and made the place spic-and-span for the next day, or for Monday when she came on Friday.

"She'll be coming tonight?"

"It's Monday."

"Where does she live?"

"I could look it up."

"Please. Her phone number too."

"Would you like for me to call her?"

"I would like for you to not call her. Understand?"

"You don't think Mrs. Motzko . . ."

Cy brought his finger to his lips. The stunned Florence nodded. She went on tiptoe to her office.

The address was less than a mile away. Cy decided he would follow up on that lead before talking with the two agents, who from time to time had stuck their heads out of their offices to see what was going on.

"How long does the average investigation last?" Wadding asked on his way back from using the fax machine in Florence's office.

"That depends."

"How long you been on this one?"

"Not long enough."

"You going to want to see me again?"

"Are you busy?"

"I'm always busy, we all are, this is a place of business."

"Don't let me interrupt you."

Wadding looked at them when they went past his office and out the back door to where the car was parked.

Mrs. Motzko's face looked like a pad you stuck pins in, and it didn't help much when she fished a denture out of her apron pocket and put it into her mouth. She worked it around until it was comfortable. "It's best if you run it under a little water first."

Cy pulled the bottle of bowl cleaner from the paper bag Florence had given him. "You ever see this before?"

She stepped back. "They called the police!"

"We're investigating it, yes."

"Who complained?"

Cy thought about it. "So you have seen this before?"

Ms. Motzko took it and her hand dropped when Cy let go, but she didn't let it fall. "I bought it."

She worked her mouth, then turned and stomped back through the house. They could see her go, so they stayed where they were. In a moment she stomped back holding a plastic bag. Cy could see an identical bottle of bowl cleaner as well as rolls of paper, cleanser, soap.

"Here," she said, shoving it at Cy.

"What's this?"

"They can have the damned stuff."

It emerged that Mrs. Motzko, when she changed a roll of paper, for instance, took what was left on the previous roll home, a kind of fringe benefit of the job. Cy took the bowl cleaner from the bag and handed the full one to Mrs. Motzko.

"What's this?"

"A trade."

"This is full."

"That's okay, this one isn't empty." He slid it into the paper bag and handed it to Monique.

"Let me know what you find out."

Tuttle's surveillance of Catherine Burger had told him what the police discovered when she showed up at Geary's funeral.

"Our stakeout has borne fruit."

"The son?" Peanuts asked. "I think so too."

"I refer to the mother and her friends. Forget about Freddy."

Peanuts put a hand over his eyes and wiped away the memory. He did this with a straight face. Sometimes Tuttle wondered what Peanuts's mental age was. Whatever mind Peanuts had been given was as good as new.

Catherine Burger was the first wife of Lorenzo Burger, the druggist. There were three locations of Burger enterprises: the Burger Apothecary in the Fleetwood Mall, Burger Pharmacy downtown next to the courthouse, and Burger Drugs, the store Lorenzo had taken over from his late father. Lorenzo and Catherine had a son, Freddy, aged twenty-four. They had been divorced for ten years. Lorenzo had married again, and again, and was having trouble with his third wife. Catherine had been given the large house on the river and lived there with Freddy.

Freddy was finding himself. That was the benign description. After finishing pharmacy school, apparently a concession to his father, he had moved into an apartment. To find himself. Or you might say he was unoccupied. Not unemployed; that suggested employability, and as far as Tuttle could find out Freddy Burger wasn't worth a hoot in hell. Except on the golf course.

He had been playing since he was a kid, starting with a set of miniature clubs. He had been club champion or runner-up in his flight ever since anyone could remember. Tuttle had gotten this from Pudge Patterson, who tended bar at the country club, which was just a mile up the river road from the Burger estate. Pudge weighed about 120 and had a kind of platform running along behind the bar so people wouldn't see how short he was. Standing more or less on tiptoe most of his life, he noticed things.

"What's the kid like?"

"As a golfer, the best."

"And otherwise."

"What was that phrase they used in the Nixon tapes?"

"Expletive deleted?"

"Something like that."

"Tell me about Mrs. Burger."

"Which one?"

All Lorenzo Burger's former wives retained membership in the club, and none had remarried. They were distinguished by Roman numerals, like popes and kings. Catherine was Mrs. Burger I.

"She has lunch here twice a week on average, sometimes alone, sometimes with friends."

"Friends."

"Other wives and widows, mainly."

"Men."

"Here? Never. My theory is that she remains a member and comes as often as she does as a rebuke to Burger. I mean, he comes in, alone or with his current wife, and there sits Mrs. Burger I looking like an actress playing the scene where the early Christians are being herded into the Colosseum."

"You've got an active imagination."

"It comes from not drinking."

"You quit?"

"You can only quit if you started. I never did. From this side of the bar, the effects of booze are awful to contemplate. Burger is a bad drunk."

"Noisy?"

"Oh no. Quiet, very quiet, like a storm about to happen. Then he picks fights. You say something offhand and he asks you very sweetly what you meant by saying that. You got two choices, drop it or begin to explain. He won't let you drop it, so you got to explain why you wanted to drop it. When he wants a fight he gets one. Luckily he's got a glass jaw. He's too drunk to remember being beaten, and he usually is."

What did all this have to do with the death of Michael Geary? Catherine Burger had been linked with Geary, but following the spoor of her husband, given his track record since the divorce, was unpromising.

"You've never seen her with a man?"

"Mrs. Burger I? Not in the way you mean. She gets married again, maybe he doesn't have to pay her as much."

"She could marry rich."

Pudge Patterson made a face.

"She's Catholic, right?" Tuttle said.

"So's Burger. At least he was."

"If she takes it more seriously than he does, she wouldn't marry again."

"She could if she wanted to. She got what they call an annulment. She's free to marry as far as the Catholic Church is concerned."

"What days she usually come for lunch?"

"Mondays and Thursdays."

"Today's Monday."

"She's at the table just inside the door, the silvery blonde, not the brunette. Mrs. Stead," he added, before Tuttle could ask.

"You know this much about all the members?"

"Someone else you want to talk about?"

"I can't afford it."

Tuttle gave Patterson the fifty and got off his stool. Mrs. Burger I and her friend were not the only people in the dining room, though it was two in the afternoon. Amos Cadbury, Fox River's most distinguished attorney, was silhouetted against the window looking out on the practice green.

"Who's what with Cadbury?"

"You know the Geary who got killed."

"I read about it."

"That's Mrs. Geary."

Tuttle left the country club. He never felt comfortable in places like that. They were for lawyers like Amos Cadbury.

Peanuts was slumped behind the wheel of the patrol car, which occupied a handicapped space in the parking lot. Handicapped parking at the golf course. There was a joke there, but Tuttle didn't want to waste it on Peanuts. Peanuts stirred into life when Tuttle shut the door hard.

"Where to?" Peanuts asked.

"Nowhere yet."

Ten minutes later, Amos Cadbury emerged with Mrs. Geary on his arm. They descended to the parking lot, talked a moment more, then parted, Cadbury to his Mercedes, Mrs. Geary to a station wagon. Peanuts looked at Tuttle, but he shook his head.

"Well, we're saving gas anyway."

"Prove it."

Peanuts was still pondering the remark when Mrs. Burger came out of the club, skipped down the steps and hurried toward a large car, which Peanuts identified as a Lincoln Town Car.

"Follow it."

Peanuts had surprising pockets of lore in an otherwise underfurnished mind. He knew all about cars. The Avanti, for example, that Gordon Furey drove. One of the last efforts of Studebaker to stay afloat. When the South Bend car company had gone belly-up, a local group bought the Avanti and produced it on a custom basis before selling out to an Ohio group.

"The body's why people buy it. Everything else is standard stuff, bought from other companies."

"Can you just buy the body?"

"And put it on a Mercedes?" Peanuts grinned at the thought, but his eyes never left the car ahead of them.

Glen, a friend of Freddy Burger, had opened up to Tuttle when he talked with him in an ambiguous bar on Walker Street.

"Former friend," he insisted.

"You know his mother?"

"Ah, La Gioconda."

"Her name's Catherine."

"I was referring to her enigmatic smile. No wonder Freddy is so screwed up, the mother's worse than the father."

"How so?"

Freddy had told Glen of the abuse he had suffered in childhood, but this turned out to be a busy father's lack of interest in what his son was doing. Then the boy himself had from an early age done strange things. He signed up for cooking in school and created a little flap when he tried to join the Girl Scouts. This was taken to be a nuisance suit until reporters interviewed Freddy. Tuttle did not wonder that Burger had been reluctant to spend time with his son. Glen said that Freddy called his mother the Virgin Queen.

"Isn't he Catholic?"

"*She* sure is. Of course he couldn't call her the Virgin Queen on that basis, could he? She is ferociously devoted, you're right. It's why Freddy lived elsewhere for a time. Of course he spied on her. We both did. It was the cement of our relationship. Hating the Virgin Queen. She pretended to be living like a nun but there was, we discovered, a man."

"Michael Geary."

"You've squashed my punch line."

"So it was Geary?"

"How did you know?"

"Intuition."

"Well, par-don me. Anyway, armed with that knowledge, Freddy moved back in. Her moral authority was kaput. So was our relationship. I think he thought his mother didn't know about him."

"Did she?"

"Oh, I made sure of that."

Peanuts would have pulled into the driveway behind the Mercedes, but Tuttle told him to drive on.

"Go up a ways and make a U."

When they came back, Tuttle had Peanuts pull into a rest area from which they could see the Burger driveway. Peanuts cut the motor and then pushed back the driver's seat and slid down out of sight.

"What's wrong?"

"See that gray sedan?"

There was a gray sedan going slowly by on the river road, heading away from the Burger house. There was a woman at the wheel. A black woman.

"Agnes Lamb?"

Peanuts nodded. "She following you?"

"What do you think?"

They repaired to Tuttle's office, where he loaded up the VCR and began to run the tapes of their surveillance, starting with the second. Peanuts put in a call to Domino's, so they were keeping only half an eye on the screen. Michael Geary's car pulling into the Burger drive caught his eye. Knowing that the driver would soon be found dead in that very car added a tragic note. Peanuts too was paying attention. He stopped chewing as his watch flashed onto the screen.

"Look at this now, Tuttle."

The camera was trained on the garage area of the Burger house where Michael Geary's car was parked. The trunk was open. Freddy appeared, carrying someone. A man. His mother, her hand over her mouth, appeared, watching him put the man he was carrying into the trunk. She turned away. Freddy shut the trunk. When the car was coming at the camera, Peanuts's watch appeared again.

"What was that?"

"You saw it."

Tuttle backed it up, checking the time and date on Peanuts's watch.

"My God, Peanuts, why didn't you tell me about this?"

"I gave you the video."

So he had. Did Peanuts understand what he had filmed, what they had just seen? Tuttle felt almost holy as he watched the tape again. Hard work had paid off. He had here on tape what everyone else was looking for. The question was, what would he do with what he knew?

Marie Murkin's resentment at Father Dowling's absence disappeared when she became the beneficiary of the visits that were paid during the interval. A good housekeeper never just turned people away from the door with a curt "The pastor isn't in," spoken in a tone that suggested getting an appointment might be a good idea. A rectory should have an open-door policy. She agreed absolutely with Father Dowling, and welcomed the change from the siege mentality that had governed his predecessor's governance of St. Hilary's. Moreover, though she knew enough to keep this a secret from Father Dowling, she was convinced that there was something like the ministry of the housekeeper, some special role assigned by divine providence to women like herself with years and years of pastoral experience. So she had waved Phil Keegan in and marched him down the hall to the kitchen.

"What do you mean, he's away?"

"He went off this morning."

"Where?"

"He wouldn't say."

"Retreat."

"He made his annual retreat last month."

"You've no idea where he might have gone?"

"I was going to ask you the same thing."

"I'll guess. He tell you about the death of this priest Melvin Gorce, up in Michigan?"

Marie narrowed her eyes and thought about it. "You know, you could be right."

"Well, he won't be back tonight, that's for sure."

"Oh. I'm sure he intends to."

"He can intend all he wants, but that's a four-hour drive or I'm a monkey's uncle."

"Well, it will do him good to get away. He's been fretting about the killing of Michael Geary."

"He's been fretting? We're back to where we started."

"Tea or coffee?"

"There any beer?"

"I believe there is."

The discovery that Michael Geary had been poisoned rather than strangled had knocked the pins out from under the assumptions of the investigation to that point.

"The whole family resented what Geary was trying to do," Phil Keegan said.

"The annulment?"

He nodded. "The wife, of course, and the daughter. Maybe the son most of all."

"What a strange man. He confessed to killing his own father when he didn't."

"Oh he would have, if Geary had still been alive, that seems clear."

"So you let him go."

"Roger Dowling may be able to talk about murdering dead bodies, but I work on a more restricted field. He had the motive and the will and seemingly the opportunity. But his timing was off. And now he's off the hook."

"And the other Gearys are back on?"

"Have you ever seen one of those devices that automatically dispenses insulin?"

"No."

"They're very new, hardly out of the experimental stage. Whoever poisoned him had to know about that and that Geary had one."

"It seems like a very complicated way to poison someone."

"But very attractive if you don't want to be in the vicinity when death occurs."

He took some beer, wiped his mouth, stared across the kitchen.

"You're thinking of Mrs. Geary."

"If she knew about the poison she would know she didn't need an alibi. Certainly not all the way to South Bend."

"But she could kill two birds with one stone."

"Who's the other bird?"

Marie had checked all the cabinets in the house since learning of the way Michael Geary had died. As she had suspected when she first heard of it, the bowl cleaner she used was as lethal as that used on Michael Geary. Hydrochloric acid was the fatal ingredient.

"Can't you just buy that straight?" she asked.

"What for?"

"I'll bet kids have that in those chemistry sets they get as gifts."

"I doubt that."

"But if I were a chemist, there must be someplace where I could purchase hydrochloric acid."

Phil Keegan was not interested in such speculation, and why should he be? They had the source of it in the bowl cleaner.

"Besides, Marie, it was not pure hydrochloric acid that was added."

Marie had found several products in the house that contained poison. There was an arsenic-based rodent poison in the cabinet over the workbench in the basement.

"Marie, murderers seldom use an exotic method. Straightforward violence does the trick—a blow, a blast from a gun, pushing the victim out a window, driving a car over them."

Marie lifted a hand to stop this grisly narrative. She could have kicked herself for not guessing where Father Dowling had gone. It was obvious, once Phil Keegan mentioned it. And they both knew why. The annulment. Father Melvin Gorce had encouraged Michael Geary to think that he had a good chance of obtaining an annulment after Monsignor Noonan had told him the opposite. So Geary had entered his plea in Michigan, rather than Chicago. That had made Gorce a possible target. And that meant that two deaths, Geary's and Gorce's, could be tied to a single motive.

"Except for one thing."

"What?"

"Father Gorce apparently died of a heart attack."

"Apparently."

"So where do you go from here?"

"Maybe Michigan."

"I keep thinking of that organist, Amanda James."

"In what way?"

"You'll think I'm being fanciful."

"Tell me."

"Well, imagine the money doesn't satisfy her. Getting it had probably been her father's idea anyway. She wants more, she wants revenge."

"Several things are wrong with that, Marie. First, Amanda is in Florida. Second, she would have had to know about the insulin dispenser, and, most important, she would have had to have access to it. I don't imagine Michael Geary would welcome her with open arms after what she did to him."

"She did to him!"

"He might still be alive and with his wife if she hadn't accused him. After all, what was it he was supposed to have done?"

Marie's indignation at what Phil Keegan was saying was tempered by her own skepticism about the charge. That Michael Geary was a bounder and had strayed from his own nest seemed beyond doubt, but that did not automatically turn Amanda James into a wronged innocent. Marie knew exactly what she or any woman she knew would do if some man made an indecent proposal to her in a choir loft or anywhere else. And, before the case went behind closed doors, with Geary's lawyer conferring with the legal advisors of the archdiocese, Geary had denied the choir loft story as well as that he had seduced Amanda. It was the second part of that denial that had enraged her father, but the first part would have let the parish and the archdiocese off the hook. The claim to sacrilege, that Amanda had been led astray in the course of her duties as organist, was essential to the settlement Amanda had received.

"She may have been in Florida, Phil Keegan, but that father of hers was not."

"I find it hard to imagine him slipping the acid into Geary's insulin dispenser."

"If it comes to that, I can't imagine anyone doing it."

Keegan sat back suddenly. "Good Lord."

"What's wrong?"

"I just thought of the most obvious person to have done that."

"Who?"

"Geary himself."

Keegan pushed back from the table and went to the wall phone and punched numbers fiercely.

"Cy? Is Geary's apartment still secure? Good. Look, do a check on the medicine cabinet, okay? Insulin. You're looking for what he supplied his automatic dispenser with."

"So you're going back to suicide as the explanation?"

"No. It's at what point the insulin was monkeyed with."

Half an hour after Phil Keegan left, the bell rang twice in quick succession. The aristocratic Amos Cadbury stood on the step, exhibiting his profile. His brows lifted as he turned to the opening door.

"Mrs. Murkin, good morning. I tried to reach you by telephone as I drove here, but your line was busy. I took that as a sign that Father Dowling is in."

Marie stood to one side and Cadbury stepped in, removing his hat and handing it to her as a priest once gave his biretta to the altar boy. He hesitated before starting toward the study.

"He isn't in, Mr. Cadbury. He's out of town."

Disappointment came and went. He smiled. "And I had been promising myself a cup of your delicious tea."

"You shall have it. Make yourself comfortable in the parlor and I'll bring it in a jiffy."

"Nonsense, I'll come with you."

Her heart actually gave a little jump as she went ahead of the distinguished lawyer. How many kitchens had he been in in recent years? He certainly would never see another as neat and clean as hers, she was certain of that.

He took a chair at the table. "Now I can watch how you go about it."

Marie wasn't so sure she wanted a kibitzer, particularly one who thought she did something special when she brewed tea. But he did note what she did.

"So you warm the pot with hot water first?"

"I think everyone does."

While it steeped, she sat. He smiled benevolently.

"It has occurred to me that it is actually better that I speak with you alone. But first let me establish the absolute confidentiality of the conversation. You are of course Father Dowling's strong right arm; I flatter myself that I am his legal confidant. I will not say lawyer, since he has no need of one. We can speak with utter frankness."

Marie nodded. It was gratifying to have her role at St. Hilary's so clearly recognized.

"As you must know, I represented Mrs. Michael Geary in her petition for divorce. My doing so excited not a little surprise in the legal community, as this is a kind of suit I have sedulously avoided in my practice. There have been exceptions, two I think in a long career. Each time there has been a very special reason. And so it was with Mrs. Geary. The divorce was meant as a preemptive strike, to dissuade her husband from pursuing an annulment. If he had sought this locally, in Chicago, I could have assured her that he would not be successful. But he sought relief elsewhere, in a tribunal that has become known, if not infamous, for swift and questionable declarations of nullity."

He paused and looked inquiringly at the pot. Marie looked at the clock on the wall, bobbed her head as the second hand moved, then picked up the pot and poured.

"How long do you steep it?"

He sipped the tea with his eyes closed, his expression that of someone awaiting some great good. A sigh as he returned the cup to its saucer. His eyes opened. "That is marvelous." His eyes went to the window. "Others get caught up in events, innocently . . ." He looked at Marie. "Perhaps no one is perfectly innocent. My concern is for a client, Catherine Burger."

"She was at the funeral."

"Was she?"

"So I'm told."

"What else were you told about her?"

Marie turned her cup in its saucer. "I think you know."

"I do. But it is not her unfortunate infatuation with Michael Geary that concerns me. She has a son."

Amos Cadbury spoke judiciously, in soft tones, but Marie sensed his opinion of Freddy Burger. She was glad when he returned to Michael Geary.

"Divorce, annulment—all that is moot now with the death of Michael Geary. I have just been told that the cause of death was poison."

"Someone put hydrochloric acid in his insulin."

"Of course you would know that."

Marie suppressed a smile. "Captain Keegan was just here."

"Was he? I suppose he and his department are now proceeding on the basis of the poison theory."

"Theory?"

Mr. Cadbury went back to his tea, as if he had been wrongfully distracted from it. When he put down his cup, his expression was once more beatific.

"Consider. At the beginning, one might have imagined that Michael Geary had committed suicide. It was a far-fetched theory, but suicides are often far-fetched, sometimes by design, sometimes not. Next, they spoke of strangulation."

His eye moved from his cup to the pot to Marie. She poured him another cup. He held it in both hands and inhaled.

Marie said, "And they had the strangler. Brian Geary confessed to the crime."

"And he was guilty, if not precisely of the crime he confessed to. Most recently, the cause of death has been discovered to be a deadly acid introduced into Michael Geary's insulin."

"I think that's certain."

"Oh, I don't contest it. But has a *murder* been committed?"

He picked up his cup and drained it.

"Do you know a lawyer named Tuttle, Mrs. Murkin?"

"Tuttle!"

"I see you do not approve of him."

"Neither would you, if you knew him, Mr. Cadbury."

"Oh, I know him. I know him all too well. It is just because I do that I am considering engaging him for a special task."

"Is that what you wanted to ask Father Dowling?"

He smiled. "Perhaps I wanted to be talked out of it. It looks as if you can fulfill that function."

"What could Tuttle possibly do for you?"

"Keep an eye on someone."

Marie threw up her hands. "Oh, he'd be perfect for that, Mr. Cadbury, sneaky little man that he is. It's what he does best, follow people about, seeking whom he might devour."

"St. Peter?"

"I don't even think he's Catholic."

"I meant your scriptural allusion."

Marie wasn't aware that she had made one. Years as rectory housekeeper had made odds and ends adhere to her mind whose origin she did not know. If she had, she might have hesitated to liken Tuttle to the Prince of Darkness.

He went to the wake for Melvin Gorce, but the following morning, having said an early private Mass for the repose of the dead priest's soul, Roger Dowling started back to Fox River. On the long drive, he had ample opportunity to review what he had learned.

Gorce had been found dead behind the wheel of his car, which was parked in his garage. His locked garage, as it happened.

"He had it rigged so that when the door was lowered it locked automatically."

"He was still in the car."

"He must have used the remote."

Lavater, the cop who agreed to tell him these things, seemed incapable of wonder or surprise, perhaps an asset in his line of work, perhaps not.

"He drove into the garage, closed the door with the remote control, thereby locking it?"

"You got it."

Although there was carbon monoxide in the body, the verdict was death due to heart failure.

When Father Dowling visited Gorce's house he was surprised to find that there was no direct entrance to the house from the garage. Closing the doors from outside, using the control in the house, and thereby locking them, made sense. But why would Gorce have locked himself in the garage?

"The car was locked too," Lavater said.

"It was!"

"We had to get a locksmith to open it."

"Isn't that odd?"

Lavater shrugged. "Most things are odd when you think about them."

What a marvelous fellow Lavater was. Too bad Phil Keegan wasn't here. Roger Dowling was certain the two men would like each other instantly. "But some are odder than others?"

"Some."

"Like a man locking himself in a garage in a locked car. It's almost as if he were afraid of something, maybe someone following him, so he double-locked himself in."

"And died of fright?"

"You may be right."

Lavater looked mildly alarmed. "I was just continuing your thought."

"That would make it less odd."

"Maybe."

Birdsell, Roger Dowling's host, mentioned that Gorce's policy on the tribunal had upset a lot of people.

"Any threats?"

"Oh, some letters you wouldn't want to receive. Most of the threats were theological."

"Theological?"

"Hoping that he would find a fiery reward in the next world."

"But no physical threats?"

"Don't you believe in corporal punishment in the next world?"

"I meant in this."

"None that I ever heard of."

The elderly retired monsignor with whom Gorce lived, Steve Adrian, seemed almost ashamed to have outlived the younger priest. "He never talked about the court. I don't think he even thought about it, if he could avoid it."

"He seem worried about anything?"

"If you had a heart like his, you'd worry too. Imagine, my heart was younger than his. Physically. It doesn't seem fair, does it? I was ordained in 1945."

"Where do you park your car?"

"I no longer drive." He widened his eyes. "If I had cataract surgery I could, but the thought of anyone operating on my eyes makes me shiver."

"Gorce kept a very secure garage."

"Oh, people have complained of someone loitering." Adrian shook the thought away. "He had the garage made secure before that."

"What do you mean, someone loitering?"

Adrian laughed. "A tall bearded man with very large eyes." He altered his voice to say this, sounding like a spooky movie.

"Bearded, huh?"

"Aren't they always bearded?" But Adrian turned serious. "He came to Mass in the morning, to mine and to Gorce's, sat in the front pew and just stared ahead. I know he got on Gorce's nerves."

"Is he still around?"

"I haven't seen him."

Father Dowling thought about it on the drive back. If the bearded man was Brian he would have intended to get on Gorce's nerves. He had strangled his father and thought he committed murder. Had he come here only to frighten Gorce and scared him to death?

After several hours, Father Dowling pushed it out of his mind. Besides, he was getting into Chicago traffic and had to stay alert. Once through the Loop, traffic moved swiftly, and finally he was at the exit that would put him on the final leg of his journey to Fox River.

Approaching his garage, he pushed the remote control attached to the sun visor and felt again a little surge of power when the doors began to lift. When he was a kid, such a gadget would have been the stuff of fantasy.

"You forgot to shut the garage door," Marie said as he approached the house.

"Is that any way to welcome me home?"

"You haven't been gone forty-eight hours."

"Don't you want to know where I've been?"

"Captain Keegan and I figured you were in Michigan, at the funeral of Father Gorce."

"Phil was here?" He went through the kitchen, dropped his bag at the foot of the stairs and went into his study. He looked around as others might have if he had never returned, been killed on the way. They would think it a very comfortable room, he was sure.

"Just before Amos Cadbury."

"Amos! Now that's a surprise."

The phone on the desk rang and Marie moved to answer it, but Father Dowling lifted the receiver.

"Yes?"

"Roger? Phil. Has Marie told you the latest on Geary?"

"I just got in. Why don't you come for dinner and tell me?"

Peanuts had once confided to Tuttle that the first time he was sent on stakeout he thought he was on an errand to a fast-food place and he was confused that he had been provided with food for the long dull hours of surveillance. He had reminded Tuttle of this more than once as they sat in an unmarked Fox River police car, keeping an eye on Mrs. Burger. Peanuts's conversational repertoire was limited.

"What're we looking for, Tuttle?"

"Just keep an eye on that driveway."

And the videocam, of course. It had helped that Peanuts assumed he knew what he was doing because there had been moments when Tuttle was ready to give the whole thing up. He told himself that he was working on spec; surveillance might or might not lead to a profit for Tuttle & Tuttle, but the fact was he had begun to feel like a damned fool. Until he saw the video Peanuts had taken on the day of Michael Geary's murder.

It was one of those times when he was certain his life was directed benevolently from above, his late lamented father putting in a word for him. He felt that he had been guided to the parking space on the river road across from the Burger house. It had been inspiration to put his videocam to use there. Now he had on tape something whose significance made him almost dizzy.

As an officer of the court, his duty was obvious. Evidence in a crime under investigation should be turned in to the police. Not to do so was to become liable to a criminal charge. So much was clear. What was obscure was the relation between what Peanuts had caught on the video and a crime under investigation.

"Who's he carrying?" Peanuts asked.

"I can't make him out."

He hoped Peanuts would remember that in any future possible inquiry. Meanwhile, he put the video in his safe-deposit box and carried on as if he knew no more than anyone else. When the police followed out the lead Catherine Burger's attendance at Geary's funeral had given them, Tuttle would find a way to profit from the video. How the police could fail to find out what he knew escaped him.

In Tuttle's experience, when people said they wanted to be free of a spouse it was because they already had a replacement in mind. Catherine Burger filled in the blank for Michael Geary. Pudge Patterson at the country club said she could marry again; she had gotten an annulment. But she wouldn't marry Michael Geary unless he was similarly free. Not just divorced, either, but the recipient of a declaration of nullity.

Obviously someone had taken Geary's application for an annulment badly. So, as Peanuts had told Tuttle, the police did the obvious thing and wondered who that someone might be. The wife? She was visiting her daughter out of state when Geary was killed. Then Brian Geary said he did it and was put in the slammer and insisted that he would represent himself.

"That's stupid," Tuttle told him, when he wangled an interview with the bearded son.

"I'm guilty."

"They're not going to let you plead guilty to murder."

"I did it."

"That doesn't matter. They'll appoint a lawyer and he'll enter a plea of not guilty."

"I'll tell the truth."

"You're in contempt of court if you open your mouth. The prosecution has to prove you did it."

"That'll be easy."

"You'll plead not guilty by reason of insanity," Tuttle said, hunching forward, eager to tell Brian Geary how it would go.

"Insanity!"

"Sure. No problem. Would anyone in their right mind kill his father?"

"I'm not insane."

About to explain the technicalities of the law to this bearded pop-eyed hermit, Tuttle paused, recognizing an opening.

"I am telling you what the court-appointed attorney will do. You can avoid that, of course."

"How?"

"Hire an attorney." Tuttle had put his business card on the table between them when he had wangled his way into an interview with the accused. Now he moved it ostentatiously around. Brian looked at the card, but did not pick it up.

"I'll plead you not guilty, but just that, not by reason of insanity."

"I'm guilty."

Tuttle spent the rest of his time trying to explain that a not guilty plea didn't mean he wasn't guilty, really, all it meant was . . . But Brian Geary had stopped listening. Well, it had been a long shot anyway. Geary's family would move in with a lawyer and protect their wild-eyed son.

"What do you think?" the guard asked Tuttle as he was leaving.

"Nuttier than a fruitcake."

"Know what he eats? Bread and water."

Tuttle stopped. "A hunger strike?"

"Naw. He doesn't believe in eating. He sits in a corner with his legs tied in knots, eyes closed, and doesn't move."

"Crazy."

"Did he really kill his father?"

"Well, the old man's dead."

Peanuts dropped him off at his building and Tuttle took the stairs to his office. He let himself in and stood for a moment with his back to the closed door, finding in the cluttered room the source of a deep contentment. On any objective basis, he was a flop as a lawyer, living from hand to mouth, seldom called on to do anything the most callow paralegal could not do. Still, as he ran his hand along the spines of his books, the gift of his father, Tuttle was certain there was one at least who appreciated what he had made of his life.

In the inner office, Tuttle removed his hat, then clamped it on again and settled behind his desk, content with his lot. He had never aspired to be an Amos Cadbury. This thought achieved mystic significance when Tuttle punched his answering device and heard a woman's voice saying she was calling for Mr. Cadbury and would Mr. Tuttle please return his call.

Tuttle rewound and played it again. The woman had to be that cold-eyed receptionist who had more than once stonewalled Tuttle when he tried to contact Amos Cadbury. Cadbury was so successful that her job was to keep potential business away. When he picked up his phone, he wished Peanuts were here to witness it.

"This is Mr. Tuttle returning Mr. Cadbury's call."

"Mr. Tuttle," the secretary announced and stepped aside, giving the visitor a wide berth. Amos Cadbury did not meet her eye. There was enmity between Tuttle and the woman that seemed to go much deeper than Cadbury's own disdain for Fox River's least distinguished lawyer.

Cadbury came around the desk, his hand extended, but he might have been fending off Tuttle as much as greeting him.

"Please be seated, Mr. Tuttle."

Tuttle sat, fitting his tweed hat on the knee of his crossed leg, and looked around in admiration. "If I had an office like this I wouldn't be able to work in it."

"Where are you located?"

"The Drexel Building."

"Is that still in use?"

"I have an unbreakable lease."

"Ah. I don't see your television ads anymore."

"They weren't cost-effective."

"That's interesting to know."

Once lawyers had conducted their business as if their right hand did not know what their left was doing. Fees? Of course there were fees, but these were discussed discreetly, almost as an embarrassment. To solicit business was unheard of. It was one of Amos Cadbury's crosses that he had lived into an era when lawyers hawked their wares like carnival barkers. Tuttle's short-lived ads had been a call to litigation, as if the courts were not already burdened with questionable cases. But it was probably the ineptitude of the ads rather than the public taste that explained their failure.

Tuttle was looking receptively at Cadbury.

"There is something I want done, Mr. Tuttle, and I immediately thought of you."

He could think of no other lawyer he would expect to perform the task. There are private investigators, of course, but the thought of employing one made Cadbury shudder.

"What I have to say is of course in complete confidence."

Tuttle nodded, uncrossed his legs, crossed them the other way, settled his tweed hat on his knee.

"It concerns the Geary family."

"Okay."

"You know what happened to Michael Geary."

"I considered representing the son who confessed to it."

"You did?"

"We had a conference. It was clear he wouldn't follow advice. He wanted to plead guilty. He's kind of a nut."

"Eccentric?"

"He got stirred up at the suggestion of a not guilty by reason of insanity plea."

"I see."

Amos Cadbury did not know what to make of this. Maureen Geary had not mentioned that Brian had sought legal counsel elsewhere. But, after all, this was Tuttle. No doubt the little lawyer had gotten an interview with Brian in order to solicit his business.

"Anyway I wouldn't touch it."

"I represent the Geary family as well as the Geary agency."

"No kidding."

"Brian was spared a trial that would have been a farce."

"How would you have pleaded?"

Cadbury brought his hands together, brought the tips of his index fingers to his lips, rested his eyes on Tuttle.

"It is not because of Brian Geary that I have asked you here."

His thoughts had evolved since employing Tuttle had occurred to him. Father Dowling, having confided in Cadbury Brian's behavior in Michigan and the possibility that he might have played some role in the death of Melvin Gorce, thought someone should keep an eye on the boy.

Brian's mother had had similar thoughts since he had been released from jail. "He is a disturbed young man, Amos."

But when Cadbury had talked to Brian he had found him eccentric but not unwell. There are those who are driven by an unslakable desire for holiness. The ordinary business of the world repels them, as a distraction from the one thing needful. Cadbury had told Brian he hoped he would find his path, and the young man had nodded and left.

There was someone else Amos Cadbury wished to have an eye kept on, and that was Catherine Burger's son. Who was the more unsettling, the facetious young pharmacist with the perpetual smile who had founded VOCL or the bearded hermit who had tried to murder his father? Cadbury knew he should agree with Father Dowling and seek to keep Brian from doing further harm. But that was not what he had decided to employ Tuttle for.

How to put this? Cadbury was not fearful that he would say it in a way that would offend Tuttle, but a lifetime in the law had made him enter into the most confidential conversations as if they would one day become public.

"Michael Geary was in the process of seeking an annulment of his marriage when he was killed. Once free, he hoped to marry another woman. That woman has a son."

It was surprisingly easy to convey his wishes to Tuttle without going into explanations that would have sounded unconvincing to himself. The scruffy little lawyer knew Catherine Burger and her son. He would be happy to keep an eye on them.

"Particularly the boy, Mr. Tuttle."

To give Tuttle any instructions would weight his investigation, and this was something Amos Cadbury was loath to do. He had no great confidence in Tuttle and he had agonized before calling him, but one factor decided him. He had heard of the odd comradeship between the lawyer and the member of the Pianone family who was holding down the family's quota on the police force, a time-honored tradition less imperative since the political fading of the Pianones, but now their witless relative was protected by contractual and other terms of employment. Cadbury had long suspected that Tuttle managed to secure such business as he did because of his ability to tap into police investigations through Pianone.

Cadbury stood and remained behind his desk. He had shaken Tuttle's hand once; he did not intend to make a habit of the performance.

"I will not ask how you intend to proceed, Mr. Tuttle. I leave it entirely in your hands. Needless to say, I should like as early a report as possible."

Tuttle dipped his head, meeting his hat halfway, and moved toward the door. There he stopped and looked back at Cadbury. "You haven't spoken to the police about this?"

"Good heavens no."

"Good."

The door closed on him, and Cadbury let himself down into his chair. He had supped with the devil with as long a spoon as he could manage and he felt exhausted. Ah, the things one does for a client. But it was demeaning to think that Amos Cadbury had allied himself with a man for whose disbarment he had twice voted, though failing to carry the others in the bar association with him. He could almost wish that he had attempted to deal directly with Pianone.

Keeping the tail on Gordon Furey had made sense until the autopsy report showed the killing of Michael Geary to be a cold premeditated act rather than the result of a flare-up argument in The Crock over lunch. Brian's confession had already weakened the case, such as it was, against Geary's brother-in-law, given the match between the boots Brian wore and the prints near the car in which his father had been killed. But the verdict of death by poison changed everything.

"He strangled a dead man," Monique Pippen said in awed tones.

"Why didn't somebody see that right away?"

"Somebody did," she said primly, giving him a significant look.

Had she? The problem was that she launched so many possible explanations of any crime that her boss, Jolson, would have been forgiven for ignoring this one. It did have the mark of one of her theories, Cy conceded to that vast anonymous audience to whom we address our unspoken thoughts.

"Did anyone suggest poison?"

Monique's favorite explanation had been that Michael Geary had died of a heart attack brought on by the excitement of the argument with Gordon Furey.

"That wouldn't have made for a strong case against Furey."

"Lieutenant Horvath, I was not thinking of making a case, but of showing that there was no case to be made. It would have been death without a crime."

"Nice."

"The poison in his insulin changes all that."

"What took so long to discover the hydrochloric acid?"

"Did you ever take chemistry?"

Cy had taken chemistry and physics and solid geometry and didn't remember a single thing from any of them. Does anyone? Keegan had said the same thing when he told Roger Dowling of the results of the autopsy. The priest began to shake his head a minute before he spoke.

"Have you forgotten that water seeks its own level, that it will freeze at thirty-two degrees, that the planets move around the sun and that if you let go of your fountain pen it will fall to the floor?"

This was oddly important to the priest and he didn't let it go until Phil Keegan agreed. "Only most of those things I knew before I studied science."

"Exactly. That's my point. You knew such things before, during and at present, when you claim to have forgotten so much."

"What's your point?"

"That you can know a death came about through unnatural causes without knowing what exactly those causes are. Dr. Jolson and his lovely assistant have refined what you already knew."

Keegan liked that, of course, but Jolson's lovely assistant pooh-poohed the thought when Cy offered it as his own. She knew that he knew there were all kinds of poisons that would leave no sign to the naked eye. No doubt. But Father Dowling's point explained why they went on watching Gordon Furey, the surveillance details reporting to Agnes Lamb.

"What a dull life Furey leads," Agnes said.

"Unlike ours."

She laughed. "You're right. What would my day look like if I were under surveillance?"

"Then you haven't noticed. Good."

"Cyril Horvath."

Just when you forgot it, Agnes reminded you how touchy she could be. Maybe she half believed that the department was out to rid itself of its only black detective and was gathering evidence to do her in.

"So he was poisoned after all."

"If his heart had failed, this was due to the hydrochloric acid being systematically injected into him. So who laced his insulin with acid?"

"The wife?"

Maureen Geary had been ruled out hitherto, because she had been visiting her daughter in South Bend at the time of the murder, but the poison did not require the presence of the poisoner at the time of death. Maureen had continued to fill her husband's prescription and make sure that he was taking care of himself. Agnes found that incredible, but then she wasn't married. Some habits are more basic than love. When couples fight the wife goes on preparing meals and the husband dutifully goes off to work. Taking care of Michael Geary's health had obviously been one of those things Maureen did without thinking about it.

"Make up your mind," Agnes retorted. She didn't like allusions made to her single status either. "Is she trying to keep him healthy or trying to kill him?"

"You know what the man said about consistency."

"The man?"

Geez, she was touchy today. Cy felt that one of his basic assumptions about life was being disproved. He had always thought he got along with people, especially women. Keegan kept telling him that, but he already knew it. Suddenly now he found himself baffled by three women, Jeanne, his wife, Monique Pippen and, today at least, Agnes Lamb. He was definitely going through a phase, and the faster he got through it, the better. Cy wanted only the comfortable and inarticulate happiness he had always known with Jeanne, but she sensed something was wrong. He was fascinated by Monique Pippen, and while he hadn't laid a glove on her, he had the feeling that if he did she wouldn't mind at all. Cy did not understand this. Women spoke easily to him because he constituted no threat. He was huge and unhandsome and reassuring and when he listened to some woman pour out her heart, whatever feelings he had were a million miles from sex. Not that he was blaming Monique. Part of her mystery was that she probably didn't know how flirty she was with him. If that continued and even escalated, it was his fault. And now it had Agnes Lamb on edge. She was the only one who had had the guts to ask him a few pointed questions about the assistant medical examiner.

"She of the golden Rumpelstiltskin hair."

"Her name is Monique Pippen."

"Monique," Agnes repeated the name as if she were entering it in evidence.

"It's French for Monica."

"When I mentioned your wife she wanted to know all about her."

"Yeah?"

"So I told Monique all about Jeanne."

"But you don't know all about Jeanne."

"Just the basics. How long you've been married, how true you are to one another, how accomplished you are in fending off predatory females."

"I thought that was going to be our secret."

"She's been warned," Agnes said. "And so have you."

If Agnes noticed, chances are others had too. Like Phil Keegan. If he had been capable of it, Cy would have blushed at the thought of Keegan imagining he would do anything to hurt Jeanne. Cy talked about it with Father Dowling. The priest wanted to know if any sin had been committed.

"No. Not yet."

"Not yet?"

"It's as if I expect something to happen and I won't be responsible but still it will happen. I won't be able to stop it."

Roger Dowling smiled. "Imagine a criminal telling you that. Not that you're a criminal. Actions start in the mind, sometimes they never make it into the real world, but thoughts themselves are real. Does the phrase 'occasion of sin' mean anything to you?"

Father Dowling put into words what Cy already knew. You sat around imagining things long enough, and before you knew it you were in trouble.

"I work with her."

"A lot?"

"I've made it a lot."

"You know the answer, Cy."

Why else do we have priests except to tell us what we already know? You had to hear it said, not just as another man's opinion, but as the way it was. The trouble was that he couldn't throw himself into his work to forget it, because doing his job was what brought him together with Monique. The only remedy he could think of was always having Agnes around when he was talking with Monique. And to insist on routine. A first item to look into was that Maureen Geary filled her husband's prescriptions. The second was the name of the druggist. Burger Apothecary. He and Agnes went down there and saw a pharmacist with "Oscar Celsius" engraved on the plastic tag pinned to his pale blue smock. He tipped it up and read it upside down.

"You're right. This is the wrong jacket."

"Who's Oscar Celsius?"

"He works the graveyard shift."

"Graveyard shift in the drugstore."

This pharmacist's name was Fraise; he had strawberry-blond hair that looked as if it had jam in it. "We're open twenty-four hours. Oscar works from ten till six in the morning."

After changing into a smock that bore the name Kenneth Fraise, he got out the file on Michael Geary. It went back a long way.

"Look who his doctor was."

"Was."

"Langsam. He committed suicide."

"Poison?" Agnes asked.

Fraise shook his head, but his hair didn't move. "You know the plastic bags your shirts come back from the laundry in? He pulled one of those over his head, after loading up on Valium."

"Was he alone at the time?"

Cy called Agnes off, gently, gently. If they ever wanted information on Dr. Langsam's suicide they had better sources than Fraise.

"Can you go on filling a prescription forever?"

Fraise was the kind of man who wanted to tell you all about his profession, now that Agnes had asked. Cy tuned him out, figuring Agnes could do the listening since she had done the asking. The area behind the prescription counter was neat as a pin. Geary's records had been entered on the computer, a database common to the three Burger drugstores, but the originals had been kept too. They went into file cabinets built into the lower portion of the counter. Maybe when the place was redecorated for the electronic age they would be removed.

"Usually the wife picked up the prescription. There's nothing wrong with that. The spouse, I mean. A sister-in-law is something else."

"Geary's sister-in-law picked up his insulin?"

Fraise was startled by Cy's questions. "I'm only going by what Oscar told me."

"When does he get the chance, if you're on different shifts?"

Fraise laughed. "He comes five minutes before my shift is over. We share an apartment too, figuring we'd never be there together."

"Is he there now?"

"He may still be in bed."

The early-morning smell of eggs and bacon greeted them when Oscar Celsius opened the door.

"I am Lieutenant Horvath, this is Detective Lamb."

Celsius nodded and went on rubbing butter into the back of his hand. "Fraise called. Come on in. I just burned myself."

He wore pajamas and his hair made him look like the real wild guy in a rock group, but this was because he hadn't brushed it since getting up. They went into the kitchen, where he went on making his breakfast.

"Michael Geary's sister-in-law filled his prescription?"

He groaned. "Why does Kenneth insist on making a federal case of that? Insulin is not a controlled substance, for crying out loud."

"It was his sister-in-law?"

There was the corner of a handkerchief sticking out of the pocket of his pajama top, and he sniffled over the stove.

"That's what she said." He sighed. "It was a time of transition. The man had a new doctor, he had a new prescription."

"We saw it in the file."

"What's the big deal?" He laid strips of cooked bacon on a paper towel.

"Weren't you surprised at the new prescription?"

"Of course not. Dr. Langsam is dead. He should have gotten one from his new doctor."

"It was your suggestion?"

"No. The woman who said she was Mrs. Furey said we had the prescription on file. Why would I doubt her? I made the mistake of mentioning it to Fraise."

"No, you didn't."

Celsius stopped scrambling eggs and stared at Cy.

"Your mistake was in not telling us."

The doctor who had written the prescription, a young man named Hawser, closed his door when he learned why they had come. He had the look of a man who did not want the whisper of malpractice to harm his fledgling career.

"He told me *he* was Michael Geary. That was the assumption all along. Geary's records were sent to me from Langsam's office when the Gearys decided to become my patients. He came and I urged him to try the experimental device I'm hoping to market. I realized my mistake when I saw Gordon Furey's picture in the paper. I told myself it was unimportant. It was a harmless deception to do his brother-in-law a favor."

"Wasn't his picture in the paper because he had been suspected of killing Michael Geary?"

Hawser looked ill. They left him to his gnawing conscience and the fear of litigation.

And so it was that they drove to the building where Furey had his office. In the garage, they checked to see if Furey's car was there. A kid in a baseball cap pointed across the crowded garage to where the

Avanti was parked. They got into the elevator and were lifted to Furey's floor.

The secretary seemed to be remembering Furey's earlier unhappy encounter with the police.

"He's gone home."

"Why do you say that?"

She was hugging an armful of files. She dropped her chin and looked at Cy over his glasses.

"Because he has gone home."

"And he isn't in his office."

"Haven't you learned that he can't be where he isn't?"

"Check it, Agnes."

The women might have been dancing with the files as she tried to get between Agnes and the closed door of Furey's office, but Agnes had it open and was inside. A moment later she looked out.

"How many ways are there out of that office?"

"You're standing in it."

"He's not there, Cy."

He didn't have to tell Agnes where they were going then. In the elevator she said she'd bet that visit to the drugstore was in the surveillance reports.

"When it rains it pours."

This was the equivalent of three cheers from him, and Agnes knew it. Whoever was tailing Furey had better know where he had gone without his car. The Avanti was so conspicuous it made following Furey easy, maybe too easy.

But Gordon Furey was in the Avanti, behind the wheel, with a plastic bag pulled down over his head, dead.

Aunt Betty had had two miscarriages, before, with the help of hormonal treatments, she had her first child, a boy. And then, as if her system had finally gotten the hang of it, she had three more children in rapid succession, prompting Gordon to say proudly that his wife was more Catholic than the pope.

"Four is it at my age," she had said to Kate, whose own pregnancy now made her the object of auntly confidences on matters maternal. "When you've had as much trouble as I did having kids, your impulse is to have as many as you can."

"To prove you can?"

Betty's hair had turned a marvelous silver gray almost overnight. "I stopped dyeing it."

"It's beautiful."

"Natural always is."

It was Aunt Betty who had told Kate about Natural Family Planning. She was a great defender of the Church's moral teaching in sexual matters and had actually read *Humanae Vitae*. It turned out that Mark hadn't. How many theologians had? Of course they rejected it, as a class, so Mark could be relying on his mentors. He had been surprised when she had told him she wasn't on the pill.

"Why not?"

"It's against your religion."

"My religion?"

He chose to pretend that it really didn't matter that she didn't go to Mass or believe anything anymore; she was still a Catholic.

"How could I stop being one?"

"What's the point?"

"Hey, that's my question."

Mark had no satisfying answer to it, but Aunt Betty considered it the most important question in the world. "I was raised a Methodist, which meant nothing. I don't mean just that my parents drank like everybody else, there was no set of things one was supposed to believe. I tried to take it seriously, but that seemed to mean getting arms to various insurgent groups. When I took instructions, before I married Gordie, I thought it was just more of the same. Then I started to read."

She had read books Kate hadn't even heard of. St. Francis de Sales, St. Louis de Montfort, the two St. Theresas.

"Two?"

"Of Avila and of Lisieux. Both Carmelites. Edith Stein too, another Carmelite."

Mark had heard of her but thought she was pre–Vatican II, meaning there was no need to read her.

"Pre–Vatican II?" Aunt Betty's smile was sad. "Most things are. I'll tell you one thing. If the Church was only what it has looked to be since the council, I'd still be a Methodist."

Expecting the baby made Kate feel even closer to Aunt Betty. She felt she had to tell her that her faith had slipped away in college.

"It sounds like what you rejected was a crazy account of the council."

Kate resisted the notion that Aunt Betty, a convert, knew more about Catholicism than her teachers and Mark and all those theologians he liked so much. The Church Betty had joined no longer existed, if Mark and his professors were right.

"There's only one Church and I joined it."

And she practiced her faith. She and Gordie were signed up for an hour a week at their parish's perpetual adoration of the Eucharist program. Betty was the one who went, from nine to ten every Wednesday evening, kneeling before the gaudy golden monstrance in which a large consecrated host was placed.

"What do you do for an hour?"

"Do you know what the Curé d'Ars said to that question?"

"Betty, I don't even know who he is."

"St. Jean Vianney. A dumb holy French priest. Anyway he said he knelt there looking at Jesus and Jesus looked at him."

She also read, those authors Kate had not read. Betty suggested the autobiography of Saint Theresa. "It's dynamite."

"What do you and Betty talk about?" her mother asked.

"Oh, babies and stuff."

"Be careful, you'll end up having a houseful of kids."

"That doesn't look so bad."

"You have to raise them and educate them, you know, not just have them."

Betty said that if God gave her four children He would also provide. "Lots of people would call that Irresponsible Parenthood, trusting God. He's a lot more reliable than we are or the economy or all the other things we depend on. Maybe raising them to be Yuppies isn't the best thing we can do for our kids anyway."

"She's a child of the sixties," her mother said.

"That's true," Betty admitted. "But I wasn't a peacenik. I lost a brother in Vietnam, his name is on the monument. He loved the Vietnamese and was there to help them. Eventually even the government forgot why we were there, but he didn't. But I did love the nonconformity. It became silly, of course, drugs and sex and all that, but there was something Franciscan about it in many cases. Out of the rat race."

"And then you married Uncle Gordie."

"And started our own commune."

Betty was a home schooler, teaching her own kids, trusting the parochial school no more than the public. "I want them all to go to heaven."

The way she said it, heaven was as real as Chicago. Which is why she dismissed the suggestion that Gordie had committed suicide.

"Nonsense. Those in despair commit suicide. He had no motive."

But all the accounts of the discovery of Gordon Furey's body behind the wheel of his Avanti, staring sightlessly through the plastic bag that had smothered him, mentioned that he had been under investigation in the death of his brother-in-law, who had also been found dead in his car.

Kate's mother lost it when she heard the news, going completely to pieces, so that it was Betty comforting her rather than the other way around. The police were buffaloed by the death of Uncle Gordie, at least Agnes Lamb was. The media referred to it as a copycat killing, meaning that like Aunt Betty they rejected suicide as an explanation.

"There's no sign of a struggle," Detective Lamb said, giving the main reason for thinking death was self-inflicted. "He had enough Valium in him to make it unlikely that he would have feared anything enough to fight it."

"I think you're wrong."

"So does your aunt."

"She would know. They were like that." The two women looked at Kate's crossed fingers.

"If he was killed we need a killer."

If Aunt Betty found relief of a sort in the midst of tragedy for herself and her four children, Kate in turn sighed inwardly at the thought that it could not have been Brian. When he had confessed to killing their father, she had believed it, believed it in the same way she could have believed it of herself. It had been devastating to learn that her father was asking the Church to declare his marriage null and void, in some sense to say those years had never been, to deny that whatever quarrels and unhappiness there had also been love and joy. Sometimes Kate could remember her childhood as suffused with happiness, with a sense of safety that enveloped the future as well as the present. Do parents ever fully realize that they are the world for their children, for better or worse? A child's notion of who and what and why he is gets taken in with his mother's milk, the do's and don't's of infancy, the preparation for the world outside the family. The child takes what his parents have given him to kindergarten. It's already settled then. Brian had lived in a kind of awe of their father that had been progressively harder to reconcile with the actual man. Oh yes, Brian could have killed him. The dope even thought he had. Somehow the image of Brian strangling a man already beyond his reach summarized the relation between father and son.

But there was no such motive in the case of Uncle Gordie. He might have been the only one in the family with whom Brian could discuss his crazy desire to punish himself with religion. Betty had told Kate that.

"Gordie actually told him he had thought of becoming a priest himself."

"Was he an altar boy?"

"I believe he was."

"Then he thought about it. That's the point of altar boys."

Kate had unwittingly furnished Betty with ammunition to use against her pastor, who was weakening in the matter of altar girls. From Gordie, Brian had received encouragement in the pursuit of his vocation.

"His vocation? He was meant to be a chemist."

It was that scientific background that had brought back Kate's fear that Brian had killed their father. About his diabetes he had been as secretive as he was about his partial plate. Kate had never seen her father inject himself with insulin; he might always have had the automatic apparatus. Once she had opened the bathroom door when he had his partial out and he was enraged.

Brian knew all about chemicals and drugs; he would have known what to mix with the insulin that would have the desired effect. When she had moved edgewise into this possibility her mother had shaken her head.

"He wasn't home, Kate."

"Do we really know where Brian was at any given time?"

"Oh for heaven's sakes. I would know if he were home."

But he had been home and she hadn't known and Kate was left with her unsettling thought that Brian had killed their father. The strangling of the corpse would then have been a diversionary act, performed with the knowledge that eventually he would be proved innocent. But this was absurd. Perhaps someone could have been that devious, but that someone was not Brian.

"What's the connection?" Agnes Lamb asked when Kate suggested that whoever killed her father had killed her uncle. The black detective seemed to be trying to match the uninformative expression of Lieutenant Horvath.

"Do you think it was an accident both were found in their cars?"

"Was your uncle poisoned?"

"Don't you know?"

"If he was, we will find out," Horvath said.

"If they had both died in bed would you attribute death to the same cause?"

Kate decided that detectives are only at ease when they are in charge, formulating the questions, defining the topic. If both men had died in bed, the chances were her father would have been in the wrong one.

"Maybe he died somewhere else and was put in his car," Agnes Lamb said deadpan, exchanging a glance with Horvath.

"Let's get back to your questions," Kate said, keeping control of herself.

"You have any more questions, Agnes?"

"No, Lieutenant."

The black detective obviously bristled at being addressed by her given name rather than her title. Or did she prefer her family name?

As far as Freddy knew, the investigation into Michael Geary's death had gone off in a safer direction, the danger that his mother should somehow be involved in it diminished. She was a woman in love with her own goodness and could not for long bear the scrutiny of her relation with Michael Geary. But she had given a frosty glance to the detective who asked how intimately involved she had been with Geary.

"Unless he were free, we could only be friends."

"By free you mean divorced."

"No."

"What do you mean?"

His mother drew back her shoulders, pointing them a few degrees to the east, while her chin was a few degrees to the west. Her joined knees, just visible below the hem of her dress, also pointed east. Her hands were folded in her lap. Her expression was that of a Boticellli madonna.

"Free in the eyes of the Church."

Oh God. Freddy did not want all that in the papers. His mother was at her smuggest when she spoke of her annulment, making her points with the precision of the grade school teacher she once had been.

Fortunately the detectives had not been interested in the subject of annulment.

"Would he have left anything here?"

"I beg your pardon?"

"Mrs. Burger, it is a matter of record that you were good friends with the deceased, that he visited you—"

"It is a matter of record only because I told you."

"That's right. And what you said has been corroborated by others."

"Corroborated?"

"Other people told us the same."

"You make it sound as if you needed some proof I was telling you the truth."

"When he visited you, did he ever leave things lying about?" The black detective opened her hands and looked vaguely around.

"I've no idea what you mean."

God, she was cool. Freddy found himself marveling at his mother's performance. Hadn't it even crossed her mind that they might have found out about Geary's partial? He would have had to replace it, God knows what he might have told his dentist. It was just such trivia that attracted the police. So Freddy sat very quietly, waiting to see whether they would ask if Michael Geary had ever left a partial plate lying about, one that got lost and had to be replaced. Of course not even she knew the whole story on that.

There were things about his mother's growing friendship with Michael Geary that Freddy could never have asked her. Even if he could, she would have made him feel ashamed for asking, as she had with the police. That his mother should be seeing a married man, a Catholic husband and father, after making so much of her precious annulment, had genuinely baffled Freddy. His talent as the secret sharer had been put to its most demanding test.

During one of Geary's prolonged afternoon visits, Freddy had entered the house silently, prepared to leave as silently as he had come; he just had to know whether the relationship was platonic. He came through the woods from the back, the river side, and crossed quickly to the lowest of the three levels of the house and let himself in. To one who entered the front of the house, where he was would have been thought to be the basement. It was a large comfortable room, one his father had designed. It might have been the thing about his marriage he had found difficult to part with.

Freddy moved the sliding door back into place, not letting it click, and felt his whole body to be a membrane receiving the sounds of the house. Through the various hums and motors and murmurs of the house he discerned voices above him. From the top of the stairs, he could tell where they were. He went up the risers as if they were beads of a rosary, praying that there was nothing wrong. From the kitchen it became clear the voices were not coming from the living room.

He wanted to leave then; he really did not want to discover such a flaw in his mother. If flaw there was. He had to know. He moved down the hallway toward the room his parents had shared. Halfway there he knew the voices were not coming from the master bedroom. It was as if his prayers had been answered.

But then his mother's throaty laugh struck him like a blow. They were on the upper level, where Freddy's room was, and the spare bedroom. Freddy floated up the half stairs as if he were a bodiless ghost and stepped into the bathroom. From there he had heard proof positive that his mother did not intend to delay the fleshly delights her love for Geary promised. The annulment would make them licit, but in the meantime, we are all sinners. He was about to burst in on them when he noticed the partial plate on the sink.

He snatched it up like a kid, somehow certain this would provide revenge enough. Afterward, he could not remember leaving the house. A few minutes later he sat trembling in his car in the little lovers' lane across the road. He buried the partial there, as if he were burying the man who had been in bed with his mother. Those phony teeth on their silver support were Michael Geary. Freddy could have found the burial spot blindfolded. In fact he had, when he dug up the partial again later.

The police had not come to Norling; he had gone to them with the information that he had made a partial denture for the man so mysteriously murdered behind his insurance agency. Freddy had made an appointment for a cleaning, but Dr. Norling checked him out before turning him over to the dental assistant. And checked out was the word. He made quite a show of pulling on his rubber gloves, getting them just right over each tapered finger. He leaned against Freddy when he asked him to please open his mouth. They met for drinks and Freddy got the story.

"Lost it at his girlfriend's. I didn't quite get why he couldn't just pick it up, or why she didn't send it, or what. Maybe the husband found it." Norling pursed his lips in a suppressed smile and look wide-eyed at Freddy.

"Ah, the follies of the heterosexual."

Norling was nervous at the prospect of frank talk in a public place.

"You'll never need a partial, I can tell you that. What wonderful shape your teeth are in."

"Thanks to my mother."

"To all mothers," Norling said fervently, lifting his drink.

Freddy excused himself and left by the back door. He had made the appointment in the name of Gordon Furey, whose surveillance of his mother had just become impossible to overlook. It was on the way home that he had the chilling thought that Furey might have been on the job when Freddy entered the house. So what if he was. Couldn't a man enter his own home?

Of course she couldn't ask him if he had seen a partial lying about the house, but for several days afterward he had sensed her perplexity. How on earth could such a thing be lost? If there was ever a time when he had been in a position to compare her facade with what lay beneath, it was then. Her composure soon returned, as well as her virginal manner.

"Are you buying insurance or something?"

"Insurance? Why do you ask?"

"Someone said he had seen you with an insurance agent."

"I don't think Mr. Michael Geary would appreciate that description."

"Doesn't he sell insurance?"

"Indeed he does. To all and sundry. He wanted particularly to talk to me about financial management."

"Better check it out with Amos Cadbury."

She laughed dismissively. "There is scarcely any need for that. You'd like Geary, I think. He is such a type, a pure type."

"Am I to meet him?"

"That was just an expression, Freddy. Of course you're not going to meet him."

"And you're not buying any insurance."

She grew serious. "Actually he made a lot of sense about car insurance. I may want to hear more about that."

Freddy felt everything that Hamlet had felt about Gertrude, his faithless mother. Ah, frailty, thy name is woman. Did she confess before approaching the altar? Of course she did. She did everything like a good Catholic, even sinning. Freddy's rage, stirred by his mother, was diverted to her faith, her annulment, her pious practices which went on even while she and the abominable Michael Geary discussed car insurance in the horizontal position. He could imagine the jokes about complete coverage, tailgating, collision. Did they say a little prayer first, grace before adultery? Oh God, God, how he hated it all.

There was therapy of a sort in getting Christopher James started on Michael Geary.

"He's courting my mother," Freddy said insouciantly and with his constant smile.

"Geary! That snake."

"He turned out to be a Lotto winner for you."

The money had been something but apparently not enough. The fact that Geary was still at it infuriated James.

"Tell your mother about him."

"She's unlikely to discuss him with me."

"Frederick, listen. She should know. If you would like, I could—"

"No. Don't. I mean it. I am truly sorry I brought it up. It was a joke in very poor taste. He tried to sell her some insurance, that's all."

"Tell her not to buy."

"How is your lovely daughter?"

James actually got a little protective, as if he thought Freddy might want to make a move on Amanda. The name he had liked, definitely, and thank God her pictures did not do her justice. Not that Freddy would have let a lack of beauty prevent his overtures. He had found in Amanda a kindred spirit; they hated the same things. No need for James to know what chums Freddy and Amanda had become. She had embraced the idea of VOCL enthusiastically, but he suggested she remain a silent member. And of course she had a morbid interest in the continuing saga of Michael Geary.

"She's in Florida," James had said, somewhat testily.

"To boldly go where no man has gone before . . . ," Freddy intoned. It was one of his charms to know verbatim the lead-ins to dozens of television shows, and he had the original "Star Trek" intro down to perfection.

"What's that?" James said, frowning.

"I was thinking of Florida."

"I've heard that somewhere before."

"Milton, isn't it?"

"If I ever read any Milton it would have been in high school."

"That's the age when memories stick."

Did they not, though. Freddy had watched his parents' marriage disintegrate before his eyes. They seemed oblivious to his being in the house. Did they think he wouldn't hear their quarrels, the threats, the angry tears, the doors slamming? Freddy watched enough television to understand that his predicament was not unknown, but he felt no fellowship with the wisecracking kids who joked through divorces and the wives of their father and new husband of the mother. His father seemed determined to play his role in such a script. What wife was he on now, so to speak? Or girlfriend, as he called them. He was getting a little tired of marrying the women he slept with, as once he had grown weary of sleeping with the women he married.

Of course Freddy took his mother's side. Children usually do. After his father moved out, finally, no more harsh words disturbed in the night, no tears. His mother's manner more than made up for the disrupting effect of the divorce. There would be just the two of them. Sometimes at night, when the two of them were first alone, he would slip into the twin bed next to hers, the one that had been his father's, and enjoy her reaction in the morning.

"I never heard you come in."

"I didn't want to wake you."

To be enfolded in her arms was like being taken into an angel's wings. Freddy developed an intense interest in his religion, to his mother's obvious satisfaction. Perhaps she saw it as a criticism of his father. Perhaps it was. But then she had initiated annulment proceedings, and soon the unctuous discussions began that Freddy had found far worse than the discussions preceding the divorce.

I am what they have made me, that was his message to the world. He had no interest in genetic explanations of his lifestyle, as if some biological freak explained it. He wanted his parents to be responsible, particularly his mother. Responsible for something neither of them apparently so much as suspected. The fact was like having his own private missile silo from which eventually he could summon a retaliation and destroy what had once been a nuclear family.

He scarcely spoke to his father, and vice versa, but he had remained on the best of terms with his mother, sustaining at a level of facetiousness and jocularity the closeness that had sprung up between them after his father's departure. Was it any wonder that he had reacted as he had to the annulment? It seemed a way for her to deny his reality. And then Geary. Of all people, Geary, the endlessly righteous. Well, they made a pair after all, whited sepulchers, disporting themselves in the afternoon.

Who else could his mother have called when Michael Geary died in her bed if not her Freddy?

Father Dowling's interest in the finding of Gordon Furey's body behind the wheel of his Avanti bordered on the joyful.

"In his car! Just like Michael Geary."

Phil Keegan shook his head. "Just unlike. The one was poisoned, the other suffocated. The body of the first was assaulted after death, that of the second wasn't. And the first was found in a Lincoln, the second in an Avanti."

Roger Dowling nodded through this litany of irrelevancies, as he promptly called them.

"The killer of Michael Geary will be the killer of Gordon Furey."

"What makes you so happy about this?"

"It can't have been Brian Geary."

"Does he want to confess to killing his uncle too?"

But Roger Dowling was not to be put off by Keegan's professional skepticism. The death of Gordon Furey wrote *finis* to the priest's fear that Brian had killed his father. Brian's scientific background would have been there to draw on if he had wanted to kill him. It was assumed that he was in Minnesota when his father died, but when he claimed to have been in Fox River, no one near his hermitage had been able to deny it, although no one could confirm his absence either. But he could have slipped in, no doubt about that, given the way he had gone off to South Bend and then to Michigan. However implausible Brian seemed to Father Dowling as a killer, there was no doubt what the young man had set out to do when he looped that wire around his father's neck and, averting his eyes, twisted and twisted, not realizing there was no life left to be squeezed from his father's body. A man who could do that could also poison him, but why do both? Because he had done neither.

"Was a statuette found with Gordon Furey's body?"

Phil Keegan tipped his head and closed one eye. "Will you be disappointed when I tell you no?"

"Are you going to tell me that?"

"There was no madonna in the front seat of the Avanti, where Furey was found." Keegan sipped his beer. "There was one in the backseat, however."

"The mark of the beast."

"Brian Geary had bought such a statue for his uncle's car."

"Then you checked."

"We check everything, Roger. Especially any tendency to jump to conclusions."

Phil Keegan could worry about the logical steps jumped, but when had pure logic ever settled anything? Besides, he had been reassured by Tuttle, sent to him by Amos Cadbury.

"But I know Mr. Tuttle, Amos," the priest said when Cadbury began a lengthy apology for sending such a creature to St. Hilary's.

"The man is impossible to avoid."

No point in telling Cadbury that if he and Tuttle represented extremes of the profession there was in the end small difference between them. Both trafficked in the suspicious and resentments of mankind, everyone jealous of his rights, sure they had been curtailed, hungry for retribution. One saw it all in the parables, the unjust steward begging a mercy he had refused to others. These were not condescending observations. Like a lawyer, a priest's business is with sinners, there being no alternative clientele. Amos Cadbury had hired Tuttle to report on Brian Geary.

"Does this shock you, Father?"

"I think we could watch someone twenty-four hours a day for years and never peer into the moral self. A person may reveal his soul to us, but we cannot otherwise be sure of it. Of course even my account of myself is not fully reliable."

"*Neque meipsum iudico,*" Cadbury murmured, startling the priest.

"Do you read Paul in the Vulgate, Amos? You astonish and delight me."

"And deceive you. I know two lines of the Vulgate New Testament. That phrase from Paul, cited several times during a semester on jurisprudence by a wise old Jesuit, and John the Baptist's words. He must increase while I decrease. *Illum oportet crescere, me autem minui.*"

"The same professor?"

"No, no. This was the motto of a bishop in another diocese. His priests thought he was recommending the motto to them, he being the *illum* of the phrase. Priests are a mordant lot, are they not, Father?"

"Like yourself, Amos. Like yourself."

"Brian travels like the proverbial salesman, though insisting on modest modes, when possible. How many people do you know who ride a bus nowadays? And I mean interurban travel."

Amos had also learned of the trips to Notre Dame and Michigan. Can anything remain unknown for long?

"What is there left for Tuttle to tell me?"

"I deliberately steal his thunder, Father. He will want to dramatize."

If Amos Cadbury felt a fastidious remoteness from Tuttle it was nothing to Marie Murkin's. She actually left him standing on the doorstep while she reported to the pastor that a man named Tuttle wished to see him.

"I'm expecting him."

Marie looked at him long enough to see he was kidding, then went grumbling back to the front door. A minute later, calling a cheery thank-you after Marie, who was retreating to the kitchen, perhaps to wash her hands of the whole visit, Tuttle took the chair Father Dowling indicated.

"All these books, Father. I told myself I only imagined there were so many, but there they are."

"Are you a reader, Mr. Tuttle?"

"Only in my field, Father. Oh, the odd paperback once in a way. And of course the newspapers."

Whereupon he reached into the tweed hat he had seemed to balance in his hand and drew forth newspaper clippings. He stood and began to arrange them on the desk, in chronological order.

"I wonder if you noticed these, Father."

Father Dowling stood next to the lawyer and saw that they were identical with Marie Mulkin's collection.

"What we have here, Father, is a series of what are now called hate crimes. You might think them random. There are similarities, but differences too. Imagine, a dead animal in a confessional."

Roger Dowling waited to see how much Amos Cadbury underestimated Tuttle. He must be careful not to take undue pleasure from telling Marie that she and Tuttle had an identical newspaper collection.

Tuttle put the tweed hat on his head, then quickly took it off. "That is not all."

Tuttle did not disappoint. He mentioned the dashboard madonnas that had been found in Geary's car. He paused for effect.

"And now a missing lawn statue has been found in Gordon Furey's car. It is the signature of the one responsible for two deaths as well as a series of . . ." Tuttle sought in thin air the word he wanted.

"Sacrileges?"

"Sacrileges!" He shook his head in admiration. "It takes a priest to understand these things. The police?" He swept his arm in an arc. "Coincidence. Some coincidence!"

"What is your explanation? But first, what can I serve you?"

"Do I smell sauerkraut?"

"In the Alsatian mode. Marie!"

Half a minute's silence, then the scraping of a chair in the kitchen. Marie appeared in the doorway and stared at a spot on the wall.

"I've found a customer for your sauerkraut, Marie. Would you bring our guest a serving, with lots of sausage in it."

But Marie's eye had dropped to the clippings on the desk, and they drew her like a lodestone.

"When did you take these?"

"Those are Mr. Tuttle's clippings, not yours. We were just discussing them. They seem to bear some relation to the killings that have been going on."

"I told you that."

"Ah well, great minds."

Tuttle now held his hat in both hands and dipped his head. "I haven't smelled sauerkraut like that since I was a kid."

"Your mother made it?"

"I never knew my mother, not really. No, it was at the home, where my father had to put me for a few years. He never forgave himself. When the meal was sauerkraut, we could have all we wanted."

Marie would have had to have a heart of stone to withstand this. Father Dowling only hoped the story was true.

Tuttle ate with such relish, with Marie standing by, that the housekeeper found it difficult to repress her satisfaction. She was regularly disappointed in the pastor's reaction to her culinary triumphs, Roger Dowling's taste in matters of food being woefully democratic. But Phil

Keegan made up for it both in the quantity he consumed and the praise he lavished on her concoctions. Marie would obviously have liked to take similar satisfaction in the famished way in which Tuttle descended on the heaping dish she brought to him on a tray. From time to time his eye lifted in eloquent testimony to her prowess.

"Ah," he exclaimed when he had finished. "That is even better than at the home."

Equivocal praise, but sufficient to prompt Marie to suggest more. But the little lawyer held up his hand. "I am here on business, not pleasure, ma'am."

Marie withdrew with the tray, her hands too occupied to close the study door. Father Dowling closed it, then looked receptively at Tuttle.

"Mr. Cadbury said you'd be coming by."

"Oh, this goes far beyond what I did for Mr. Cadbury, Father."

"I had thought it might."

"And I don't just mean those clippings, either, though I did not share that with Cadbury. A lawyer's life is a dog's life, Father, unless of course one is established in the manner of Amos Cadbury. The main lot of us have a more difficult time, waiting for the public to seek us out. Of course we can advertise now, but that does little good except in luring people who want to sue for millions on little basis. I can't afford to take on clients on the remote hope that years from now some money will be forthcoming. So I keep a sharp lookout."

"I've no doubt of it."

"As often as not it's some item of information that proves to be the Open Pumpernickel. Take the case of Michael Geary. The man had separated from his wife, she had filed for divorce, he himself had appealed to the Church for an annulment. Well, experience tells me that in a situation like that, the old rules are best. *Cherchez la femme.* A man gets rid of his wife not to be a bachelor, but to take on another wife. It's human nature."

"And there was another woman?"

"There was. Catherine Burger."

"Good heavens."

"You know her?"

"Yes I do."

"A Catholic woman, I believe. You understand my interest began before the unfortunate death of Mr. Geary."

"And what prompted your interest?"

"Divorces, alas, make up much of one's business, Father. It's not a matter of approving or disapproving, they're simply a matter of fact.

Statistical fact. One in two marriages ends in the divorce courts, Father Dowling, make what we will of it. And divorces involve lawyers."

"You represented Michael Geary?"

"Not exactly. I was looking into the background, you might say. I had an intermittent stakeout at the Burger residence. How regular he was. Geary I mean. You could set your watch by him, which considerably eased my task. I would take up my post half an hour before he would arrive."

"He came to see Mrs. Burger?"

"He favored afternoons, Father. Wednesday at three, Monday or Friday during the noon hour."

Which was sadder, these furtive meetings or the fact that they had been recorded with such exactitude? Roger Dowling imagined the sanctimonious Michael Geary keeping his assignation. It was more difficult to fit Catherine Burger into the picture, but as Tuttle had observed, it was human nature. How sad, however, to think of the little lawyer-voyeur, hoping to profit from the weaknesses of others.

"On the fateful day, a Monday you remember, he arrived at one o'clock. We know now that he had lunched with his brother-in-law, Gordon Furey. They had exchanged words and parted on an angry note. Michael Geary arrived at the Burger house just as I was about to leave, thinking he would not be coming. He seemed upset and preoccupied when he turned in the drive. I made a note of the time and settled down to wait. The average length of stay was one hour and fifteen minutes."

So short a time? But illicit passion must take the time that is offered. Tuttle recounted this matter-of-factly, without any sense of intruding on the privacy of others. Perhaps technically they were breaking the law. Is adultery still punishable as a crime? But these two would be more aware of the Law of God.

"When an hour had passed, I became alert. The son drove in about that time, and I made a note of that. This had happened before."

"While Geary was in the house?"

"That's right."

"But surely that puts a very different light on things."

"Not necessarily. Freddy, as he's called, is an odd one. He could make a fortune as a private detective, I think. But on this day there was no effort to conceal his arrival. Something was afoot, I was sure of it."

Half an hour later, Geary's car had come down the drive from the house. "Freddy was at the wheel."

"Alone?"

"Alone. Several possibilities occurred. It might have been a practical joke, of a kind. Removing the man's car while he was seeing the boy's mother. But something in his expression as he turned onto the river road told me otherwise. I followed him."

"And where did he go?"

"He turned in at Michael Geary Insurance."

"Good heavens."

"Here I must blame myself, Father. I ended my pursuit and returned to my office. You can imagine my chagrin when I heard the news of Geary's being found dead in his car behind the agency."

"So he didn't die there."

Tuttle nodded approvingly, as if Father Dowling were gaining his approval. "Exactly. He died when he was with the woman and she called her son to remove the body."

"Have you told anyone else of this?"

Tuttle shook his head. "Not until this moment. And now, Father, I ask your advice. As a lawyer, I might be thought to have concealed evidence relevant to a criminal investigation. My defense would be that I would have to make inferences any defense attorney would get laughed out of court. It would be argued that Geary left the house in some other fashion and that the son was simply returning his car to him. What happened in the parking lot behind the agency? I can only speculate. But your study is not a court of law, Father Dowling. What should I do?"

"What had you thought of doing?"

"Coming here."

"Nothing else?"

One thinks of the betrayer as malicious, but treachery comes from weakness or some lesser desire—for money, perhaps, or some small notoriety. Thirty pieces of silver was enough to buy a plot of ground, and how could that compensate? Tuttle's problem seemed to be that he could not decide on the one he would betray. Catherine? Her son, Freddy? Perhaps the Geary family, who had been put through enough and would not want this bizarre story made public. What after all did it contribute? But of course Geary had been killed, and if his death had occurred at the Burger house, then Tuttle was obliged legally as well as morally to make this known. Father Dowling told him as much.

"But think of the family, Father."

"Which family?"

"I suppose neither is much of a family anymore."

Father Dowling picked up his telephone and began to dial.

"Are you calling Captain Keegan?" Tuttle did not protest. Rather, he sat back with the air of one who has accomplished his mission.

"Catherine Burger."

The little lawyer leapt to his feet, clamped his hat on his head, removed it, seemed about to dance up and down in his excited disappointment.

Daddy never figured the hour's difference in time when he tried to call her, and then when he did get through he adopted such an accusatory tone, as if she were supposed to be sitting by the phone twenty-four hours a day, waiting for him to decide to call.

"Daddy, I was sitting by the pool."

"At eight o'clock in the morning?"

"No, at nine. This is the Eastern Zone."

A pause. "Why don't you take the portable phone I gave you down to the pool?"

"Did you try to reach me on that?"

"Of course."

"What on earth was so urgent?"

The doors of the balcony were open and the curtains moved wraithlike in the afternoon breeze, as did the palm tree whose top just reached her balcony. The sea was dark blue with occasional whitecaps; the sky was sky blue and the sand stretched white in the sun. Because the sun was behind her apartment now, it was possible to have the balcony doors open while she listened to Daddy giving her the latest incredible installment from Chicago.

"No one knows this yet, not even the police, so whatever you do don't say anything."

Poor Daddy. Did he think the indolent inhabitants of Marco Island cared about what was happening in Fox River, Illinois? But then there must be as many centers of the universe as there are people.

"I never talk about home." Her voice was level as she spoke, but she knew he would take her remark to indicate the continuing trauma of the sexual harassment by Michael Geary that had made her financially comfortable before the age of forty.

"You never need work again," Daddy had said when the archdiocese settled.

"Is it so much?"

"Capital is always more than an amount. It is possibility. With proper investment, it will increase in value even as you live on it."

That seemed a strange objective, but then unlike Daddy she had no one to whom to leave what money she amassed. Was he counting what would come to her on his death? But of course Daddy never thought of dying; that was why he was immune to the attractions of religion. Amanda had started to go to Mass again. The church on Marco Island had been added to several times to accommodate the retired faithful from the North. There were even balconies overlooking the original nave, and of course Amanda was reminded of the choir loft at Blessed Sacrament. What her father had accused Michael Geary of seemed almost as real as what had actually happened there.

"Wh should I be interested in Catherine Burger or her son?" she asked, interrupting what Daddy was saying.

"Just listen. She came to me because a priest had told her to talk to the police. Obviously she doesn't want to do that."

"Why did she come to you?"

"Her son recommended it."

"I should think he's the one who would be in trouble."

"If any of it happened, Amanda. That is the point. It is a fantastic story. I don't believe it, I don't think anyone would."

"Why would she tell you such a thing if it wasn't true?"

"She may think it's true. People believe things happened that didn't."

It was fitting that he should stop himself there. How he had insisted that she remember what Michael Geary did to her, and in church. It was an abomination, they could not let it pass. If she agreed, it was because it seemed a way of paying Michael back for no longer wanting to take her home. She had come to live for those drives, his tenor voice, his arms about her.

"Why did her son tell her to go to you? Does he believe it happened too?" If Catherine Burger was cast in Amanda's role, let her son play her father's.

"She refused to go to her regular lawyer. Small wonder. That is Amos Cadbury."

How remote all these events seemed. The excitement, even urgency in her father's voice was vaguely comic. But of course he saw that the drama of what he was telling her lay in a priest's urging the woman to go to the police.

"Who is the priest?"

"Roger Dowling."

Her father said this almost angrily, as if it were irrelevant. All priests were the same to him. Did anyone take religion more seriously than her father?

"What have you advised her?"

"I would like her to go away, perhaps to spend some time with you."

"With me?"

"Not in the same apartment, but in that complex. Away from here. It is important that she escape the influence of that priest."

"What if she's telling the truth?"

"All the more reason for her not to tell it. Amanda, what earthly difference does it make now? Taking her story at face value, a man died in her house and in a panic she asked her son to remove him, to avoid scandal." He paused. "She is a very pious Catholic. That is why she is so susceptible to the suggestions of this priest."

"Having a man die in her bed does not sound pious."

"And even if she told this story, it would be dismissed. How could such a thing be proved?"

"By asking the son."

"He will say nothing."

"How did the priest learn of it?"

"I don't know. But surely he can't go to the police with something like that."

"Did the woman tell him?"

"How else would he know?"

Obviously this was the point that bothered Daddy. Outside, far below, half-naked bodies moved upon the sand, and Amanda felt irrestistibly drawn by the prospect of mindless hours in the sun, just watching the water come, watching the harmless clouds form and re-form overhead, watching the people.

"It all sounds so interesting I almost want to come home."

"I want you to enjoy yourself."

"It is lonesome," she lied.

"Poor darling. If only I could get away . . ."

She encouraged him to think she missed him. He seemed to believe that now they would live their lives together, this healing period in Florida once over. Now that he considered her as lacking in faith as himself, they could be bosom companions, father and daughter. He only sang in the shower, horribly off-key, but even with absolute pitch his voice would have grated on the ear.

Tuttle asked so often that Peanuts got mad and it didn't help that the insistent questioning made it sound as if Tuttle thought his policeman friend was too dumb to learn whether there were any new twists to the investigation into the death of Michael Geary.

"It's Gordon somebody now, the guy's brother or something. They found him dead in his car in a downtown parking lot."

"Like Geary."

Peanuts frowned. "That wasn't downtown."

"But he was found dead in his car too."

"Yeah."

"You check it on the computer?"

"I told you I did."

Finally he went downtown and brought up the file himself and Peanuts was right. There was nothing new. Tuttle wondered if he should call Father Dowling and ask him whether he had talked to the police. When Father Dowling had dialed Catherine Burger after Tuttle had told him, she hadn't answered, and the priest had refused to call the police.

"Maybe I will, but I want to talk first to her."

Tuttle imagined the call, he imagined it several ways, and he didn't like it. The visit to the rectory had been a gamble. What he had to tell the priest was pretty wild, let's face it, and all the while he had expected disbelief to break out and put him on the defensive. Had Father Dowling listened that carefully when all along he had thought Tuttle wacko for bringing him such a story?

Nothing in Tuttle's past presented an obstacle to the interpretation.

"There are no video games on that computer, Tuttle."

The little lawyer looked up from the screen at Cy Horvath. He was with Agnes Lamb. Tuttle looked around. Peanuts was nowhere in sight; he couldn't stand to be in the same room with Agnes. He might at least have given a warning.

"What are you doing on a police computer?" Agnes wanted to know.

"Someone brought up the Geary case and I thought I'd take a look at it."

"That doesn't answer my question."

Tuttle addressed Cy Horvath. "You reached some sort of impasse or what?"

"You want to confess?"

"I never use poison."

Agnes reached over his shoulder, punched several buttons and cleared the screen. "If I ever catch you on the computer again I am going to bring charges."

"It says that you tracked it down to one of Burger's pharmacies."

"Did you hear what I said, Mr. Tuttle?"

He nodded at Agnes. "And you're perfectly right. But it was completely inadvertent. If things are left on the screen they are likely to catch the curiosity of people passing through."

"Where were you passing to?" Cy Horvath asked.

"Have you seen Peanuts Pianone?"

"Try the lounge."

"That's where I was going. Which Burger drugstore was it?"

The second mention of Burger got no reaction from either of them, though it would take the end of the world to get a rise out of Cy.

"Beat it, Tuttle."

In the press room, under a nimbus of cigarette smoke, his tie pulled loose, Netsky sat reading a rival newspaper.

"What's new on Geary?"

"Read the *Tribune*," Netsky said, not looking up.

"That's why I ask. What are you reading?"

Netsky tossed the paper aside. "You should be asking about Furey, Geary's brother-in-law, he's the news now."

"Terrible tragedy. The poor family."

"You know how I got it figured."

Tuttle pulled out a chair and sat. Maybe if he listened to Netsky's bullshit he could figure out a way to put a bee in his bonnet.

"Furey goes after Geary because of the way he's treating Furey's sister. That's Mrs. Geary." The reporter squinted knowingly through the smoke. "He's got motive. He had opportunity. He couldn't account for the time when Geary got it. The simplest way is to suppose he killed the guy. In a rage, out of his mind. Then the dust settles, and his conscience starts to work on him. All these people are Catholic, you realize that? Finally he can't stand it anymore. He walks out of his office, goes to his car in the parking garage, and pulls a plastic bag over his head."

Tuttle nodded through this nonsense, if only to hurry Netsky along. "Too bad his conscience didn't prompt him to write it all down before he checked out."

"Is that a criticism?"

"I'm just making an observation."

"Let me tell you that's a helluva lot better than anything the police have come up with."

"Then you haven't heard?"

Netsky looked at him suspiciously. Tuttle pushed back and stood. "Ask Captain Keegan where Geary went from the restaurant."

"Geary! I'm talking about Furey."

"I know. That's your mistake."

Tuttle sailed out of the room, the reporter's protesting voice following him. He had just poured himself a cup of coffee in the lounge when Netsky spoke at his elbow.

"Keegan really have something?"

"He'll deny it."

"So how the hell do you know about it."

"I have my sources."

Netsky's expression showed that he was hooked. "Pianone."

Tuttle smiled. "I never reveal my sources."

He left Netsky in the lounge, carrying the Styrofoam cup of coffee down the hall to the john, where he dumped it in the sink and smiled at himself in the mirror. He made a small adjustment to his tweed hat, but why tamper with perfection? His visit to headquarters had turned out to be useful after all.

The Alitalia flight from Rome to Chicago left at eleven-fifteen. Cardinal Hildebrand had been taken directly to the VIP lounge with Monsignor Tracy in tow; their tickets were processed, they were upgraded from business to first class over the cardinal's apparently sincere objections. They would be escorted aboard minutes before takeoff, to minimize any possibility of a commotion.

In street clothes, wearing a Borsalino and with the collar of his overcoat upturned, the Prince of the Church had passed within feet of a ragtag group of protestors outside the terminal, the signs they carried resting in the crooks of their arms like lowered flags. A woman Monsignor Tracy recognized as someone who had been trying in vain for months to gain entrance to the Congregation's offices stared vacantly ahead, the sign she held in both hands upside down. LIBERTÉ, ÉGALITÉ, SORORITÉ. God knows what she would have done if she had realized that the man she abstractly hated was passing by a few feet from her.

"Herodia was out front," he told the cardinal.

"You mustn't call her that."

But it seemed a pro forma demur. The woman was from Bayonne, New Jersey, and she claimed to have had a vision in which it was revealed to her that she would be the first woman to be ordained a priest. The file of her letters to the prefect was thick, beginning with a calm statement of what the Blessed Mother's instructions for the Congregation of the Faith were. As the one-sided correspondence grew, the prophetic and oracular tone of her missives crescendoed. The earthquake she had prophesied had failed to occur, but she explained that in great detail. Her claim evolved into the assertion that she had been ordained, miraculously, by divine intervention, during a vision, and that the cardinal's role was simply to acknowledge this. Twice she had managed to get to the main altar in St. Peter's and begin to say Mass, going directly to the offertory in the hopes of pronouncing the words of consecration before she was hauled away by the basilica guards.

"She wants your head."

But then so many did. Tracy had found Hildebrand a pleasant man, serious, intelligent, a man of prayer, devoid of much of a sense of humor, perhaps, but nothing like the caricature of him in the dissident Catholic press.

"I'm surprised she isn't on our flight."

Tracy smiled at this pleasantry, but as soon as they were aboard he made a tour of business and tourist classes and was relieved to find that Herodia was not aboard. But his relief was not total. Had she been a harbinger of what awaited them in Indiana?

Hildebrand always referred to their destination as Indiana—not America, not South Bend, not Notre Dame. Doubtless it conjured up for him the Westerns he had watched as a boy in postwar Germany. Had he sided with the Indians, imagining the cowboys as those who had taken charge of his native land? Monsignor Tracy had found that, despite all the counterevidence, Europeans clung to the notion that the United States was a place where gunfights in the streets were a daily occurrence. Or was this because of the evidence?

Tracy had been on the phone to Ambrose Ravel daily over the past week, taking the morning call from Chicago in the Roman afternoon, trying to tell whether there was another message hidden in the auxiliary bishop's cheerful reports that things were going well.

"The Catholic press seems to be of another mind."

"That's just the *NCR*, and America, of course. The usual Vatican III crowd."

"There won't be any agitation?"

"Monsignor, there are dozens of places we can hold the meeting if anything arises."

"Not at Notre Dame?"

"On the campus. The seminary on the other side of the lake has been suggested."

"I understood that the university insists this meeting does not involve them."

"Monsignor, you understand this political nonsense far better than I do. Please assure the cardinal that we are looking forward to his remarks to the commission. Although the meeting will be secret, closed, that message will be publicized far and wide. Incidently, suggest that he use the phrase 'family values.' "

"It sounds like a supermarket sale."

The episcopal laugh was incommensurate with the faint wit of the remark. Tracy prepared himself for the worst, but he decided not to bother the cardinal. Now, aboard Alitalia 874, they were lifting slowly but surely into the air, and the die was cast.

Hildebrand worked for the first hour of the flight, having asked for mineral water when the flight attendant came around. Tracy had some white wine, hoping it would relax him. The cardinal picked at his lunch and then read until the movie began. Startled by the display of flesh, he tipped his seat back, adjusted his eyeshade and fell asleep. Tracy got out his laptop and worked "family values" into the presentation the prefect would make to the Bishops' Committee on Marriage and the Family.

Bishop Ravel met them at O'Hare with the news that the archbishop was out of town so there was no reason to delay their departure for South Bend. There was no way to tell from Ravel's expression whether the archbishop's absence was diplomatic or genuine—it was a risky thing to seem to be an ally of the prefect of the Congregation of the Faith. Ravel took them out to a stretch limousine.

"This will be at your disposal throughout your visit, Your Eminence." The driver was a middle-aged man wearing a gray suit, the jacket of which would not have buttoned over his belly. He wore a democratic expression that fended off the suggestion that the people he drove were any better than himself; he didn't care if they were big shots from Rome or local hierarchy. His name was Berlioz.

"Leo is a Knight of Columbus," Ravel said, making a little bow to the driver.

"We are in good hands," Hildebrand said. He was ready if Berlioz sought to shake his hand, but the moment passed.

Ravel sat on the seat facing Tracy and Hildebrand. They would drive immediately to South Bend, where they could sleep well in readiness for the meeting tomorrow.

"Would you like something to drink, Your Eminence?"

Ravel displayed the little fridge, with its soda and beer. He slid back a panel to reveal a cache of liquor.

"Is there water?"

There was. Tracy, not trusting his bladder, declined, and Ravel, disappointed to have dispensed so little from the car's cornucopia, poured himself a Coke. Perhaps Hildebrand would have been disappointed if Ravel had not shown a preference for the national drink.

The cardinal murmured appreciatively when he saw the sign announcing they were entering Indiana. He scanned the horizon but saw no signs of ambush by Native Americans. Tracy wondered if the state would have to change its name under the pressure of current ideologies. When religious faith went, far more rigorous dogmas took its place. On the Toll Road Cardinal Hildebrand began systematically to quiz Ravel. The questions were meant to get corroboration for facts that were in his address, whether explicitly mentioned or presumed. Tracy knew this was Teutonic thoroughness rather than any doubt about his own research.

"Give me some background on the members of your committee."

This put Ravel on the spot, of course. No matter how he described his fellow bishops he would be sticking his neck out. He obviously knew that Hildebrand would not settle for circumlocution.

"All of them were made bishops by the Holy Father."

Hildebrand nodded. Given the present pope's long reign, it was the rare active prelate who had not been elevated by him. Nonetheless, it was a good beginning. What Hildebrand wanted to know was the disposition of members of the committee on the scandal of annulments in the United States. The word "scandal" appeared in the remarks the cardinal would make.

"Perhaps not all of us would use the word 'scandal.' "

"Would you?"

"If I were not uneasy I would not have asked you to address us, Your Eminence."

"It is time we leave psychology to the psychologists and return to a theological interpretation of matters of faith and the acts of the faithful. Recall the number of laicizations granted in this country befor the Holy Father stopped it."

"There are some who should have been let go."

Ravel seemed to have expected a more festive drive to South Bend in the comfort of the limousine. He was obviously alluding to the spate of suits brought against clergy for various forms of sexual misconduct.

"They can be suspended. There certainly must be some sort of rehabilitation before they can function again as priests."

"Counseling is a must," Ravel agreed.

"I did not mean counseling. It is absurd to suppose that sin is just an odd name for a psychological malfunction. As if the soul were a machine that can be taken in for repairs. A prolonged retreat would be more to the point, under a wise spiritual director."

Ravel's eyes flickered to Tracy. How was he to acknowledge these remarks without accepting them? Obviously their host was going to be as surprised as anyone when he heard what the cardinal had to say to his committee.

Identifying himself as the secretary of the cardinal archbishop of Chicago, Freddy had called Alitalia to ask if Cardinal Josef Hildebrand was on the flight to Rome.

"We cannot give out that information, sir."

"Monsignor Wippel," Freddy said, hoping the repetition of his assumed name would impress the person on the phone. It didn't. She repeated the same message. She might have been a machine. Then Freddy remembered Barleduc, a sometime friend who was with Air France. Ten minutes later he knew that the cardinal was coming in the following day.

Freddy was there to meet him, so to speak. When he was crossing from the parking lot to the terminal, he noticed the line of stretch limos there to pick up incoming passengers. He had not thought there were as many such vehicles in Chicago. When a clerical figure got out of one and tucked his pectoral cross under his suit jacket, Freddy put on the brakes. He let the bishop go inside, then went over to the driver of the limo.

"Wasn't that Bishop Grace who just went in?"

"Naw. Ravel. Ambrose Ravel."

Freddy snapped his fingers. Of course, Ravel. "This his car?"

"It's my car."

"No kidding. What's a thing like this cost?"

He slapped his forehead and staggered backward when the driver named a figure. He waved, smiled, shook his head and, before returning to his car in the garage, noted the license number of the limo. All limos look alike, after all.

He left the garage and circled around and came to a halt behind the row of limos. The narrow street was clogged with taxis, private cars, microbuses from hotels and the rental-car outfits. No one could object to his stopping; there wasn't much movement anyway. He opened his door and stood, making sure that the limo was still in line.

When the driver got out and went around to open the passenger door, Freddy was on the alert. Bishop Ravel emerged with two other clerical figures, the taller of whom had a Borsalino pulled jauntily onto his head. His hair was as white as Freddy had heard. There was a little pas de deux before they got into the car, and then the driver went around the front of the car, walking at a list, like Broderick Crawford in an old series that was rerunning on cable. The driver looked around to see if anyone was impressed with his passengers, then slipped behind the wheel.

"Ten-four," Freddy murmured, and then they were away.

Freddy put in a tape, one with a subliminal message that was supposed to increase his self-esteem. For all he knew it was just Muzak, but he was psychologically prepared to have his image of himself enhanced, and he could almost feel the effect of the music on his subconscious. It occurred to him that with the cause subliminal and the effect subconscious, tapes of this kind were sure winners. But he was in no mood for skepticism. When it came to tinkering with the psyche, Freddy was as credulous as a primitive snake worshipper.

His addiction to such therapy was his own secret, of course. Which of his friends would not consider it a great joke if Freddy said he was trying to build up his self-esteem? It would sound like an effort to make the Sears Tower imposing. His smiling cockiness was a facade. It hid his self-doubt as well as his seething indignation, whose object sometimes seemed everything in the world and out of it. The trouble with being an atheist is that you have no God to hate. That left the Church, however, and Freddy had made a minor art of expressing his loathing in lighthearted witticisms. The poet has been described as a man enclosed in a bronze animal which is then placed over a flame. As the heat increases, the imprisoned man screams in agony, but the animal is so constructed that all sounds that emanate from it are the sweetest music.

"Sing for us some more," the people cry, ignorant of the agony they are asking of the poet.

Even his mother laughed or at least smiled at what she took to be Freddy's innocent irreverence toward the Church she loved so much. After all, its court had freed her from his father, and there was always the sacrament of reconciliation to restore her innocence after her bouts with Michael Geary. To indulge his semisacrilegious jokes was to acquiesce in the suppressed rage out of which they arose.

"He'll get hard if I leave him in your bed," he had said when he looked at the dead body of Michael Geary in his mother's bed. "But then I suppose he always did."

"Freddy!"

"I refer to rigor mortis, not to rigor vitae."

That was wasted. It is said that Catholics can't sing. They no longer know Latin either. His suggestion that he get Geary out of the house both repelled and attracted her.

"Where will you take him?"

"Well, not to Emergency. It's too late for that."

She covered her mouth with her hands and stared peekaboo at the dead Geary.

"Where does he usually go from here?"

"What do you mean, usually?"

It was very tempting to tell her how he had monitored her adultery, but what the hell, she was suffering enough at the time.

"I suppose he would have gone back to work."

"Good. That's where I'll take him."

And he did, driving bold as brass into the driveway and past the remodeled house in which Michael Geary had made his modest fortune and into the parking lot in back. When removing a body from the trunk of a car and putting in behind the steering wheel, act matter-of-fact, that was Freddy's advice. Don't hurry, don't act furtive, don't look around. Just do it as if it were the most natural thing in the world. A minute after parking the car Freddy was loping down the alley.

Was recalling all this an effect of the subliminal message on the tape? God knows he was proud of the way he had brought it off. His mother was beholden to him as never before; the police were obviously baffled by what had happened. But then so was Freddy, until the verdict of death by poisoning came.

Ahead of him the white limo gathered speed as it cleared the Loop, and soon it was swinging off onto the Indiana Toll Road. *Wunderbar.* How could he lose them on a tollway? He punched the button, took his ticket and crept up the ramp behind the limo. Soon they had settled in at a prudent sixty-five. The tape had finished, but Freddy put it in again.

The limo went on to the second South Bend exit. While the driver paid the toll, Freddy caught a glimpse of the dome at Notre Dame, all lit up, impressive. A couple of stoplights, couple of left turns and they were on their final approach. The golden dome was directly ahead now, seeming to lift through the overhanging branches of the trees. The limo's turn signal went on when the Morris Inn came into view, but suddenly it slowed considerably, almost stopping. They had seen the pickets waiting by the entrance of the campus inn.

The turn signal went off, and the limo moved ahead and swung into the gate. Freddy began blasting his horn at the group in front of the inn, but they just stared at him. He swung into the inn drive and braked at the entrance. Sliding across the seat, he rolled down the window and shouted, "Hildebrand just went through the gate onto the campus."

Dumb expressions; then someone turned and noticed the limo, and cries of indignation went up.

"Corby," someone yelled. "They're taking him to Corby."

Freddy had come to be a witness of the cardinal's reception. If he had not sounded the warning, it was obvious Hildebrand would have been stashed away somewhere on campus while these idiots milled around with their signs waiting for Godot. Maybe he could chalk this happy consequence up to the subliminal tape. Or maybe it was just his native shrewdness. He liked that. That showed real self-esteem.

When Father Dowling told Marie that he thought a small valise would be sufficient for his trip to South Bend, the housekeeper exploded.

"And when are you leaving?"

"This afternoon."

"And you come back?"

"On Saturday. Not in time for the evening Mass, but . . ."

She waved this away. "Exactly. Thursday, Friday and Saturday. Three days."

"Three nights."

She pointed out delicately that a stay of this length would require more than a valise could carry, pajamas, underwear, shirts, socks, handkerchiefs, collars . . .

"You're right, Marie."

"Of course I'm right."

"I'll want to dress appropriately for the game. My windbreaker, a turtleneck sweater, maybe that pair of corduroys."

Marie threw up her hands. "I had forgotten the game. Oh, you'll need your large suitcase *and* the valise."

"Maybe you should do the packing."

She looked at him as if this had been settled all along.

"Just the valise, Marie. I can hang up the other things in the car."

"And just leave them there until Saturday?"

"I'll take them inside, of course."

"You'll carry them in, on a hanger, into a hotel!"

Not only was she annoyed, she was embarrassed. On such occasions Roger Dowling got an intimation of what marriage must be like, a marriage of long standing, when the couple have become just aspects of one another. There was something ritualistic in Marie's wanting to prepare him for the journey, as if this were imprinted in her genetic code. When he had gone off to school each fall, his mother had fussed like this, counting the items as they were packed, estimating the number of things he would need, reminding him to make sure his laundry went out each week. She seemed to need to see him as a callow boy who couldn't find his way to the corner alone. That was the role Marie was playing—a maternal, not a spousal one. This made her manner only slightly more tolerable.

"Before I board the cruise ship, I'll buy an entirely new outfit."

"What cruise ship?"

"I thought you had noticed the brochures. Sail the cerulean Caribbean, dine and dance under the stars, stops at six ports with opportunities to shop. It sounds wonderful."

She clamped her mouth shut and looked patiently at the wall, waiting for him to finish. He left her to the packing, once more insisting that he would take only a valise.

"And a briefcase."

"Ah." She took this for a concession.

"I'll need to bring books."

"Books!"

She stomped up the front stairs and he went into his study. Books. Among them the new *Code of Canon Law*. Its appearance in 1983 had seemed to write a definite *finis* to his blighted career as a canon lawyer and permanent member of the tribunal. The code that had been replaced would forever stand in his mind, paragraph by paragraph, phrase by phrase. As a student, he had been urged to memorize it, a considerable chore, but he found that this was happening almost unintentionally anyway, so he completed the task intentionally. Some paragraphs were stored in bolder type than others; those dealing with marriage had been his guide. On his shelves were the canon law journals he had subscribed to during those years. His collection stopped in the year he left the tribunal. They were a reminder of the decisive break in his priestly life, when he had left the tribunal in disgrace because he had sought in alcohol a buffer against the sadness of the job. But God is good and Father Dowling was soon able to give thanks for his happy fall, the *felix culpa* that had brought him to St. Hilary's parish in Fox River, the Siberia of the Chicago Archdiocese. It was no Ars and he was no Jean Vianney, but it was here that he would work out his salvation.

He felt again, as he had when Ambrose Ravel first asked him to attend the meeting with Cardinal Hildebrand at Notre Dame, that he was in danger of being drawn back into that other life. Not the drink, thank God, that had been merely an instrument of oblivion. He had put it behind him easily once he was free of the tribunal. He had also avoided the big men in the archdiocese, not just the cardinal and his auxiliaries—who but Ambrose Ravel would he have been likely to see?—but the movers and shakers, the Noonans, the Egans, the insiders and the outsiders, Andrew and the rest. Obscurity became a passion with him. His fear was that Ravel would think it a waste of his education and experience to leave him in Fox River now that he was so far beyond his troubles. What had overcome his misgivings were the two tickets to the Notre Dame–Southern Cal game.

He took the tickets from under his desk blotter and contemplated their polychrome fronts. He had sold his soul for these? Now it would be too cruel to prevent Phil Keegan from going, but he could feign sickness, give Keegan both tickets, and he and Cy could enjoy the game. Once admitted, this thought became more and more attractive.

Above him, Marie clomped around, busy with the packing. Again he was reminded of his mother. No wonder. His great idea was like a kid's trying to keep from going to school. In the seminary, there was a special skill some acquired to convince the sister in charge of the infirmary that they were ailing. Boys gargled with hot water, scalding their mouths, in order to achieve a fever temperature. Others did push-ups until their hearts thumped and then staggered into the infirmary. There was an epidemic of this before exams. Did he now plan to get a letter of excuse from his doctor?

Phil Keegan looked in before noon Mass. "Don't bother about blankets or seat cushions, Roger. I'll bring those." His face was alive with excitement. "Did you see the *Trib* this morning?"

"What did it say?"

"Are you inviting me for lunch?"

"What else?"

Keegan disappeared, hurrying off to the church. Roger Dowling followed in a few minutes.

He said his daily Mass at noon largely as a convenience to the senior citizens who came to the school, now a parish center under the direction of Edna Hospers. As a convenience, not an obligation. As many as a dozen came most every day, and then there were the parish stalwarts who did not think of themselves as senior citizens. St. Hilary's had been a residential parish in its golden years, but with all the changes in Fox River it functioned for some almost as a downtown church, and the noon Mass drew a number of people on their lunch hours. Phil Keegan was a regular at Mass and almost as regular at the table in the rectory afterward.

"I'm surprised you can get away, what with people dropping dead all over the place, Captain Keegan," Marie said. She seemed to have hit upon resentment as the appropriate reaction to this weekend of recreation.

"All over the place? The only ones I can think of didn't drop at all, just died at the wheel of their cars. Luckily they weren't moving at the time."

"Have you made any progress?"

Phil Keegan frowned. He was an avowed champion of routine in his work, while at the same time insisting that detection almost never involved the kind of complicated inferences popularly associated with it. By and large, the killer was known and the task was to provide the prosecutor with sufficient evidence to prevent the judge and jury from flying in the face of the facts. The great unknown was not who did it but whether the court could be persuaded to hold him responsible for what he had done. Listening to him, it occurred to Roger Dowling that what had happened in ecclesiastical courts reflected in some degree what had happened in civil courts. There had been a general flight from the traditional notion that human beings are responsible for what they do. The deaths of Michael Geary and of his brother-in-law, Gordon Furey, had seemed to fit into the usual object of investigation, but this was now less clear.

"Admittedly, we seemed to have a choice of killers in the case of Geary. I can tell you now, I was certain it was Furey. Then the son confessed, and that made sense, largely because of the boot prints, until that damned Jolson finally got around to finishing the autopsy and told us Geary had died of poison."

"Hydrochloric acid added to his insulin."

"So that makes it sound like the wife, right?"

"The wife!" Marie stuck her head in from the kitchen.

"The woman he was married to. What kind of pie is this?"

"It's not pie. It's quiche."

"What?"

"Quiche."

"As in, quiche me, you fool?"

Marie made a noise and disappeared, out of sight but not out of hearing. Phil Keegan might have been addressing her while he developed the reasons why anyone of minimal intelligence would suspect that Maureen Geary had done in her exasperating husband.

"The prescription," Marie called.

"Right. The prescription. That took us back to Gordon Furey. He renewed his brother-in-law's prescription and permitted the doctor to think he was Michael Geary; he had every opportunity to draw out some of the insulin with a syringe and inject hydrochloric acid."

"Is that how it was done?"

"So I'm told."

Maureen Geary had blandly told them she had asked Gordon to run the errand for her, explaining it by saying that she still treated him like her little brother at times, "just ask his wife if you don't believe me."

"Was she protesting too much or had you expressed doubt?"

"Both, I thought. Furey seemed our man. God knows he had provocation. Imagine having a brother-in-law like Michael Geary. I'd call him a Pharisee if that didn't make me one. Anyway, Furey had motive, opportunity and the means. It was going to pose a bit of a problem, showing he put the acid into the plastic package of insulin, but any half-competent prosecutor could make that seem the inevitable sequel of what we did know for sure. And then Gordon Furey shows up dead."

"Was it suicide?" Marie called.

"No."

"Thank God. How can you be sure, Phil?"

"The passenger door of the Avanti was open and the seat pushed forward. Someone had been hiding back there and then got out as soon as he had snuffed the life out of Furey."

"The way Brian Geary got into the backseat of his father's car."

"The Avanti is a two-door."

"Who would want to kill Gordon Furey?"

Phil Keegan shrugged. "You can see why I want to get away and forget all this."

He would drive to South Bend Saturday morning and they would return that night. It did not seem like a prolonged absence from his work. But of course the football game would absorb him and he would completely forget the puzzles that awaited him in Fox River.

Marie came into the dining room, drew out a chair and sat. "Maybe it was someone who thought what you did, that Gordon Furey had killed Mr. Geary."

"You mean Mrs. Geary."

"No, I do no mean Mrs. Geary."

"That leaves the son and the daughter. The son is a wacko and—"

"He is not! Why does any man who has interests out of the ordinary, who has a profound devotion to St. Anthony, for example, strike you as strange?"

"You wrong me, Marie. I was speaking only of Brian Geary."

"He is a nice man."

"Maybe you'd like to hire him to work here at St. Hilary's, Roger," Keegan said. "He could be a lot of help, puttering around the church, keeping the school clean. He eats like a bird, so he'd be no trouble to Marie."

She had her hands flat on the table, the tips of her thumbs and index fingers touching. "Brian Geary did not kill anyone."

"That leaves the daughter."

"She is expecting!"

Keegan sat back and regarded the chandelier. "You may have something there, Marie. She visits Fox River often enough, apparently. She had opportunity to kill them both, her father and her uncle. Dad's no problem, a little toilet bowl cleaner in his insulin pouch, but Uncle Gordon presents a difficulty. Of course it's easily overcome. She sneaks into the backseat of his car, waits until he is settled, then, zoom, over his head with the plastic bag and lets him squirm himself to death."

Marie had her hands over her ears as she rose from the table. She glared at Keegan, trying to think of something that would really hurt him. And then she had it.

"I hope Notre Dame loses! Do you hear? I hope they are beaten and you have to sit there and watch."

Keegan went ashen and watched her leave the room with dread in his eyes.

"She got you there, Phil."

"Roger, wouldn't that be awful?" He was whispering. "Imagine losing to Southern Cal in South Bend and we're there."

"It could happen."

"Don't say that." There was agony in his eyes. He stood, stared at the kitchen.

"Was that a curse, Marie? You got a Lou Holtz doll you stick pins into or something? You want Our Lady's school to be beaten by a bunch of heathen?"

Marie reappeared. "It's for us to be on Our Lady's side, not for her to be on ours."

And she withdrew.

"How did Gordon die?" Mark asked Kate when the news first came.

"Mark, I didn't even ask."

"Was he ill?"

"Not that I know of."

"How did she put it?"

"What are you getting at?"

"Hey, take it easy. It just seems odd she didn't tell you how he died."

"Mark, she's not very good at telling people her husband is dead, okay? This is her first shot at it. Give her time and she'll be as good as you or me."

"Whoa."

He put his arms around her, but she was unyielding. What he meant was that her father's death was mysterious, presumably murder, and that this sort of thing ran in the family. Prolonged study is a danger to the soul, there was no doubt about that in Kate's mind. She had watched Mark become facetious, wary of seeming not to know all about everything, faking his way through conversations lest others suspect there might be some topic on which he was not an authority. That was the approved stance, to speak with authority, to know it all. And this induced a contempt for authority, so that it was obligatory to snicker about the pope and Cardinal Hildebrand and anyone else outside the magic circle. She had been particularly annoyed at the way he fell in with those going ballistic about the so-called secret meeting at the CCE. He had been one of the pickets who were stood up at the Morris Inn when the cardinal didn't show up.

"Remember that guy who came down here, Freddy?"

"Yes."

"He was there. We were standing in front of the inn when he drove up, honking his horn and saying the cardinal had gone through the campus gate. In a limo. Barbara claimed to have seen it. What were we supposed to do, go chasing after it on foot? Beiler said he could check it out."

"Who was going to take the pictures?"

"We had *The South Bend Tribune* there." He made a face. "And their TV channel."

"What about WNDU?"

He made another face. "The university owns them."

"Now what?"

"We'll be at the CCE before the meeting starts tomorrow."

The point was to show that the Theology Department, at least some of them, perhaps most, were incensed at the thought of a Roman cardinal flying into their university to tell Americans what to think.

"They're restorationists. They want everything back to where it was before. The only difference between the people in the Vatican and the Lefébvreites is that the people in the Vatican have power. There isn't a lira's worth of difference between them, doctrinally."

"Isn't the topic annulments?"

Mark looked wise. "That's what they say. I suppose they think it's less controversial than other subjects."

"Freddy wants them to go back to the way it was before."

"I wonder how serious he is."

"About what?"

"About anything. How about that smile?"

"I don't think he started VOCL as a joke. As far as I can see, the other members are deadly serious about easy annulments."

"I think there's a lot of sadism in that. People made a promise so they're stuck with it, no matter how awful it gets. I think they like the thought of people leading miserable lives."

"They think their own lives have been made miserable by annulments."

He had more to say, lots more, but he made a visible effort to curtail it. "In any case, that's just a cover. Hildebrand will lay down the law to one bishops' conference, then another, and the lid will be clamped down tight."

There were things Kate decided not to say as well. Increasingly now, she occupied Betty's shoes when she heard Mark and the others going on about how awful the Church was. Betty thought the Church was fine, the problem was its members didn't try to become what they ought to be. Rules and regulations could be empty of meaning, but maybe this was because one lost the sense of what they were aimed at. Of course it wasn't fair, but putting side by side in her mind Betty making her hour of adoration every week and their living room full of chattering academics, Kate knew which sounded more genuine to her. Mark seldom went to Mass and didn't seem surprised that she never went. Except to funerals.

"I can take the South Shore, Mark."

"Why don't you drive?"

"You may need the car."

"How long will you be gone?"

"That's what I don't know."

"Isn't the car easier on you than a train?"

Her heart melted at his concern for her, and for their baby. Oh, God, why wasn't he an electrician or something? Why wasn't he all excited about Saturday's game? But it was academically infra dig to acknowledge that the university had a team that was vying for number one in the nation.

She took his hand and placed it on her stomach so that he could feel the stirring within her. Once she might have denied that she would make a big deal out of pregnancy. Watching expectant mothers, it had always seemed to her that many of them became mysteriously aloof, as if they were colluding with the cosmos. Well, now she knew how they felt. She had become a house whose occupant was now giving her little kicks to establish his otherness. He, she—Kate didn't want to know for sure beforehand. Whichever, it was someone different from her and from Mark yet somehow both of them together. She was in awe of what was happening to her, nor did reminding herself that this was the way in which every one of the billions of people on earth had gotten here diminish her sense that this was a unique endeavor. Nobody else had ever carried her baby.

"Does it hurt?"

"Only when he laughs."

Christopher James looked forward to his trip to Notre Dame the way he imagined a Hasidic Jew might anticipate a visit to the University of Damascus. Freddy's suggestion that, as counsel to VOCL, James request an opportunity to address the meeting to which the Vatican was sending the head of what in more honest days was called the Inquisition, had seemed to James to be but a gesture, but then Freddy thrived on gestures.

"Should I send it to the pope?"

Freddy thought about it. "Just a copy. The letter itself can be addressed to Bishop Ambrose Ravel. He's head of the bishops' committee that organized the secret meeting."

"Some secret."

"Send a copy to Monsignor Noonan as well. He's on the Chicago tribunal and has been invited to the meeting."

"Who else will be there?"

"Locally? Father Roger Dowling will also be there. He's the pastor of St. Hilary's here in Fox River."

"Why him?"

"People think highly of him. Amos Cadbury, for instance."

"Ah."

So James wrote the letter and was answered by a phone call from Bishop Ravel. James expected the bishop to convey some of the anger the archdiocese must feel toward a man who had forced the settlement he had. This was an impediment he had not mentioned to Freddy. If he had, he would have suggested that Freddy write the letter, but the young man was a loose cannon and James only believed in actions that had some chance of success. The letter he himself wrote was a model of respectful inquiry and, the settlement for Amanda apart, would have been assured of an equally respectful answer. The telephone response was a surprise.

"There is merit in your suggestion, Mr. James. The experience of members of families involved in annulments is very relevant to the aim of our meeting. Incidentally, how did you learn that there was to be a meeting?"

"It's no longer a secret, sir."

The slightest of pauses. The "sir" was a mistake, but James was damned if he was going to call a fellow American "Your Excellency." He had been judiciously deferential in representing his daughter, but saw no need for violating his personal principles now.

"Perhaps it's just as well. Perhaps you also know that some kind of demonstration has been threatened at Notre Dame. Your own suggestion seems constructive. I can schedule you for fifteen minutes."

"That's not very much time."

"It will not be a very long meeting. Actually, I would have to squeeze you into an agenda that was agreed to some time ago."

"I will take what time you give me."

"Fine. We will be meeting at the Center for Continuing Education, on Notre Dame Avenue, just west of the stadium and east of the Morris Inn. I'm sorry I can't supply you with a ticket for Saturday's game."

"If you could I would have to warn you I will be rooting for Southern California."

"Perhaps Cardinal Hildebrand will be too."

"Church politics," Freddy said, when James asked him what the bishop had meant.

"Explain it to me."

Freddy's laughing account made the Church of Rome sound as if it were crumbling from within. Catholic institutions declaring their independence of the Church, teachers of Catholic doctrine disputing what the pope said and advising Catholics they could ignore him and remain in good standing, agitation for married priests and women's ordination.

None of this matched James's abiding image of a threatening monolith, an institution whose members either moved in lockstep or were given the thumbscrew treatment. Finally he decided that this must be one of Freddy's jokes. No organization as riven with dissent as the one Freddy described would last for a week. Christopher James did not question the account, of course; that would be to play into Freddy's mischievous hands. But he decided that he would approach the Notre Dame meeting with his longtime assumption of the nature and character of the Church of Rome.

"I'm going to Notre Dame to address a cardinal from Rome and a committee of American bishops," he said to Amanda on the phone.

"Is it about the settlement?"

It hadn't occurred to him that she would think this. He chortled and assured her that it was on an entirely different matter. For the first time he told her of his role as counsel for VOCL.

"Daddy, you'd better be careful. The next thing you know you'll be taking instruction."

"Ho ho."

"Don't underestimate the attraction."

"If it is even fractionally like Freddy Burger says, I am as likely to be attracted to it as to the Ku Klux Klan."

"What did Freddy say?"

"Have I mentioned him to you before?"

"What did whoever Freddy is say?"

"I wouldn't begin to try to tell you." He paused. "How is everything with you?"

"Fine."

"You know what I mean."

"Now what do you think? After what I've been through."

She was not being frank with him. What she had been through and what he had managed to convince the archdiocese's lawyers she had been through were very different things. Unless of course she meant her disenchantment with Catholicism as a result of the legal proceedings. Christopher James developed the certainty that his daughter was falling back into the embrace of the Whore of Babylon.

"I wish I could come down there now."

"You can always ask me to visit you."

"Would you like that?"

"Well, what do you think? I lead a very lonely life, Daddy."

It broke his heart to hear her say that. Whatever Michael Geary had or had not done to her, the way the Church had worked on her, breaking her resistance, drawing her in, had to leave her psychically scarred. He drove from his mind all memories of his wife's turn to religion. She was beyond his reach, but he could still help Amanda.

"Get on the first plane you can."

"I thought I might drive up."

"That will take days."

"When do you go to Notre Dame?"

"On Thursday."

"I guess I will fly. I want to see you in action."

"It's not an open meeting, Amanda."

"I'll carry your files or something. Don't bring your secretary."

"Come home and we'll talk about it."

Maybe a look at the inner workings of the Church would be the best antidote of all. The meeting would try to reconcile the public claim that Catholic marriages are forever with the way in which those same marriages are regularly declared never to have existed.

He drafted a fifteen-minute statement and discussed it with Freddy. Smiling and humming, the founder of VOCL rapidly turned the pages.

"It reads like a lawyer's brief."

"It's addressed to lawyers."

"You make the right points."

"Thank you."

"My own taste is for bombast. What a chance, to lay it on the line to the second man in the Vatican."

"Is that what he is?"

"That's who he is. He'll be pope himself if the present one ever decides to accept the fact that he's mortal. The two of them have been there together from the beginning. There'll be people picketing at Notre Dame who think Hildebrand is a fascist who rules with an iron hand. Some iron hand. This meeting looks like a first effort to lower the boom on the American Church."

"There'll be pickets?"

"Don't worry. They're harmless."

"If Cardinal Hildebrand tells them to shut down the annulment mills, what will happen?"

"Probably not much."

"They'll defy him?"

"Oh no. Not the bishops. They don't defy anything but common sense. They'll agree and then waffle."

"How about the others, the pickets?"

"After Hildebrand goes, they'll say the bishops are weak and caved in to Rome."

"So the bishops can't win."

"They don't even know there's a war on."

"Freddy, you're such a cynic, I don't know why you remain a Catholic."

"It's the only church that accepts sinners."

Wednesday after midnight Amanda showed up at the door. He had been frantically trying to figure out what flight she was on, assuming she was en route when he couldn't raise her at her apartment on Marco Island.

"Chicago Air has the best fares and leaves at odd times. I would have had to wait until tomorrow for an airline you've heard of."

She had arrived at Midway, making the trip from the airport twice as long, but what struck James about her daughter was how fresh and young she looked. Almost forty, she had apparently decided to enjoy the youth she had missed during her extended religious period. He put his hands on her shoulders and looked tenderly at her.

"You look wonderful."

"A tan is a great disguise. Daddy, why don't you pack it in and move to Florida? Surely you have enough money?"

Did she mean the settlement? But she would know that was hers alone. Another lawyer would have taken a big slice of it, but of course he had not. She would also inherit money that would make her a very wealthy young lady.

"I'll retire when you marry."

She looked at him from the corner of her eye. "You are the only man I can abide."

"Very well. Find someone like me."

She hugged his arm and nuzzled her cheek against his. "If only I could."

Now that she was here he realized he did not want her to make the trip to Notre Dame.

"I have to leave early in the morning and you've been traveling how many hours? I'll be back tomorrow night."

"Then you didn't get tickets for the big game."

"So you heard about that?"

"Daddy, it's the talk of the country. No one is indifferent to Notre Dame, they hate it or they love it. So everybody has a side."

"You too?"

"Don't you?"

"The last time I heard, tickets were going for five hundred dollars apiece."

"I thought we were rich."

"Look, I'll see what I can do. How about this? I go down in the morning and if I can get tickets, we'll both go on Saturday."

"Why go back and forth? We can stay there."

"You couldn't get a motel within a hundred miles of the place."

In the end he agreed that she would come with him and just lounge around the Morris Inn while he represented VOCL at the no longer secret meeting of a committee of the American bishops and Cardinal Hildebrand at Notre Dame.

"By train!" Noonan cried. "Not on your life."

"It's very convenient," Roger Dowling said.

"What is it, Amtrak?"

"No, the South Shore."

"Is that still running?"

"Well, they sold me a ticket."

Noonan was genuinely surprised. He could remember the North Shore that had run between Chicago and Milwaukee, up through Great Lakes and Waukegan. The Noonans had often gone that way to visit relatives in Milwaukee, but that line, like so many other things of his youth, was no more. Why had the line to South Bend survived when the other hadn't? Noonan felt indignation, as if his memories were being trifled with.

"Commuters, students," Roger Dowling explained, and Noonan felt like arguing the point. There must have been at least an equal number of commuters to the north of the city.

"You worried about game traffic?"

"Phil Keegan is coming down and I'll drive back with him."

"I haven't found a ticket."

"You're probably lucky. Imagine paying that much and remembering it the next day."

"You should talk."

The fact that Roger Dowling had been given tickets to the game of the half century by Ambrose Ravel increased Noonan's sense of discontent. Obviously Dowling had offered the other ticket to Phil Keegan. Noonan had been told that Keegan had spent some years at Quigley, but he couldn't remember him. "I didn't either," Roger Dowling disarmingly said. "Not at first. He has far sharper memories of the place than I have."

Not than I have, Noonan thought. He prided himself on the way in which he made a shrine of the past, evoking it in melancholy moments when he felt that his life had not gone the way it might have, that great chances had passed him by, that he was still doing what he had been doing when Roger Dowling was on the tribunal. It was a dead end, and he could admit it, at least to himself. Being made a monsignor? A consolation prize at best. Sometimes, however, he imagined himself in Ravel's place and wondered if he would have been content with it. Not that Ravel would remain long in Chicago. Arranging meetings with Hildebrand was no small thing, and it would probably put Ravel on a fast track to his own diocese. If the meeting went well.

Here was the deepest source of uneasiness and discontent. If the meeting went well, if the point of bringing Hildebrand over was reached, Noonan and his court would come under fire. Oh, it hadn't escaped him that Ambrose Ravel was not too subtly suggesting that the tribunal as it was when he and Roger Dowling were members of it had been a far trimmer ship than it became with Noonan as the senior member. Maybe they had loosened up a bit, accepting grounds for nonconsent that would never have passed muster with Dowling and Ravel. Noonan wondered if either of the other two men could remember what a grim thing hearing cases had once been. Even when your heart bled for some poor husband or wife, there was nothing to be done then. They sat there and said no and the majority of such plaintiffs just went out and got a civil divorce, drifted away from the Church, probably embittered by their experience.

Ambrose Ravel had developed an episcopal silence that enabled him to express disapproval without saying anything. Noonan wished he would say something, would comment on some particular case, so that he could walk the bishop through it and find out if he really would want to do things differently. General disapproval was both unfair and impossible to respond to, particularly when it was conveyed by silence. Since Ravel began to emerge as a force in the National Council of Catholic Bishops—how could he not, given his patron?—his pet project had been the nation's marriage tribunals. He had obviously tapped a source of discontent, although that might be little more than bishops echoing Rome without any intention of doing something. The joint meeting of Ambrose Ravel's committee and representatives of the Canon Law Society, and the persuading Cardinal Josef Hildebrand to attend, were not just a coup; they looked like the first serious efforts to squelch annulments. The Vatican could do this with the stroke of a pen, of course, as it had with laicizations, but that would risk reactions that would be at least softened if the move were made by the NCCB itself.

Noonan decided he could not miss such a meeting. If the tide was going to turn, he wanted to be there when the surf was up and ride it rather than fight it. But he would have preferred not to be in the situation he was in. A moment had come when he should have stepped down from the tribunal, sat down with the archbishop and got around to what a man who had given such devoted service over so many years might be offered as a reward. The problem was that he was past the age when a huge prosperous parish looked attractive. He could imagine himself sweeping up the aisle of his church, preaching to his beloved people, living high off the hog with plenty of help, but inevitably he thought of the sense of responsibility he would have. Even if he got away to Cancún for a few days he would know that back there in Chicago everything depended on him. By comparison, life on the tribunal was a piece of cake. The cases all looked alike after a while; there seemed to be no surprises left in the marital sweepstakes; and now when decrees of nullity could be granted with a minimum of red tape, he was no longer haunted by those who begged to be declared unmarried.

Noonan clicked off the television, which had been running on mute, and picked up his breviary. It was his affectation to say the Breviarium Romanum that had been his daily prayer since his subdiaconate. This volume was from the same set of four he had bought then, and its pages were interleaved with memorial cards. Old Tuohy's was there now. Noonan wondered when his own would be a bookmark for men as yet unordained.

He did not like to think of the future. The Church and the priesthood were irrevocably different now than they had been. No one suspected Noonan of being saddened by this, just as no one would imagine he continued to say the office in the Latin as it had been established under

Pius XII. When Noonan had been a young priest, there had been older men who grumbled about the new translation, some of whom were permitted to use the version they had grown up with. Had that amused him at the time? He was like those old guys now, only he saw no reason to make it public. He dreaded the thought that he would be the object of amused condescension by the young.

He was distracted as he said vespers, but his mind got into gear with the Magnificat and then with Compline, his favorite hour; he could close his eyes and recite it from memory, the day being one that used the Sunday office. He closed the book and did not open his eyes. *Dixit Dominus domino meo, sedit a dexteris meis . . .* In memory he was back in the chapel at Mundelein, Sunday vespers, all of them in cassock and surplice, putting on and taking off their birettas, the stir of visitors in the loft. Noonan had carried the contentment of such moments into his priesthood. He opened his eyes. It was that he was being robbed of by this damned meeting at Notre Dame.

And he didn't even have a ticket to the game.

Actually, he had never liked sports, although he feigned an interest so as not to have to explain it. What was one supposed to make of a system of higher education when big-time athletics were the main means of identification by the public at large? College basketball, football—these provided standard fare on television, and people who had never seen the inside of a university or strolled the campus walks were furiously pro or con a given team. This was notorious in the case of Notre Dame, whose subway alumni stretched from coast to coast. For American Catholics it was *their* school, its victories a compensation for who knew what inadequacies. How ironic that this role had not been altered by the increasingly antipapist noises coming out of the campus. Apparently it was still possible to think of such dissenters as freaks rather than the standard. From what Monsignor Noonan was told, it was the papal Catholic who was the oddity there; certainly such Catholics were never heard from.

The effort to turn Ambrose Ravel's meeting into another occasion of protest, apart from the little shiver of morose delectation that Ravel might come out of this with egg on his face, annoyed Noonan. In the circumstances of the meeting, he dreaded the idea that his policies on the tribunal would be in any way linked with the radicals who spoke of Cardinal Hildebrand in terms that would once have been considered libelous, to say nothing of sacrilegious. *Der Eisenkardinal.* The man was actually called a fascist, a Nazi. Monsignor Noonan did not want the prefect of the Congregation of the Faith thinking that such people were his allies.

Noonan had half a mind to take the train with Roger and show up arm in arm with the canonist Ravel had pulled out of retirement for this meeting.

The ride through the South Side and then into East Chicago and Gary was not calculated to keep the passenger's nose pressed to the window, but after that it got better. Once the country around Fox River had looked like this, rural, rolling fields, farm buildings off on the horizon, but now through the valley one housing development after another sprouted from the prairie, and the main crop seemed to be sod for the new lawns.

Roger Dowling found that Fox River was moving with him along the rails, rather than the prospect of the meeting that lay ahead advancing toward him. Of course he was looking forward to meeting Cardinal Hildebrand. He nurtured few ambitions of knowing the ecclesiastical greats, but Hildebrand was an exception. It was a sign of the times that the cardinal's levelheaded, traditional explanation of and defense of Church doctrine was regarded as somehow retrogressive. For too long there had been too many whose idea of progress was equivocal at best. But it was the death of Gordon Furey, coming on the heels of Michael Geary's, that weighed on Father Dowling. He had spoken to Furey's widow, a wonderful woman, who reminded him that he had met her niece, Kate.

"She's coming up to be with me."

"Good."

"How well do you know her, Father?"

"Not well at all. She came to talk about her parents and the way their marriage was falling apart. I couldn't blame her for worrying. I think she thought I was urging her father along in his effort to get an annulment."

"Poor Michael."

And now poor Gordon. Poor Betty Furey.

"Kate is very wobbly in her faith. As a priest, you should know that."

It was the kind of confidence that was seldom welcome, one person reporting on the spiritual condition of another, but in Betty Furey's case, Roger Dowling sensed that she was not trafficking in churchy gossip.

"I came into the Church when I married Gordon and it always amazes me that cradle Catholics seem to have so little appreciation of what has just been handed them. Gordon wasn't like that."

"Sometimes people have to earn what's been given them. Young Catholics drift away, but with marriage and a family they begin to think of what it is they can offer their children. Many come back then and are stronger for the wandering. Not that I would recommend drifting away, of course. But then people who do, don't do it on the advice of a priest."

"I wish you'd talk to Kate."

"It's ironic that while she's here, I'll be at Notre Dame."

"Maybe she'll still be here when you return."

The unexplained death of Betty's husband would still be there. Father Dowling waited for her to give some indication of what had happened to him, but all she said was that she was as sure as one can be that he had been ready to die.

"He'd made a retreat just a week ago. After Michael's death."

One sometimes encountered a fierce desire on the part of the bereaved to know the condition of the departed. Father Dowling did not find this in Elizabeth Furey. She took consolation in the thought that her husband had so recently been on retreat, where presumably his mind and heart would have been on eternal things. Of course no mortal can read the secrets of another heart, and in those moments before the drama is done, the mystery of human freedom will write the ending, for good or ill.

But it was the role of others, or at any rate another, in these deaths that added to their mystery. Tuttle's claim to have been an eyewitness to the transfer of Michael Geary's body from the home of Catherine Burger to the parking lot behind Geary Insurance had sunk to that part of his mind where Father Dowling kept things told him in the confessional or outside of it in a confidence he considered almost equally binding, which is why he had avoided bringing it up voluntarily. He did not feel bound to secrecy in this instance. What constrained him was Tuttle's meager track record for frankness. The little lawyer's tale revealed him as an ambulance chaser of shameless proportions. It was Tuttle's seeming amorality that had prompted Amos Cadbury to employ his services. As if Tuttle required any spur to stalking potential clients. Did all this discredit Tuttle's story?

Of course Tuttle could simply be trying to enlist a priest in some scheme whose purpose was hidden to all but him but would surely turn out to be profitable to the firm of Tuttle & Tuttle. Had Tuttle been waiting since his visit to the rectory for Father Dowling to play his part, inform the police, and turn their investigation in a surprising direction, but one that Cy Horvath must have been thinking of when he and Agnes experimented with drive-bys at the insurance agency? Having established that someone other than Geary could have driven by the window and been assumed to be Geary by Florence Lewis, Cy had taken it no further. If Tuttle's story was true, exactly what Cy had shown to be possible had actually occurred.

But Tuttle, with his pipeline into police headquarters, doubtless knew of the tests Cy had r at the agency. The story he had brought to Father Dowling might then have suggested itself to him, and he had expected Father Dowling to go to the police. Instead he went to Catherine Burger.

"Why was he watching my house?" she had asked. It seemed an odd first reaction to hearing Tuttle's claim.

"He's not an ordinary lawyer."

"How do you mean?"

"Let me put it this way. Amos Cadbury holds him in low esteem. Will you do this? Tell Amos what Tuttle told me. You should be prepared if this were ever made public."

That was all he had done, otherwise keeping his own counsel. If Tuttle's story was true he would have to do eventually what he should have done at first—take it to Phil Keegan.

"Say they are connected," Keegan replied to the suggestion that it seemed rational enough to assume that there was a link between the deaths of Michael Geary and Gordon Furey. "You and I can sit here and come up with all kinds of ways they might be connected. So what? I don't have to tell you we can't act on the basis of mere possibility."

If Keegan were to permit himself to speculate, he would favor a domino theory. Furey killed his brother-in-law by contaminating his insulin supply and was subsequently killed himself. If his death was connected to Geary's, this suggested a falling apart of allies. Or the revenge of someone who knew what Furey had done.

"Taking us back to the Geary family. Did the wife kill her brother?"

Maureen said that she and her sister-in-law, Elizabeth Furey, were together at the time Furey was slain in his Avanti. Brian? Apart from the fact that he couldn't possibly have hidden in the diminutive back seat of the sports car, he had been talking with the rector of Mundelein Seminary when his uncle was killed.

"The daughter is very pregnant and besides was at her home on the Notre Dame campus when someone slipped the plastic bag over Gordon Furey's head."

"That accounts for the whole family."

"So who could have been allied with Furey in doing away with Geary? And who was the woman who picked up his insulin from Oscar Celsius?"

Father Dowling puffed on his pipe and thought of Freddy taking the body of Michael Geary out of his mother's house and driving it, in the trunk of Geary's car, to the insurance agency. There were other figures in the background of these events, among them Catherine Burger. The investigation would inevitably turn to her, but if she was the one who had filled Geary's prescription, there need be nothing ominous in that, given their relationship. If there was truth in Tuttle's story, it would come out without any intervention by Roger Dowling.

Or Tuttle would have to take the direct and potentially not very profitable route of simply telling the police what he claimed to have seen.

Joggling along on the South Shore—however sleek and new the cars, the roadbed was far from smooth—Father Dowling found himself unable to put aside wondering who had brought about the deaths of Michael Geary and Gordon Furey.

"I don't know," Elizabeth Furey had said. Just that. She didn't know, nor was she inclined to speculate.

As for Michael Geary, Marie Murkin wondered if it might not have been a disgruntled client. "You know what insurance agents are like, Father Dowling."

Noonan had a mordant suggestion. "The archdiocese might have employed a hit man to do away with Geary because he had cost them so much money by his philandering."

"What ever happened to the woman in the case?"

"I understand she is living in sybaritic luxury where the sun always shines."

"Poor Panzica."

"Are you kidding? He got off scot-free. The archdiocese assumed the burden of the settlement."

"Who was her lawyer?"

"Her father. A man named Christopher James."

The South Shore terminated at the airport, where Roger Dowling boarded a shuttle for the campus. When he checked in at the Morris Inn there was a note for him from Ambrose Ravel asking him to call. Roger Dowling made the call when he got to his room, but there was no answer. He tried several more times and then feel asleep in his chair. The ringing of his phone brought him awake.

"Roger? Ambrose. Would you come to room three-twenty-three across the street?"

Ravel's voice did not sound as if he were alone. And he wasn't. The tall man wearing corduroy trousers and a white cable-knit sweater proved to be the formidable Cardinal Josef Hildebrand. Noonan was there, and a Monsignor Tracy. Ravel introduced Roger Dowling to the cardinal as his special advisor, a former member of the Chicago tribunal. While this was going on, Roger had the undivided attention of Hildebrand.

"Former member?"

"Father Dowling is now pastor of a parish."

"Ah," Hildebrand said. "How I envy you."

He spoke of the pastoral work he had done as a young priest. "During my years of study, I sometimes helped the chaplain at one of your bases in Germany. There were young families there. I formed a very favorable impression of American Catholics."

Other participants in the meeting to be held the next day came in and, if they had not previously met the cardinal, were introduced. Ambrose Ravel drew Roger Dowling aside. He sighed a muted theatrical sigh.

"So far so good."

"How did you get past the pickets downstairs?"

"You obviously did."

"Just barely. Someone said something in German and when I turned my arm was grabbed. I think for a moment they thought I was the cardinal."

Ambrose Ravel smiled sternly. "Did you notice it?"

"What?"

"Your resemblance to Hildebrand."

Ravel was serious, but height, hair gone white and leanness seemed a flimsy basis for such a mistake.

"In the night all cats are black."

"The pickets prove it, Roger."

"And disprove it. Only momentarily were they misled."

A very unflattering thought occurred to Father Dowling, and he looked closely at Ambrose Ravel.

"Why exactly did you ask me to this meeting, Bishop?"

Ravel held up his right hand with its heavy episcopal ring as if he were deposing himself. "Roger, it only struck me when you came into the room and were talking with Hildebrand."

To doubt him was unattractive. Besides, as Ravel pointed out, the invitation had been extended long before there had been any possibility of negative reactions to Hildebrand's visit.

"It was not to be public at all. He would fly in, speak to the meeting, fly out, and only the participants would know."

All that had long since gone up in smoke, of course, and now Ravel confronted the problem of assuring the cardinal's safety.

There is a tunnel that connects the Morris Inn with the Center for Continuing Education across the road. This was designed for pedestrian traffic, but there is also a network of heating tunnels beneath the campus, connecting the various buildings to one another and eventually to the power plant, which over the years has expanded to meet the growing needs of the university. Because of the pickets at the entrance of the Morris Inn, Cardinal Hildebrand had been taken first to Moreau Seminary, on the far side of one of the campus lakes.

"Given the circumstances, Hildebrand preferred that. But he couldn't stay there. Roger, it is amazing how different things look when you are concerned with someone's safety. There is an east-west public road that runs beyond the seminary. If the protesters learned Hildebrand was there, it would be impossible to keep them away with less than an army of police. So he is being lodged in the rector's quarters on one of the residences."

"Which one?"

"It doesn't matter."

The cardinal could be spirited out of the Morris Inn via the tunnel to the CCE, and he could leave the CCE and go by heating tunnel to the DeBartolo classroom building, to Engineering or to O'Shaughnessy Hall. Emerging, he could be driven to his campus quarters.

"Come here, Roger."

From the window, Ravel pointed to the stretch limo in the parking lot.

"That's why the pickets think he's here."

"Won't they know of the tunnel?"

"We have to assume so. But chances are they will not realize the heating tunnels can be similarly used."

"So the limousine is a decoy."

"We must be wise as serpents and simple as doves."

Roger Dowling wondered whether serpentine logic rather than mere coincidence had prompted his invitation, no matter what Ravel said. He looked down at the long sleek car, a decoy, and felt a certain kinship with it.

What had struck the cardinal, and Monsignor Tracy could only agree, was the flatness of the terrain. Hildebrand had been born in Innsbruck, where one had to look straight up for unimpeded vision in a town that was a scattering of toy structures under the looming mountains. Northern Indiana was flat as a pancake and gave to anyone used to mountains the sense of being exposed. Now, with the threatened nuisance of the protesters and picketers, the flatness of things added to the difficulties of providing the cardinal with security.

Tracy had been given rooms just above the elegant quarters provided for Hildebrand in a building festooned with signs urging the defeat of Southern Cal on Saturday. One or two of the signs surprised Tracy, but the cardinal would have had to know American scatological vocabulary to decipher them.

"Southern Cal Sucks," he read.

"Just a slogan."

"I don't understand it."

"It's an Indian word." Tracy supposed the Indians had a word for it, in any case.

Far from being put out by the need to be moved about through heating tunnels and asked to dress in nonclerical clothes, Hildebrand seemed to be enjoying himself. Perhaps he had the sense of dwelling in the catacombs under a hostile imperial city, keeping out of harm's way but doing the Lord's work nonetheless.

"You prefer the big car, Monsignor?"

"This is fine."

They were being whisked along a campus walk in a golf cart. Hildebrand fit right in with the visitors who already crowded the campus in anticipation of the big game. Hildebrand had shown interest in the idea that he should see the game.

The president came like Nicodemus in the night to welcome the cardinal to the campus, where he was now unequivocally a guest. It was a brief pro forma visit, cordial enough, but the lanky priest looked warily at the cardinal, of whom he had obviously heard so many criticisms. Was he disarmed by a man who so easily fell in with the need for precaution, but who even in lay clothes retained the mien of a prince of the Church? The president emeritus also came and entertained the university's guest with stories of other distinguished visitors. Montini before his election, as earlier Pacelli before his.

"We're still trying to get your boss to come."

"You'll have to settle for me. At least for now."

Away from the Morris Inn, away from the noisy little group of protesters, Monsignor Tracy relaxed. What had threatened to become a disastrous visit now fell into a routine.

In the morning, first Hildebrand, then Tracy, said Mass in the beautiful chapel of the residence hall. Mullioned windows, stained glass of great artistic merit, a raftered ceiling of brilliant red, rich woodwork complementing the marble—it was an impressive place of worship. Without, however, a lot of worshippers at this hour, a boon to security.

A Continental breakfast was to be served in the CCE before the meeting opened. Again, Hildebrand obviously enjoyed being taken through heating tunnels and emerging unheralded into the building, where the voices of breakfasting participants were audible. Now that they had entered upon the schedule of the day. Monsignor Tracy relaxed. The hours ahead were all accounted for; there was no need to leave the building until after the final session in the afternoon; predictability was the keynote.

Ambrose Ravel opened the meeting. The three other bishops on his committee were there and an equal number of representatives from the Canon Law Society, two of them with obvious chips on their shoulders. The third, Corkery, unreadable, suave, was purportedly the éminence grise behind the intractability of the Church in the United States. When the new code was issued, he had written the downputting statement issued by the society; he was behind the scenes in the translation efforts of International Commission of English in the Liturgy, thanks to which the Universal Catechism had been delayed nearly two years, while elsewhere in the world it was having the hoped-for effect of clarifying the teaching of the Catholic Church. He showed up regularly on ternae, although there was no chance that he would ever become a bishop. But he had been at ease and respectful in talking with Cardinal Hildebrand, chatting with him about his successor in the diocese Hildebrand had had to give up when he answered the pope's summons to Rome.

The tables had been arranged in a square with Hildebrand and Ravel and Dowling, flanked by the three bishops and the three canonists. Noonan and a middle-aged woman, a nun, sat behind the canonists; there were some aides from Washington behind the bishops, and Monsignor Tracy sat behind the cardinal, on the qui vive should anything be needed. The fourth side of the square, opposite Ravel, was soon occupied by Christopher James, who had asked permission to speak on behalf of a group calling itself Victims of Canon Law.

"I wondered what VOCL meant," Hildebrand said.

"The claim to be a victim is often made," James replied. "I think you will agree that it is clearly applicable to those I represent."

There followed a terse, well-constructed tale of horrors—husbands finding to their amazement that their marriage had been declared null and void, the trauma of children of such nonexistent marriages, the questionable grounds that were allowed, the difficulty or impossibility of the noncomplaining partner's testifying, the want of zeal in many defenders of the bond. The account was anecdotal, studded with direct quotes, and James read it with a dispassionate yet intense voice.

Throughout, the bishops paid close attention, while two canonists frowned and Corkery wrote what appeared to be notes on what James was saying.

"Thank you very much, Mr. James," Ravel said. "That was a well-prepared presentation."

"Do those you represent concede that annulments are sometimes justly granted?" Corkery asked.

"They claim that in the cases they know about, justice does not seem to have been the overriding concern."

"But it is conceivable that no valid marriage was entered into even though one party thinks so."

"It takes two to tango," James said. "But it is when a declaration of nullity is made without the other partner being heard that many of my clients become particularly concerned."

"Any other questions or discussion?"

After James had been excused, the real discussion began. The bishops as well as the canonists, discovering that further statements would be presented, began to move toward the collective view that James, however eloquent, had given a distorted view of things.

"Admittedly, mistakes have been made, or apparently made," Bishop Velleity said.

"How often would you say that has happened?" Hildebrand asked.

"I don't have a number in mind, Your Eminence. Or even a percentage. I am thinking of general human fallibility."

Corkery sought the floor and began to shuffle the notes he had been making when he was recognized.

"I couldn't help think, while listening to Mr. James, how easy it would be to make a presentation that would give an entirely different picture of what tribunals have been doing in this country. I make no claim for the uniqueness of the United States, but I think it safe to say that certain tendencies are more pronounced here. Believers must function in a cultural atmosphere which sustains values often opposed to their own. Freedom and autonomy are cherished here as perhaps nowhere else. In good and bad forms. Catholics come to the altar with their heads and hearts full of assumptions that are simply part of the air they breathe. What tribunals have discovered is that there are warring conceptions of marriage in the minds of people even as they stand before the altar."

Corkery's remarks controlled the discussion for the rest of the morning. Hildebrand followed the discussion with rapt attention, and sat sideways in his chair when Father Dowling spoke.

"The difficulty I see in this," Roger Dowling said, "is that it is equally applicable to people when they apply for a declaration of nullity. Are they then presumed to be seeing marriage as the Church does, free of the intangible influence of the surrounding culture? If this is possible at one end of the process, it seems possible at the other. In all my years on the tribunal, I encountered two, perhaps three, cases where an annulment seemed justified."

"When did you leave the court, Father?" Corkery asked.

"Before the new code. Not that I see anything in the new code to explain the astonishing number of annulments granted in this country."

"Forty thousand a year," Hildebrand noted.

"I believe that's correct."

"Out of fifty thousand total throughout the world."

Corkery's fellow canonists looked at Roger Dowling as if he were a traitor to his class, but the cardinal's remarks gave pause to the bishops. In any case, the stage was set for the afternoon.

There was an hour break for lunch, and everyone but Hildebrand and Monsignor Tracy went to the Morris Inn. Tracy led the cardinal back through the heating tunnels to the meal that had been catered in the rector's quarters within the residence building where they were staying. When they returned to the CCE, participants were standing outside the meeting room looking down at the great lobby of the center.

"Hark, we are observed," Corkery said, looking out a window.

Tracy was not gratified to see the number of pickets now moving back and forth along the walk in front of the CCE. Last night there had been a dozen; now there seemed to be hundreds. The legends on the signs indicated that the protest had become general, all the grievances against an allegedly oppressive church reduced to slogans on signs that rose and fell with the movements of their bearers. Proponents of the ordination of women, opponents of celibacy, champions of homosexuality, far outnumbered the representatives of the group represented by Christopher James.

Trucks from television stations were visible, camera crews moved about with shoulder-mounted equipment, recording the event. Behind the protesters were others in great number, puzzled football fans who wondered what the commotion was about or, insofar as they understood, exhibited something less than sympathy for the protesters. It was not that they much cared about the protest as such, but this was not the sort of festive activity they wanted during a football weekend.

Freddy learned from Christopher James that Hildebrand could be spirited back and forth between the Morris Inn and the CCE via a tunnel that connected the two. ("That's the way I got there," James said.) No wonder the stretch limo hadn't moved from the parking lot since it had mysteriously appeared there. No one had seen it arrive.

Freddy went to check it out, as much as he could, given the tinted windows in the limo. Only the windshield was clear, and he leaned against the hood to look inside. All he could see was the front seat; the divider between the front and back was down. Hildebrand could be in there and no one would know. Except that Freddy knew he was across the street in the CCE.

"What do you want?" a voice asked as Freddy continued to look over the limo.

He swung around, but he was alone. There was the sound of laughter. It came from inside the limo. Freddy knocked on the tinted window and in a moment it slid down.

"Some rig," Freddy said. The driver did not seem to recognize him from O'Hare, perhaps because of the football fan costume Freddy now wore. "Is it yours?"

"You want to rent it?"

"Aren't you hired?"

"Where you from?"

"I was going to ask you the same thing."

"You mean you didn't notice the Illinois plates when you were looking her over."

His name was Leo Berlioz, and he warmed to Freddy's curiosity. "Come on in and see what luxury's really like."

The door unlocked and Freddy got in. There was a television going; the bar was open and Leo was having a bourbon and water. Freddy said he'd have the same.

Leo was a type Freddy had always gotten along with, and before long he was getting the story of the big shot from Rome the driver had brought down from O'Hare.

"We nipped right past the inn, though. No one expected those pickets. Now look at them over there."

"What's it all about?"

"You tell me."

"This is great bourbon."

"There's more where that came from."

And so there was. As Leo got progressively more sloshed, he went on and on about the limo, so that when he turned away and Freddy brought the empty bourbon bottle down on his head, Freddy knew all there was to know about the car. He hit the driver again with a full bottle, then released the trunk. It took an act of faith to believe that while he could see out no one could see in. When the coast was clear, he carried Leo back to the trunk. He got adhesive tape from the first-aid kit and secured his arms behind his back, and sealed his mouth up too. He was moaning when Freddy closed the trunk, proof enough that he was able to breath despite his taped-shut mouth. Then Freddy locked the limo, pocketed the keys and went back to the inn. In the lobby, James was standing at the check-in counter with a tan young woman wearing sunglasses who apparently had just arrived.

"I could have told you there are no rooms, Amanda. This is a football weekend."

"That's why I came. I want to see that game."

James was in agony. He had no tickets, he had no room. By this time Freddy had recognized James's daughter in her Florida outfit, and he joined them. Amanda took off the sunglasses when Freddy was introduced as if she wanted to enjoy her father's unawareness as much as Freddy would. Freddy gave her the soupçon of a wink with the eye James could not see, even as he told himself that Amanda had looked younger with the sunglasses on.

"How did it go?" he asked James.

"Fine, fine. I'll give you a full report."

"What's the problem?"

"Amanda wants to see the game tomorrow."

"No problem."

"Are you serious?"

Freddy removed from his pocket the tickets he had taken from Leo before closing the trunk door. He handed them to James.

"With my compliments. But you won't get a room here, you know."

"So I'm told."

James gave it some thought. "We could return to Chicago and then come back in the morning."

Amanda moaned at the prospect.

"I guess it's my day to be the Good Samaritan. You can have my room at the Holiday Inn."

He explained that it was a large room, with two double beds. Not ideal, but better than driving back and forth to Chicago.

"But what will you do?"

"Maybe I'll kidnap the cardinal and hold him for ransom."

And they all laughed about that.

The Jameses, father and daughter, went to check out the motel room Freddy had turned over to them. Freddy took a seat in the lobby and got out his crossword puzzle magazine—only the tough ones, a real challenge—and settled down. He had a view of the stairway up which people came from the tunnel leading across the street. There was a big beefy guy, probably a cop, sitting on a straight-backed chair, his hands on his knees, looking inscrutably ahead. One Across was a five-letter word for Wise Ones, and One Down was a Tiff. Freddy settled down. This puzzle would be an absorbing piece of cake.

At noon, the participants came back, through the tunnel as Freddy had expected. He had bought a paper in the interval and now peered over its top at the clerics coming eagerly to their meal. There was no Cardinal Hildebrand.

From the entrance of the inn, Freddy looked across the street at the pickets milling around, a picture of futility and ineffectualness. Imagine if he had decided to rely on them. Academic rhetoric feared no excesses, but action left everything to be desired. Freddy took out his portable phone and put through a call to Sedge.

"I've got the limo, but I don't know what good it will do. Big Bird is nowhere in sight."

They discussed it a bit. The cardinal could still be over there in the CCE. Freddy doubted it. Why?

"Intuition."

"That's my department."

"So intuit where the hell he is."

"Maybe there are other tunnels."

And maybe there is such a thing as intuition. Freddy rang off and went out to the limo, where he put on the chauffeur's cap and rolled out of the parking lot. The guard at the gate waved him through with a grin, and Freddy proceeded along the campus road, past the grotto, up a little rise, and then he saw the smokestacks of the heating plant. Heat must be pumped from the plant to the various buildings. There had to be underground tunnels connecting all the buildings to the power plant and, in some cases, to one another.

Freddy hung a right at the firehouse and went up a narrow road to where it stopped. He pulled into a restricted parking space and turned off the motor. He sat, gathering his thoughts, and became aware of a muffled sound. He got out and went around back and bent over the closed trunk. Leo was trying to yell through the tape as he kicked at the door.

Looking around, not liking all the windows of the building behind him, Freddy decided not to do anything about Leo for the moment. Instead, he crossed a road to a building that was just east of the CCE and went inside. A classroom building. A tour was under way for those visiting for the weekend, and Freddy fell in with it.

The girl leading the tour had straight hair and an adenoidal problem and chirped her account in a rote way. She was big on the state-of-the-art audiovisual teaching aids available to the faculty in this building.

"How is the building heated?" Freddy called over the intervening heads.

The interruption threw her off. "Heated."

A little guy in his fifties wearing a Notre Dame jacket and cap, brand new from the bookstore, nodded. "Yeah, how do you heat this place? How do you heat all these buildings?"

The girl gave a kind of helpless smile, then had the solution. "Let's ask."

She marched them downstairs to the office of the director of maintenance. A tall guy with surprised eyes and an overbite, he was more than happy to show them the mysteries of the heating and cooling of his building. And so Freddy was introduced to the tunnel system.

He stayed behind when the group went off, pulled open the door to the tunnel, and stepped in. It was hot and airless and the light seemed doubly artificial. He crossed to the door at the end of the tunnel, opened it and looked inside. Proof positive. He had stepped back into the tunnel when he heard voices coming toward him through it. He opened the door again and entered the CCE and found himself facing a guard.

"They're coming," he said, nodding toward the tunnel. "Everything secure?"

A nod. Freddy was still wearing the chauffeur's cap. Perhaps it was this that disarmed the guard. Freddy was holding the door to the tunnel open, and through it now emerged a tall white-haired figure wearing civilian clothes. Hildebrand. Well, well. A species of disguise. He was followed by a shorter man with an Irish face and questioning eyes.

"Where's Leo?"

"I've replaced him. The car's on campus now, I got it out of the parking lot."

The man didn't like that. And Freddy, intuiting effortlessly now, saw why. The car had been a decoy.

"Should I take it back?"

"Where is it now?"

"By your building."

"Morrissey? Get it away from there. I don't care where else you park it, but get it out of there."

Freddy touched his fingers to the bill of the cap and disappeared into the tunnel. Odd how whistling echoed in the tunnel.

He emerged in the classroom building, went out the east door and started toward the spot where he had left the limo. There were half a dozen people standing around it, looking at the trunk, jabbering to one another. Whoops. Freddy took off his cap and deposited it in a trash can, cut away from the scene and got out his portable phone.

"Problems," he said when Sedge answered. He explained about the limo.

"You're lucky the guy's still alive."

"No. He's lucky."
"So what do we do?"
"It may be easier to accomplish our objective now."
He gave careful directions as to how Sedge should do it.
"Without a car?"
"There are cars all around the campus."

Noonan, sitting behind those at the table, watched the reactions to the cardinal's declaration. The bishops, up to that point cooperative, almost obsequious, began to squirm, trying not to look at one another. Doubtless they were thinking of the reaction to the new rule among their fellow bishops and the criticism that they should have said something at the time. The mouths of two of the canonists dropped open, but Corkery, who should have been affected most negatively, seemed positively happy, as if his worst predictions had been realized. He had the look of a man eager to get the meeting over so that he could get on the phone. Ambrose Ravel leaned toward the cardinal, as if wanting to make sure that what he was reading was actually on the paper he held. A great idea was in the process of blowing up in Ravel's face.

Acting with the assent and authority of the Holy Father, the Congregation for the Doctrine of the Faith reserved the final judgment on all declarations of nullity to the Sacred Rota in Rome. As under previous procedures, local tribunals could admit appeals and undertake preliminary investigations and then recommend for or against nullity. But the declaration itself must from now on come from Rome. The Congregation, with the assent of the Holy Father, acted in defense of the marriage bond and the sanctity of the sacrament of matrimony.

Hildebrand invited no discussion when he was done. He bowed his head as Corkery led the prayer. His statement had obviously been prepared before his coming to the States. Reading it had been his purpose when he had agreed to attend the meeting. Participants were informed that copies of the decision were already in the mail to the bishops. This was a lowering of the boom. Noonan was not yet sure what his own reaction was.

"What do you make of it, Roger?"

"We were asking for something like this."

"It'll be the old story over again."

Roger Dowling nodded. "The new story was worse."

Noonan let it go, drifting to Corkery, with whom he had had lunch. They had been on the same wavelength, and it surprised Noonan that Corkery still seemed happy as a lark. Didn't he recognize a slap in the face when he got it?

"This one's for the bishops," Corkery said. "If they sit still for this, well . . ."

Well what? Noonan found it impossible to imagine the American bishops rebelling against a decision that many of them, like Roger Dowling, would likely think the tribunals of the nation had provoked. Dissent from canonists and theologians was one thing, but it is not open to bishops to separate themselves from the Vatican.

Roger Dowling was in conversation with Cardinal Hildebrand. Noonan was struck by the resemblance between the two men, an outer as well as an inner resemblance. The conversation did not look as if it would soon break up. Noonan, wondering why he had accepted Ravel's invitation, took the elevator to the basement and went through the tunnel to the Morris Inn.

He wasn't staying, he had no room in the inn, he might as well get started back. The bar was unappealing; besides, he wasn't sure what the local practice was on the matter of clerical drinking in public places. The thought of his own rooms, quiet solitude, a scotch and water, drew him outside. Across the street, the pickets seemed subdued. And then he saw Corkery. He seemed to be handing over his copy of Hildebrand's statement to a picket wearing a Roman collar. The aim was obviously to cause trouble—so much for Corkery's remark that it was up to the bishops to react to the cardinal's decision. Well, Hildebrand had not stated any restrictions on the use and dissemination of the document.

On the drive home, Noonan treated himself to imagined scenarios of what might have happened. In the silence following Hildebrand's bombshell, Noonan rose slowly to his feet; heads turned and soon all eyes were on him. His expression was serious, almost sad.

"Your Eminence, I respectfully suggest that you are making a tragic mistake. Those of us who have served on tribunals seem to be in the dock here. Is that fair? Monsignor Corkery has already drawn our attention. . . ."

The exact words he might have spoken did not emerge clearly from his imagination, but the electrifying effect of his speech on others was obvious. Cardinal Hildebrand, chin in hand, listened with close attention. Soon he put a few questions to Noonan, who, with consummate diplomacy, dignified deference, responded. Soon the cardinal stood, looked around the room, picked up the statement he had read and tore it to pieces. Applause broke out . . .

Noonan in his abstraction had gotten trapped in a middle lane with a lane of trucks to his right, a high semi ahead, another behind, and to his left a ceaseless flow of cars. It was claustrophobic, and he sought to extricate himself, to pull off the road, relieve his bladder and have a cup of coffee. It took him ten miles to accomplish the extrication and another twelve before an oasis appeared. It was with a sense of escape that he took the exit ramp.

The oasis bridged the interstate so that, sipping his coffee from a paper cup, Noonan watched the traffic sweep beneath the restaurant. It seemed an odd way to provide respite from the road. Travelers came and went, the eastbound and westbound mingling in this aerie over the highway, men and women, children, young and old; they were an adequate sample of the race, of the Church. Hildebrand's surprising announcement affected the people, not just canonists like himself. What would be the effect of making annulments all but impossible of attainment? Broken marriages would be escaped by divorce. Annulment had provided an alternative that enabled the Catholic to remain in good standing with the Church, as of course civil divorce did not. But Noonan could not disguise from himself the fact that Hildebrand's announcement gave him a sense of relief.

"Can the tribunal make a mistake?" Noonan had been asked more than once by disgruntled children or spouses after an annulment was granted. And sometimes by the successful petitioner.

"Our judgment was reached with great care."

"But is it infallible?"

"You have no reason to doubt its validity."

"But could you be wrong?"

Of course the tribunal could be wrong, but the recipient of an annulment, acting on the tribunal's judgment and remarrying, could scarcely be guilty of anything. Had the tribunal ever knowingly cut corners?

Such a question was difficult to answer. Noonan remembered the vertigo he had felt the first time a decision of nullity had been reached. That sense diminished and then disappeared with time. Had this been the acquisition of an erroneous conscience? On retreat Noonan had been bothered by such thoughts, and he had resolved them as best he could and gone back to work. Cardinal Hildebrand, by reserving all final judgments to Rome, had lifted a burden from Noonan, one heavier than he had permitted himself to think.

When finally he did get home and, slippered and sweatered, sat at his desk nursing a drink, he slid out the drawer that contained letters he had not opened. Experience had taught him to recognize what he thought of as crank letters from their envelopes. Sometimes he was fooled and opened a letter and started to read it before he pitched it into this drawer. He took a handful of letters and shuffled through them. He stopped and went back, struck by a return address. "Brian Geary, La Crescent MN." The scrawled address had earned it quick consignment to the drawer. After hesitation, Monsignor Noonan opened it. The message was prefaced by no salutation.

"What God has joined together, let no man put asunder."

After Roger Dowling had exchanged pleasantries with Cardinal Hildebrand, he told him that his decision, while apparently harsh, seemed called for.

"At least temporarily. Perhaps, with appropriate prudence, discretion can be returned to local tribunals after a time."

"I hope so, Father. We will of course increase staff in Rome, I hope with the support of the American bishops, so that unacceptable delays before judgments can be avoided."

"That is wise."

"We will want a good representation from this country, of course."

Roger Dowling changed the subject and got away from the speculative regard of the cardinal. He looked around for Noonan, but he was nowhere in sight. Perhaps he could catch him at the Morris Inn.

"Roger," Ambrose Ravel called, stopping him. Ravel hurried up. "Don't go. We've been asked to the cardinal's rooms."

"Surely not me."

"By name."

Roger Dowling's heart sank. It was absurd to think he was in danger of being drafted for the larger team Hildebrand had spoken of, but he could not quell the fear.

"I really should get back to my room, Ambrose." He felt like a kid and was on the verge of pleading an imaginary illness when he thought of a serviceable truth. "I want to call Phil Keegan."

"Roger, this is a command performance."

Ravel turned and went back to the little group around Hildebrand. Monsignor Tracy came up to the cardinal and suggested they leave now. Going off with Tracy, even if it was to the cardinal's quarters, seemed to get him at least temporarily out of harm's way.

They took the elevator to the basement of the CCE, and when Father Dowling turned toward the tunnel leading to the Morris Inn, Tracy took his arm.

"This way."

"We'd better use the tunnel, unless you want to run the gamut of those protesters outside."

"Oh, we're going by tunnel. The cardinal and I are not staying in the inn. For security reasons."

Tracy nodded to the guard, who opened a door into a tunnel much different from that going to the inn. It was lined with pipes and offered but a narrow passage. Tracy moved along at a great clip, apparently accustomed to this way.

"The cardinal likens these tunnels to the catacombs."

"These are better lit, if I remember rightly."

"Ah, you've been to Rome."

"When I was young."

Tracy gave him a quick look. "Are you so venerable?"

"Almost as much as Bede."

Clerical humor, just the sort of thing he wanted to avoid. He didn't want Tracy or Hildebrand to think he was interesting, diverting, a fine fellow to have around.

At the end of the tunnel, Tracy pulled open a door with a practiced hand and they emerged into a building the monsignor identified as DeBartolo. "I've become quite an expert on the campus."

"Many of the buildings weren't even here a few years ago."

Tracy's progress slowed. "Speaking of the campus, there's no need for us to keep using the tunnels. It's the cardinal we're spiriting underground."

"I find this fascinating. I wish my parish plant had tunnels like these."

Tracy made a dismissive gesture. "It's okay with me. But I do want to just stroll around this campus before we leave."

"It's beautiful. This may be its best season. Fall."

Tracy had turned from the stairway that had been his destination, and they entered a hallway that took them to the door of the next tunnel. This one was larger and seemed to have been made with an eye to traffic, but Tracy had been assured by campus security that these tunnels were never used as they were using them.

The lights went out.

Roger Dowling walked into Tracy, who had stopped abruptly.

"Maybe that's why they're not used."

"This never happened before." There was a quaver in Tracy's voice. "Maybe we should go back the way we came."

"Listen."

Behind them there was the sound of a door closing. Someone else had entered the tunnel. There was a pinpoint of light and then darkness. A flashlight. Dowling took Tracy's elbow and whispered, "Can you find your way ahead?"

How could they lose their way in a tunnel?

"If we go slowly." They began to pick their way forward in the dark, while behind them the sounds of someone approaching grew closer. "I forgot to tell you I hate to be in places like this. But in the dark . . ." Tracy actually shivered.

"Think of the catacombs."

"I'm trying not to. I have never been able to take a tour of any of them."

"Spelunkophobia? *Cave cavem?*"

"Don't."

Tracy really was taking this badly. Suddenly he stopped. The tunnel ahead of them was flooded with light, and then there was the sound of a door closing and darkness descended.

"Who's there?" Tracy cried out.

There was no answer either before or behind. Tracy had come to a dead stop, and it was clear he did not intend to move. Quite apart from his fear of such places, Tracy had lived since coming to Notre Dame under the threat of something happening to Cardinal Hildebrand. Until now, Roger Dowling had assumed that meant merely a threat to the dignity of his office, being hurried past pickets hurling impossible demands and accusations at him. It had not occurred to him that the danger might be physical. Getting away from Fox River had seemed, in the light of recent events, an escape from violence and unexpected death. Tracy was trembling now as if certain he was *in ictu mortis*. Roger Dowling tightened his grip on Tracy's arm.

From time to time, in front of them and behind them, narrow beams of light would appear, then disappear, like meteors in the night sky. There were at least two others in the tunnel with them, and they were converging slowly on them. The lights might have been signaling one another.

"Who is there?" Monsignor Tracy cried again, and his voice shook with emotion and echoed back to them.

"Tell them who you are."

"They know that," Tracy said, his voice a whisper of despair now. "This is what they feared."

Roger Dowling said aloud, "If you think Cardinal Hildebrand is here, you are mistaken. I am with Monsignor Tracy, the cardinal's—"

A light shone suddenly in his face, blinding him.

"That's him," a voice said.

A push sent Roger Dowling stumbling, and his grip on Tracy's arm was broken as he instinctively put out his hand to break his fall. His head hit a pipe, painlessly, and he might have regained his balance if someone had not pushed him again. Then something pressed against his face, covering his nose and mouth, suffocating him. The odor caused him to hold his breath and close his mouth, but it invaded his nostrils and finally he had to breathe, and when he did his head was filled with an alien mist; he felt that he was desperately climbing a ladder in his mind, toward some diminishing objective, until the dark was replaced with a flash of reddish light and he went limp.

Scuttling along the leafy campus walks, his tweed hat pulled low over his eyes and a green scarf he had found on a bench wrapped around his throat, Tuttle looked like any other fan in for the big game the following day. The difference was that the rest of them could probably afford it, while he was here on spec. He didn't have a ticket either, but Peanuts Pianone had been given a name by an uncle and was over at the Joyce Athletic and Convocation Center trying to wangle passes.

Ahead of Tuttle on the walk was Freddy Burger, loping along, a real puzzler, that kid. Tuttle told himself that his surveillance of Catherine Burger's son was an assignment from Amos Cadbury, or at least a plausible extension of the assignment he'd been given. But that bird Brian seemed to spend most of the day in church, and unless he was jimmying the poor box there didn't seem any point in continuing to follow him. You've seen one church, you've seen them all. It was Tuttle's fiction that he himself preferred to worship in the great cathedral of nature, and the campus, its trees golden and red and tan, the brisk bracing air, the sound of a band in the distance, made the little lawyer feel he was in church, his kind of church.

For the past hour, Freddy had been leading him a merry chase around the campus, looking speculatively at buildings, obviously not knowing where the hell he was going. At Corby—with Fair Catch Corby on the lawn out front, a Civil War chaplain who had been at Gettysburg and was depicted blessing the troops, one hand lifted high as if in a signal—Freddy went up the walk and was climbing the steps to the porch when a priest came out. Freddy tried to engage him in conversation, but his charm must have failed him. With a downturned mouth and a frown, the priest shook his head.

Freddy came down the steps with the priest and walked beside him to the road. Tuttle had to give it to the kid for guts.

"My mother met him once in Rome," Freddy was saying.

"He must be at the Morris Inn," the priest said. "He isn't here."

Freddy shook his head, smiling, then fished in his pocket and brought out a rosary.

"She wanted me to get the cardinal to bless these. Could you do it, Father?"

A request he couldn't refuse, even though he was obviously anxious to get into his car. He put out his hand; Freddy dropped the rosary into it, and then the priest began to mumble some prayers while making the sign of the cross over the beads.

"I'm no cardinal, but those are now as blessed as they can be."

"Thank you, Father. What's your name?"

Guts. Tuttle smiled. He didn't catch the priest's answer. Freddy stood in the middle of the road, waving as the priest drove away. He was still smiling when he turned and started to come straight toward Tuttle. The best defense seemed to be an offense. Tuttle walked toward Freddy but craning his neck, looking up at the steeple of the campus church. He had the feeling Freddy was looking him over pretty good, but nothing was said. Freddy danced up the steps of the church, wrestled open the big door and disappeared inside. Thinking of Brian Geary, Tuttle groaned.

The sight of an empty bench under a tree offered an alternative to going into the church. He beat an elderly couple to it and sat at one end, indicating he would share it with them. The old guy had a Class of '44 button on. They didn't sit, but Tuttle had already made himself comfortable, adjusting his hat, ready to keep an eye on the church door.

The bell struck the quarter hour, then the half, and Tuttle smelled a rat. Freddy did not look like the kind of guy who would put in extended periods in church. He got off the bench and accelerated as he went toward the church. The thought was growing in him that Freddy had deliberately shaken him.

For ten minutes, Tuttle searched the church, followed around by a guy in uniform who looked closely at Tuttle as he told him it was customary to remove one's hat in church.

"I'm Jewish," Tuttle said.

"Everyone is welcome here," the guard said.

"I'm looking for my son, young fellow, always smiling, came in maybe twenty minutes ago."

The man looked at him and Tuttle was afraid he was going to get a lecture on how many people visited the church, particularly on game weekends, and how busy the guard was and all the rest, so he waved his hat and started up the aisle.

Freddy was clearly not in the church, and he had had his choice of several possible exits. Outside again, Tuttle decided to return to home base, meaning the Morris Inn. Freddy was registered there; the meeting was across the street from the inn; he had to go back there. Maybe he already had. Tuttle went bumping along the walk, seeming to be going against the stream of the traffic.

Freddy was in the parking lot checking out a stretch limo. Tuttle, relieved to have caught up with him, decided he had better take extra precautions and stay out of sight. There was a hedge running along the walk in front of the inn that would provide cover enough. He got behind it, took off his signature hat, and to his consternation found that Freddy was no longer in the parking lot. But the back door of the limo was just being pulled shut. Tuttle decided it was a safe assumption that Freddy had gotten into the passenger section of the limo.

This guy was incredible, that had been clear from the time Tuttle saw him haul Geary's body away from his mother's house.

"You see the body?" Peanuts had asked.

"It had to be."

"He came home, found the guy with his mother and whacked him?"

"That could have been it."

Tuttle hadn't believed it then, but now that he knew Freddy better he could imagine the kid doing damned near anything. Of course Tuttle knew about VOCL—by rights he should be its legal counsel—and he knew James was representing the organization at this meeting with the big shot from Rome. Freddy's interest in the limo dated from the trip from O'Hare yesterday, Freddy following the limo and Tuttle following Freddy.

"Where's this guy going?" Peanuts had asked.

"Where that limo's going."

"Where's the limo going?"

"Notre Dame."

"If you know that, why follow him?"

Tuttle put a finger beside his nose. "Instinct."

"Bullshit."

"That's your instinct, Peanuts. But I ask you, when have I been wrong?"

"You mean the last time you was?"

"Ever."

"When you ever been right?"

"Trust me."

"I can't be driving a Fox River patrol car through Indiana."

"Call in and report it stolen."

While Peanuts had pondered that possibility they had crossed the Indiana state line and the point had become academic. Tuttle had told Peanuts he was on special assignment.

"You'll get a citation for this."

"I'll get suspended." Peanuts shook his head. "Naw, they can't touch me."

"You bet they can't. When you explain to them how Geary and his brother-in-law died, they'll tell you to keep this car."

"I don't want this car. Listen to the motor."

"How we doing on gas?"

"What's this trip got to do with Geary and the other guy?"

"You'll see."

"Who's in the limo?"

"Someone very big. From Italy."

"Yeah. Sicily?"

"Not directly."

Peanuts buttoned his lip. There were certain things you never talked about, never. And family connections with the old country were definitely one of them. The silence gave Tuttle time to think. When he said he was following instinct he meant it, but from the time he had seen Freddy put that bundle in Geary's trunk and drive off Tuttle had known something was up. When he'd learned that Geary had been found propped up behind the wheel of his car in the parking lot behind his agency, Tuttle had figured out what Freddy had put in the trunk of Geary's car. This was going to be bigger than he'd thought.

What exactly it was, he didn't know. He didn't pretend he did. There were simple explanations. Carting a dead body around like that was some sort of crime, no doubt about that, but who was going to blame a kid for trying to spare his mother some scandal? Not Tuttle, by God. But there was the possibility Peanuts had mentioned. Say Geary was still among the living when Freddy got home and an outraged son put him into the next world.

Only that didn't jibe with the cause of death, which was poison from Geary's drip drip insulin dispenser. Whoever did that did it in cold blood, not in a fit of passion.

The problem was that Freddy kept on doing funny things. Not his lifestyle, though that had come as a surprise to Tuttle. Maybe he was a switch-hitter, because there were dames, no doubt about it; they seemed to come out of tanning parlors. He wasn't thinking of Geary's daughter, though Freddy had been to see her, and seemed part of the VOCL thing, like James's daughter, business connections, so to speak. People with a beef.

Now, from behind the hedge, Tuttle saw the lid of the trunk pop up and then, sure enough, Freddy stepped out of the limo and smiled at the world. He dipped back inside the limo and dragged something out. A body! Freddy rested his burden and put something on his head. A chauffeur's cap. Quick as a fox, Freddy cradled the guy in his arms and took him around the car and put him in the trunk. He spent some time before closing the lid. Then he slid behind the wheel and backed the limo out of its parking space.

Tuttle raced through the parking lot to where Peanuts was snoozing at the wheel of the unmarked Fox River police car. Tuttle knew from naps Peanuts had taken in the offices of Tuttle & Tuttle after a feast of ordered-in Chinese that his friend was a troubled sleeper who came awake swinging. He pounded on Peanuts's window, rounded the car, and piled in beside him.

"Follow that limo."

Peanuts had the car going and out of the parking lot before he could have had any idea what he was doing. The limo was just being waved through the gate.

"Tell him it's police business."

"It's a her."

"Show her your badge."

The gate guard came out of her shack and stood beside the car. Peanuts had trouble getting his wallet out of his pocket. Tuttle leaned across the seat.

"We're police officers on official business."

She laughed. She thought it was a joke. Considering the still fumbling Peanuts, she had a point. Finally he flipped his wallet at her. It closed immediately, and he opened it and showed her the badge.

"Is that real?"

"Take a look."

She did. "Fox River, Illinois. Where is that?"

"Where it says. Illinois."

"Near Chicago?"

"Right. On the Fox River."

"What kind of business could you be on here?"

Tuttle got her attention. "You know that stretch limo you just let through?"

"What about it?"

"It's stolen. We got to get going."

She hesitated, looked back at her telephone, finally decided to lift the gate and let them through. The limo had long since gone out of sight.

They took a couple of wrong turns, one of which took them out to a cemetery where uniform white crosses stood over the graves of former members of the community, another of which took them to the maintenance building, but finally, just when Tuttle was about to suggest they turn back, he saw the limo parked ahead. Peanuts pulled up behind it.

A man who had passed the limo now stopped and was looking back at it. Tuttle went immediately to the trunk and tapped on it. A groan from within and a kicking sound. The man who had stopped came back, scratching at his beard.

"Is someone in there?"

"It sounds like it."

"Good Lord."

Tuttle asked Peanuts if he knew how to open the trunk and Peanuts waddled to the driver's door and pulled it open. A full minute went by and then the trunk door began to lift. Inside was a bound and gagged man. Tuttle reached in and pulled the tape off his mouth, bringing the man screaming in pain to a sitting position. He swore fervently.

"It's the only way," Tuttle assured him. "What happened?"

Peanuts came up and showed the man his badge. He asked to see it more closely. By now a crowd had collected. The bearded man began removing the tape from the man's wrists. Tuttle walked away, looking for Freddy. When he saw the building just across a mall from the CCE, he knew where he was going.

Phil Keegan was standing at the check-in desk of the Morris Inn when the clerk took a phone call he could not help overhearing. Someone was anxious to get in touch with Father Dowling. "I'll put you through to his room."

"I was just about to ask you what room Father Dowling is in."

"My, he's popular."

The phone rang again, and she picked it up, her brows lifting as she listened. "He doesn't answer. Well, he must be out then. No, he didn't leave a message." More listening. She rolled her eyes at Keegan and readied her pencil. "Bishop who?"

Even upside down, her writing was easy to read. "Ambrose Ravel."

"Here, I'll talk to him."

She didn't want to give up the phone at first. This was all quite irregular. Keegan showed her his badge. She gave him the phone.

"Bishop Ravel. This is Captain Phil Keegan. I just got in and I'm looking for Father Dowling. We're going to the game tomorrow, thanks to you."

"The phone in his room rang forever. He was supposed to be here talking with Cardinal Hildebrand."

"He didn't make it to the meeting?"

"The meeting is over. We are in the cardinal's room."
"Here?"
A pause. "On campus. Not in the Morris Inn."
"Maybe he's on his way."
"He left before we did, together with Monsignor Tracy, the cardinal's chaplain."
"Well, the campus is pretty crowded."
"Are you going to be there for some time, Captain?"
"I'm just checking in."
"I may get back to you."
"When Roger shows up, tell him I'm here."
Keegan handed the phone back to the clerk.

Something was wrong, he had a feeling and he couldn't shake it, but he went up to his room and washed up and waited for Ravel to call him. He kicked himself for not asking Ravel to give him a number. The inn operator had no idea where Cardinal Hildebrand was staying. Phil got out of his shoes, lay on the bed and, against all expectation, dropped off.

The room was dark when he awoke and in the moment it took him to figure out where he was the vague anxiety returned. He turned on the light and then the television. It was on the local news.

A young man with a pointed face and a slight lisp was talking of the kidnapping of Cardinal Hildebrand.

"This station was contacted within the hour. We have agonized over how to handle this situation." His face reenacted the agonizing. "We have decided that we should read the message given us. This is it. 'Cardinal Josef Hildebrand is in our custody. No harm will come to him. He will be returned when a ransom is paid. Further instructions will be given on this channel.' "

The announcer looked helplessly into the camera. "That's it. Is this a hoax? Has the cardinal really been kidnapped? Needless to say, anyone with information on this subject is urged to contact this station without delay."

Phil Keegan was on his feet, angry that a television station would allow itself to be used in such a way. The guy wondered if it was a hoax! The only possible explanation for such a stupid announcement was that the announcer was himself being threatened. Keegan worked his feet into his shoes and picked up the phone.

"Give me Roger Dowling's room."
"Others have been asking for him. He's not answering."
Down in the lobby he asked where he could get a cab. He didn't

want to search for that television channel. Coming toward him as he started for the door was Bishop Ravel.

"Captain Keegan. Have you seen Father Dowling?"

"He didn't show up?"

"I can't believe it. The cardinal's secretary also failed to show up."

"Was the cardinal there?"

"Of course."

"There was an announcement on television minutes ago. Someone is claiming to have kidnapped Cardinal Hildebrand."

"How long ago?"

"Just now."

"But that's impossible. He's in his room."

Keegan looked at Ravel and Ravel looked at him. Maybe the cardinal wasn't missing, but his secretary and Father Dowling were. It was Ravel who said it.

"They must have taken Roger for the cardinal. There is a resemblance, I was struck by it earlier today."

"Who is they?"

Keegan listened to Bishop Ravel's account of the protesters who had been outside the CCE during their meeting.

"They shouted some pretty severe things whenever we went by. They were furious that Cardinal Hildebrand didn't come out."

"You think they went after him?"

"And took Roger Dowling and Monsignor Tracy? I don't know."

Keegan contacted the local police, suggesting that someone must have been putting pressure on the television station for them to broadcast an uncorroborated claim to have kidnapped the cardinal. A man named Zweck came for him, a sergeant, about Cy Horvath's age, and they drove to the station. The lisping telecaster was called to the reception area by a pretty excited receptionist.

"They were here. They threatened me. I had to read that message."

"You still got it?"

A nod. "But it's in my handwriting. She made me write it down."

"She?"

"You'd have to see her. Besides she had the kind of gun everyone wants to make illegal."

"What were they driving?"

"Bikes."

Zweck and Keegan exchanged a look.

"Bikes?"

"Motorbikes. Hondas. Powerful." Did there lurk behind the makeup, the impeccable attire, the life devoted to surface and appearance, a wild desire to roar off into the unknown?

"Which way did they go?"

Two bikes had gone off in opposite directions. No help there. "What did they look like?"

An androgynous cameraperson whose ponytail was no cue to gender raised a hand for attention.

"I think I got them on tape." She—her name was Juanita—patted her camera.

And so she had. A minute later, the tape was run for Zweck and Keegan. "Is that a woman?" Zweck asked.

"Can't you tell?"

There were two of them, booted, jeaned, the one Zweck had discerned to be female wearing a bandanna pulled tight and low over her forehead, just above the silvered reflecting glasses. She held an Uzi as if she meant to use it. Her companion might have been her twin, except for the drooping mustache.

"Which one dictated the message?"

"Dick?"

Dick was the telecaster. He pointed at the woman.

"What was she like?"

"Not a good voice, but monotone. Bad diction. Of course we were all pretty excited."

He acted as if she were auditioning. He added, "Kind of Southern, wasn't it, Juanita?"

"I don't know. After we swam the Rio Grande, we came north quick."

This was a joke. The studio as a whole seemed a facetious place to Phil Keegan, and he was anxious to get some indication as to how these bikers would react when they realized they had the pastor of St. Hilary's in Fox River rather than the prefect of the Congregation for the Doctrine of the Faith. Everyone in the studio agreed that however ferocious their appearance, the gun-toting intruders had been polite.

The trip to the studio had at least kept his mind busy. Back on campus, he called Cy and told him what had happened.

"You want me to come down there."

"I wish you were here, but I don't know what you could do. I don't know what I can do."

"Have you seen Peanuts?"

"Peanuts!"

"He called in to say he was in hot pursuit of a car headed for Notre Dame and would keep us advised."

The thought of Peanuts in hot pursuit of anything but food boggled the mind. Keegan told Cy he hadn't seen Peanuts but if he did he would send him in hot pursuit of hell.

"How much you want to bet Tuttle is with him?"

A minute later, Keegan got a flash from Zweck, and went with him to where a man had been found locked in the trunk of the limo that had brought Cardinal Hildebrand from Chicago.

"How do you know that?" Zweck asked the cop who reported to him. The cop, whose height should have disqualified him for the force, turned.

"Hey you. Butler. Come here."

"Tuttle," the little lawyer corrected, and came smiling up to Phil Keegan. "Good to see you, Captain. The poor fellow might have suffocated in there."

Rubbing his wrists and looking about angrily, Leo Berlioz, whose limo it was, told the world that this man had saved his life. He clamped his hand on Tuttle's shoulder. "I was dumped in there and left to die."

Keegan detected the aroma of booze as the man talked. Tuttle took off his hat and studied his shoes modestly as the chauffeur expressed his thanks. Then, seeing a camera pointed at them, he clamped his tweed hat on his head.

"Go Irish," someone yelled in the distance, and there came the sound of the marching band that was now wending its way through the campus, whipping up excitement for the evening rally.

"Go Irish," Tuttle said, and was cheered for wit as well as grit.

"How'd you know he was in there?" Keegan asked Tuttle. His tone made the little lawyer uneasy.

"You got jurisdiction here, Keegan?"

"How did you know?" Zweck asked.

"I heard him. So did he." Tuttle pointed at a bearded fellow wearing jeans, a sports jacket and a dress shirt. Professor Weber said yes, he had heard something when he went past the car.

"It shouldn't be parked here, of course. I assumed it was some dignitary here for the game."

"Peanuts got the trunk open."

There was a round of applause for Peanuts too. Zweck talked to the driver, trying to find out what had happened.

"I was parked in the lot by the Morris Inn. I was sitting in back."

"Drinking?"

"I had a drink, sure. Anyway, someone pulled open the door and hit me over the head. The next thing I know, I got tape on my mouth and my hands are taped behind me and the trunk door is shutting on me." He looked around, to ask everyone to imagine the terror.

"What did he look like?"

"I never got a good look at him."

Professor Weber scratched his bearded chin. "Anything can happen around here on a football weekend."

They left it there for the moment at least. Someone had played a dangerous practical joke on Leo the chauffeur.

Cardinal Hildebrand was under even more security than he had been, but he had the look of a man who wished that it was he rather than his secretary and Father Dowling who was in the hands of kidnappers. He had been told of the ransom demand but said to Zweck that he thought it was simply a bid for publicity.

"All day there have been protesters. What does a protester accomplish? His point is to be seen, to make his message known. I think this is part of that."

Bishop Ravel thought that possible. "If it's true, Father Dowling and Monsignor Tracy are in no real danger."

If, if, if . . . But the hypothesis suggested interviewing those who had been involved in the protests, and Keegan started off to do that.

"Captain Keegan," Tuttle whispered. "Could I have a word?"

"Did you persuade Peanuts to bring you down here in an official car?"

"You have a room here, haven't you?"

They left Peanuts in the lobby, fascinated by the pregame festivities, and went upstairs, where Tuttle had his say. Keegan just listened. He hadn't joined in the applause at the limo when Tuttle was acclaimed a hero, but he had trouble concealing his gratitude to the little lawyer now.

"Who the hell is Freddy?"

"Catherine Burger's son. He started this organization for people who've had annulments. VOCL."

"Were they protesting the cardinal?"

"That's right."

"But why did you follow him?"

"I was on special assignment."

"Come on."

"I can say no more. The important thing, Captain, is this. I saw Freddy put the chauffeur in the trunk. He put the guy's cap on and drove through the gate, bold as brass. Me and Peanuts followed."

"In hot pursuit?"

"Exactly." Tuttle took off his hat, fit it onto his knee, and leaned forward. "Captain, I have withheld information relevant to a criminal inquiry."

"So what's new?"

"I am serious. I did tell Father Dowling, which doesn't count of course, but I know you will appreciate the sentiment that prompted me to do so. I gather he has not passed what I told him on to you?"

"I don't know."

"If he had, you would know."

"Tell me."

"The man who put the chauffeur in the trunk of that limo was Freddy Burger."

"You already told me that."

"That was not the first time I saw him put a body in the trunk of a car."

Keegan sensed that this was indeed important.

"Before I go on, I want your assurance that I will not be punished for coming forward, however belatedly."

"Go on, Tuttle. I'm not the prosecutor and you know it."

"I also know that the prosecutor will take his cue from you."

"Okay, okay, I'll tell him you're not a crook. Get on with it."

Tuttle got on with it. He couldn't have stopped himself from going on now. Listening, Keegan controlled the impulse to wring Tuttle's neck for not immediately making known how Geary's body had been transferred from the Burger house to the parking lot behind the insurance agency. Cy's testing now looked even shrewder, but there was no way they could have acted on it as merely a possibility. Tuttle wasn't the only one who had screwed up this investigation. That nitwit Brian clomping around the car in his cowboy boots and looping a wire around his dead father's throat and then, after a delay, confessing to the crime, had permitted leads to go stale. It was only human nature to stop asking a question when you thought you had the answer.

"That's it," Tuttle said.

"Interesting."

"I was sure Father Dowling would tell you and you would act on it . . ."

"Sure."

Only he wasn't sure what this meant. The verdict on Geary's death was poison, and the poison had been slowly administered over a period of time from a contraption he wore as a diabetic. Where the dose took its final effect seemed unimportant, or at least not decisive.

"What are you going to do?"

"I won't arrest you until we get back to Fox River."

"Come on, Keegan."

"Get out of here, Tuttle."

"You sure are grateful."

"You got your applause when you let the driver out of the trunk."

He slapped Tuttle on the back before he closed the door, letting the little lawyer know he appreciated his coming clean. But the pressing question now was: Where is Father Dowling?

Zweck had people checking through the heating tunnels on the campus, but they had outlets in every building and the campus itself was now crawling with people getting hyped for tomorrow's game. The supposition was that Roger and Monsignor Tracy had been snatched when they were making their way through the tunnel to the cardinal's quarters.

The fact of the matter was that there wasn't a darned thing Phil Keegan could do to help find his old friend. But that wasn't true! There was Freddy Burger.

Presumably he was still on campus. But before leaving his room Keegan put through a call to Cy Horvath and told him to go check out Catherine Burger. He gave Cy a short account of what Tuttle had told him. That done, he left the room and went down to the lobby. He wanted to make sure the desk clerk told him whether Freddy was registered at the hotel.

Roger Dowling watched Monsignor Tracy move from trembling terror to cool fatalism.

"They're going to kill us."

"Oh, I doubt that."

"They'll get whatever money they can and then kill us."

"They won't get any money for me."

Tracy whispered in his ear. "They think you're you know who."

Roger Dowling whispered back. "If they're that dumb, we're safe."

This conversation was taking place in a mobile home parked east of the Notre Dame football stadium. Across the living room of the unit their guard, armed with a wicked weapon, presumably watched them, though it was difficult to tell because of the mirrored sunglasses he wore. Father Dowling still felt woozy from the substance that had disabled him, but he had been conscious enough before being pushed into this mobile home to know what was happening. He figured it had been no more than five minutes from their being taken into custody and being locked up here.

Around them in the lot were other early arrivals, tailgating their pregame-day dinner. The smell of charcoal made its way into their place of captivity. From time to time, their guard drank water from a plastic bottle.

"What are we waiting for?" Roger Dowling asked.

The head moved and Father Dowling looked at his two reflected selves in the mirrored glasses.

"You've made a big mistake, you know." The glasses if not their wearer reflected on this. "My name is Roger Dowling. I am a priest from Fox River, Illinois. My friend here is a priest of the St. Paul archdiocese. Clearly you think we're somebody else."

"You speak English pretty good."

"It's my mother tongue."

"And mine," piped up Tracy. "Ask me the lineup of the Chicago White Sox."

White Sox? Roger Dowling frowned at Tracy. But then the monsignor began to rattle off the names of that odious band. This brought the man in the mirrored glasses to his feet.

"Check my ID," Roger Dowling said. "You'll find my billfold in the inner pocket of my jacket."

In a moment the man dug into the jacket and pulled out the billfold, letting it open in the hand that held it. The multicolored ends of the football tickets caught the invisible eye, and he drew them out.

"These are for tomorrow's game."

"My driver's license will tell you who I am."

"Who do you think we are?" Monsignor Tracy asked, unwisely. A puzzled expression while checking Roger Dowling's driver's license turned to anger at Tracy's question. He gave Tracy a push, toppling the monsignor into a corner. He took the football tickets from Roger Dowling's billfold, then threw it at him. He let himself out the door and locked it after him.

"It worked," Tracy said, getting himself seated again.

"We don't want to be here when he gets back."

When Tracy toppled over, Father Dowling saw that his wrists were bound with rope. Presumably his own were as well. Roger Dowling got to his feet and moved in a hopping motion toward the kitchen area, where he turned and pulled open a drawer, then looked over his shoulder. He found what he wanted in the second drawer he opened. Turning to remove the butcher knife from the other utensils, he felt like the claw in one of those machines children manipulate in order to get a particular prize. He kept grasping the wrong thing, a spatula, an eggbeater, a basting tube, but finally he had what he wanted. With a firm grip on the knife, he hopped back to Tracy and sat beside him.

"Turn your back to me."

"Be careful."

"I'll try not to hit an artery."

When he got the blade behind the rope, he asked Tracy to move his hands, tightening the rope. It seemed to take forever, moving the blade up and down.

"This is hardly sharper than a butter knife."

But even as he said it, Tracy, who had been pulling his hands, apart as well, felt the rope giving. Several more moves and Tracy's hands were free. He immediately started to work on his ankles.

"Release my hands first."

Tracy hesitated, complete freedom exerting a powerful attraction, but then he agreed. But before he could begin cutting the rope that bound Roger Dowling's hands, there was the sound of the door unlocking.

A young man with a broad smile bounded into the room and threw up his arms.

"Thank God, you're safe."

"Who are you?" Tracy asked.

But the young man was untying Father Dowling, humming as he worked.

"Freddy Burger," he said.

"How did you know we were here?"

"The main thing now is to let people know everything is fine, that you're all right. Come, come."

He took Tracy's elbow and steered him through the door. Father Dowling followed with a thoughtful look on his face.

Cy Horvath got the whole thing in a condensed version from Keegan as soon as he arrived in South Bend. No one listening to Keegan would think Father Dowling was anyone he knew, let alone a close friend.

"How did the cardinal get back to his room?"

"The way he had come."

"Through the heating tunnels."

Keegan looked at Ravel, who nodded.

"Roger had already left with Monsignor Tracy?"

Ravel didn't think that was possible because Father Dowling was supposed to come see the cardinal and the cardinal hadn't left yet so there wasn't any point in himself leaving yet.

"But he had," Phil Keegan said.

"He may have," Ravel conceded. "But it doesn't make sense."

What made sense to Ravel was that a simple priest should wait around cooling his heels until his superior moved. Cy thought Keegan was right. Beside, he had last been seen with the cardinal's aide, Monsignor Tracy.

"I'll check the route," Cy said.

A guard who said his name was Wiener would be his guide.

"Wiener?"

"Vee-en-er, if it were pronounced the original way. Someone from Vienna. I know a little German so they put me in charge of the way the cardinal would come and go."

"Why don't you pronounce it Vee-en-er?"

"Would you want to tell anyone that was your name?"

"No. But then my name is Horvath."

They had gone through a tunnel from the Morris Inn lined with photographs of the early days of the university and come into the basement of the CCE. Off to the left, around the corner, Wiener opened the door to the heating tunnel, flicking on the light as he entered. The ceiling seemed low to Cy, with caged bulbs at intervals, and pipes of various sizes with white housing on them taking up half the passageway. It was the kind of place that gave Cy the heebie-jeebies.

"Watch your head," Wiener said, starting down the tunnel.

"How long is this thing?"

"Maybe a hundred yards, just to the next building."

Halfway through, Cy told Wiener to hold it.

"What's wrong?"

Cy had crouched and now asked Wiener not to block the light. It was a book, bound in black leather, gold edges, ribbon markers in various colors. Cy lifted the cover. "Roger Dowling" was written on the first blank page. Cy had Wiener come see the signature before picking it up.

"I wish I had a plastic bag."

"What's it mean?"

"That Dowling and the monsignor never made it through this tunnel before they were grabbed."

"Grabbed?"

Did Wiener think they had simply gotten lost?

"I opened the door for them when they went in."

"And closed it afterward?"

"It closes itself."

"You let anyone else through?"

"No one got into this tunnel on my end."

"Was there a guard on the other?"

Wiener shook his head. Cy quelled his anger. Who knew whether the threat to the cardinal was serious? They had taken precautions, but they hadn't handled it as if Hildebrand were a head of state or a political figure, and who could blame them for that? Cy put the Book of Hours under his arm and preceded Wiener down the tunnel, but there were no further signs of what had happened here. Roger Dowling might have deliberately left the book as an indicator.

When Cy exited from the tunnel, a door directly in his line of vision was closing. When Wiener came out, Cy pointed at the door.

"Is that the tunnel out of here?"

Wiener shook his head. "We have to go down another level and to the other side of the building."

Cy went to the closed door and tried the knob. Locked. He knocked, hard.

Wiener said, "That's not the tunnel."

"What is it?"

"Maintenance."

Cy pounded on the door. "Police," he shouted.

Wiener was saying that there was no way to know if anyone was in there when the door opened.

"What is it?" the man asked angrily, and then, "Wiener?"

Cy looked around the man into the room. "This where you work?"

"Who are you?"

Wiener explained.

Cy said, "You got a pretty good line on that heat tunnel door."

The man laughed. "I can see the wall too, and those sprinklers on the ceiling."

"Two priests were grabbed in that tunnel and taken away by force. Did you see anything?"

"I heard about it on the radio. They got some big shot from Rome."

"The one we've been guarding, Jude," Wiener said.

"This guy know you were using the heat tunnels?"

"Hey," Jude said. "This is my building."

"Why did you assume one of the priests taken forcibly from that tunnel was Cardinal Hildebrand?"

"You asked."

"I didn't mention any big shot from Rome."

Jude looked helplessly at Wiener. "Who else is it going to be? Look, we don't normally use these tunnels."

"Were you in on it?"

"In on what?"

"What did they give you to set the thing up?"

Jude's face was a mask of shock. He was beyond anger now. Obviously he had never dreamt anyone would imagine he could do such a thing.

"Maybe you just mentioned it to the wrong people."

Wiener said, "You tell anyone we were taking the cardinal back and forth through the heating tunnels, Jude?"

His expression changed as he thought about it. Cy waited.

"Look, it isn't as if I went around blabbing about it."

"What was it as if?"

Jude had mentioned the unusual use of the heating tunnel to a couple of graduate students in engineering when they came to talk with him about the heating and cooling of his buildings.

"When was that?"

"This afternoon."

"Were they taking some class that brought them here or what?"

"It must have been a class. They had blueprints."

"You get their names?"

"I don't remember them."

Cy turned to Wiener. "Where's engineering?

It wasn't fifty yards distant. The offices of civil engineering were at the end of the building they entered. The sight of Cy at the counter lifted a secretary from her chair. "Yes?"

"What professor would have sent students around to check the heating tunnels on campus?"

The question drew a blank, and the other woman behind the counter wasn't much help.

"Maybe Professor Carberry?"

"Call him."

"His office is just two doors down."

The sound of a woman in pain emanated from the door of Carberry's office, so Cy just turned the knob and looked in. A sparrowlike man, eyes closed, was moving in rhythmic accompaniment to the music. His eyes opened and he saw Cy, but at first there was no reaction. It was clear he was waiting for the song to end. When it did he turned off his CD player.

"What can I do you for?"

"Two men who claimed to be engineering students have been inspecting the heating tunnels on campus. Do you know if any professor gave them that assignment?"

Carberry's shirt looked as if he changed twice a day. He wore a bow tie. He fiddled with his mustache.

"Wearing sunglasses?"

"You know them?"

"They came by a few hours ago and asked me about heating tunnels."

"They're not students?"

"They said they were researching for a movie they planned to make."

"Could you described them, Professor? As accurately as possible."

"What have they done?"

"They think they kidnapped a cardinal."

"A Southern Cal player?"

"That's Stanford," Wiener said.

"I can do better than a description. I got them on tape."

Carberry had two cameras mounted unobtrusively in his office, a precaution, he explained, against sexual harassment charges.

"I kid you not. Even an old geezer like me isn't safe. I am a cautious man."

Meanwhile he rewound the tape and then let Cy have a look through the viewer. Two spaced-out-looking guys, wearing sunglasses, waving their arms as they talked, appeared. How could anyone mistake them for students?

"Can I have that tape?"

"Be my guest."

The men on Carberry's tape matched the male who had shown up at the television station. Carberry's tape made the evening news and was shown at half-hour intervals thereafter.

It had been Freddy's contention all along that the success of the plot did not depend upon its success, so to say, and a good thing too, given the way things had suddenly fallen apart after getting off to such a good start.

"It started with the limo," Amanda said.

"I should have tied his ankles."

"Didn't you?"

"How do you think he was able to kick and get attention?"

"He was rescued by two men from Fox River, Tuttle and a policeman named Pianone."

"Down for the game."

"And they just happened to come along a moment after you had left the limo and they heard the driver kicking and yelling in the trunk."

"I love working with you, Amanda. Total support, shared responsibility, rolling with the punches."

"I'd say you just received a knockout."

"I defer to your expertise," Freddy said, doing the Groucho waggle with his brows. "It looks that way, but it isn't."

The two thugs Freddy had hired in a questionable bar in Old Town had performed better than Freddy would have imagined. They had made the snatch cleanly in the tunnel and got the cardinal and his aide into the mobile home in the parking lot, lost in the sea of the people revving up for the big game tomorrow; they had got the message on television in short order.

"They were almost perfect."

"Except for the fact that they were taped doing it."

"Hey, you're in a TV studio, cameras are going to run. I don't fault them for that."

"And in the professor's office."

"You heard that guy." Carberry had responded gleefully to a reporter's questions as to why he had his office wired and equipped with surveillance cameras.

"It could happen to anyone."

"Like Michael Jackson."

"Who's he?"

Swan Lake provided background music for the interview; the camera had ranged along the shelves of CD albums, not a single twentieth-century composer represented. That the musicophilic professor should know that popular music existed, let alone recognize the name of one of those made into megamillionaires by it, was unlikely.

"Of all the professors of engineering they happened to go into his office. You can't calculate for such things, Amanda."

He argued his case again. Even failed, the kidnapping and ransom demand had made the point Freddy and Amanda had wanted to make. They were sending a signal to the Church, expressing their discontent with its annulment policies. Hildebrand was in the country to discuss the matter. The wackos Freddy had met at Notre Dame through Kate and her husband talked as if Torquemada had landed and repression was just around the corner. Freddy had become, despite himself, a student of the Church since Vatican II. The chances of a crackdown were nil as far as he could see. If the Notre Dame meeting went like previous such occasions, there would be a stern statement—and there had been—which would be talked to death for a few days and then somehow would fall into oblivion, never to be heard of again. Besides, from the time it became clear that they thought any pressure was exerted by parading around with signs while inside the CCE the meeting went comfortably on, Freddy knew he was with the wrong bunch. Of course he did not say so. The pickets were an ever ready disguise into which he could disappear if things went awry.

"The ransom would have hurt them," Amanda said. "It's the only thing that does, taking money away from them."

Did she really believe that? Freddy detected echoes of her father. Beneath that borrowed cynical exterior beat the heart of a true believer, Freddy was sure of it. That was the reason for her support of VOCL, if only as corresponding member, so to speak. It was the reason for his own zeal too, perhaps. Sometimes Freddy thought that he himself loved the Church more sincerely than any of her faithful adherents. It pleased him to think of himself as a great sinner, singled out for the nature and extent of his iniquity. He wondered if Augustine, during his wild days in Carthage, had tasted doubly forbidden pleasures. Surely he must have; he had hit bottom, that was his almost boast, and then he had been lifted up up up . . . In some imaginary future, Freddy too would change his ways, yield to grace, become a saint. Make me chaste, Lord—but not yet. How like Augustine he was, really.

But the worst was yet to be. In a special news program, Cardinal Hildebrand was interviewed by the anchor of the network, who had been in Chicago and jetted down for the occasion. Freddy and Amanda fell silent and watched with quite different reactions.

"So rumors of your kidnapping were exaggerated, Cardinal Hildebrand."

"They were false, yes. But only because someone else was mistaken for myself."

"I must say that, on the face of it, that's unlikely."

"It was perhaps more the hair than the face. And other things, height, weight . . ."

"Then you know who was in fact kidnapped?"

Cardinal Hildebrand turned to Ambrose Ravel. "The look-alike is Father Roger Dowling of Fox River, Illinois. He bears a striking resemblance to the cardinal."

"And he was acting as decoy during the visit?"

"They also took my secretary, Monsignor Tracy, into custody."

Freddy felt Amanda turn to him when Ravel was asked whether Roger Dowling had been used as a decoy. A mistake was one thing, but being outfoxed was another.

"Are they safe and sound?"

The cardinalatial brow darkened. "Pray God they are."

"Haven't they been released? I understood that the kidnappers had been apprehended."

Ravel was uncomfortable. "When I last talked to the police, the kidnappers had not yet revealed the whereabouts of the two priests they did take."

Freddy was on his feet. "They don't know, that's why they haven't told them. Come on."

Amanda was still sprawled in her chair. "Come on where?"

"I want you to meet our captives."

Marie was in her room, wearing robe and slippers, fresh from her bath and settled down for an hour of reading with half an eye on the television set, when the special interview with Cardinal Hildebrand flashed on the screen.

Marie got onto her feet but, unable to hold her balance, sat down again abruptly, causing her rocking chair to tip backward in a great arc until she was dumped unceremoniously on the floor. She uttered not a sound; during all this her eye had never left the screen of the television; she was desperate to get her headphones on so she could hear distinctly what was being said. They hung on a device atop the set. She clamped them on her head and flicked the button behind the right earpiece. A terrible crackling sound. She turned on the sound just in time to hear Bishop Ravel say, "The look-alike is Father Roger Dowling of Fox River, Illinois. He bears a striking resemblance to the cardinal."

"And he was acting as decoy during the visit?"

"A decoy!" Marie said aloud, not realizing that she had. She stomped across the room, getting out of range of the television, then hurried back to look down at what at the moment seemed to her the fatuous expression on Bishop Ravel's face. He had not answered the question, but Marie knew the answer with a certainty that left her breathless. It was all clear to her now. How hollow her fears of the time seemed, thinking they meant to lure Roger Dowling back to the marriage tribunal. It was ridiculous to think they would waste a man of his caliber on a job like that. And oh, those tickets he had been so delighted to get, him and Phil Keegan as well. Now the reason was clear as clear. Bishop Ravel had seen a resemblance between Roger Dowling and Cardinal Hildebrand and, knowing the danger the cardinal would be in, had had the gall to use Roger Dowling as a decoy.

Marie had never been so angry in her life. There was no possibility that Father Dowling could knowingly have participated in such a charade. He had been gulled.

Maybe he would have done it for those tickets, she objected to herself, but she didn't believe it.

The horrible thought struck her that all over the parish people would be watching this same program and would learn that their pastor had been kidnapped at Notre Dame. How many of them would even have known he was away for the weekend? Imagine the situation she would have on her hands tomorrow when people came storming the rectory to demand to know what happened. The thought of being unable tell them was a bitter one for Marie Murkin. A portion of her anger with Bishop Ravel transferred to Father Dowling, since she could not help imagining how he would enjoy seeing her exposed to the parish as ignorant of the whereabouts of the pastor. That was insufferable. But what to do?

Her prebedtime mood was gone, of course. She stepped into her closet and pulled the door shut behind her before turning on the light. This was her dressing room; here she was hidden from any prying eye that might scale the back fence, creep across the yard and get atop the garage to see what could be seen through the drawn shade of her bedroom. She told herself it was silly to hide in the closet like this. She could cavort around naked in her room and the world would never know. But a modesty ingrained in her when she was a girl and only enhanced by her brief and tragic marriage sent her to a closet whenever she must expose even a modicum of flesh.

Dressed as she would have been the following morning, she went down the stairs she had thought she'd climbed a final time that day, to her kitchen. The situation called for tea, lots of it, and for heavenly aid. She lit the fire under the kettle and with the same match touched into flame the vigil light before her statue of St. Anthony of Padua.

"Find him," she said to the gaudy painted image. "Go find him and bring him back here safe. Please."

She was almost sorry she had added "please." She had once been told that St. Anthony never acts more swiftly than when ordered to do so without ceremony. At the same time, she wanted to ask the saint if he'd like a cup of tea.

It was not yet nine o'clock; she had gone upstairs early since there was nothing to do downstairs except answer the phone, and she had switched calls to the phone in her room. As if to confirm this, the phone began ringing upstairs. She took the receiver from the wall phone, her heart in her throat, expecting to hear the voice of the pastor.

"Marie? This is Edna Hospers. Have you been watching television?"

"You mean about Father Dowling?" Marie asked in casual tones it cost her much to adopt.

"Has he really been kidnapped?"

"Edna, everything is under control. You heard the bishop and the cardinal . . ."

"They're the ones who said that Father Dowling is still in custody. Are you alone?"

"Yes."

"I could come over."

"And just leave your kids?"

"Junior can watch things. I'll be there in a jiff."

A stronger person would have refused and told Edna to remain with her family, Marie Murkin would soon bring order out of chaos. But the fact was that she welcomed the prospect of having another woman, especially Edna, with whom to share this dreadful news.

Keegan and Cy talked over Tuttle's claim to have seen Freddy Burger take the body of Michael Geary from his mother's house to the insurance agency.

"In the trunk of Geary's car?"

"The chauffeur," Cy said.

"Like that, yeah. Tuttle was in on that too. Maybe we better put the collar on Tuttle, Cy."

"Is Freddy down here too?"

Keegan thought about it. "Let's find out."

Step one was to get the tag number of Freddy's car and put out a bulletin. Step two was to see if by any chance he was registered in a local motel. Needless to say, he wouldn't have gotten a room in the Morris Inn. Cy began calling around. The Skyway was the fifth motel he called.

"No Burger. You say Burger?"

"Yeah."

"From Fox River, Illinois."

"That's right."

"I got a Michael Geary from Fox River."

Geary! Cy said thanks a lot for the trouble and hung up.

"No luck?" Phil said.

"Michael Geary from Fox River is registered at the Skyway."

It was odd enough to warrant a look. The fellow behind the desk propped himself up on crutches when they came in.

"I just called you about a Burger being registered."

The guy shifted his weight on the crutches, not liking this. "I told you he wasn't here."

"What room is Geary in?"

"What's this all about?"

Cy showed him the badge. "You're from Fox River."

Cy turned to Keegan. "You want to see the extradition papers?"

"You're not going to make a scene, are you?" the guy asked.

"Not unless you keep stalling."

Geary was in unit 21, on the second level, overlooking the parking lot. Light seeped from the pulled blind and leaked from under the door as well. Cy knocked, and Phil Keegan took up a position to the left of the door. Inside, the sound of television diminished. Cy knocked again.

In a moment there was the sound of a chain, the turn of a lock, and the door opened and Christopher James squinted into the dark. "Amanda?"

"Lieutenant Horvath, Mr. James. This is Captain Keegan."

"You're from Fox River!"

"We'd like to talk to you," Cy said, stepping forward. James, surprise still on his face, admitted them.

"You're registered in the name of Michael Geary," Keegan said.

"What!"

"Michael Geary of Fox River."

James was in shirtsleeves, his tie loosened, and in stocking feet. He looked back and forth between Keegan and Cy, then sat on the bed.

"This isn't my room."

"Then what are you doing here?"

"The room was offered me by someone else. I came down here for a meeting, as the representative of—"

"Victims of Canon Law," Keegan said. "Founded by Frederick Burger."

"He rented this room. He offered it to me so I could stay for the game tomorrow."

"Where is he now?"

"I don't know."

"Who is Amanda?" Cy asked.

"My daughter. She and I are going to the game tomorrow."

"Where is she?"

"On the campus. She wanted to walk around . . ."

"With Freddy?"

James didn't know, but the question did not please him. Keegan told him they would wait for the return of his daughter.

"My daughter! What is the meaning of this?" James seemed suddenly to remember that he was a lawyer and he didn't have to admit policemen to his room and answer any question they might put to him. He stood up and began to wriggle his feet into his shoes.

Keegan ignored the question, unwrapping a cigar and taking a seat on the other bed.

"There's been a kidnapping."

"A what?"

The bed looked as if James had been napping, but he had turned down the television when he heard the knock on the door. The set was mute, a soundless game show on. Perhaps he hadn't heard the news. He seemed genuinely not to know what Phil Keegan referred to.

"The cardinal you would have seen at the meeting. Kidnappers have demanded a million dollars for his return. Not very intelligent kidnappers. They have been taped in action twice."

"The cardinal has been kidnapped!"

Cy said, "Tell us all you know about it."

Something in James's expression prompted Cy to say this. It turned out to be a hunch worth trusting. James plumped down on the bed again and looked abjectly at Keegan.

"And you think Freddy is behind it?"

Keegan just looked at him, saying nothing. Cy too waited. James looked distractedly around the room and said, aimlessly, "This is his room. He said we should take it."

"When do you expect him back?"

"Why would he come back here?"

"To bring Amanda."

"Why do you think Amanda is with him? She doesn't even know him." But even as he said it, he seemed to doubt the truth of what he was saying. He looked vacantly ahead, apparently asking himself what he did and did not know about Freddy Burger.

"He is your client."

"I represent VOCL, yes."

"Did he accompany you to the meeting?'

"No!"

On the television, a rerun of Cardinal Hildebrand talking to the press appeared, and Cy moved to get between the set and James.

"But he is here?"

"He gave you this room," Cy added.

Keegan pressed it. "He planned to kidnap the cardinal and demand—"

"I knew nothing about that."

Keegan tucked in his chin and looked skeptically at James. "You don't expect us to believe that, Mr. James. You are one of the smartest lawyers in the Chicago area. You knew what kind of group VOCL was when you agreed to represent it."

"Amos Cadbury recommended that I agree to do so."

"Maybe we should telephone him."

"Don't be silly."

"We can talk to him later."

James was clearly considering what representing Freddy might do to his professional reputation. He had not rejected the notion that Freddy was the one behind the attempted kidnapping of the cardinal.

"I know absolutely nothing about any kidnapping efforts. I repudiate and abhor such an action."

"They botched it, of course."

"What do you mean?"

"They took the wrong man."

James's relief was short-lived. Phil Keegan went on. "They have taken Father Roger Dowling and the cardinal's secretary into custody . . ."

Outside there was the sound of footsteps on the porch that connected the units. Cy flipped the switch beside the door and pointed at the bathroom. Keegan put his finger to his lips and indicated that James was to go into the bathroom and shut the door. Cy switched off the television.

James stood in the bathroom doorway, but did not close the door. Instead he turned off the light and the unit was plunged into darkness.

Voices were audible and then stopped outside the door, a man, a woman. Silence. Then a tapping.

"Daddy?"

James started from the bathroom, but Keegan stopped him. There was the sound of a key in the lock. The door opened and several figures were pushed in; then the light went on and a young woman stared at James, while Freddy Burger, still unaware of who was in the unit, put the safety chain in place.

"Hello, Phil," Father Dowling said. "This is Monsignor Tracy."

Saturday dawned clear and cool and the campus was still asleep when Father Dowling walked from the Morris Inn to Sacred Heart Basilica to say his Mass. A tap on Phil Keegan's door had brought no response, and he had decided to let the Fox River captain of detectives sleep in. Yesterday had been harrowing and, for Keegan, had continued into the early hours of today. When Father Dowling returned along the campus walk, the smell of charcoal was already in the air and the banners and pennants moved with anticipation. By midmorning, the oompah oompah of bands was heard, and Father Dowling put down the breviary Cy had returned to him and looked out over Notre Dame.

Soon he would be swept up in the excitement of the game, but for the moment he wanted to reflect on the events that had begun in Fox River and reached their culmination in South Bend.

Freddy Burger was in custody downtown, a courtesy to Phil Keegan until he could arrange for his transfer to Illinois. The initial questioning in the Skyway suite had been supplemented later when Monique Pippen had flown in with a laptop full of the findings of the medical examiner, bringing along Agnes Lamb, who spent the first ten minutes on terra firma vowing she would never go up in such a small plane again.

"It's no bigger than a hang glider," she said and shivered.

Monique, who had been permitted to take the controls when they were over the lake, was eager to climb back into the clouds.

It was Freddy's pharmacy background and access to Burger Apothecary that, together with Tuttle's witnessing of his transferring Michael Geary's body from his mother's home, had put the investigative focus on him. To Agnes Lamb's initial dissatisfaction. She had been arranging an encounter between Oscar Celsius and Betty Furey, to corroborate the pharmacist's claim that Geary's sister-in-law had picked up insulin for him. "The murder weapon, remember?" But since the death of Gordon Furey, Agnes's enthusiasm for the idea that it had been the Fureys, husband and wife, who had killed Michael Geary was not shared.

"Did you kill Gordon Furey too?" Phil Keegan asked Freddy in the Skyway.

"If I killed Michael Geary I killed Gordon Furey."

"Was he alive when you dumped him into the trunk of his car and drove him away?"

Freddy's smile went on and on, like a toothpaste ad. "You sound like an eyewitness."

"You were taped by Tuttle," Father Dowling said. Phil Keegan was more surprised by this than Freddy. Apparently Tuttle had not told him everything. Freddy threw up his hands in mock despair.

"You got me."

"Why would you kill him?" Father Dowling asked.

James and his daughter had withdrawn to a corner of the room when the questioning began. Freddy was handcuffed, and from time to time he smiled down on them as if he were an Olympian deity finding amusement in the foibles of mortals. He turned his smile at Father Dowling, but the priest noticed how vacant the young man's eyes were.

"It seems an odd way to protest the Catholic Church, doesn't it?"

"Kidnapping cardinals makes more sense."

"Unless you mistake a Fox River pastor for a cardinal."

"It was dark in the tunnel."

Freddy bowed at the concession. From the corner Christopher James wished to have it understood that nothing Frederick Burger was now confessing had anything to do with the purpose and activities of VOCL.

"Don't worry," Freddy said cheerfully. "I won't implicate you."

Amanda turned away with a little sob, and her father comforted her. Had she thought her father was involved? Phil Keegan, in the interests of thoroughness, gave a complete rationale for Freddy's arrest. Suspicion of two murders, a kidnapping . . .

"Two kidnappings," Cy said.

"That's right. Father Dowling and Monsignor Tracy."

"I was thinking of Leo the chauffeur."

Phil Keegan nodded. "You were lucky there, Freddy. Leo has a weak heart. He might have had the big one after you slammed down the lid of the trunk on him."

"Was that taped too?"

"Tuttle was on the scene," Keegan said ambiguously.

Freddy chuckled. "I was going to blame this on the ineptitude of the confederates I brought into it. Have they been arrested, by the way?"

"We'll find them. They were taped too."

Freddy yelped with laughter. "I feel I've been on location! Can I have copies of all this tape?"

When Zweck arrived with a car in which Cy accompanied Freddy to the St. Joseph County Jail, the events of recent weeks seemed accounted for. At the Morris Inn, Father Dowling spent some time in Phil Keegan's room while his old friend sipped bourbon and water and frowned over the latest newspaper previews of the game.

"Notre Dame by three points!" he said in disgust.

"It would be psychologically better if they weren't favored at all."

"You call a three-point spread being favored?"

"I'll be more than happy if ND wins by three points."

"I want a blowout," Keegan said.

But they were interrupted by the arrival of Monique Pippen and Agnes Lamb. Cy's confidence caused Father Dowling to look at Monique with new interest, although of course he would not in any way manifest Cy's temptation in her regard. It was unclear in any case whether the attractive young woman realized the confusion she sowed in the breast of the seemingly impassive lieutenant.

"The guy had a cache of stolen religious objects in his apartment."

"I thought he lived with his mother."

"He had a long-term lease and kept the place. He lived a double life," Agnes added in a neutral voice.

"Well, he certainly kept busy."

Agnes glanced at Monique and then at the ceiling. Then as if reminded by the recent terrors of flying, she dropped her gaze to the floor.

"Religious objects?"

"Dashboard statues, plastic madonnas."

"We found a little statue in Geary's car," Monique pointed out. "And in Gordon Furey's."

"His signature."

"What was the point?"

"He hates religion," Phil Keegan said.

"Oh, I wouldn't say that," Roger Dowling remarked. "Let's just say he was obsessed with it."

"Wasn't a dead animal left in a confessional at St. Jude's?"

"We'll have to ask Freddy about it," Phil Keegan decided.

The link between Freddy and the insulin contraption that had been used to poison Michael Geary seemed something they had always known. He would have had access to the device in his mother's home when—Cy could think of no delicate way to put this—Geary had removed it before making love to Catherine Burger.

"We found a partial denture in Freddy's apartment," Agnes said.

Monique added that it matched one Michael Geary had worn.

"Did he have an extra?"

"He lost one. Mislaid it. Apparently at Catherine Burger's."

"He removed his partial before he went to bed?" Phil Keegan found this incredible.

"Well, it ended up in Freddy's apartment."

Agnes's mouth opened as if she were about to speculate on something, then closed. She shook her head.

Connecting Freddy with Gordon Furey, the telltale dashboard madonna apart, was chancier. No Tuttle had witnessed his entrance into Furey's Avanti or recorded it with a video camera.

"He confessed to it," Keegan said.

But what Roger Dowling remembered was a conditional statement: "If I killed Michael Geary I killed Gordon Furey." If the protasis was true, the apodosis followed by *modus ponens*. The others just looked at him when he developed this thought.

"Just a logical point."

"Thanks, Roger," Phil Keegan said with uncustomary irony.

His phone was ringing when Roger Dowling finally got to his own room in the Morris Inn. Marie's half-hysterical voice flooded his ear when he said hello; she was angry and relieved and happy and furious and why hadn't he called her?

"I'll need ransom money, Marie. You've got a little nest egg, haven't you?"

"Ransom."

"I'm being held in the Morris Inn at outrageous prices. I'll have to buy my way out of here after the game—"

"Stop that, Father Dowling. You stop that right now. Half the parish has been calling here and if it hadn't been for Edna Hospers I don't know what I myself would have done. Tell me you're all right."

"I'm all right."

"Tell me what happened."

"That will have to wait until I get home."

"You are all right."

"The cast on my leg is an annoyance, and the head bandage makes me feel like an oil sheik, but—"

"Fa-ther Dow-ling."

He stopped teasing her. He realized that his inclination to do so was in part delayed relief at having escaped harm. Monsignor Tracy had shown his fear, which was probably healthier. Roger Dowling had been more affected than he knew by the monsignor's predictions of imminent physical harm, even death. Marie urged him to put everything else out of his mind and enjoy the game.

"Who's playing?"

"Good night."

"Good night, Marie."

Phil Keegan was still not up when Father Dowling returned from Mass, so he went down to the Morris Inn dining room, where he was surprised to find Christopher James and his daughter waiting for a table.

"I thought you might have wanted to return home after last night's excitement."

"What have they done to Freddy?" Amanda asked.

"They've taken him downtown."

"Don't worry about Freddy," her father counseled, glancing at Father Dowling. The father was obviously awed by the magnanimity of the daughter.

"Are you going to the game?"

They were interrupted by the hostess, who wanted to know if they were together. They decided they were and were taken to a table in the lower section, next to the window, looking out over the golf course. A squirrel scampered importantly about on the other side of the glass.

"There's a cardinal," Amanda said.

The bird. James's first reaction had been somewhat like Roger Dowling's, looking toward the door to witness the presumed entrance of Hildebrand, garbed perhaps in scarlet, scattering blessings as he went. Amanda laughed at their interpretation.

"About the game, Father," James said, reaching into an inside pocket. "I believe these are yours."

He handed two colorful football tickets to Father Dowling, who sat back and shook his head.

"No. I have mine." To prove it, he brought them out. At the other tables, diners smiled at this display of enthusiasm for the coming game.

"Freddy gave me these."

"They must have been his to give."

James had scrambled eggs and a double order of bacon, to the accompaniment of his daughter's disapproval. She had juice, decaffeinated coffee and a bowl of cream of wheat. Father Dowling half expected to be chided when he ordered French toast.

"I have prepared a letter of resignation as VOCL's counsel," James said.

"That's silly, Daddy."

"I know what I would think of a lawyer who had a client like Freddy Burger."

"Maybe he's innocent," Father Dowling suggested.

James snorted. "You heard him. He killed two men."

"If he killed one."

"What do you mean?"

"That's what he said. He made no confession."

"He's a shrewd fellow. I'll give him that. He led me a merry chase, I'll tell you. I came down here at his insistence. It was a waste of time."

"Maybe that tireless smile is the clue."

"Clue to what?"

"He's not serious. He's kidding the police."

"He was arrested for suspicion of murder."

"And reasonably so."

"I don't get your point."

"I'm not sure I get it myself." He dismissed it with a wave of his fork. "You live in Florida," he said to Amanda.

"Yes, Father."

"Miami, Sarasota . . . ?"

"Marco Island."

"Really. That's where many retired priests winter."

"I haven't noticed any."

"Oh, you wouldn't. They dress like natives. You'll see them all at Mass on Sunday, concelebrating, helping out."

Amanda bent over her bowl of cream of wheat.

"Where on the island do you live?"

Amanda's answer was vague until her father urged her to specificity. He seemed happier that his daughter had moved to Florida than she did.

"It's an older crowd, isn't it?"

"I don't mind that."

"All Amanda does is sit in the sun and read," James said indulgently.

"How long have you known Freddy?" Father Dowling asked the sugar bowl, looking at neither father nor daughter. But it was Amanda who answered.

"I don't know him at all."

"He seems to know you."

"Why do you say that?" James asked, frowning.

"I suppose he heard of her from you."

"Not from me."

"Did he say something about me?" Amanda asked.

Father Dowling wrinkled his nose. "The events of yesterday are difficult to keep separate from one another. I must be thinking of what he said at your hotel room."

"What was that?"

"Oh, it wasn't what he said so much as his manner. He seemed to know you."

"We ran into him earlier at the Morris Inn. That's when he gave Daddy the use of his motel room."

"That must be it," Father Dowling said.

It was as a distraught mother that Catherine Burger called Father Dowling. Freddy had called her, rather than a lawyer, to tell her what had happened.

"He said he is accused of killing Michael Geary and Gordon Furey. Father, that's absurd."

"He hasn't confessed to anything."

"He hasn't? Thank God. It's so difficult to follow Freddy. He seems to think the whole thing is a joke."

"He was taped removing the body of Michael Geary from your house the day Geary died."

"My God."

"The assumption is that he drove the body to Geary's insurance agency and propped him behind the wheel of his car."

"I should not have let him do that. He did it for my sake."

"Removing the body?"

"Yes. Father, he didn't kill Michael. He couldn't have."

"It was a very indirect method. Poison in his insulin dispenser."

After a long silence, she said, "I still don't believe Freddy was capable of such a thing."

"Did Michael Geary lose a lower partial there?"

"That was a long time ago." She drew in her breath. "Father, I don't know if I could admit these things to you if we were face to face."

"If we were face to face, I would be acting as your confessor."

"I have already confessed these sins."

"The lower partial was found in Freddy's apartment."

"It was?"

She did not dispute the suggestion that Freddy must have entered the house on that occasion and played this little joke on his mother's visitor.

"The police would have been mad not to arrest Freddy, Catherine. The business with Geary's lower partial proves he could enter the house without your knowing it. Poison could have been introduced into the dispenser with a syringe, I'm told."

"Why would he do such a thing?"

Father Dowling forbore suggesting that a son might easily react violently to his mother's secret lover. When he finally put down the phone, he felt he had not offered her much consolation. Perhaps she should suffer through a period of anxiety. Catherine said she had confessed her sins, but it was difficult to see that she felt much remorse for them. She was sorry that what she had done was a nuisance now, but remorse is more than that.

Tuttle had actually sent Peanuts Pianone to Fox River in the wee hours of the morning to fetch the video he had taken of the removal of the body of Michael Geary from Catherine Burger's house.

"I don't have a VCR," Father Dowling said.

"You can watch it through the viewer. It's a small picture, but very sharp.

Father Dowling had been squinting into the viewer for twenty minutes when Phil Keegan knocked on his door. He and Cy had breakfasted, and Keegan at least was eager to get out onto the campus and into the pregame festivities. He lifted his brows when he noticed the video camera.

"You taking that to the game?"

"I don't think so."

Keegan looked relieved. "Where'd you get it?"

"It belongs to Tuttle. This is the tape he made of Michael Geary's body being removed from Catherine Burger's house. Take a look."

Keegan looked, backing the tape up several times and peering at the crucial scene, then handed the camera to Cy.

"That's the first useful thing Tuttle ever did."

"The case against Freddy looks pretty tight?"

"I'd feel better if he'd stop grinning."

Cy put down the camera and Roger Dowling asked him what he thought.

"Who's the woman?"

"That's the mother," Phil Keegan said.

Cy let it go, but Roger Dowling was glad Cy too had caught the glimpse of the girl who had been briefly visible in the backseat of the car when Freddy slammed down the lid of the trunk. The experiences of the past two days enabled Roger Dowling to identify the woman as Amanda James.

"Cy, why don't you use my ticket? You'll get a lot more out of the game than I will and I can watch it here on television."

Both Phil Keegan and Cy erupted at this suggestion, urging the need for Roger Dowling to go, the tickets had been given to him in the first place, Cy hadn't expected to see the game, so there was no need to feel sorry for him.

"I might wangle a stand-up spot in the press box anyway."

Roger Dowling pressed the ticket into Cy's hand. "Look, you'll miss all the excitement if we stand here arguing about it. Go on, both of you. Listen to that music."

The marching band was passing the Morris Inn, playing the fight song, and Phil Keegan was drawn out of the door and down the hall. Roger Dowling went down with Cy, returning the ticket each time Cy put it into his pocket or pressed it into his hand. It was in Cy's possession when the two burly cops walked out of the inn into the mounting pregame hubbub. Father Dowling went up to his room and put through a call to Florida.

Monsignor George Kelly didn't know Amanda James, but he would ask around and call back.

"What's your number in Fox River?"

"I'm at the Morris Inn, George."

"Notre Dame. Isn't today a home game?"

"That's why I'm here."

"Say, what's this I hear about Hildebrand attending a meeting there?"

"I'll tell you when you call back."

Quid pro quo was clerical currency, and Roger Dowling was willing to pay if George Kelly could be of help. And he was. A golfing partner was an airline executive; he made a few calls, and sure enough Amanda James was a frequent commuter between Naples and Chicago.

"Midway."

"Thanks, George."

"Tribunal business?"

"Not really."

"Tell me about Hildebrand."

Roger Dowling gave him a quick sketch, concentrating on the statement the cardinal had read in the afternoon. George Kelly was delighted and would have liked to go on, but Roger Dowling, feeling disingenuous, reminded him that there was a game on.

"Are we going to win?"

When it came to football, the Church in America was as one—unless of course Boston College was the opponent.

Amanda and Freddy were allies, and the woman in supposed Florida exile made frequent trips to Chicago without the knowledge of her father. Any doubt Roger Dowling might have had that it had been Amanda seated in the back of Geary's car was gone. He remembered Cy's account of the inquiries at the insurance agency. The client who had been waiting for Geary to return, Mrs. Rockhurst, waiting patiently to see Geary, had said she thought there was someone in the backseat of the car that went past the window, but no one had paid any attention to her, not even after one of Cy's experiments had included Agnes Lamb in the backseat.

So what did it all mean? If Freddy had access to the house while Catherine was misbehaving with Michael Geary, this was equally true of Amanda. At the very least, she was in collusion with Freddy. But Father Dowling remembered the careful way Freddy had phrased what had wrongly been thought to be his confession. If A, then B.

Whatever motive Freddy was thought to have would be more than shared by Amanda. Freddy's animosity toward the Church, and toward flamboyant members of it like Michael Geary, had been prompted by his reaction to his mother's annulment. Disturbing as that must have been, Amanda had suffered personally from Michael Geary and it was far easier to link her with him than Freddy, for whom Geary was simply one of a type. No, not quite. He had after all been courting Freddy's mother. Such thoughts led inevitably to Christopher James, Amanda's father and counselor of the organization Freddy had formed to focus attention on the practices of the Church's tribunals.

The sound of the band had dwindled, and so had the shouts and cries of fans as all converged on the stadium. A huge blimp floated above, providing aerial shots of the game, and small planes flew over the fans, trailing banners on which commercial and other messages were lettered. Car dealers, commemorations of birthdays, as well as proclamations *urbi et orbi* of undying devotion were flown across the November sky. One banner pleaded with Liz to marry Tom. Such a proposal seemed grounds for future annulment. Father Dowling turned the sound of the television up.

In the stadium, Phil Keegan and Cy Horvath were wedged into seats shaded by the press box and overlooking the fifty-yard line. Below them in the presidential box, his white hair visible despite the billed ND cap he wore, was Cardinal Josef Hildebrand, smiling benignly and uncomprehendingly at the activity on the field.

Notre Dame had elected to kick; the receiver had bobbled the ball but managed to fall on it, but Southern Cal began its first drive on its own seven-yard line. On second down a pass into the flat was intercepted and run into the end zone: 7–0, Notre Dame.

When they settled down again after the frenzied cheering, Phil Keegan had a triumphant look on his face. "A three-point spread," he growled at Cy.

A game is seldom decided in its opening minutes, however, and by the quarter Southern Cal had amassed ten points and Notre Dame had been held to its original lucky seven. The home team seemed unable to get a sustained drive going. Phil Keegan began to complain about the officiating.

Several sections over, Cy noticed a man in a uniform cap leading two security men upward.

"There's Leo," Cy said.

"Who's Leo?" Phil Keegan asked, not taking his eyes from the field.

Cy kept an eye on the three men climbing the steps with determined expressions. Leo stopped and pointed toward the middle of a row. Security men had also gone up the stairs at the opposite end of the row. The two groups now converged. The activity on the field had brought the fans to their feet again, and Cy, standing, got a glimpse of Mr. James and his daughter being unceremoniously ushered down the steps in the custody of the guard. The place in which they had been sitting was now occupied by Leo, who glared around in triumph.

In the office of security beneath the stands, with constant thunder from above, Christopher James was being interrogated by a very fat man with a lantern jaw and an expression of ineradicable skepticism.

"They were given me by a client."

"How much did you pay?"

"They were a gift."

"Someone just handed you two tickets to this game. Well, they belonged to someone else who had the good sense to write down the numbers."

"They were given me by Frederick Burger."

A guard stopped and whispered into the ear of the grand inquisitor. He looked up at James.

"Frederick Burger."

"Yes."

"The guy who was arrested last night on suspicion of murder."

Oh God. James looked at Amanda, who seemed undisturbed by this humiliation.

"My father knows Cardinal Hildebrand," she said.

"Who's Cardinal Hildebrand?"

"He's with the president."

"Clinton?"

"The president of the university. They're watching the game together."

The fat man, Foley, thought this was interesting. "Maybe we ought to go up there and straighten this whole thing out."

"Officer, I am a member of the Illinois bar, I practice law in Fox River, Illinois."

"This your identification?"

"Of course it's my identification."

"You got anything with your photo on it?"

He searched his wallet frantically. Where was his driver's license? He felt as felons must feel when they are brought before the judge, suspicion establishing guilt.

"Father Dowling will vouch for us," Amanda said.

Unimpressed by the claim to know Cardinal Hildebrand, Foley seemed open to the possibility that James might be known by a simple priest.

"Where is he?"

"He's staying at the Morris Inn."

The skeptical expression had not wavered when Foley picked up the phone and called the Morris Inn.

"You got a Father Dowling registered there?"

He listened and for the first time showed surprise. "He's in his room? Sure, put me through."

Ten minutes later, they were on their way to the Morris Inn, James and Amanda in different cruisers. At this point James would not have cared if they had turned on the sirens, but the roar from the stadium made that pointless in any case.

* * *

The shouts from the stadium were accompaniment enough to the televised game, so Father Dowling pushed the Mute button and settled back. And fell asleep. He didn't realize this until he was wakened by the phone and asked by stadium security if he knew a man claiming to be Christopher James.

"Claiming to be?"

"Well, he's got ID of someone named James. We rousted him and a young woman out of seats whose holder had been robbed of his tickets. He claims to know you."

There was obviously a lot of claiming going on at stadium security. The description sounded like James and his daughter.

"Why don't you bring them over, Officer? I wouldn't want to make a mistake about a thing like this."

He turned up the sound of the television and tried to get back to the game. A score flashed on, indicating that Notre Dame was fifteen points behind and the first half had five minutes to go. Roger Dowling had been thinking how Phil Keegan would have ragged him for falling asleep while Notre Dame was playing, but with that score Keegan might envy him.

Chrisopher James stepped into the room and gripped Father Dowling's hand as if they were long-lost friends. "Would you tell this man who I am?"

"I know who I am," Amanda said, smiling prettily and following her father in.

"Are you Officer Foley?"

"Leonard Foley, Father. What kind of way is this to watch a game? I'll take you back to the stadium and make room for you."

"Oh, I'm getting used to this. As you can see, I know Mr. James and his daughter. I hope you're not going to bring charges against them."

Foley laughed this suggestion away, repeated this invitation to smuggle Roger Dowling into the game, and finally rolled away down the corridor.

"He had no doubt who I was," James said, angrily. "He did that deliberately."

"It wasn't so bad as being hustled out of our seats."

"Where did you get the tickets?"

"From Freddy Burger! I'd like to wring his neck."

Freddy must have taken the tickets from Leo after he dumped him into the trunk of the limo.

"Your connection with him has certainly been a nuisance."

While James went on about no longer serving as counsel to Freddy Burger's organization, Father Dowling offered to share his soda with father and daughter.

"Could I order something else?"

"Of course."

James ordered a double scotch for himself and a margarita for Amanda. He scowled at the game. "What's the score?"

"Notre Dame is trailing."

"Good."

"Daddy!"

"I wonder how long room service will take."

"On a football Saturday?"

James decided to go fetch the drinks. When he was gone, Father Dowling again pressed the Mute button.

"Do you mind?"

"Me?" Amanda rolled her eyes. "I hate sports."

Father Dowling turned on the videocam and brought it to Amanda. "Just look through the viewer?"

She looked up at him with a puzzled expression.

"It's a tape Tuttle made."

Amanda put her eye to the viewer, and Father Dowling pressed the button. Long after the sequence had been shown, Amanda kept her eye to the viewer.

"I'll rewind it so you can see it again."

She put down the camera. "What is it?"

"Freddy Burger putting the body of Michael Geary into Geary's trunk. It was taken the day Geary died."

"What house is that?"

"Don't you know?"

"Should I?"

"You were there. There is a quite distinct view of you in the backseat when the trunk is closed."

She picked up the camera and, unassisted, rewound the tape and watched it again. And again.

"It could be anybody."

"But it's you."

"Even if it were, and I don't say it is, Freddy has confessed to the murders."

"Has he?"

"Last night. You were there."

"He said, 'If I killed the one, I killed the other.' "

"So?"

"That's not a confession."

"The police thought so."

"But we know better, don't we?"

"We?"

"I've found out about your regular flights from Florida. Into Midway. Your father wasn't aware of them, of course, but Freddy was."

"Are you going to tell Daddy?"

"That is the least of your problems."

"Do you seriously think that I harmed someone?"

"You knew Michael Geary, didn't you? Of course I've heard all about your unfortunate experience from Father Panzica. And the handsome settlement your father won from the archdiocese. Were you angry that he had taken up with someone else?"

"He was trying to get an annulment."

"Yes."

Thoughts flickered across her face, among them certainly that Michael Geary might have thought of that a year ago when he had been interested in Amanda.

"Were you and Freddy partners?"

"Partners? No. I didn't even belong to his organization. But I supported him. I approved of what he was doing. And Daddy represented them."

"You were obviously involved when he took Michael Geary's body out of his mother's house."

Amanda said nothing; her eyes were dragged to the television, where a player was streaking untouched down the field, a Notre Dame player, but her gaze continued to the window.

"Did you go into the house with him? Did you watch while he put poison in Geary's insulin dispenser?"

"No." Calmly, as if she wondered whether his questions would become more difficult to answer.

"Did you yourself inject the poison?"

"No."

"Oscar Celsius, the pharmacist, will identify you as the woman claiming to be Geary's sister-in-law and picking up insulin for him."

This long shot had no time to land. In the hallway, Christopher James announced his return; Father Dowling opened the door and James, hands full of drinks, backed into the room.

"I brought you another soda, Father Dowling. What's the score?"

He brought up the sound; yet another runner had broken free. With a field goal the first half ended, in a tie. James became absorbed in the halftime review of the game thus far, while Amanda, sipping her drink, looked warily at Father Dowling. She had nothing to fear, not now. There was little point in telling Christopher James of his daughter's involvement with Freddy and of her presence at the Burger home on that fatal day.

At halftime, Cy went for popcorn and hot dogs, down through the crush of people, waiting in line, somehow not minding it because of all the excitement. Phil Keegan's reactions to the fortunes of the game made it clear that a loss would be a major disappointment. Whenever Cy had watched a game on television with Keegan and Roger Dowling at St. Hilary's rectory, he had found the two older men impassive, or perhaps fatalistic, but then they were Cubs fans and used to disappointment. Notre Dame was always a potential winner, however, so it was a very different story.

A man in plaid pants, a green hat and jacket and a leprechaun look turned from the counter with his hands full of junk food, and his eyes met Cy's. A moment during which each man tried to place the other and then Cy had it.

"Hello, Doctor."

Only then did Dr. Hawser recognize him, and his boyish joy diminished.

"Down for the game?"

"Who you rooting for?" Cy kidded. Hawser must have cleaned out the bookstore to get that outfit.

"I'm a Domer," the doctor said, deciding Cy would not ask him any embarrassing questions here.

The line moved forward, and Hawser went off with his load of food.

"I keep seeing people I know," he said to Phil Keegan when he got back to their seats.

"Or look-alikes. There are only so many different faces."

"I saw Hawser downstairs."

He reminded Keegan about the doctor who had taken on the patients of Langsam, among them Michael Geary.

"The guy who thought Gordon Furey was his brother-in-law."

That made Hawser sound dumb, but he had had no way of knowing that Furey was not Geary.

The third quarter was scoreless, and in the fourth a wind came up, reducing the possibility of passes, so the game became largely running plays and the clock seemed to run twice as fast. Phil Keegan kept muttering that he didn't want a tie, but Cy sensed Keegan would settle for that. What he was worried about was a score from Southern Cal with not enough time for Notre Dame to match it.

The worry was realized when Southern Cal scored with two and a half minutes left. They tried for two points and were stopped. There were less than two minutes on the clock when Southern Cal kicked. They had the wind at their back, and the ball lifted high and then hung there, driving the receiver into the end zone to catch the ball. He hesitated for a moment, about to take a touchback and start from the twenty, but suddenly he began to run. Phil Keegan and thousands of others had been shouting for him to stay in the end zone. Now he seemed to be the only Notre Dame player on the field, with the whole Southern Cal defense vectoring in on him. It looked as if he would be tackled within the five-yard line.

But miraculously he burst through the defense and the whole expanse of the field lay before him, the only defender the kicker. Suddenly the game was reduced to a contest between the man with the ball and that lone defender. The Southern Cal kicker launched a tackle and managed to get a grip on the runner's leg, but his hands slid down the leg to the foot and the runner stumbled free but started to fall. His free hand went out, hit the ground and then seemed to lever him forward, and then he was running again; the stadium was in a frenzy as yard by unimpeded yard he went down the field and crossed the goal line.

The fans were still celebrating the goal when the extra point was scored and Notre Dame had a one-point lead. There were forty seconds on the clock.

Those forty seconds turned into the longest period of the game. An onside kick was recovered by Southern Cal, putting them at midfield. Then, despite the wind, the visiting team did nothing but pass. Completed passes stopped the clock when the receiver got out of bounds with the ball. Incomplete passes of themselves stopped the clock. With seven seconds left, the Southern Cal team lined up on the Notre Dame ten-yard line. The quarterback dropped back; the end zone was flooded with possible receivers and Notre Dame defensemen. Suddenly there seemed nothing between the quarterback and the goal line. In the years that followed, fans of both teams would debate what would have happened if he had chosen to run. But he passed. A receiver momentarily broke free, and the pass went toward him like a rifle shot. Total silence, and then just before the pass would have been gathered in, a defender got his fingertips on the ball, deflecting it. When it struck the ground, uncaught, there was a massive sigh of relief. And then the cheering began.

Phil Keegan didn't want to leave. Almost no one did. Notre Dame fans and Southern Cal fans, knowing that either team could have won, mingled philosophically. On the field the band formed and played the Southern Cal anthem, saluting the valiant visitors, and then, wheeling toward the west side of the field broke into the fight song.

Finally they left, moving slowly down to the exit. Below them, Cy got a glimpse of Cardinal Hildebrand and Fathers Hesburgh and Joyce, but they seemed anonymous in the enormous crowd of people.

Epilogue

Kate brought Aunt Betty to the rectory, and when Father Dowling came into the parlor he found Marie explaining to the visitors how the former parish school had been transformed into a center where senior parishioners congregated.

"It's been very good for them," Marie said, speaking as if she herself were decades younger than those who frequented the center.

Kate started to get up when Father Dowling came in, but he stopped her with a gesture.

"It's my good Catholic upbringing."

It was not, he noticed, an ironic remark, but it occasioned an account of how her aunt had come into the Church.

"Marry a Catholic, become a Catholic, that's all I thought at the time."

Kate listened with obvious attention to her aunt.

"Just stay away from theologians," Kate advised.

"I wouldn't know one if I saw one."

Kate's kidding description brought to mind Gustave Doré's illustrations of Dante.

"Can I see the center?" Betty asked.

Marie offered to take her over to the school and introduce her to Edna Hospers.

"That was arranged," Kate said, when her aunt and Marie were gone.

"Oh?"

"Betty wanted me to talk to a priest. You were my idea."

Father Dowling looked receptively at her. There followed an account of the way Kate had drifted away from the faith, first in college, then as the wife of a graduate student.

"And as daughter of Michael Geary?"

"The super-Catholic? Oh, I don't blame anyone else."

Staying these few days with her aunt, plus the wonder of carrying her baby, had made Kate feel the faith of her childhood reviving.

"Betty is a very bright woman, but she is so simple in matters like this. Good simple, I mean."

It was the false sophistication of the campus that Kate had rejected. This is what being with her aunt had led her to believe. Now, with the return of faith, her problem was how to foster it in the rarefied environment in which she and her husband lived.

"They were behind that picketing. They really think that's big stuff, telling the pope's man you don't want him on campus. For the Dalai Lama, they would be out strewing flowers in his path." She shook her head. "I've got to stop complaining about it."

Later, when talk turned to her baby, Father Dowling asked if her mother would be going to South Bend to be with her as her time approached.

"I couldn't keep her away if I wanted to, which I don't." Kate stopped and stared at him. "I'm just beginning now to grieve for my father."

"I'll say a Mass for him. And for your uncle."

"Isn't it odd that it should have been Freddy Burger who was responsible? Freddy came to see us, wanting us to join his organization. Of course he was all excited about picketing the cardinal. I wonder if that gave him the idea for trying to kidnap him."

Marie returned with Mrs. Furey and Edna; Father Dowling went outside but after a moment left the women to themselves. In his study, he filled his pipe slowly and, having lit it, sat puffing thoughtfully.

Freddy had not confessed to killing Michael Geary and Gordon Furey, but only repeated his engimatic conditional, "If I killed Michael Geary I killed Gordon Furey."

Father Dowling, after his conversation with Amanda in the Morris Inn, was certain that she had been Freddy's partner, but he did not want to be the one who pointed the finger at her. Phil Keegan had the tapes

Tuttle had made, and they contained the evidence that Amanda had been with Freddy the day he removed the body of Michael Geary from his mother's house.

Catherine Burger refused to believe her son had done these awful things.

"Oh, he has done some dreadful, inexcusable things. Kidnapping a cardinal! Father, I am mortified."

"How do you think I felt?"

She put a hand over her mouth and tried not to laugh. "It does have its comic side, doesn't it, Father? But that is very different from killing someone."

Freddy's treatment of Leo Berlioz, the driver of the stretch limousine, could hardly be classified as gentle. And inserting a syringe filled with poison into the plastic sack of insulin meant for Michael Geary's dispenser might have seemed very remote from violence. But Freddy, with his pharmaceutical training, would have known what he was doing.

Christopher James, not trusting himself in so delicate a matter, had engaged defense counsel for his client.

"He came to me with a professional courtesy request," Amos Cadbury told Father Dowling. "After all, at my suggestion he had agreed to serve as counsel for VOCL. In any case, I am not a criminal lawyer, as Christopher in his lucid moments would have realized."

So a flamboyant courtroom performer named Lothar had been flown in from Florida. He was Amanda's suggestion. She had met him by the pool of the condominium in which she stayed on Marco Island, and was struck by the mane of gray hair gathered into a ponytail. Tuttle was trying to join the defense as one steeped in the local culture.

After a visit to Burger Drugs, Father Dowling telephoned Christopher James's apartment, calling when the lawyer should be in his office, and reached Amanda.

"I would like to continue the conversation we were having at Notre Dame."

"You haven't told anyone, have you?"

"I am a priest, Amanda, not a policeman. Where can we meet?"

She came for him in the car she had rented at Midway when she flew in from Florida. She drove with both hands on the top of the wheel, as if she were about to bring them down on a keyboard rather than guide the car. She drove out of the city and along the river road to the country club.

"There is Catherine Burger's house," Father Dowling said when they passed it.

Amanda nodded. She wore a little smile.

"You asked if I had spoken to anyone about our conversation, Amanda."

"It was more of an inquisition, wasn't it?"

"Is that how it felt?"

She lifted her chin. "I assume you want to continue it. Well, Father," she said, glancing at him, "I am prepared to set your doubts at rest."

"I have little doubt left, Amanda."

"Well, as you said, you are a priest."

Her jaw set and she fell silent. Had her experience with Michael Geary, whatever it had been, embittered her and turned her against the Church? The convert expects so much of the Church, of its members, of its priests, that disillusion is almost inevitable. Almost. Betty Furey had retained her simple but lively faith through her terrible ordeal.

Amanda turned into the driveway of the country club and wound up its asphalt road to a parking lot below the tennis courts. She turned off the motor but looked straight ahead, her little smile back.

"I used to play tennis here."

"How long has it been since your last confession?"

She wheeled toward him with a startled expression. "What kind of question is that?"

After a moment, he said, "I repeat, Amanda. I am a priest. Acknowledge what you have done, confess your sins . . ."

"I don't believe any of that anymore."

"Don't you?"

"No! No. Daddy was right all along. I should have listened to him."

"Tell me about your father."

Her shoulders slumped and her expression changed. "What an odd man you are."

"I'd like to hear it."

She took it as the path of least resistance, telling him of her father's opposition to her interest in the Church.

"It was only later, after the terrible business with Michael Geary, that he told me about my mother. The fact that she had apparently returned to the Church on her deathbed devastated him."

"I wouldn't advise you to wait, Amanda."

"Father, what exactly is it that you think I have done?"

"I would prefer that you tell me."

"Sure you would. You would like me to confess to all kinds of things I haven't done, tell you that I helped Freddy do what he did."

"What did Freddy do?"

"Oh, come on, Father Dowling. It's in all the papers."

"I know what he's accused of. I think he may be innocent."

"You should be telling Freddy this. I'm sure he would find it more interesting than I do."

"It was when he said, in answer to Captain Keegan's accusation, that if he killed Geary, then he killed Gordon Furey, that I realized he was stating his innocence."

"I hope Lothar can convince the jury of that."

"He will need your help."

"What good would it do Freddy if I should say I helped him?"

"At the moment, I am thinking of the good you can do yourself. When I described you to Oscar Celsius he was certain I was describing the so called sister-in-law who picked up Michael Geary's last supply of insulin."

"You told him it was me?"

Father Dowling just looked at her. From the tennis court came the oddly echoing bong of balls being hit back and forth across the net.

"It's not a crime to buy insulin at a drugstore. As a favor."

"A favor to Freddy?"

"How else would I have known where to go? Freddy is the pharmacist."

"He has denied any knowledge of your going for the insulin."

Agnes Lamb kept worrying like a bone what she and Cy had learned from the pharmacist and Dr. Hawser. Even though Gordon Furey was dead, she wanted to test her thought that the Fureys had been involved in the death of Michael Geary, he getting the new prescription, she getting it filled. Finally Cy had put the question to Freddy and had drawn a total blank. Followed by a buttoned lip. He didn't want to talk about it anymore.

"What did he say?" Amanda asked, dropping her hands to the top of the wheel. Father Dowling half expected to hear a chord, but there were only shouts from the tennis courts.

"Amanda, this can be a confessional; nothing you say to me will go beyond it. I think you should worry less about what Freddy said to the police and more about what you must say to God."

"That I killed Michael Geary?"

"That you injected the poison into the insulin you purchased from Oscar Celsius, yes."

"And you would give me absolution?"

"God's pardon and peace, what a priest can give, as you know."

"I really believed that once. I believed it all."

"Because it is true."

She looked at him, looked away, then took her hands from the wheel. She bit her lower lip, and tears formed in her eyes. She shook her head as if to stop them, then opened her purse. The gun she took from it was hardly larger than her hand. She shifted in her seat and pointed the gun at him.

"Swear to me that you have told no one else about this."

Perhaps the experience of being kidnapped at Notre Dame had inoculated him against fear. The gun she held seemed hardly more than a toy.

"I am not the only one who knows, Amanda."

"You're just saying that."

"God knows what you have done, Amanda."

Her expression no longer that of a benign musician. "You and God know? Well, that is how it is going to remain."

"I have already assured you that I have no intention of telling these things to the police."

"Would you like to know what exactly 'these things' are? I suppose I can enjoy some of the therapeutic aspects of the confessional by telling you."

Once she began, she was eager to talk. It was Freddy who had joked about killing Michael Geary by doing something to his insulin. Freddy had motive but nothing like Amanda's. It was clear that the woman who had received a large sum of money as the victim of Michael Geary saw herself as a woman scorned. When she had learned that her former lover had someone new and was applying for an annulment, she had been furious.

"Daddy would have acted very differently if we were going to marry. But Michael fell back on the fact that he was a married man. An unhappily married man, but nonetheless . . ." She pressed her lips tightly together and shuddered in her anger.

Amanda had acted on Freddy's half-humorous suggestion about poisoning Michael Geary's insulin. Had Freddy suspected anything when she asked about the pharmacy and prescriptions? Amanda didn't know.

"For an intelligent man, he is still such a kid. His idea of defiance was stealing dashboard madonnas."

Amanda had injected some toilet bowl cleaner into Geary's insulin and, in a manner she had heard of from Freddy, slipped into the house during a rendezvous between Catherine Burger and Michael Geary and put the poisoned insulin in his dispenser.

"Then it was just a matter of time."

She had remained in Fox River, wanting to be there when the poison took effect, and had been with Freddy when his mother called frantically. Freddy told Amanda to wait in the car parked in the driveway while he went in to bring out the body of Michael Geary.

"Did you ride with him to the agency?"

"I followed in his car, to pick him up when he had left Michael behind his agency."

Freddy had thought that it had been simply a heart attack that had carried Michael Geary off in Catherine's bed. "He kept quoting *Hamlet* after I picked him up."

She was much more matter-of-fact about Gordon Furey. She had hated him since the time he had come to her and accused her of breaking up his sister's marriage. That confrontation, far more than her father's rage when he found Amanda and Geary together, had been the death of her affair with Michael Geary.

"You're going to let Freddy be punished for what you have done?"

She smiled grimly. "I think Lothar will win an acquittal. Freddy doesn't. I think he likes the thought of himself as a dual murderer."

She looked beyond him, thinking. "We are going to get out of the car now. Do you see that cart path over there? It runs out to the driving range. There is a shed there."

"I should tell you that you will be found out whatever you might do to me."

"You said you had told no one."

"I haven't. You saw the video in which you are quite clearly visible in the backseat of Michael Geary's car."

"You are the only one who thinks so, apparently."

"Ah, but there are other tapes. Many others. No doubt including one that will show you arriving to put the poisoned insulin in Michael Geary's dispenser."

She looked at him. "There is no such video."

"Isn't there?"

"Have you seen it?"

"Amanda, put away that gun. For God's sake, think of your immortal soul. You have cruelly killed two men and harming me will only worsen your condition."

She was filled with indecision; she lifted the gun, she lowered it, then lifted it again. He could have grabbed her wrist and taken it, perhaps, but that was not the way he wanted this confrontation to alter.

"Tell God you're sorry, Amanda."

She looked at him, eyes wide, trying to say something, but unable to.

"Are you sorry for killing those two men?"

Her chin lifted; she was about to nod; for all eternity Roger Dowling was sure she was about to nod and ask God's pardon. But suddenly both doors of the car were pulled open. Roger Dowling's arm was grasped and he was pulled out of the car, while Amanda was overpowered by Agnes Lamb.

"You all right, Father?" Cy Horvath asked.

Roger Dowling scrambled to his feet. On the other side of the car, Agnes was putting handcuffs on Amanda, who looked at Father Dowling with an expression of total disillusion.

"We came just in the nick of time," Cy said.

Father Dowling wanted to protest, to berate Cy and Agnes for coming here, to explain to Amanda that he had nothing to do with this, to beg her to make the confession she had been on the point of making. But that moment had passed forever.

"What if Tuttle hadn't filmed her going into the Burger house?" Marie said in awed tones.

"Officer Pianone took the pictures," Phil Keegan said.

"Are you saying you assigned him there?"

Keegan glanced at Roger Dowling. "Peanuts is on roving assignment."

Marie made an irreverent noise.

Roger Dowling had never felt worse about the solution of one of Phil Keegan's cases. Murder charges had been dropped against Freddy, though of course he faced a number of other charges, kidnapping being the most serious. The young man with the perpetual smile seemed chagrined at losing the role of chief defendant. Lothar had moved to the defense of Amanda James, so Freddy chose Tuttle for his lawyer.

"The boy has a death wish," Amos Cadbury confided to Father Dowling. "Imagine, allowing himself to be indicted for murders he didn't commit, and now putting his fate in Tuttle's hands. At Catherine's request, I will be represented at the defense table."

"Personally."

Cadbury, eyes closed, shook his head. "Not unless it becomes absolutely necessary. A young associate of mine will be at Tuttle's disposal."

The cases had been separated, of course, and Amanda went first to trial. Lothar devised an imaginative defense. The murder of Michael

Geary had been provoked by the mental damage he had caused the defendant, and the killing of Gordon Furey had been an inevitable result of the same damage; Gordon's interference, at a time when Amanda, in Lothar's passionate description, was dangling from an emotional precipice, had created a ticking time bomb of resentment, bound to go off eventually.

Following this incredible defense, Roger Dowling wondered if the nature of human action had ever been so thoroughly caricatured.

"The jury will buy it," Phil Keegan said morosely, but years as a Cubs fan had inured him to defeat.

Father Dowling tried to visit Amanda, but her father kept constant vigil. Unnecessarily, as it turned out. Father Dowling managed to have a note delivered to her. It came back unopened with "Judas" scrawled on the envelope.

He could not blame her for thinking that he had arranged to have the police follow when she came for him. He had guessed at the existence of the damning video when he talked to her; it was the tape's discovery that had made her the object of a police search, a dozen cars searching for the rental automobile. Thus he was prevented from getting Amanda to see that he had not betrayed her, and he was equally prevented from telling Cy and Agnes Lamb why he had been so upset at their arrival. Contrition and remorse had been in Amanda's eyes; acknowledgment of her sins had trembled on her lips. Father Dowling prayed that the moment would count as her confession. As she was being taken away, he had murmured the prayer of absolution after her.

Marie was saying that a young woman who would sue the Church on trumped-up charges of sexual harassment could be expected to do what Amanda had done.

"You weren't surprised?" Father Dowling asked.

"Were you?"

"I thought it was Brian."

Brian Geary had shaved his beard and returned to his classroom in Berkeley. Elizabeth Furey was staying with Kate in South Bend until the baby came. Despite his scheduled role in Freddy's trial, Tuttle was being investigated by a committee of the bar association because he had sold copies of his videotapes to television, and he was being sued by rival networks who claimed they had paid for exclusive rights.

"He may have compromised the trial of Frederick Burger," Amos Cadbury explained. "At least that is the charge."

"You sound skeptical."

"The charge against Tuttle will be dismissed."

Since Cadbury was chair of the committee this prediction carried weight.

And then one day a large envelope, sealed with wax and festooned with foreign stamps, arrived at the rectory. Before bringing it to Father Dowling, Marie weighed it in her hand, noticed the stamps were from Vatican City, saw that it was from the office of Cardinal Hildebrand. Reports of Father Dowling's role in the Notre Dame meeting had been eclipsed when he and Monsignor Tracy had been kidnapped, but Marie remembered them and felt terror. She was certain the pastor would be whisked away from Fox River to some scene more appropriate to his talents. She laid the envelope on the pastor's desk as if it were a letter bomb. He did not look up.

"A letter for you, Father."

"Thank you, Marie."

"From Rome."

He glanced at the letter and pushed his chair back. It was not reassuring to Marie that he shared her apprehension. He looked up at her, as if blaming her for the letter.

"Open it."

He opened it. The message was folded square and was typed on very thick paper. As he read it, a smile grew on Father Dowling's face.

"What is it?"

He handed her the letter. Monsignor Tracy thanked Father Dowling on behalf of Cardinal Hildebrand for taking part in the recent meeting. In his own name, he asked the pastor of St. Hilary's if he would purchase an item of clothing with the Notre Dame emblem on it, a cap, a sweater, a jacket, and send it to the monsignor's nephew, whose address was enclosed. Marie was smiling now too.

"I think I'll ask Father Panzica for supper, Marie. Is that agreeable?"

"Agreeable? Of course it's agreeable. You're the pastor here, Father Dowling."

And in her kitchen, she said a little prayer to St. Jude, asking that Father Dowling would remain pastor here for many a year.

8-96

lph M.

ffense.